Cyrion

watched the demon-beast, by the light of its vast eyes, slink towards him. He watched, motionless, leaning on his sword.

Then a sinewy taloned forefoot, lengthy as a column, struck at him, and Cyrion was no longer in that spot, motionless, leaning on his sword, as he had been an instant before. Away in the shadow, Cyrion stood again unmoving, sword poised, negligently waiting. Again, the batting of scythe-fringed death; again missing him.

The jaws clashed, and slaver exploded forth, like a waterfall. Cyrion was gone, out of reach. Stone had returned to lightning. The fourth blow was his. He neither laughed at the seriousness of his mission, nor frowned. No meditation was needed, the target no challenge, facile. . . .

Cyrion swung back his arm, and sent the sword plummeting. . . .

Auxia
CYROAM
Andriok
Aphria
MARREAN SEA
(Mareuna of the Remusans)
Heshbel
Daskiriom
Tynt
Cassireia
Teboras
Jebba
Bakrad Road
Heruzala
Askandris
Desert
KYROS

Cyrion

Tanith Lee

DAW BOOKS, INC.
DONALD A. WOLLHEIM, PUBLISHER
1633 Broadway, New York, NY 10019

Cover art by Ken W. Kelly.

FIRST PRINTING, SEPTEMBER 1982

1 2 3 4 5 6 7 8 9

DAW TRADEMARK REGISTERED
U.S. PAT. OFF. MARCA
REGISTRADA. HECHO EN U.S.A.

PRINTED IN U.S.A.

Contents

DEDICATION:

To *Carol McShane*,
Who knows why.

PROLOGUE—*The Honey Garden*

The plump young man with the bright ginger hair caused something of a sensation as he entered the inn. It was not intentional.

Dazzled by the hard sunlight of the streets, he judged the three steps of the threshold as two. Finding otherwise, and breaking into an involuntary leap to save himself, he sprang upon an unwitting figure just then in the process of crossing the area, bearing with him two flagons of wine. With cries of surprise and discomposure, both toppled into the clutches of the brass Qirri who guarded the entrance. And, inevitably, struck the brazen gong suspended from her hands. A loud clang echoed through the building, followed by the crash first of one wine jar, then of a second wine jar.

A silken curtain was thrown aside to reveal the major chamber of the inn, and two male customers, prepared for combat. One was a burly, black-browed fellow, the other a blond Westerner, clad in mail and obviously a soldier, drawn dagger already in professional evidence. From a passage the innkeeper had also come flying. At their feet, two persons writhed and struck about them feebly.

"Are they killing each other?"

"The scoundrel is attacking my poor slave!"

The dark man, who wore the badge of a master mason, at this point intervened, hauling the ginger young man in one direction, while the stunned slave rolled in another. The innkeeper bent over him, cooing. "Speak to me, Esur. Are you dying? And the price of slaves just doubled in the markets."

The soldier had already sheathed his dagger. With amusement on his attractive, neatly bearded face, he remarked, "A mistake, I think." He turned and walked back into the body of the inn.

Ginger-cheeked now, the plump young man began to explain his error, and produced money to pay for the spilled wine and the spilled slave. The mason stood looking on, toying with the gold coin in his ear.

Leaving the slave, the innkeeper had gone to examine the brass Qirri. A copy of some pagan statue of the bee goddess—imported when, centuries before, the Remusans had occupied the city—she was the symbol of this inn known as the Honey Garden. Superstitiously, the innkeeper felt her over, was satisfied, kicked the slave to his feet and, taking the proffered money, decided to forgive and forget.

"You are welcome, sir. The Honey Garden, sweetest inn of Heruzala, lies before you. What may we bring for your delight?"

Wiping his forehead, Ginger-Hair ordered fresh wine.

"And roast spiced kid, glazed with honey—our speciality—"

"Later," said the plump young man. "Meanwhile. . . ."

"Yes?"

"I am looking for a man. A particular man. I was told I might find him here."

"His name, dear sir?"

"Cyrion."

The innkeeper wrinkled his face.

"This name I have heard. He is a swordsman, is he not? We do not encourage brawlers."

"A swordsman, but rich," said the mason, in an undertone.

"You know him?" Ginger-Hair demanded.

"*Of* him."

"He is famous in Heruzala?"

"Perhaps. And in a few other places, I believe."

"They say," said a new voice, female, a smoky contralto, "that he resembles an angel."

The mason, the innkeeper and Ginger-Hair stared after a tall and graceful woman who, having imparted her wisp of information, had gone directly by them, and up toward the street. Her midnight hair was heavily pearled, and her heavy scent remained behind her on the air to interest them for some while. (Unlike the latest arrival, she did not misjudge the steps.) A maid hurried after her.

"As you see," said the innkeeper, "we entertain only the very best clients. But if, as you say, he is rich and couth, this Shirrian, then he may well have stayed here—"

"Cyrion," the plump young man corrected. He fixed the mason with a determined, if plainly shortsighted eye. "If you will tell me what you know, I will reward you with gold."

"Will you now? I know very little."

But Ginger-Hair urged him back into the main chamber, and the mason, with a nod of resignation, led him to the table he had occupied before the interruption.

The table was spread with the complex papers of architectural design, a pen, some ink and a small abacus. It would seem a pleasant enough spot to work. Directly above, a high window pierced the wall, and here a bird in a cage sang melodiously.

The rest of the large room, its plaster washed by a blue-dye of Tynt, and altogether well-appointed, had few occupants this morning. In a corner the soldier had resumed his own seat and returned to his wine. Farther off, tucked in an embrasure, two men in dark robes seemed to be debating the teachings of the prophet Hesuf, somewhat vigorously. They did not glance at the newcomer, nor at their wine when it was brought.

Ginger-Hair sat down.

"My name is Roilant." Jewels burned on his fingers and collar, and the light from the window described his fine clothes, only slightly sullied by spillage and dusty brass. "The name of my family is, at this point, immaterial. But you can assume I am well able to pay you, if you help me. I trust this will not insult you."

"No." The mason moved his writings and the abacus out of the way as the grudging slave, Esur, approached and banged down a flagon and cups. "However, I prefer to earn my wages, and I am uncertain I can. This inn is a fair one, as inns go. But not the best in Heruzala. You might do better to try for your man at the Rose, or the Eagle."

The slave grunted agreement, adding something about falling upon *their* slaves, who were notoriously savage, before limping theatrically away.

Roilant did not hear.

"But I was told he came to the Honey Garden."

"Well. He is not here now. You cannot, it seems, miss him.

Young, handsome, blond as ice, and dressed as splendidly as King Malban himself, if with rather better taste."

The soldier at the nearby table, catching the mason's comment, grinned. "Poor Malban. Under the Queen Mother's thumb."

Ginger Roilant bridled. "I have met the king. My family has loyal connections with the imperial house of Heruzala, and I would ask you—"

His request was drowned by sudden altercation. The more elderly of the two debaters in the embrasure had risen, smiting a fist on his tabletop.

"This line, as any intellectual knows, has been mistranslated from the Remine. Have you no wits, young sir?"

The other, a man in his late fifties, ignored this youthening, and exclaimed: "You are very wrong."

"I tell you the word 'meek' is an error. This has been known for decades—"

Their voices dropped again.

The soldier, having finished his own wine but keeping cup in hand, now wandered over to the mason's table and sat down companionably by Roilant.

"The old holy man over there," said the soldier, "has a great many rings. Not uncommon, of course, with such people as the nomads, who must carry their wealth with them. But unusual for a sage, which is what I take the man to be—"

"To return to Cyrion," said Roilant.

"You see," said the mason, "this Cyrion of yours is elusive. And rather more than merely a swordsman, it would seem. Now he is reported as outriding with some caravan. Now he is studying in one of the great libraries. Now he is outwitting a demon on a mountain."

The soldier took up the rhythm. "Now he is in Heruzala. There he is in Andriok. Here he is in the desert. Where now? In thin air."

"I have been trying to locate him for two weeks," said Roilant. He, the mason and the soldier all drank deep of Roilant's wine. "I—need to know his qualifications for a particular reason. This is not idle curiosity. Yet all I hear are rumors."

"All I can offer you is little better," said the mason gravely. "I got the story on the coast, in the port of Jebba."

"*Jebba!*" Roilant cried. "Do you mean he is there?"

"Maybe. Maybe not. But it seems he has been, now and then."

Roilant sighed. His weak chin sank and his worried eyes dropped.

"If you will tell me what you heard, I suppose I will listen."

"Well," said the mason, "I render no guaranty of truth. This concerns, for one thing, a form of sorcery. You may not credit such stuff."

"Oh." Roilant shuddered. He collected himself with an obvious effort. "I do."

The mason and the soldier exchanged involuntary looks.

The mason touched the coin in his ear.

"I want no payment for a tale, then. But I will tell it you, since it describes your Cyrion for you. It begins in an inn at Jebba far superior to this one. . . ."

CYRION IN WAX

"Cyrion, be wary of that man."

Cyrion raised guileless eyes.

"Why, and whom?"

Mareme, the beautiful courtesan, lowered her own eyes swiftly beneath turquoise lids. She was young, lovely, wealthy and accordingly difficult to obtain. Being only for a few, she had learned something of the habits of those few, both in the bedchamber and out of it. This one she believed she knew well enough to judge that the thing he appeared unaware of was frequently what had gained his utmost attention. Besides, their game of lotus-and-wasp on the painted ivory board was beginning, she thought, to veer too readily in her favor.

In addition, the behavior and appearance of the man in question were difficult to ignore.

Dark of hair and with the silken olive complexion common in the region, his forehead was bound with gold and his scarlet robe, long as that of a scholar or physician, stitched with bizarre golden talismans. Three pale purple amethysts trickled from his left ear. Satanically glamorous as an eagle, he had stalked into the cool garden of the expensive inn, two human jackals coming after, plainly a bodyguard, a pair of leering sadists, scarred and welted from ancient battles, and clearly keen for more as they smashed forward through the tubs of flowers and the unlucky patrons. Their hands rested ready to their Swords and their fingers were coated with spikes. And nobody challenged them. They mounted the steps beside their master, and stood over him as he seated himself. The seat was on the upper terrace nearest the kitchen wing, among the mosaic pillars and under the scented shade of the orange and cinnamon trees, not ten feet from where Cyrion bent his silver sun of a head and Mareme her coal-black one over their intellectual game. Below, from the open court with its flowers and the palm tree which made a necessary umbrella against the noon sky, men and women had broken off their talk uneasily, and rescued it only in whispers. Those who had been pushed flat arose and resumed their seats in silence. And, strange in this great coastal city of Jebba, where to stare was as natural as to breathe, eyes slid narrowly sideways and no more.

Presently, the inn's proprietor himself came hurrying. You could note, from a deal less than ten paces, the sweat making mirror of his suddenly greenish face. He bowed to the dark man.

"What can I serve you with, Lord Hasmun?"

The dark man smiled.

"Eels fried in butter, some quince-bread. A jug of the black, very cold."

The innkeeper took a quarter step back, or tried to, on shaking unreliable legs.

"We have no—eels, Lord Hasmun."

One of the jackals stirred eagerly, but Hasmun checked him with an idle finger.

"Then," said Hasmun softly, "get some eels in, my host."

The innkeeper fled as fast as jelly would permit, into the kitchen wing behind the house. A minute later, some boys crept from thence into the garden with quince-bread, black Jebba wine packed in ice, and the news that others scoured the fish-market.

Hasmun sampled the wine. The jackals fidgeted.

Hasmun laughed, mellowly.

"Fine living is not for you, lads, eh? Well, go out and play in the streets for a while, my honeys."

The bodyguard went, but, in the garden, the conversation grew no louder, and not a head was raised.

Till Cyrion raised his to ask across the board of lotus-and-wasp: "Why, and who?"

"I should have held my tongue, I perceive," said Mareme, very low, "but I thought you had marked him."

"The innkeeper? Oh, we are old friends," murmured Cyrion. He seemed to have remembered the game, and annexed two of Mareme's pieces neatly before she could fathom the move. When she had fathomed it, she said, "Beautiful as the angels you may be, my soul, but transparent, to a cunning lady of the night. Leave it alone, beloved."

Cyrion, having won the lotus-and-wasp, decided to let Mareme win the other game they were playing.

"I have already caught a rumor here of Hasmun. But not why I must beware of him."

"Not only you, my darling. All of us. They call him the dollmaker. Did you know?"

"He makes dolls then. No doubt a charming trade, the toy business."

"Not those dolls that children play with," huskily mouthed Mareme, as if her voice were trying to reach the very nadir of her throat. "The kind of doll a magus constructs of one he would slay, and then sticks a needle in its liver."

"Hasmun is an apothecary, though the rumor says magus. Does the trick work?"

"Trick!" squeaked Mareme, as if her voice, having reached the nadir, had there changed into her own pet dove-rat. "There are three dead already, and others who have crossed him have gone blind, or their limbs pain them and they cannot walk—Ah, God bless me. *He is looking at us.*"

Cyrion leaned back in his chair, and slowly turned his head. The noon sun, raying through the orange trees, fired his elegant silk clothes, and revealed his hair as pure light. It was a fitting halo for the marvellous face Mareme had compared to an angel's—though whether of the heavenly variety or one of the descended sort, it was somehow hard to be sure. Hasmun was indeed looking in their direction, openly, and with amusement. Now he met this face full on and next Cyrion's dazzling smile. Hasmun's eyes half closed, enjoying it all, just as Cyrion seemed to be doing.

"I heard my name mentioned," said Hasmun. His words carried throughout the garden, and were meant to. Faces greyed further among the flower tubs. "Can it be my humble person is known to you?"

"Everyone knows Hasmun the dollmaker," said Cyrion courteously. Kindly, he added, "but take heart, no man can help his smell."

The sensuous enjoyment snapped off Hasmun's face. It became perfectly still. Perhaps this too was enjoyment; a different form of enjoyment.

"I think you must be tipsy," said Hasmun.

"I think I must be entirely sober," corrected Cyrion, rising, "for what I am about to do requires a steady hand."

Cyrion crossed the not quite ten paces with a mercurial speed that stunned the eye, and all in the fluid motion of it, as he reached Hasmun's table, the jug of Black Jebba seemed to soar up of its own accord into Cyrion's hands, contriving next to up-end itself over the magus' head.

Bathed in a black-red ichor of the wine, Hasmun yelped once like a trodden-on dog. Then stumbling up, sent the table and its contents flying.

Cyrion was distressed, incredulous.

"How can I have been so clumsy—"

A crash resounded hard on the table's crashing. Hasmun's bodyguards were returning through the garden. They had apparently got no farther than the intimidating of a girl in the doorway of the inn, and hearing the row, had come running, with prayers of thanks to the Fiend, no doubt.

Cyrion waited until the two were careering up the steps, then lobbed the wine jar, slippery with wine and ice, casually amid their feet. One bellowed, lost footing and thudded backward among the scented shrubs. The second went down on one knee, righted himself, and, sword dragged bare, leapt for the terrace.

Cyrion's sword was at his hip. He had seemingly forgotten it. He ducked under the first ham-fist blow, spun negligently and kicked into the base of the bully's spine. The man screamed and plunged forward to land writhing on the terrace in the spreading pool of liquor.

The other thug had meanwhile extricated himself from the shrubs. As he bounded back up the stair, sword and one spiked fist much in evidence, the innkeeper emerged ingratiatingly from the opposite kitchen end of the terrace, bearing a spluttering dish of fried eels. Cyrion turned on his heel as if bored with the whole matter, skimmed the dish of scalding sea-worms and bubbling butter, and cast it unerringly over his shoulder into the face of the bodyguard. Buttered and blinded, dropping the sword with a clatter, the fellow again left the terrace in a backward manner. In passing, his skull met the rim of one of the stone tubs. He did not now get up.

Cyrion smoothed his finery with ringed left hand and ringless right one. For a man who had been hurling liquor and fried seafood about, he was surprisingly unspotted. As if resenting the fact, the writhing kicked bully on the terrace made a final token grab at Cyrion's ankle. Cyrion kicked once more, this time into the grab. A bone snapped somewhere followed by a thin howling.

Cyrion glanced at Hasmun.

"A great uproar, master apothecary, over a little spilled wine."

Hasmun, soaked and perfumed with Black Jebba, had had the space to string his nerves and his wits together. He straightened himself, startlingly the same height and build as Cyrion himself, but otherwise opposed as shadow to light.

"Choose," Hasmun said to the bodyguard with the broken wrist. "Be quiet or die." The howling ceased. "You, on the other hand," Hasmun continued, "will die in any case."

"As the priests lesson us, life is but the briefest kindling of sweet light doused in the darkness of eternity," quoted Cyrion philosophically.

"You are wrong," said Hasmun. As the wine dripped in his eyes, he actually managed a smile. "Your dousing will be rather prolonged and definitely not sweet. It will begin tonight. If you would see for yourself how I can break you, come to my Apothecarium and look. Your whore will tell you where."

And he nodded to Mareme, who had covered her painted face with her powdered hands.

The white daylight gradually reddened. The sun went bathing in the ocean. Jebba became an amber city at the edge of a sea of golden coins. Then the dusk filtered shoreward from the desert, and blue-dyed the windows of Mareme's exquisite apartment.

On the silken bed, Cyrion was stretched, the flawless model for a young god, naked, beautiful and mildly drunk. Mareme sat upright beside him, nervously plucking at the silks.

"Are you not afraid?" she suddenly blurted.

"Oh, I thought I had made you forget Hasmun."

Certainly, he could generally make her forget anything for a while. Even the touch of his hand on her face had the power to do that. The moment she had seen him, a year before, a casual meeting, by chance, Cyrion had possessed her thoughts, dominated not merely heart but also mind. She was slyly cool-headed enough with others, had had to be. But never with Cyrion. She had refused his money always. Instead, meticulously, he always sent her gifts. His scrupulous fairness disturbed her. She wanted Cyrion to love her, not pay her. Once, stupidly, she had sought to procure a love potion, but this venture had had none of the desired results.

"How could I forget Hasmun?" she said now. "Listen, my lord, I have not told you everything. His Apothecarium is in the Street of the Three Walls. Those who pass by sometimes see a small man-formed doll inside the front of the shop, set out as if to display its craftsmanship. And in the doll are stuck jewelled pins. Presently there is a pin in the heart, someone is buried, and the doll vanishes from the shop."

"I heard as much," said Cyrion. "Does no one ever go there, effect entry, appropriate the doll, extract the pins?"

"How could they, when the magus keeps watch? Even when he vacates the premises to sleep, ten of those human beasts of his guard the place."

Cyrion reached for the cup of blue crystal at his side, while the stars, as apparently impervious as he, evolved in the window.

"Tell me," said Cyrion, "do you know how the dolls are fashioned?"

"Who in Jebba does not? Hasmun boasts of his art. He requires nothing from the victim, only to have seen him once. He constructs the doll in the image of the one he would harm, then casts a foul spell on it to link doll and man together. While the spell is active, he tortures the doll with his pins. Then removes the spell. Without the spell, the doll is passive, only a doll. The man ceases to feel his hurts, rejoices, thinks Hasmun has forgiven him. Then Hasmun makes the spell again, and hurts him more, till he is crippled or dies screaming. And this, my wise master, you chose to pick a quarrel with. Why did you *do* it?"

"I am," said Cyrion humbly, "a masochist."

The window was now radiant with its stars. From a gilt cage, the little dove-rat cheeped imperiously to be let out. Softly albescent as any dove, round-eared, delicate of feature and with two large golden eyes, the dove-rat was the second love of Mareme. Minute though it was, she would sometimes lead it about the upper thoroughfares of Jebba on a long gilt leash. It had a habit of thieving bright objects, which might have proved embarrassing had not Mareme, versatile in many modes, turned trouble to advantage. Often, in former less-exalted days, she had let the dove-rat steal from the tumbled and discarded clothes of her patrons—earrings, buttons, coins. Next, herself running daintily after the client on the street, to return the items with a charming apology for her pet. Thus, she gained her not entirely founded reputation for honesty.

Mareme arose from the bed and let the dove-rat from its cage. It scampered instantly to her cosmetics table, to sit among the tall onyx pots of powder, colored unguents and black kohl, sometimes staring at itself in the mirror of rare silver-framed glass—Cyrion's latest gift. The crystal bottles and the tiny shiny paring knife had been shut away from the dove-rat's greedy gaze. Once, Cyrion had watched the minuscule animal drag an emerald torque twice its size from Mareme's jewel box to its nest in the cage, then come back for the pearls.

Mareme knelt by Cyrion.

"What will you do, Cyrion?"

The light was going fast, and the lamps not yet lit. At first she did not see the whiteness around his mouth, the fixed unblinking emphasis of his eyes. Then he said, offhandedly:

"Half a minute ago, I should have said I was going to wait, to see if Hasmun could make good his threats. I no longer need to wait, however. He can."

Mareme shuddered.

"What is it?" she hissed. "Do you suffer pain?"

"Somewhat. I assume he has one of his damned pins in my wax ankle."

He shut his eyes and opened them. His face had paled under its light fair tan, but his features were composed. Suddenly, he drew a deep breath and said, with indifference: "A demonstration. He forgoes the pin. He will give me the briefest respite before demonstrating further. But not too much tonight, I hazard. He means me to—to visit his toyshop tomorrow. He wants me to beg his pardon and his—mercy."

On this occasion, beyond the slight stumble in his words, he gave no sign.

"How can I help you?" Mareme cried.

"Not in the usual way, I think," he murmured. "Take your lyre from its peg, and play to me instead. Music soothes all pain, they say. Let us try if it does."

Over the three white walls for which the street was named, fig, palm and flower trees shook their fragrance and their piecemeal shadows. In the noon heat, the street was empty and innocent, and halfway down it, between the courts of the gold workers and the sellers of silk, gaped the hole of Hasmun's Apothecarium.

The door was open, and strings of blue ceramic beads hung over the entrance. Inside, incense rose in streamers on a shade that was infernal even by day.

As the bead curtain rattled, and a silhouette brushed by into the shop from the sun-drenched street, two of Hasmun's bullies surged from the interior to intercept.

"Peace, my cherubs," said a friendly and musical voice. "I am here to gratify your master's sweet tooth. Leave the damage to him, or he will make dollies for you, too."

The guard fell back, grunting, and Cyrion passed on into the depth of the shop.

In the gloom, black flagons on shelves were just discernible, and black caskets, and bottles of leaden green stoppered with parchment and cobwebs. A lusterless cobra, stuffed and placed on a stand in the attitude of striking, barred the way through a curtain of lion-skin. Beyond, a cell, similarly stacked, but picked out in the reddish light of a depending lamp.

Under the lamp's glow, Hasmun sat in a chair of ebony. On a lacquer table at his elbow lay Cyrion, in miniature, naked, blond, and with two fiery-glinting red-jeweled pins thrust one through the right ankle and the second through the lobe of the left ear.

"Not on display at the shop front, as I was told," said Cyrion blandly. "I had hoped to be the spectacle of Jebba."

"That is for later," said Hasmun, exactly as bland. "Did you enjoy your night?"

"I have had some dealings with the desert nomads. They teach a method of converting pain into delicious pleasure."

Hasmun, unruffled, called the bluff.

"I am glad that you reckoned it pleasant. Tonight should be more pleasant still. The jawbone—I have a topaz pin for that. The wrist and shin—sapphire. I keep the diamonds for your eyes, my beautiful. But blindness is not yet. Nor death. This will be a long game. Revel in it, my dear."

Cyrion had bent to examine the doll. He seemed to find its cunning likeness appealing, though you could see now it was not a perfect replica. Without the activation of the relevant spell, the pins caused no pain to him, even when he twisted them himself in the lightly pigmented wax flesh.

"Of course," Cyrian remarked, "I could steal the doll from you. Or kill you, perhaps."

"Try," invited Hasmun the magus. "I should like you to. Please."

Cyrion had already glimpsed four thugs, rippling the lion-skin as they lurked the other side of it. He had seen also the solitary narrow window high up among the shelves of the cell, wide enough to admit a man's hand, but no more. For Hasmun, psychic sparks played round his fingers.

"Try," Hasmun said again, winningly. "It will discomfort you a good deal, but not so much as these pretty pins, whose hurt you can turn to ecstasy."

Cyrion abandoned the doll. His face was unreadable.

"How if I ask for clemency?"

"How if you do."

Cyrion turned and walked out again through the lion-skin. The thugs, attempting a little idle bruising as they jokingly saw him from the shop, found him somehow too quick for them. One, kicked on the thigh by another who had expected to kick Cyrion, abruptly no longer between them, must console himself that at least, Cyrion could not be quick enough for the magus.

Dusk came again, the constant and reliable night. Many in Jebba who had fallen foul of Hasmun had had cause to dread that reliable return, darkness which brought jeweled stars and jeweled pins and pain jeweled with tears and sweat.

In the hours of that night, white-faced, Mareme paced and prowled her exquisite apartment. She could not rest, and sometimes, in an instinctive memory of her primitive beginnings on the waterfront, she tore her hair.

Two hours before dawn, a cat's-paw rap on the door galvanized her. She flew to the door and, pulling it open, admitted Cyrion, whiter than she and gaunt as a man after a month of fever, who smiled at her companionably. He was closely wrapped in his cloak, in one hand a couple of the slender clay wine jars that were sold at all hours along the harbor.

"I cannot bear this—" Mareme cried out.

"Softly," he said, and shut the door. "I have had an interesting sojourn in a ship-shed and scared the rats with my writhings. The apothecary has finished with me for another night."

"I will kill myself," said Mareme. "You hid in a ship-shed so I should not see your agony. But your suffering is mine—"

"Not quite," said Cyrion. "Be glad."

"Have you no plan?" she wept.

"I plan to drink some harbor wine."

Still cloaked, he unstoppered a jar, poured liquor into the two blue crystal cups, handing her one. The girl drank unwillingly and reflexively, then, with a sigh, dropped the cup on the rugs and dropped full length beside it. A faint scent rose from the spilled wine, the perfume of the drug pellet Cyrion had crushed in it. He lifted Mareme and laid her on the bed. Then stepped noiselessly over to the cosmetics table, above which the dove-rat chirruped in its cage.

Hasmun's ten shop guard sat dicing in the murky room between the shelves of potions and poisons, presided over by the stuffed cobra. Three or four lamps burned fitfully to show the players their casts. In another hour, the sun would bound up from the desert at Jebba's back and the daylight guard would replace them. There had been some more fun tonight. The muttering of the spell, the drone of unseen pipes, the hot rushing of the air that betokened the arousal of unwholesome forces. Then the strategic interested silence of the magus beyond the lion-skin curtain, twisting the pins. None of Hasmun's thugs had ever witnessed his sorcery. They knew better than to spy, and indeed had no ambitions in that area. They made the odd jest concerning Cyrion's fate, but their eyes grew fixed when they spoke of it, and the dice clattered more loudly.

It was a nasty complex dicing they were having, with money and probably a fight resting on its outcome. Now there was quiet, as one nursed the dice and entreated some ratty noxious personal demon to be generous.

And in that quiet, a vast commotion began. It seemed fantastically to originate inside the shop, and to the rear. A smashing of pottery and a shouting and roaring, in which the name of Hasmun had mixed itself with imprecations.

The guards ran to the lion-skin and through into the cell, which crunched underfoot but gave no other evidence of an intruder. Soon the depending lamp was lit, to reveal the floor carpeted in sharded clay pottery from a jar which had apparently been flung through the window into the cell. The shouting had meanwhile ceased. Before any of the guards could hoist themselves via the shelves to the narrow window, a sharp and alarming report went off, from the front of the Apothecarium. As a single organism, the ten guards veered from the red-lit cell and plunged once more through the shop and thence through bead strings to the door. The door, unbarred and flung wide, revealed a second vessel, this one filled with burning tar, which had just now exploded it into a thousand bits in all directions. As the guard kicked hot debris, swearing, an apparition appeared, dancing wildly along the street.

It was the thin and wretched figure of the poorest sort of sailor. Head bound in the sailor's striped head-cloth—optionally filthy, as this one was—clad otherwise in revolting disarray and copious flapping pockets, all of it reeking of bitumen and corn spirits, and with a dark brown, black-stubbled face contorting insanely, the sailor cursed Hasmun with a multitude of curses.

Three guards sought to obtain the apparition, but it danced aside.

"Upon Hasmun, the Swine of Rancid Smell, be vomited the manifold punishments of the Fiend!" wailed the sailor. "And you, his reeking minions, rolled from the dung of pigs and quickened by dog urine, may you be pickled in your own rottenness till the sea requires its salt!"

Five guards chased the sailor, who promptly fled, though encouraging them to pursuit with further elaboration upon their merits. Half down the street, all but two halted, recalling their duties to the magus' shop. The two who thundered on in the sailor's wake, galloped about a corner and into an unlit alley. Next second, both were spun, gagging and half strangled, to the ground, their gullets having made horrible connection with the thin cord which some minutes before the sailor had tied across the way, and subsequently ducked himself on his return.

When, yet choking and blaspheming, the failed rear-guard action had reentered the Apothecarium, having lost their quarry, a violent discussion was in progress regarding the sailor's identity. Presently, they thought to douse the depending lamp in the magus' cell.

Bleary as they were, involved in rampaging anger to boot, the chances were they might not even have noticed. But one, blundering into the lacquer table, looked down. And beheld an empty space where previously the wax effigy of Cyrion had lain, impaled by its pins.

Cyrion had come on the sailor in the ship-shed, one of the scores dotted here and there about the port, sleeping off the night's drink and drugs before weaving shipward at sunup.

Now, however, this frightful, spirit-stinking vision of a sailor was not heading, weaving or otherwise, toward the harbor, but along one of the comelier streets of Jebba. Presently, reaching a stair, the sailor went agilely up it, unlocked a door with a key taken from a girl's creamy neck, and pushed through into the apartment of Mareme, the beautiful courtesan. Arrived, and having kindled a lamp with some familiarity, the sailor dragged the striped head-rag off and wiped his face with a cloth, thereby revealing the blond hair, stubble and skin of Cyrion.

The drunk sailor in the ship-shed, who would awake in the finery Cyrion had exchanged him for his own anti-social garb, could have few complaints. Perhaps he might miss his nearly empty wine jars, though, one having been tossed through the window of the magus' shop, the other exploded by a stick of fired bitumen outside.

Mareme, still sleeping, had not observed the transformation Cyrion had worked on himself, partly with the aid of her own cosmetics. Nor did she now observe Cyrion take from the left flapping sailor's pocket a velvet bag which squirmed, and from the bag the reason for the squirming—the incensed dove-rat.

Having stroked the creature into a better humor, Cyrion removed the gilt leash and replaced the rat in its cage. Then, from the sailor's dexter pocket, he lifted the wax doll.

He had carried the rat to the wall of the goldworkers which neighbored Hasmun's cell window. There, he tied the end of the rat's long leash to a convenient overhanging tree bough. His first clamor and smashing of pottery brought the guard to the cell and caused the lighting of the lamp. Next, the jar he had already primed with a red-hot coal, burst at the shop's front. The dove-rat had found itself elevated to the window of the cell, and put through onto a shelf. Cyrion meanwhile bolted to distract the guard about the doorway. Having lost and half-throttled his followers, Cyrion sped by a circular route back into the Street of the Three Walls. Quieter than a leaf, this time, he alighted against the cell window.

The dove-rat, which could be relied on to steal anything bright, had already completed its mission. Illuminated sparklingly by the depending lamp, the jeweled pins through the doll's body had attracted the rat immediately. It had climbed down to the lacquer table, the length of its chain. Having tried to pull the pins free and failed, the rat had gripped the whole doll in its predaceous teeth, and climbed up again to the window embrasure. The chain, secured to the bough, prevented its wandering. Then, as always happened, someone, currently Cyrion, took away its hard-won prize.

It had been a long night, and it was not yet done.

Cyrion placed the lamp on Mareme's cosmetics table, and stood there, turning the wax image, of such a near-likeness to himself, over in his ringed left hand, his bare right hand.

Mareme woke, her body soothed and comforted, her head clear, her heart like lead.

She understood what had been in her wine. Sometimes she had used it on others, or in the slight quantities that produced euphoria, for her own enjoyment. If she had not been distrait, its perfume would have warned her from drinking—yet, Cyrion had been kind to her, ensuring her forgetful sleep. Her eyes flooded again with tears, and through the tears she saw him gazing at her from beside the window. He was immaculate in the way that only he was capable of, like new-minted silver. Shaved, bathed, combed, unique and magical—and clad in the dark nomadic robe of the desert he affected when traveling. The garment which meant he was going away.

"Yes," she said, "that is clever. For once, I am glad to see you leave me. In the desert, perhaps, you will be safe. When do you go?"

"Soon," he said quietly, "but there is something to do first. You had better rise, my love. Hasmun will be here shortly."

Her eyes widened, then flicked across the cosmetics table.

The pots of unguent were not as she had left them. The tall pot of kohl lay on its side, And, as he moved, she beheld the ornamental brazier had been lit, the smoke rising against the blue-skied window. There was the smell of tar, distinct and unusual in the luxurious room.

"What have you done?"

"Guess," said Cyrion.

She was knotting the robe of pearl-embroidered silk together about herself, when blows hammered into the door. No permit for admittance was asked. A few moments the door was a barrier. Then it burst inward on shattered bars. Five of Hasmun's thugs edged grinningly aside, and Hasmun, the Doll Maker, strolled into the chamber.

To Mareme he nodded politely. At Cyrion he smiled with love.

"As a rule," said Hasmun, "I have had to deal with cowards and idiots. To meet a sheep that bites the butcher's blade is fresh. I like your novelty. I almost feel inclined to spare you. But still, on the whole, I think I should prefer you dead. To snuff a candle is pleasing. But to finish you, my dear, is to blot out a sun. How can I resist it?" Cyrion, poised in an attitude of nearly sublime indifference, was expressionless. "And now, sir Beautiful," said Hasmun, "where is the wax doll?"

"Look," said Cyrion gently, "up your arse,"

Hasmun shrugged. He waved his guard forward, then stayed them with the precise checking finger by which he demonstrated the power of his brain over their brawn.

"Mareme," said Hasmun, "possibly you would prefer to tell me where your client has hidden the doll. It would save the rude handling of your furniture and person by these ruffians. It is difficult for me, you are aware, to control them."

Mareme shrank.

"Please—" she said, but no more, which left the single impotent word to drop between them like a slain pigeon.

"Oh come now, Mareme," said Hasmun. He appealed to Cyrion. "This seductive night-lady of yours is not always so squeamish. But, of course, she loves you. I should know, having been privy to the secret. She once came to me for a love potion, when my reputation in Jebba was young and spotless. She did not get her potion. Such silly muck is not my trade. Though she did get something. She got, in fact, more than she yearned for. Did you not, my darling? Shall *I* tell," Hasmun inquired, "or shall *you* tell *me*?"

Mareme buried her face in her hands.

"I always considered it rather too opportune," said Cyrion, "that Hasmun the Apothecary arrived at the inn in conjunction with my own visit."

"Opportune and planned. She told me you would be there. And she made sure you would tangle with me, too. You could not resist the bait, this reputation of mine. It inflamed your vanity, Cyrion. As your reputation inflames mine. Jealousy. You must destroy wicked Hasmun and his wax, and rule alone in the cities of the coast. Eh, my honey? As I must, and will, destroy Cyrion."

Mareme shrieked through her hands at Cyrion: "He threatened me, to make my effigy in wax and torture me too—I was afraid. I could not master my fear. Oh, Cyrion—I love you as my life, but I could not die for you. And I swear I trust you would outwit him. In God's name, I swear that I did!"

"But you did not trust me enough to offer me the truth," said Cyrion, soft as arsenic sifted through a fine gauze.

Mareme took up the weeping she had set aside.

Hasmun said: "Cry tears of emerald if you must, beloved. But inform me where he has hidden the doll. Remember, I can still make your image. If I have seen Cyrion, I have seen you. One sight is sufficient. I need nothing else. The sight, the wax, the spell, the pin."

"The pot of kohl!" Mareme cried, then threw herself down before both men, the dark and the fair, her face in the rug.

Hasmun walked, as if he savored each footfall, to the cosmetics table. He took up the pot of kohl.

"Such exceedingly dark kohl," said Hasmun. "Yet not so black, for I see a speck of white here." He scraped at the stuff. "And so hard, for kohl, so sticky, so gritty to smear about the doe-eyes of a lovely woman. And it does not smell like kohl, either. Perhaps it is not? Could it be tar from the ship-sheds, I wonder? The kohl scooped out, the tar heated and poured in the pot. Then the wax figure thrust home into the cooling substance—just the speck of a white wax sole left showing. This pot now, is the exact size for such a doll—"

Hasmun dashed the pot suddenly onto the piece of bare stone floor beside the smoking brazier. The thin onyx, already weakened by heat, cracked. Hasmun retrieved from the two portions of the pot the solid lump of bitumen, and held it tenderly.

"Oh, my Cyrion. How miraculously sage you had been—if I had missed it. But as I have not missed, you have not been sage. Can you imagine, when I activate the spell—everything the bitumen has done to your image, you yourself will feel—burned, asphyxiated, blinded. Death in your nostrils and your mouth. I could almost experience compassion. A worse end even than I had devised for you. Do you wish to pray?"

Still expressionless, Cyrion said: "How long will I have for my prayers?"

"I have decided to be lenient," said Hasmun. "Rather than leave you in a nausea of dread all day, I will make the spell this instant. You shall die now."

Cyrion looked away. He stared into the blue sky beyond the window. He said nothing.

On the rugs, Mareme did not lift her head. At the door, the five bodyguards had excised their grins and were retreating in evident unease.

Hasmun raised his arms. He began to chant, in a voice far deeper and more vibrant than that he utilized during speech, the phrases of the spell. Sulphurous and bitter, these phrases splashed in searing drops about the room. The gleams of silk and sun faded; the window itself darkened as if with a premature dusk. In its cage, the dove-rat effaced itself in a quivering ball of fur. The atmosphere of the chamber shook, warmed dryly and terribly. The notes of pipes were heard, withering the eardrum. The air surged, gushed, became the air of a desert where no shade had ever been.

A wind blew through the chamber.

Chaos touched the chamber, and the hot breath of Hell.

Then all was still.

The spell was set on the doll. No need for more. Hasmun gave a crow of triumph, irrepressible. A crow that snapped, was amalgamated and disintegrated in a scream of anguish, which in its turn was stifled.

Hasmun fell to his knees. He clawed at his eyes, his nostrils and his mouth. His face congested; his hands seemed to freeze against his face. On his knees he staggered, and as he staggered, a desperate whining came from his lips. It might have been a resumption of the scream. Only Cyrion deciphered the fatal noise as a reversal of the spell, somehow got out through jaws of clamped stone, by sheer will alone. And Cyrion, a lightning bolt, was first in one spot, then another. In a split second he had wrenched from the magus' grasp the lump of bitumen with the wax doll inside it. A split second further, and Cyrion had hurled the black cake into the brazier. An eruption of fire leaped at the impact. At once the tar began to melt. Within, the wax was melting too. His spell was lost to Hasmun now. He floundered some way across the rugs in his attempts to scream, and tiny squeakings came from his throat. Till finally, all movement and all sound deserted him, and he reeled backward against the table of cosmetics, sending its exotic load into motion. As a rain of powder and rouge descended on him, Hasmun did not stir. The unguents spilled upon his blackened breathless face. The silver mirror slithered slowly from its stand and crashed to fragments at his shoulder.

He lay dead, and as the last atoms of wax and tar swirled together in the brazier, a dim smoke rose from his pristine clothing and from his unmarked flesh.

In the doorway, the guards groveled, saw Cyrion paid no attention, reversed themselves and ran. They no longer had a master. They had a story, of Cyrion the Magus.

Cyrion glanced at the girl. Through fingers and the fringe of the rug, she had watched. Falling rose powders had smudged her. With one rose cheek and one plaster white, she now watched Cyrion.

"You are a sorcerer, too," she muttered. "Will you kill me, as well?"

"No sorcerer," said Cyrion. There was the most fleeting trace of tiredness in his eyes.

"But—" said Mareme, emerging a fraction more from her prone position, "but how else—"

"I had the doll," said Cyrion. "He had formed the wax so it should resemble me. I reformed it with heat and a woman's paring knife, and colored its skin and hair with pigments from her jars. When I had finished, it resembled Hasmun as much as it had ever resembled me. By the nature of his spell, that was enough. He was meant to find the thing. You made my task the easier. So he worked his magic, and discovered himself asphyxiated, burned and blind inside a chunk of bitumen."

She sat up.

"I had faith," she said, "you would destroy him."

"My faithful Mareme," said Cyrion.

She trembled suddenly at his caressing tone. "But you forgive me—it was my fear—"

"I forgive you," said Cyrion. He glanced now at the smashed glass by the dead magus. Taking coins from his nomad's robe, he flung them across Hasmun's corpse, lightly and pitilessly into her lap. "Buy yourself another mirror," he said.

Her tears were silent in the silence that followed his departure. She knew he was gone for good.

1ST INTERLOGUE

When the mason had finished his story, it was discovered by the blond soldier that they had also finished the wine. After a few moments of idly upturning his cup on the table, and tapping the flagon, the soldier said, "Dry work, story-telling. Eh, Master Mason?"

The mason rolled up his papers and collected the abacus.

"Perhaps. I will leave you to discover."

"Wait—" Roilant came out of his ginger trance and caught the man's sleeve. "I must ask you some questions."

"Why?"

"Why?" Roilant was at a loss to explain the self-evident.

"He," said the soldier, winking, "does not believe your tale."

"That is not my reason," protested Roilant, "necessarily."

"Sir," said the mason, rising, "I informed you at the beginning I could offer no guaranty of the authentic. Suffice it to say, the adventure was current in Jebba. And I do know, for a fact, there had been an apothecary in the city of very ill repute, who mysteriously vanished from the thoroughfares. His shop was looted of its potions, and a large stuffed snake appeared in the market-place. None bought it. It was reckoned to carry the magus' curse."

Roilant, seeming troubled, began to speak.

The soldier interrupted him quietly.

"Maybe, the offer of more wine. . . ."

Roilant instantly called the morose slave, Esur, who had been lurking in the vicinity on the pretense of looking for something, and sent him for further refreshments.

"Dine with me," said Roilant to the mason.

"I am already contracted to dine at the house of an illustrious architect. I can scarcely refuse at this late hour."

"No. Then, for God's sake come back this evening."

"There really is no purpose, sir. I have told you all I can."

Roilant gave way and watched as the mason bowed and left the room. The young man with the ginger hair, though patently an aristocrat, appeared to possess none of the aristocrat's autocracy. Generally taken advantage of by all, he seemed to know it, with a sort of good-natured despair, and indeed to expect nothing else.

When the wine came and the soldier fell to drinking it, Roilant gazed over, without much hope, at the two still-debating philosophers in the embrasure. One looked to be of the variety of traveling scholar who now and then frequented the city, pausing to investigate the Imperial Library before passing on to the rather more illustrious one at Askandris in Kyros. The second man, older and less kempt, might well be a sage, the kind who wandered and was often mad. That such a type had entered the inn at all seemed peculiar, yet the straggly unclean beard and stragglier uncombed locks were highly sage-like. So much for the quality of the Honey Garden's guests. Unless the sage were a figure of popular standing, there could hardly be any kudos in serving him.

Roilant's attention was recalled with a start.

The slave, Esur, was whispering moistly in his ear.

"I said," Esur repeated, "if you want to pay gold for a story of Cyrion, I know a story of Cyrion."

The soldier laughed. "Oh, be *sure* he does."

Esur glowered.

"I am only a slave, fit merely to be kicked and thrashed and jumped upon for no good reason. But I still hear things."

Roilant said, "I suppose I owe you something anyway for knocking you down. Your life must be bad enough without that."

"It is—it is—if you knew. An orphan at two years, my parents lost to me, sold at three years in the market of Heshbel, where a child fetches less than a sheep—"

The soldier spluttered into his free wine.

Esur settled himself with great dignity and appropriated Roilant's own cup. "If *he*—" presumably the innkeeper—"comes, you must tell him I am helping you, or he will beat me. Again."

Esur nodded his rather well-groomed head, poured the wine straight down his throat, and commenced. . . .

A HERO AT THE GATES

The city lay in the midst of the desert.

At the onset it could resemble a mirage; next, one of the giant mesas that were the teeth of the desert, filmy blue with distance and heat. But Cyrion had found the road which led to the city, and taking the road, presently the outline of the place came clear. High walls and higher towers within, high gates of hammered bronze. And above, the high and naked desert sky, that reflected back from its sounding-bowl no sound at all from the city, and no smoke.

Cyrion stood and regarded the city. He was tempted to believe it a desert too, one of those hulks of men's making, abandoned centuries ago as the sands of the waste crept to their threshold. Certainly, the city was old. Yet it had no aspect of neglect, none of the indefinable melancholy of the unlived-in house.

Intuitively, Cyrion knew that as he stood regarding the city from without, so others stood noiselessly within, regarding Cyrion.

What did they perceive? This: A young man, tall and deceptively slim, deceptively elegant, which elegance itself was something of a surprise, for he had been months traveling in the desert, on the caravan routes and the rare and sand-blown roads. He wore the loose dark clothing of a nomad, but with the generous hood thrust back to show he did not have a nomad's pigmentation. At his side a sword was sheathed in red leather. The sunlight struck a silver-gold burnish on the pommel of the sword that was also the color of his hair. His left hand was mailed in rings which apparently no bandit had been able to relieve him of. If the watchers in the city had remarked that Cyrion was as handsome as the Arch-Demon himself, they would not have been the first to do so.

Then there came the booming scraping thunder of two bronze gates unbarred and dragged inward on their runners. The way into the city was exposed—yet blocked now by a crowd. Silent they were, and clad in black, the men and the women; even the children. And their faces were all the same, and gazed at Cyrion in the same way. They gazed at him as if he were the last bright day of their lives, the last bright coin in the otherwise empty coffer.

The sense of his dynamic importance to them was so strong that Cyrion swept the crowd a low, half-mocking bow. As he swept the bow, from his keen eyes' corner, Cyrion saw a man walk through the crowd and come out of the gate.

The man was as tall as Cyrion. He had a hard face, tanned but sallow, wings of black hair beneath a shaved crown, and a collar of swarthy gold set with gems. But his gaze also clung on Cyrion. It was like a lover's look. Or the starving lion's as it beholds the deer.

"Sir," said the black-haired man, "what brings you to this, our city?"

Cyrion gestured lazily with the ringed left hand.

"The nomads have a saying: 'After a month in the desert, even a dead tree is an object of wonder.' "

"Only curiosity, then," said the man.

"Curiosity; hunger; thirst; loneliness; exhaustion," enlarged Cyrion. By looking at Cyrion, few would think him affected by any of these things.

"Food we will give you, drink and rest. Our story we may not give. To satisfy the curious is not our fate. Our fate is darker and more savage. We await a savior. We await him in bondage."

"When is he due?" Cyrion inquired.

"You, perhaps, are he."

"Am I? You flatter me. I have been called many things, never savior."

"Sir," said the black-haired man, "do not jest at the wretched trouble of this city, nor at its solitary hope."

"No jest," said Cyrion, "but I hazard you wish some service of me. Saviors are required to labor. I believe, in behalf of their people. What do you want? Let us get it straight."

"Sir," said the man, "I am Memled, prince of this city."

"Prince, but not savior?" interjected Cyrion, his eyes widening with the most insulting astonishment.

Memled lowered his gaze.

"If you seek to shame me with that, it is your right. But you should know, I am prevented by circumstance."

"Oh, indeed. Naturally."

"I bear your gibe without complaint. I ask again if you will act for the city."

"And I ask you again what I must do."

Memled raised his lids and directed his glance at Cyrion once more.

"We are in the thrall of a monster, a demon-beast. It dwells in the caverns beneath the city, but at night it roves at will. It demands the flesh of our men to eat; it drinks the blood of our women and our children. It is protected through ancient magic, by a pact made a hundred years before between the princes of the city (cursed be they!) and the hordes of the Fiend. None born of the city has power to slay the beast. Yet there is a prophecy. A stranger, a hero who ventures to our gates, will have the power."

"And how many heroes," said Cyrion gently, "have you persuaded to an early death with this enterprise, you and your demon-beast?"

"I will not lie to you. Upward of a score. If you turn aside, no one here will speak ill of you. Your prospects of success would be slight, should you set your wits and sword against the beast. And our misery is nothing to you."

Cyrion ran his eyes over the black-clad crowd. The arid faces were all still fixed toward his. The children, like miniature adults, just as arid, immobile, noiseless. If the tale were true, they had learnt the lessons of fear and sorrow early, nor would they live long to enjoy their lessoning.

"Other than its dietary habits," Cyrion said, "what can you tell me of your beast?"

Memled shivered. His sallowness increased.

"I can reveal no more. It is a part of the foul sorcery that binds us. We may say nothing to aid you, do nothing to aid you. Only pray for you, if you should decide to pit your skill against the Devil."

Cyrion smiled.

"You have a cool effrontery, my friend, that is altogether delightful. Inform me then merely of this. If I conquer your beast, what reward is there—other, of course, than the blessing of your people?"

"We have our gold, our silver, our jewels. You may take them all away with you, or whatever you desire. We crave safety, not wealth. Our wealth has not protected us from horror and death."

"I think we have a bargain," said Cyrion. He looked at the children again. "Providing the treasury tallies with your description."

It was noon, and the desert sun poured its merciless light upon the city. Cyrion walked in the company of Prince Memled and his guard—similarly black-clad men, but with weighty blades and daggers at their belts, none, presumably, ever stained by beast-blood. The crowd moved circumspectly in the wake of their prince. Only the rustle of feet shuffling the dust was audible, and no speech. Below the bars of overhanging windows, here and there, a bird cage had been set out in the violet shade. The birds in the cages did not sing.

They reached a market-place, sun-bleached, unpeopled and without merchandise of any sort. A well at the market's center, proclaimed the water which would, in the first instance, have caused the building of a city here. Further evidence of water lay across from the market, where a broad stairway, flanked by stone columns, led to a massive battlemented wall and doors of bronze this time plated by pure flashing gold. Over the wall-top, the royal house showed its peaks and pinnacles, and the heads of palm trees. There was a green perfume in the air, heady as incense in the desert.

The crowd faltered in the market-place. Memled and his guard conducted Cyrion up the stairway. The gold-plated doors were opened. They entered a cool palace, blue as an under-sea cave, buzzing with slender fountains, sweet with the scent of sun-scorched flowers.

Black-garmented servants brought chilled wine. The food was poor and did not match the wine. Had the flocks and herds gone to appease the demon-beast? Cyrion had spied not a goat nor a sheep in the city. For that matter, not a dog, nor even the sleek lemon cats and striped marmosets rich women liked to nurse instead of babies.

After the food and drink, Memled, near wordless yet

courteous, led Cyrion to a treasury where wealth lay as thick as dust, and spilling on the ground.

"I would have thought," said Cyrion, fastidiously investigating ropes of pearls and chains of rubies, "such stuff might have bought you a hero, had you sent for one."

"This, too, is our limitation. We may not send. He must come to us, by accident."

"As the nomads say," said Cyrion, charmingly, innocently, " 'No man knows the wall better than he who built it.' "

At that instant, something thundered in the guts of the world.

It was a fearful bellowing cacophony. It sounded hot with violence and the lust for carnage. It was like a bull, or a pen of bulls, with throats of brass and sinews of molten iron, roaring in concert underground. The floor shook a little. A sapphire tumbled from its heap and fell upon another heap below.

Cyrion seemed interested rather than disturbed.

Certainly, there was nothing more than interest in his voice as he asked Prince Memled: "Can that be your beast, contemplating tonight's dinner?"

Memled's face took on an expression of the most absolute anguish and despair. His mouth writhed. He uttered a sudden sharp cry, as if a dreaded, well-remembered pain had seized him. He shut his eyes.

Intrigued, Cyrion observed: "It is fact then, you cannot speak of it? Calm yourself, my friend. It speaks very ably for itself."

Memled covered his face with his hands, and turned away.

Cyrion walked out through the door. Presently, pallid, but sufficiently composed, Memled followed his hero-guest. Black guards closed the treasury.

"Now," said Cyrion, "since I cannot confront your beast until it emerges from its caverns by night, I propose to sleep. My journey through the desert has been arduous, and, I am sure you agree, freshness in combat is essential."

"Sir," said Memled, "the palace is at your disposal. But, while you sleep, I and some others shall remain at your side."

Smiling, Cyrion assured him, "Indeed, my friend, you and they will not."

"Sir, it is best you are not left alone. Forgive my insistence."

"What danger is there? The beast is no threat till the sun goes down. There are some hours yet."

Memled seemed troubled. He spread his hand, indicating the city beyond the palace walls. "You are a hero, sir. Certain of the people may bribe the guard. They may enter the palace and disrupt your rest with questions and clamor."

"It seemed to me," said Cyrion, "your people are uncommonly quiet. But if not, they are welcome. I sleep deeply. I doubt if anything would wake me till sunset, when I trust you, prince, or another, will do so."

Memled's face, such an index of moods, momentarily softened with relief. "That deeply do you sleep? Then I will agree to let you sleep alone. Unless, perhaps a girl might be sent to you?"

"You are too kind. However, I decline the girl. I prefer to select my own ladies, after a fight rather than before."

Memled smiled his own stiff and rusty smile. Behind his eyes, sluggish currents of self-dislike, guilt and shame stirred cloudily.

The doors were shut on the sumptuous chamber intended for Cyrion's repose. Aromatics burned in silver bowls. The piercing afternoon sun was excluded behind shutters of painted wood and embroidered draperies. Beyond the shut doors, musicians made sensuous low music on pipes, drums and ghirzas. All was conducive to slumber. Though not to Cyrian's.

In contrast to his words, he was a light sleeper. In the city of the beast, he had no inclination to sleep at all. Privacy was another case. Having secured the chamber doors on the inside, he prowled soundlessly, measuring the room for its possibilities. He prised open a shutter, and scanned across the blistering roofs of the palace into the dry green palm shade of the gardens.

All about, the city kept its tongueless vigil. Cyrion thoughtfully felt of its tension. It was like a great single heart, poised between one beat and the next. A single heart, or two jaws about to snap together—

"Cyrion," said a voice urgently.

To see him spin about was to discover something of the nature of Cyrion. A nonchalant idler at the window one second, a coiled spring let fly the split second after. The sword was ready in his bare right hand. He had drawn too fast almost for a man's eye to register. Yet he was not even breathing quickly. And, finding the vacant chamber before him, as he had left it, no atom altered in his stance.

"Cyrion," cried the voice again, out of nothing and nowhere. "I pray heaven you had the cunning to lie to them, Cyrion."

Cyrion appeared to relax his exquisite vigilance. He had not.

"Heaven, no doubt, enjoys your prayers," he said. "And am I to enjoy the sight of you?"

The voice was female, expressive and very beautiful.

"I am in a prison," said the voice. There was the smallest catch in it, swiftly mastered. "I speak to warn you. Do not credit them, Cyrion."

Cyrion began to move about the room. Casually and delicately he lifted aside the draperies with his sword.

"They offered me a girl," he said reflectively.

"But they did not offer you certain death."

Cyrion had completed his circuit of the room. He looked amused and entertained.

He knelt swiftly, then stretched himself flat. A circular piece was missing in the mosaic pattern of the floor. He set one acute eye there and looked through into a dim area, lit by one murky source of light beyond his view. Directly below, a girl lay prone on the darkness which must itself be a floor, staring up at him from luminous wild eyes. In the half-glow she was more like a bloom of light herself than a reality; a trembling crystalline whiteness on the air, hair like the gold chains in the treasury, a face like that of a carved goddess, the body of a beautiful harlot before she gets in the trade—still virgin—and at her waist, her wrists, her ankles, drawn taut to pegs in the ground, iron chains.

"So there you are."

"It is a device of the stonework that enabled you to hear me and I you. In former days, princes would sit in your room above, drinking and making love, listening to the cries of those being tortured in this dungeon, and sometimes they would peer through to increase their pleasure. But either Memled has forgotten, or he thought me past crying out. I glimpsed your shadow pass over the aperture. Earlier, the jailor spoke your name to me. Oh, Cyrion, I am to die, and you with me."

She stopped, and tears ran like drops of silver from her wild eyes.

"You have a captive audience, lady," said Cyrion.

"It is this way," she whispered, "the beast they have pretended to seek rescue from is, in fact, the familiar demon of the city. They love the brute, and commit all forms of beastliness in its name. How else do you suppose they have amassed such stores of treasure, here in the wilderness? And once a year they honor the beast by giving to it a beautiful maiden and a notable warrior. I was to have been the bride of a rich and wise lord in a city by the sea. But I am thought beautiful; Memled heard of me. Men of this city attacked the caravan in which I rode, and carried me here, to this, where I have lingered a month. You arrived by unlucky destiny, unless some of Memled's sorcery enticed you here, unknowingly. Tonight, we shall share each other's fate."

"You are their prisoner, I am not. How do they plan to reconcile me to sacrifice?"

"That is but too simple. At dusk a hundred men will come. You do not seem afraid, but even fearless, before a hundred men you cannot prevail. They will take your sword, stun you, bind you. There is a trick door in the western wall that gives on a stairway. Through the door and down the stair they will thrust you. Below are the caverns where the beast roams, bellowing for blood. I too must pass that way to death."

"A fascinating tale," said Cyrion, "What prompts you to tell it me?"

"Are you not a hero?" the girl demanded passionately. "Have you not promised to slay the beast for them, to be their savior, though admittedly in return for gold. Can you not instead be your own savior, and mine?"

"Forgive me, lady," said Cyrion, in a tone verging subtly on naïveté, "I am at a loss. Besides, our dooms seem written with a firm hand. Perhaps we should accept them."

Cyrion rose from the mosaic. On his feet he halted, just aside from the hole.

After a moment, the girl screamed: "You are a coward, Cyrion. For all your looks and your fine sword, for all your nomad's garments, the wear of those they name the Lions of the Desert—for all that—*coward* and *fool*."

Cyrion seemed to be considering.

After a minute, he said amiably: "I suppose I might open the trick door now, and seek the monster of my own volition, sword in hand and ready. Then, if I slay him, I might return for you, and free you."

The girl wept. Through her tears she said, with a knife for a voice: "If you are a *man*, you will do it."

"Oh no, lady. Only if I am your notion of a man."

The stair was narrow, and by design lightlessly invisible—save that Cyrion had filched one of the scented tapers from the room above to give him eyes. The trick door had been easy to discover, an ornamental knob that turned, a slab that slid. Thirty steps down, he passed another kind of door, of iron, on his right. Faintly, beyond the door, he heard a girl weeping.

The stair descended through the western wall of the palace, and proceeded underground. Deep in the belly of the caverns that sprawled, as yet unseen, at the end of the stair, no ominous rumor was manifested. At length, the stair reached bottom, and ceased. Ahead, stretched impenetrable black, and from the black an equally black and featureless silence.

Cyrion advanced, the taper held before him. The dark toyed with the taper, surrendering a miniature oasis of half-seen things, such as trunks of rock soaring up toward the ceiling. The dark mouthed Cyrion. It licked him, rolled him around on its tongue. The lit taper was just a garnish to its palate; it liked the light with Cyrion, as a man might like salt with his meat.

Then there came a huge wind from out of the nothing ahead. A metallic heated blast, as if from a furnace. Cyrion stopped, pondering. The beast, closeted in the caverns, had sighed? An instant after, it roared.

Above, in the treasury, the roaring had seemed to stagger the foundations of the house. Here, it peeled even the darkness, and dissected it like a fruit. The broken pieces of the dark rattled on the trunks of rock. Shards erupted from the rock and rained to the ground. The caverns thrummed, murmured, fell dumb. The dark did not re-congeal.

There was a new light. A flawless round of light, pale, smoky red. Then it blinked. Then there were two. Two flawless rounds of simmering raw rose. Two eyes.

Cyrion dropped the taper and put his heel on it.

This beast you witnessed by its own illumination. It swelled from the black as the eyes brightened with its interest. It was like no other beast; you could liken it to nothing else. It was like itself, unique. Only its size was comparable to anything. To a tower, a wall—one eye alone, that rosy window, could have fit tall Cyrion in its socket.

So radiant now, those eyes, the whole cavern was displayed, the mounting rocks, the floor piled with dusts, the dust curtains floating in the air. From the dust, the beast lifted itself. It gaped its mouth. Cyrion ducked, and the blast of burning though non-incendiary breath rushed over his head. It was not fetid breath, simply very hot. Cyrion planted his sword point down in the dust, and indolently leant on it. He looked like a marvelous statue, For someone who could move like lightning, he had chosen now to become stone, and the pink fires settled on his pale hair, staining it the color of diluted wine.

In this fashion Cyrion watched the demon-beast, by the light of its vast eyes, slink toward him. He watched, motionless, leaning on his sword.

Then a sinewy taloned forefoot, lengthy as a column, struck at him, and Cyrion was no longer in that spot, motionless, leaning on his sword, as he had been an instant before. Away in the shadow, Cyrion stood again unmoving, sword poised, negligently waiting. Again, the batting of scythe-fringed death; again missing him.

The jaws clashed, and slaver exploded forth, like a waterfall. Cyrion was gone, out of reach. Stone had returned to lightning. The fourth blow was his. He neither laughed at the seriousness of his mission nor frowned. No meditation was needed, the target no challenge, facile. . . .

Cyrion swung back his arm, and sent the sword plummeting, like a straight white rent through the cavern. It met the beast's left eye, shattered it like pink glass, plunged to the brain.

Like a cat, Cyrion sprang to a ledge and crouched there.

Black ichor spouted to the cavern's top. Now, once more gradually, the light faded. The thunderous roaring ebbed like a colossal sea withdrawing from these dry caves beneath the desert.

On his ledge, Cyrion waited, pitiless and without triumph, for the beast, in inevitable stages, to fall, to be still, to die.

In the reiterated blackness, blind, but remembering infallibly his way, as he remembered all things, once disclosed, Cyrion went to the demon-beast and plucked out his sword, and returned with it up the pitchy stairway to the iron dungeon door set in the wall.

The iron door was bolted from without. He shot the bolts and pushed open the door.

He paused, just inside the prison, sword in hand, absorbing each detail. A stone box the prison was, described by dull fluttering torches. The girl lay on the floor, pegged and chained as he had regarded her through the peep-hole. He glanced toward the peep-hole, which was barely to be seen against the torch murk.

"Cyrion," the girl murmured, "the beast's black blood is on your sword, and you live."

Her white and lovely face was turned to him, the rich strands of golden hair swept across the floor, her silken breasts quivered to the tumult of her heart. Her tears fell again, but now her eyes were yielding. They showed no amazement or inquisition, only love.

He went to her, and raising his sword a second time, chopped the head from her body.

Thirty steps up, a door crashed wide. Cyrion stooped gracefully, straightened, took the thirty steps in a series of fine-flexed leaps. He stepped through the trick door and was in the upper chamber, the sword yet stark in his bare right hand. And in his left hand, mailed with rings, a woman's head held by its shining hair.

Opposite, in the forced doorway of the chamber, Memled stared with a face like yellow cinders.

Then he collapsed on his knees, and behind him, the guards also dropped down.

Memled began to sob. The sobs were rough, racking him. He plainly could not keep them back, and his whole body shuddered.

Cyrion remained where he was, ignoring his bloody itinerary. Finally Memled spoke.

"After an eternity, heaven has heard our lament, replied to our entreaty. You, the hero of the city, after the eternity, our savior. But we were bound by the hell-pact, and could neither warn nor advise you. How did you fathom the truth?"

"And what is the truth?" asked Cyrion, with unbelievable sweetness, as he stood between blotched blade and dripping head.

"The truth—that the monster is illusion set to deceive those heroes who would fight for us, set to deceive by the bitch-sorceress whose head you have lopped. Year in and out, she has drained us, roaming by night, feasting on the flesh and blood of my people, unrelenting and vile she-wolf that she was. And our fragile chance, a prophecy, the solitary weakness in the hell-pact—that only if a heroic traveler should come to the gates and agree to rid us of our torment, might we see her slain. But always she bewitched and duped these heroes, appearing in illusory shackles, lying that we would sacrifice her, sending each man to slay a phantom beast that did not exist save while her whim permitted it. And then the hero would go to her, trustingly, and she would seize him and murder him too. Over a score of champions we sent to their deaths in this manner, because we were bound and could not direct them where the evil lay. And so, again, sir hero, how did you fathom truth in this sink of witchery?"

"Small things," said Cyrion laconically.

"But you will list them for me?" Memled proffered his face, all wet with tears, and brimming now with a feverish joy."

"Her proximity to me, which seemed unlikely if she were what she claimed. Her extreme beauty which had survived a month's imprisonment and terror, and her wrists and ankles which were unchafed by her chains. That, a stranger to this place, she knew so much of its by-ways and its history. More interesting, that she knew so much of me—besides my name, which I did not see why a jailor should have given her—for instance, that I wore a nomad's garment, and that she thought me presentable, though she could not have seen me herself. She claimed she beheld my shadow pass over the peep-hole, but no more. She knew all our bargain, too, yours and mine, as if she had been listening to it. Would you hear more?"

"Every iota of it!"

"Then I will cite the beast, which patently was unreal. So huge a voice it could make the floors tremble, and yet the house was still intact. And the creature itself so untiny it could have shaken the city to flour, but confined in a cavern where it had not even stirred the dust. And then, the absence of bones, and its wholesome breath, meant to impress by volume and heat, and which smelled of nothing else. A cat which chews rats will have a fouler odor. And this thing, which supposedly ate men and drank their blood and was big enough to fill the air with stink, clean as a scoured pot on the stove. Lastly, I came above and saw the peep-hole would show nothing of what went on in this room, let alone a shadow passing. And I noticed too, the lady's sharp teeth, if you like."

Memled got to his feet.

Halfway to Cyrion, he checked and turned to the guards.

"Inform the city our terror has ended."

The guards, round-eyed, rushed away.

Memled came to Cyrion, glaring at the head, which Cyrion had prudently set down in a convenient bowl, and which was beginning to crumble to a sort of rank powder.

"We are free of her," Memled cried. "And the treasury is yours to despoil. Take all I have. Take—take this, the royal insignia of the city," and he clutched the collar of swarthy gold at his throat.

"Unnecessary," said Cyrion lightly. He wiped his sword upon a drapery. Memled paid no heed. Cyrion sheathed the sword. Memled smiled, still rusty, but his face vivid with excitement. "The treasury, then," suggested Cyrion.

Cyrion dealt cannily in the treasury. The light of day was gone by now, and by the smooth amber of the lamps, Cyrion chose from among the ropes of jewels and skeins of metal, from the cups and gemmy daggers, the armlets and the armor. Shortly, there was sufficient to weigh down a leather bag, which Cyrion slung upon his back. Memled would have pressed further gifts on him. Cyrion declined.

"As the nomads say," said Cyrion, " 'Three donkeys cannot get their heads into the same bucket.' I have enough."

Outside in the city, now ablaze with windows under a sky ablaze with stars, songs and shouting of celebration rose into the cool hollow of the desert night.

"A night without blood and without horror," said Memled.

Cyrion walked down the palace stairway. Memled remained on the stair, his guards scattered loosely about him. In the market-place a fire burned, and there was dancing. The black clothes were all gone; the women had put on their finery and earrings sparkled and clinked as they danced together. The men drank, eyeing the women.

Near the edge of the group, two children poised like small stones, dressed in their best, and Cyrion saw their faces.

A child's face, incorrigible calendar of the seasons of the soul. Men learn pretense, if they must. A child has not had the space to learn.

Cyrion hesitated. He turned about, and strolled back toward the steps of the palace, and softly up the steps.

"One last thing, my friend, the prince," he called to Memled.

"What is that?"

Cyrion smiled.

"You were too perfect and I did not quite see it, till just now a child showed me." Cyrion swung the bag from his shoulder exactly into Memled's belly. Next second the sword flamed to Cyrion's hand, and Memled's black-winged head hopped down the stair.

Around the fire, the dancers had left off dancing. The guards were transfixed in stammering shock, though no hand flew to a blade. Cyrion wiped his own blade, this time on Memled's already trembling torso.

"That one, too," said Cyrion.

"Yes, sir," said the nearest of the guard, thickly. "There were the two of them."

"And they diced nightly over who should batten on the city, did they not, your prince-demon and his doxy. He could not avoid the prophecy, either, of a hero at the gates. He was obliged to court me, and, in any event, reckoned the lady would deal with me as with the others. But when she did not, he was content I should have killed her, if he could escape me and keep the city for himself to feed him. He rendered himself straightly. He never once uttered for his own demonic side. He acted as a man, as Memled, the prince—fear and joy. He was too good. Yet I should never have been sure but for the children's agonized blankness down there, in the crowd."

"You are undeniably a hero, and heaven will bless you," said the guard. It was easy to see he was a true human man, and the rest of them were human too. Unpredictable and bizarre was their relief at rescue, as with all true men, who do not get their parts by heart beforehand, when to cry or when to grin.

Cyrion laughed low at the glittering sky. "Then bless me, heaven."

He went down the stair again. Both children were howling now, as they had not dared do formerly, untrammeled, healthy. Cyrion opened the leather bag, and released the treasure on the square, for adults and children alike to play with.

Empty-handed, as he came, Cyrion went away into the desert, under the stars.

2ND INTERLOGUE

Esur, who had fallen into a kind of trance during his sing-song story-telling, reached for the wine flagon and was prevented by the soldier, who had got to it first.

"By the Choirs of Heaven," said the soldier, "what a tale that is." Esur glared, and the soldier drank. "Is any of it to be believed? Where is this demon city? Does it exist? Plainly an invention of the most—"

Affronted, Esur rose, and the soldier broke off, grinning. Esur stared at Roilant.

"You asked for a story. I gave you one. Where is my gold?"

"Actually, I asked for information on the whereabouts and character of Cyrion," said Roilant.

The soldier gurgled in his cup, and emerged to declare:

"He told you something. Cyrion is capable of sentiment over small children. And can remain unblinded by the prettiest woman."

Roilant frowned. He produced a piece of gold from a wallet and handed the money to Esur, who promptly bit it ferociously with surprisingly white teeth.

"Sound coinage," said Esur, pleased. "Thank you, generous lord."

"Wait," crowed the soldier, "tell me what is a gresher, a gerosha—"

"He means a ghirza," said Roilant. "A musical instrument with strings, I believe."

"Ah," said Esur. "I always wondered."

The soldier hiccupped.

"Wonderful wine here. Bring some more. Make up another lie as you fetch it."

"The story is real. I vouch for it," said Esur. "I heard it some while ago on a forced march from the slave market of Cassireia."

"A minute ago it was Heshbel."

Esur showed his teeth again.

"If I were a free man—"

"But you are not," said the soldier, and hurled the quarter-filled wine cup at him.

Esur ducked with alarming agility and the cup, somehow seeming to gain more liquid as it flew, landed in the lap of the scholar, who leapt up with a shout.

"Oh God," said the drunk sailor, and buried his head in his hands, refusing to participate in what came next.

It was Roilant who, taking resigned responsibility, arose, crossed the room, and begged the scholar's pardon. The scholar, recovering his equilibrium, shook the wine from his long robe.

"It is nothing. A shock to cool my heat in argument; the reprimand of God, I fear. This gentleman and I have been in earnest discourse regarding certain religious teachings."

Across the table in the embrasure, the sage, as tangled and unsartorial as he had appeared from the far side of the room, and perfumed faintly, though only faintly, you noticed with relief, by an odor of goat, paid no heed, poring on over the unrolled parchment he and the scholar had been studying.

"Nevertheless, my deepest apologies," said Roilant. "My own table has become somewhat rowdy. I have been asking after a man—"

"—Named Cyrion. Yes, I caught a word or two. Cyrion of Cyroam. Or some say of Nowhere At All."

"You know him?" The disappointed Roilant was cautious now, uneager.

The scholar touched a beautiful enameled amulet at his throat. His face was aesthetically pale, handsome under its lines and weathering. One of his fine, tapering hands came from the amulet and briefly patted Roilant's arm.

"I am sorry I too must fail you. Like your other informants, I have heard stories of Cyrion. But know him? Of course, how many of us can say we know even ourselves."

"I am," said Roilant, "becoming desperate."

"Oh, do not become that. I see your third flagon has arrived, much to the approval of your warrior friend. And soon the noon dinner will be served. The kid is excellent."

Roilant's relief at finding company in a more cultured mode was evident.

"Will you join me for dinner? To recompense for the sudden arrival of unasked for wine."

The scholar smiled.

"You are most kind. Certainly I will. This wise sage is fasting, and consumes only wine, milk and water for the rest of the week. I do not think he would care to dine."

"A great pity," said Roilant, without regret.

The sage, looking up, shot him a wild, woolly glance, and returned to the parchment with a mutter—"mine, actually," the scholar confessed, as he and Roilant crossed the room to the other table. "But I fancy he is not done with it, and might become somewhat dogged. Rather than have it torn in half, I will temporarily surrender it."

The soldier now showed neither shame nor any sign of incipient apology.

"No one," announced the soldier, "is permitted to sit down here unless he pleshes, plebers—*plodges*—a story concerning Skiriom, Spyrion, Cyripom. You see?"

"I do indeed see," answered the scholar, "a knack I think you are about to lose."

"Eh?"

"But I will pledge a story, if my host desires it."

"Why not," said Roilant mournfully. "It seems to be all I am to get."

There was a noise beyond the curtain, footsteps, laughter, and the imperative summoning clang of the gong.

Despite himself, Roilant gazed at the doorway, and was rewarded by a mass entry, the innkeeper and two fresh slaves hurrying in its wake. Roilant's face did not fall, but it set. The arrivals comprised three merchants in gaudy habit, complete with two ladies of sprightly bearing who were unlikely to be their wives or sisters, but were quite young enough to have been their granddaughters, plus a caravaneer—by his comments—who seemed in some disarray and a great deal of dust. Not one of these persons was even blond, let alone of the whip-lash, quicksilver elegance Roilant was coming, even by hearsay, to associate with the creature of the tales.

"Courage," said the scholar gently, "have faith. If your

destiny decrees you find him, he will come here. Or you will meet him elsewhere."

"I need to meet him today." Roilant shook his head. "I can wait no longer."

"It seems you require his services urgently."

Roilant now looked evasive.

"I did not intend to pry. Let me advise you. Even from a group of myths, it is possible to learn a reasonable amount. The very fact that he has become the subject of myths says much of Cyrion. And who knows, the tales may be true. I have learned to credit sorcery, just as I credit the power of God. And God is the Master of all balances. If there is evil in the world, some men must arise with the natural facility for defeating it. How else may we survive?"

Roilant agreed politely. The soldier burped, and said it seemed to be the hour for dining.

Seated at a central table, the merchants were laughing uproariously and the young women squealing and clinking their earrings and bangles. Over the din, the caravaneer could be heard confiding to the innkeeper about lost wheat, and a thieving steward who had run off with half his profits and his servant girl.

Suddenly the sage surged upward in the embrasure. Pointing at the merchants' female companions, he shrieked: "Unclean and monstrous! Oh users of men, Oh cows of vice, Oh heifers of the Devil! There shall come upon you weeping and misery all your days, and after them shall wait an unquiet grave."

The two women sniggered nervously. One of the merchants, the largest, got to his feet and bellowed. The innkeeper rushed to pacify and the sage relapsed, salivating, and was presently brought some milk, probably goat to complement his aroma.

The scholar murmured, "another misquotation, I am afraid."

" 'Squaishen," agreed the soldier.

"Kid, with the honey," said Roilant to one of the new slaves. "For three," he added tiredly.

"Have you ever visited," said the scholar to Roilant, "Teboras. . . ?"

ONE NIGHT OF THE YEAR

"Proceed no farther that way! You must come with us."

The voice, scraping as harsh from the scented darkness as sharp sword from soft scabbard, not surprisingly halted the traveler. Yet, pausing, he did not turn. He was swathed in a hooded cloak of finest black Askandrian silk, that concealed both appearance and attitude. His own voice, musical and exceedingly mild, inquired: "And why must I do that?"

A brash laugh sounded.

"To commence, because there are two of us and but one of you. To continue, because a reward awaits your compliance. To conclude, because my Lord Jolan bids you, and I am here to add weight to the bidding."

At that, a profile appeared, pale in the dark, between the hood and the shoulder. A chiseled profile, startlingly handsome, and an eye of long-lashed innocence.

"Suppose," said the profile, "for the sake of argument merely, that I refuse."

The brash voice grunted and there came a swirl of motion, abruptly checked. The harsh voice exclaimed wildly: "No, Radri! No violence—" But the silken traveler had already altered in every particular. The black cloak flew back, the slim body within it seemed to spin. A demoniac angel stood suddenly face to face with the two men, a drawn sword in his right hand flickering at the throat of one, his ringed left hand stroking a lethal little knife in the air, over the ribs of the other. Both men jerked and froze with choking surprise. The angel said, apologetically, "And now, gentlemen, perhaps you would care to explain your request more fully."

It was midnight in Teboras. Midnight all across the quiet and ancient city, perfumed with its oleanders, ghostly with its magnificent ruins, harped through with the faint strumming of its deep blue lake. In this quarter, high in the fine streets above the old Remusan Forum, you might expect falling blossoms, the occasional well-to-do courtesan with her litter and attendants, even a stray phantom, perhaps, from one of the arcane temples. But generally not robbers. Nor did this duo look like snatch-purses. The taller of the two was richly dressed, his big shoulders bulging sleeves of brocade and gold embroidery—this was the brash person who had wished to rush the traveler. The shorter and more slender man, young and attractive as his voice was not, and yellow-haired, wore the clothing of a prince, and pendant from a huge gold collar about his neck shone a finely painted antique portrait of some lady, set round with large sapphires and larger rubies.

This Yellowhair, presumably the Lord Jolan, now cleared his throat, but did not clear it of its grating quality. "Forgive us, sir. I fear we were peremptory. It is ineeed a *request*, not a demand, that you go with us. But Radri spoke truly when he promised you a reward." The traveler's innocent and luminous eyes did not even blink. "But, of course, the reward depends on your accompanying us."

"Where?"

"Why," Jolan moved his hand cautiously, "only into the house there."

A high stone wall, broken by two stout gates and brimmed over by courtyard trees, seemed to indicate an important dwelling. It resembled several others the length of the street, all showing a blank windowless facade to the public gaze. Actually, the traveler's business had been some steps farther up the way, where a Remusan fane interrupted the present with its archaic pillars and its ghosts. It was well known there was a haunt in the vicinity. There had even been a hushed rumor of fresh human bones intermittently left scattered over the years on the open ground beside this temple. The traveler's nature was such that notoriety of that kind occasionally intrigued him. But to be interrupted possibly intrigued him more.

"In the house," he now mused, still delicately balancing sword and knife in their uncivilized positions at jugular and lung, "what shall I be called on to do?"

Jolan sighed.

"Sir, you will be called on to make a fair judgment."

"Between whom?"

"Between four persons, of whom I and my steward, here, are two."

"I confess, you fascinate me. A judgment relating to what?"

"A—family matter. I shun discussion of it on the street. If you will enter—? Should you decide the thing satisfactorily, you will be doing us a greater service than you could dream. And the reward will be in gold, silver and gems."

The traveler sheathed his sword in red leather and his knife in silk. His hair seemed made of silk, too, and blond as the moon that was now slowly rising over the forum below.

"Gold, silver and gems are an irresistible argument."

The steward, Radri, thrust one of the big gates open. The tree-filled court revealed itself, somewhere sprinkled by an invisible fountain. The front of the house was obscurely sketched by a pair of dull torches set either side the portico, but a threat of red light dripped down the steps; the bronze-faced door stood ajar.

"Please enter," said Jolan. "And, since you consent to do so, may I ask your name?"

"Cyrion."

The house was of somewhat unusual design, but Teboras was inclined to borrowings. A marble basin dominated the entry, ornamented neither by fish nor flowers but by mats of dead leaves. Beyond was a candle-lit room with painted walls and rich draperies. Yet something indefinably unkempt presided over the chamber, an air of neglect. It was, however, occupied.

Both figures rose instantly. The nearer of the two was a man, dressed in the somber robe indicative of the priest, though contorted, pearl-studded talismans on his breast pointed to a perhaps unorthodox canon. His countenance was long, melancholy and sallow, with a contrasting mouth of tiny, greedy redness. The second figure was that of a young woman, small in stature and very slender. Her leaf-yellow hair was arranged in an elaborate style reminiscent of the Teboran vogue for copying Remusan frescoes. She was clad in plain black, but like Jolan had a golden collar, hers of filigree. Gold bracelets encircled her wrists, while both her hands were heavily ringed with precious stones. Her face was at once serious and sensual, with large guarded eyes.

No servant, beyond the steward Radri, was in evidence. The late hour and the quiet of the house suggested its staff were all abed, or else had been ordered from the premises.

Jolan announced the visitor solemnly.

"And this," he said, next turning to Cyrion, "is my sister, Sabara. And this, our religious, Naldinus, a scholar, also skilled in physic. Together, we make up the four you are to judge."

Neither the priest nor the young woman seemed amazed by the proceedings. Clearly, the entire family was eccentric.

Radri had meantime gone to a carved table, and poured a dark red wine into five goblets of hammered silver. These he now handed round, taking the ultimate cup himself.

Cyrion breathed the vintage. Its plummy sweetness interested him.

"To our guest—" Jolan pronounced the toast with intense gravity. "And to justice, that she may deal fairly with us. At last."

The taste of the wine interested Cyrion further. The other four drank deeply, but only Radri coarsely emptied his cup. That he joined the drinking at all was a sign of his intimate involvement in this family gathering.

"And now," said Jolan. He glanced at Cyrion. "If you are ready—"

"I am ready," said Cyrion, "for an explanation."

"You shall have it. Very shortly. Before that, I must show you something. It is the reason for your being here. The reason that we demanded—I mean, naturally, *asked*—that you would come in. Radri, lead the way."

The steward took up a candlebranch, holding it, with muscular carelessness, by its heavy pedestal, and walked forward without a word, pushing aside a drapery as he went. The priest glided after him at once, followed by the girl. Jolan made anxious gestures that Cyrion should emulate them, then fell in behind him. The room opened, rather unexpectedly on a garden. Passing along an avenue between tall shrubs, in the wake of Radri's light, they reached a small pillared building. It might have been, at casual glance, a summer pavilion, but the lack of windows gave it away. It was a sepulchre.

"You must not be alarmed," said Jolan hastily. He peered

at Cyrion, but Cyrion showed no trace of anything beyond polite attention, even though Radri was busily unbolting the sepulchre door. Perhaps the guest was noting the odd automatic quality his hosts displayed in their acceptance of him, in their stroll to the tomb, and now in their orderly filing inside. As if this were not the only time such things had happened. As if, in fact, they had happened frequently.

The inside of the sepulchre was also unusual, mainly because it had been arranged as a bedchamber. There were further paintings and drapes, lamps and candles, which latter Radri methodically lit. Cushioned couches, chairs and little tables poised on rugs. A canopied bed dominated the scene, the curtains closed. Jolan now strode to these curtains and dragged them aside. Then, he stepped back and proclaimed, his hoarse voice grown yet hoarser: "My other, elder, sister, Marival."

She lay on the embroidered sheet, her round chin tilted, her warm lips smiling, her barely covered breasts glowing, as if but recently caressed. Her skin was whiter than the marble, her hair had been poured round her from the night. She was dressed in a bygone fashion that suited her to perfection, and jewelled in a way that would have been grossly exaggerated, had she been alive. But, since she was demurely deceased, even an artist could hardly have quarrelled with it.

Jolan began to sob, leaning against the wall. Radri cursed and would not look at the bed. The priest muttered some unrecognizable prayer at the back of his throat. Sabara, the living sister, walked forward, and said to Cyrion: "She is lovely, is she not? Do you think so? Everyone always thought so. Beautiful Marival. Marvelous Marival. Do you think her marvellous?"

"I think," said Cyrion, "she is dead."

"Oh, yes. But her glamour lives on. Listen to my brother, crying like a child. And to Radri's oaths. Even Naldinus is affected."

"And you?" Cyrion inquired.

"I," said Sabara, "am jealous of her, even now."

The priest spoke to Cyrion for the first time.

"This house, sir, is wise in certain magics, certain sciences. When Marival died, I used particular medicine of Aigum, wherein I am versed, to embalm and preserve her flesh."

"So she died and you preserved her," said Cyrion. "Why is judgment needed in connection with that?"

Jolan flung about from the wall, his eyes inflamed.

"One of us, one of the four here with you in this place, killed her. One of us *poisoned* Marival. You must determine which one."

"*Must* I?" Cyrion was frankly incredulous.

Jolan smeared the water from his eyes with his sleeves.

"Yes. Must. It is too late now for any retreat. One of us is sick of guilt, yet will not, cannot—confess. We are all in hell, and you must free us. You must detect which of us is the murderer."

Cyrion was touchingly ingenuous. "How?"

"By hearing our accounts of our actions and deeds on the afternoon of her death."

"I surmise," said Cyrion, "you would do better to seek redress from the law. The governor in Teboras is adept, I hear. Or you could take your case to the king at Heruzala—"

"*No.* The law is no use to us."

"Possibly, neither am I."

Jolan smiled unpleasantly, and finally his appearance matched his unattractive voice.

"You no longer have any choice. Naldinus spoke of sciences and sorceries known to this family, and he spoke well. I will tell you now, this house is not quite as it appears to you, neither are we. Even our names have been altered, in order that you might enter without prejudice. Why should we go to such trouble if we were not in earnest? And the same phenomena which cloak us, are capable of keeping you in this chamber, our prisoner, till you have done as we ask—no, as we *demand* of you. Try the door."

Cyrion looked quizzically about. The magically disguised (if they were) denizens of the house stared back at him intensely. To oblige them, he walked to the sepulchre door and toyed with the handle. The door did not open. More. At the third rattle, it slowly, but undeniably, *vanished*. The wall was a blank, the handle was air—maybe it was only an illusion, but if so, an illusion that included touch and hearing with sight. The deaf silence of total enclosure wrapped round the interior of the tomb. The wall was smooth and seamless against Cyrion's palm.

Cyrion turned and regarded his captors reasonably.

"With magic at your disposal, you should be able to discover by yourselves which one of you killed Marival."

"Where emotion clouds magic, magic becomes unstable and unusable," said Jolan. "We could not—were not able—"

"We require," said Naldinus suavely, "a dispassionate witness. If you will, it is a fate laid on us. We cannot help ourselves, yet we are desperate for help. Even the murderer," Naldinus hooded his cunning sorrowful eyes, "even he—or she—is desperate, perhaps, for a conviction. *To be found out.*"

"Suppose I determine which of you is the transgressor, and the transgressor, contrary to your hopes, Father, refuses to concur?"

"We—are promised a sign," said Jolan, avoiding Cyrion's eyes. "An unmistakable omen, once the true facts are unearthed. You need only be right."

"And do not forget," said Sabara crisply, "the gold, silver and gems which are to be your reward."

"And what if I fail in my judgment?" The wooden silence deepened. Cyrion listened to it a moment, and said: "The reason I mention it is that I have extravagantly taken the notion that you have forced midnight travelers in off the street before, to act as judges. And since I now am here, I can only assume my predecessors were unsuccessful. What then, is your reward for *un*success?"

Radri the steward grinned across the lamplit tomb.

"Death."

It would have been obvious to any by now that the family were not merely eccentric, but stark crazy. Brooding on murder had turned their brains like milk. It appeared they would currently kill, repeatedly and without conscience, in order to expunge the original crime, which had assumed such fanatical significance. You might have thought the threat an addled lie, and that bad enough from the lips of mad magicians. But Cyrion had not forgotten the rumors of human bones occasionally scattered but a few steps up the street, beside the Remusan temple. Tales of a haunt were one thing; here might reside the real and grisly truth.

As for the omen, if it were feasible, doubtless its source was as dubious as the atmosphere.

Cyrion smiled his most enchanting smile, and seated himself with simple and exquisite elegance in the nearest chair.

The mad family glanced at each other tautly. However many victims had been coerced into this predicament, there had never before been one like this one.

"Well," said Cyrion, with a slight but quite charming impatience, "you had better begin, my friends. One by one, your accounts of your dealings with the dead woman, and of her last afternoon in your company. In whatever order pleases you most. I shall ask you questions, as I think fit."

There ensued a brief and restrainedly savage argument. At length Radri was prevailed on to start the proceedings.

Radri had been, he declared, a soldier, and it was on the battlefield that he had initially served under Jolan's father. This lord had subsequently employed him as steward to the house. Radri had been treated more as relation than servant. The late master's offspring, Jolan, Sabara and the eldest child, Marival, had continued the practice. Indeed, Marival, whose beauty was the talk of the city, had shown Radri especial favor. Indeed again, Marival, who might have had her pick of the rich aristocrats of Teboras, had spurned them, preferring Radri. "They," Marival had avowed, "are lapdogs, marmosets, good for nothing but to be given dishes of cream. They swoon at blood. They can think of nothing but the latest love tune. They have the strength of crushed flowers. But you," she murmured to Radri, "are strong as a lion. You are a *man*."

"You are a *liar*!" Jolan yelled at this point. "As ever, Radri, you foul the name of my sister with this absurd and filthy nonsense."

"Foul her name? She had me in her bed, and not the bed only," roared Radri. "She could not get enough of me. She laughed at the others, as she laughed at you. It was well enough when I was *your* friend, lord Jolan, but when I turned to her—as what man would not?—then there was a different song sung. I often wondered," snarled Radri, "who you were most envious of: myself having Marival, or Marival having me."

Jolan, yellow as his hair, clutched at a jeweled dagger in his belt, then drew his hand despairingly away.

"Let him go on," he muttered, "I shall have my say later."

Radri, with another oath, continued.

Radri said that Jolan, due to this same perverse possessiveness just now demonstrated, had at last hit on the idea of shutting the household up inside the house. For this he had invented some lunatic pretext. Presently, the other servants left the establishment, unnerved by the obsessive qualities lord Jolan was displaying. Jolan promptly barricaded the doors and locked the gates. It had seemed best to humor him. Sabara had secluded herself, as was her wont; Naldinus had gone about his religious and scientific studies as was his. Jolan had alternately fumed and moped. As for Marival and Radri, they had had each other, and passed the time in diverse sensual entertainment. Finally, however, one ploy of Jolan's began to bear dark fruit. He had been storming at his elder sister saying she must contract a marriage with a particular nobly-born pip-squeak of the city. Since she was beneath her brother's jurisdiction, he being master of the house, Marival had become dejected. That afternoon she was listless and ill-tempered, refusing to sport with Radri, saying she must get acclimated to forgoing the joy of his embrace, since her brother would have it so. A quarrel had ensued, its outcome being that Marival had cast herself after all into Radri's brawny arms, begging him to carry her off from the house which had become a jail. Radri, though loath to betray his former master's trust, eventually agreed. With impassioned pledges, the lovers had parted, planning to meet again in the dead of night. Radri would then forced the gates, and he and his lady would fly to their new life, eschewing fortune, content with love.

Leaving Marival, Radri said, he had had an uneasy thought that perhaps their plot had been overheard. Along the corridor, he had encountered the Lady Sabara, who announced that she was just then on her way to her sister's apartment. It seemed possible to Radri that Sabara might have been listening at Marival's door, then run off a way, realized Radri would overtake her, and so retraced her steps to imply she was only that moment arriving. Sabara had a natural and enduring hatred of her sister's great loveliness and power over men, being herself too bookish and overfastidious to attract them. On the other hand, rather Sabara as eavesdropper than Jolan—Radri had put uncertainties from his mind, and set about organizing his escape with Marival. But at dinner that evening, Marival had suddenly gasped, clutched her throat and next her side, and dropped in a faint from her chair. The faint soared into a racking fever, and fever sank into a coma. Her skin burned, then turned icy cold, her pulse galloped and then stumbled, she cried aloud in pain, and then she cried aloud no more. Naldinus attended her, but skilled physician though he was, at midnight she died.

The symptoms of sudden poison were all too obvious to the remaining quartet. The fatal tincture, perhaps, had been administered at dinner. Radri had served the meal, there being no other servant in the building, but he had had nothing to gain by his beloved's death, and all to lose. Others had also passed her dishes; Jolan, for one, had poured wine into her cup but a short while before she collapsed. Then again, Sabara had gone into Marival's apartment. With the family's knowledge of witchery, there were other methods of execution. An envenomed ring, a doctored glove, even a vial of scent with death in it. Sabara's hatred might well have got the better of her. Perhaps she had had designs on Radri herself—

Radri's account was slashed by a low but razor-edged laugh, of obviously genuine amusement. Sabara, with a look of contemptuous steely hilarity, turned her back on him.

"Or," shouted Radri, "the bitch ran to her brother, and lord Jolan, damn his weak and worthless hide, took his warped revenge on us."

"Thank you," said Cyrion, with the utmost courtesy. "Who is going to tell their story next?"

The slight emphasis on the word 'story' left the company unmoved. It was Jolan who accepted the cue.

It was untrue for a commencement, said Jolan, nervously striding about the tomb, that Radri had ever been anything more to any of them than a servant. (Radri swore vigorously and with melodramatic hauteur.) Certainly, Jolan had shown him occasional friendliness, but only because it was not in Jolan's character to be overbearing with underlings. (Radri bellowed with raucous derision.) That Radri lusted after Marival Jolan had come to understand, but had attempted to ignore, out of delicacy toward them both. He trusted the steward to repress his unsuitable appetite. Marival, who was accustomed to love and admiration from all men who saw her, would scarcely notice. Then Jolan began to perceive that Radri, rather than honorably suffering in silence, had started to press his attentions on Marival. Becoming aware of the uncouth streak that was now manifest in the steward, Jolan grew alarmed. A marriage was about to be arranged between Marival and one of the richest and most well-born men of the city, and she herself was eager for the union. One morning, Jolan had come on Radri in the process of what was obviously an attempted rape upon the girl. Marival herself, plainly shamed and distressed beyond bearing, could say little. Jolan would have dismissed the man instantly, but a groveling apology, the sight of Radri literally upon his knees in contrition, and the memory of his former years of excellent service, delayed Jolan's decision. (Radri made a noise that seemed unlikely to be due to tears of gratitude.)

"Then," said Jolan loudly, in his hoarse grating voice, "fate took a hand. A sickness broke out in the poorer quarter of Teboras. It was invariably fatal. Such things can spread like wildfire, and whoever can afford it is inclined to retreat from the city. But who leaves their house donates it to the mercy of looters. Accordingly, I sent our servants away to an estate of my late father's some miles from the city. This house is self-sufficient, having its own internal well, and I hastily provisioned us with meat and bread. Like most others who were able, I meant to shut our family within doors, having no outside contacts, until the plague had burned itself out. When Radri refused to leave with the other servants, what was I to do? I am afraid I let sentiment blind me, and permitted him to remain with us. I foolishly thought, I suppose, that loyalty to our name and house would overcome his low-born villainy."

"Did you?" thundered Radri. He lunged forward, red-faced, his muscles bulging as if independently alive and intent on causing harm. "And did you also expect we would credit your infantile make-believe? *Plague!* What plague? I never saw any trace of it. It was a lie to wall us up at your command, under your thumb. But you were too weak to rule us even then. Your sisters had to humor you, and I—I stayed to protect Marival, but I failed in that." By now he had caught Jolan by the neck and was starting to wring it through the collar. Jolan in turn had grabbed out his dagger. Sabara had averted her face stiffly. Cyrion sat immobile and watched. It was the priest-physician, Naldinus, who glided forward and placed his long limp paws on both men's shoulders.

"No, no," he murmured unctuously, "not now. You must

not fight now. This gentleman is here to make judgment. How can he judge if you take up the time brawling?"

Jolan and Radri sprawled apart. Radri threw himself on to a couch and began to rub his chest in a simian fashion, morosely. Jolan, no longer striding, hung his head and resumed his version of events.

Being shut up together, with a scarcity of diversion and no means of present escape, the participants of the drama had quickly brought things to a head. Marival had spilled her scorn and loathing upon Radri in an exchange of words that Sabara had heard clear across the garden in her own rooms. Subsequently, Marival had come to Jolan, admitting that she feared some retribution from the depraved steward. Jolan determined that, whatever the risk, Radri must be seen off the premises, and resolved to tell him so directly dinner was at an end. However, during the dinner, Marival was taken ill. At midnight, she died, Jolan could never forgive himself for not acting sooner. He had been caught unawares, imagining Radri would prefer physical violence to the more subtle means of poison. But many herbs and medicines, some lethal, were stored in the cell of Naldinus, and the steward was probably a cunning pick-lock, It would have been but too easy to procure some deadly granule, and let it fall into Marival's cup of wine as he served her. Rather than allow her to enjoy a happy marriage to another of her own station, the wretch had slain her in the most painful and prolonged manner he could devise.

Jolan began to weep again. He strewed himself at the end of the same couch occupied by the sulking Radri, and buried his head in his arms and the cushions.

"I think," said Sabara, moving about the couch to confront Cyrion, "that you must be forming a most romantic and endearing picture of my beautiful dead sister. I am sure you are half in love with her already, despite the fact that she is a corpse. Before we proceed further, I have an uncharitable but burning wish to correct your impression." Sabara looked over her shoulder a long hard moment at the embalmed woman who lay on the bed. Sabara's eyes dwelled on the limpid animal curves, the midnight stream of hair, the exquisite face that seemed only waiting for a lover's kiss to wake it. "She," said Sabara, "was no less than a demon. Do you credit demons, sir? They exist. If she lived, she would show you.

Because you she would have had to have." Cynically, Sabara's eyes, freckled by their black shade-lashes, returned to Cyrion's. "Your looks, you see, would have provoked her. Although my sister, to be just to her, was concerned to have the approbation of every man she met. Whatever his profession or calling or birth; whatever his appearance, Marival must bring him to her feet. And next, to her bed." At her back, Radri growled; Jolan's sobs momentarily increased, but Sabara paid neither any heed. "You must not think," said Sabara, "I minded her lack of morals. She was a harlot, and with none of a harlot's honesty, but I do not condemn her for that."

"No," Radri sneered, "you condemn her for her beauty, you scrawny lizard."

"Oh, no. That was the thing I hated her for, her beauty. Because no man who came to this house would ever look at me, if he might have her to look at; because, since I was thirteen years of age, I have been cheated of those few men I might have wished to court me—yes, that is what I *hate* her for. But it is not the thing for which I condemn her."

Sabara condemned Marival, she said, for the havoc Marival had caused in their own household. The grooms, the gardeners, the kitchen boys she systematically seduced and then cast aside, who consequently came to blows with each other. Sabara condemned Marival for the foolish indulgences she had elicited even from their own father, and later from their brother Jolan. For even Jolan had been turned into a sort of swain, hopeless and frantic as the rest.

"I do not know," said Sabara coolly, "if he ever lay with her, but it would not surprise me. Nor would it shock me, if she had been other than she was. But then, to set Radri and Jolan at each other's throats—"

Radri had been Marival's favorite, presumably for the simple reason that he was a boorish and unsubtle brute. Of all the legion of men Marival played games with, he alone treated her roughly, and the novelty must have been sweet. But in the end, even Radri's barbarism ceased to please. So Marival permitted the secret to come out, which all this while only Jolan, blindfolded by adoration, had been unable to see. She let Jolan come on them, Radri and herself, among the garden shrubs against the wall. She let Radri overhear her speaking ill of him to Jolan. Marival clamored to be wed to a rich nobleman. She told Radri Jolan would procure her this marriage, which would not be to a pig like Radri, either, whose artistry in bed caused her to vomit; she told Jolan he was a milksop at whose funeral she would dance in Radri's arms. The two men had been friends once, in their way. She put paid to that. Marival brought them to a juncture where at any moment either might slay the other, or slay her, or each attempt both deaths. It had been only a matter of time. And Marival had reveled in it.

"I am afraid," said Sabara, "I have been the witness in this house. I have been largely ignored, but I have seen it all. Whoever slew her is unable to admit the deed, fearing the further dislike of the others. But in fact, it seems to me a service. She was a devil. She herself was responsible for the death of some who slew themselves, or their rivals, all through her meddling, or else she ruined their lives so well each became a living death. I have observed it often. She would have done more and worse. Her arrogance and her mischief were maturing. No, whoever killed her should not be abashed. She deserved poison. It was necessary, unavoidable, that she be removed."

There was a pause. Sabara lowered her eyes.

Cyrion said quietly:

"And did you eavesdrop on the argument between Radri and your sister?"

"Little need. I heard the tumult clear across the garden. How else should I know how she described his lovemaking? And later, I heard a similar war between her and our brother. She had strong lungs, my sister to conduct two such battles in one day. Though she was particularly irritable that day, I remember. Everything was at fault, even the weather was too hot, though it was mild enough; even the wine tasted sour. She could hardly wait to see Jolan and Radri with drawn blades. She used every means to touch them off."

"And did you," inquired Cyrion conversationally, "go to your sister's room in the aftermath of Radri's visit?"

Sabara's eyes came up, guarded as if with iron shields. She held herself very still, and said,

"I did. I went to beg her to ease the tension in the house. Only she could do it. She would not."

"And that was when the wine tasted sour?"

Sabara's eyes and mouth narrowed.

"She said it did."

"Perhaps," said Cyrion idly, "something had fallen in her cup."

Sabara flinched. The pulse in her throat flickered the light rapidly across her golden necklet.

"Are you accusing *me*?"

Cyrion smiled, captivatingly.

"How could I be? There is another left yet for me to hear."

The priest Naldinus seemed to have combined with the shadows beside the bed, almost vanishing as the supernatural door had done. Now, with a small quiver, he shook himself free of darkness, and slid a pace or so forward as if on oiled runners.

"I am, sir, most willing to speak. But really, there is no chance of any blame attaching itself to me. I am sure you will appreciate I had nothing to gain by murdering the lady Marival. I am here merely in the capacity of religious mentor to the house. And its physician. I have attended them all, at one time or another."

"Exactly," said Cyrion. "Tell me about your skill with herbs."

Naldinus made a modest gesture. His tiny red mouth sucked in the air, reminiscent of one of those blooms which close upon and devour flies.

"I am something of an experimenter and innovator. I spend a great deal of my time investigating ancient writings. You would be astonished at the knowledge one may glean by going back rather than forward, in research of this sort."

"Not necessarily," said Cyrion. "The embalming of the lady, for example, is most impressive. You performed the entire procedure yourself?"

"Why yes. The uninitiate would find it somewhat unpleasant, I fear."

"But you are initiated."

"I have performed such work before. Oh, not on the human dead, you understand. But on animals, experimentally."

Cyrion seemed entranced.

"Like the true scientist, you are able to rise above such paltry interferences as the wholly debatable pain suffered by the subject. So many clever men have let such stupid considerations stand in their way. The result—nothing."

"Indeed," Naldinus smiled, stretching his mouth to its little utmost. His melancholy face lighted. "Of course, one does not wish any animal to suffer unduly—but where I must be firm, I can be firm."

"Animals, after all," added Cyrion, "were placed on earth to be of service to man. Their ornamental quality is purely incidental." Naldinus positively beamed. He had found kindred. Any instant his minuscule mouth might split. "But do tell me," said Cyrion, and the priest leaned forward a fraction, amenably, "were you never tempted by the extreme erotic potential of the lady Marival?"

Naldinus' countenance petrified, congealed.

"Sir. I am a priest. I am celibate."

"Agreed. But if, as has been postulated, Marival required tribute from all the male gender, then, astounding though it may seem, even you may not have been exempt from her attentions."

Naldinus said, proudly and coldly: "I will admit it, then. She tried her wiles, even with me. But in a man whose intellect is stronger than his appetites, to deny her was no huge matter."

"Quite so. Much more delectable to be dissecting a living mouse than playing bears with a woman's honey-pot." Naldinus blinked. "And yet, said Cyrion, "she tried to board you, did she not? Did you not find her beautiful?"

The tiny mouth was sucked in and for a second disappeared, returning moist and avid. "She was—well formed. But I have explained. I am celibate and disciplined."

"However," wondered Cyrion, "did she get by your guard at all?"

"Oh, she would come to me in my role as physician—I attend the entire household, even the servants—and say her head ached, or her heart beat too quickly. After the first examinations, when I learned her drift, I was wary. Though she constantly approached me."

"Remarkable. When was the last time she tried this foolish assault on your virtue?"

"The day before her death. The usual tale. She put my hand upon her breast before I could snatch it away." Naldinus breathed heavily. "I found it easy to refuse her."

"Despite your ministrations, she died of the poison. Did that disturb you?"

"No. I did my best for her, but the—the corruption was too far advanced. I was powerless."

"Dear me," said Cyrion.

He rose and stretched, catlike. The four in the tomb, and maybe the fifth dead one, waited for him in a vast new soundlessness.

"I have," said Cyrion, "just a single question. It concerns you all."

Jolan, who had sat up, his head upon his fist, said dully:

"You had better ask it, then."

"We have established," said Cyrion, "that I am not the first passerby you have forcibly elected to judge you. What I should like to know is the number of my predecessors."

Radri snapped out: "You need not trouble with that. Suffice it to say they got the answer wrong. And paid for it."

"If I assure you," said Cyrion, with enormous patience, "that the answer to my question profoundly affects my judgment, will you consider telling me then?"

Jolan got up. He glared at Cyrion, distraught, and rasped defiantly:

"Do you want an exact number? There have been—over forty."

Cyrion nodded. "That will do." He reseated himself. He said: "And now I am ready to tell you the identity of the murderer."

"To begin with," said Cyrion, "my opinion of Marival is that she was indeed all Sabara supposes her, and maybe more. But that a woman so driven by unconfidence, despite such beauty, to prey on and destroy the lives of those around her, in order to have proof of her ability, is more to be pitied than hated. On the other hand, if any laid this fate on you, this anguished and interminable search for the truth, it was she. Though she is free and you remain in torture, I think it was her final jest with you, an ultimate demonstration of her power over you. You are still her slaves. And she has seen to it that all of you have other deaths to burden you, aside from hers—the hapless judges you killed when they failed to solve the mystery and set you at liberty from guilt and indecision. As the nomads say, you have torn down the wall in seeking the broken brick.

"But now I will tell you the real story of the afternoon and the night of Marival's death.

"In the afternoon, Radri forced his way into Marival's chamber. She was restless and reluctant to join him in their normal duet, and an argument ensued. During this argument, the lady informed the steward that she was done with him, being about to make a splendid marriage amid her peers. Radri, who for some while had scented imminent retirement from her service, had a desire to snap her neck. Aside from her physical enticements, he had spent his life worming into the family's good graces, hoping eventually not merely to be treated as its son, but actually to become such. Marival had semed as eager as he was, and he had even once put to her, to stress the genuine burnish of his feelings, a scheme that they run away together and wed. Radri had hoped every day to get his mistress with child. He, perhaps too trustingly, believed Jolan could not dispossess her, but would settle on them both a generous marriage endowment. Now, with Marival's retreat, Radri beheld disappointment no less crushing for being feared. But he did not dislocate her neck, which in any event would have been an act something obvious of its instigator. Radri is vain. He had an idea that aloof Sabara might be yearning for him, and that he need only bend his charms on her to win her. There would be no point to that, however, if he had only her paltry share of the inheritance to look forward to. Conversely, though, if Marival were dead, Sabara would succeed to Marival's portion in the general way. Of course, her death must be of natural appearance—but blood poisoning is hardly uncommon. Radri had already planned, and doubtless had the remedy about him for some time. He got it the way any in the house might get it, by going to the priest on some pretext of indisposition. To rummage among the herbs might be a trifle incriminating, but, while Naldinus tinkered over a healing potion for an invented complaint, what could be more simple than inadvertently to wipe up a smear from his dissecting bench, ripe with the toxics of decayed tissue. Many know the poison inherent in mortified flesh, particularly those who have seen the soldier's side of a battlefield, which Radri has. This rather nasty bane Radri either introduced into the wine or food of Marival at dinner, or, more probably, clasped against her skin. The smallest scratch would be sufficient doorway to let in almost certain death."

Radri rose slowly from the couch. His eyes bulged, his face was convulsed.

"You say it is I, then?"

"I say," said Cyrion, "that you used poison against Marival. Now sit down, and let me continue."

Staring, his mouth open, Radri crashed back on the couch.

Cyrion went on.

"Sabara had heard the quarrel from her own apartments, and her fury with her sister reached its summit. Her desperation was mainly to protect Jolan, her brother, whom none of you, even she, have ever properly noticed that she loved. No doubt her self-admitted envy of Marival (a misguided envy, for Sabara has twice the resource and fascination of her pathetic sister, had she only realized) played a large part in what she determined to do. Entering Marival's room, Sabara reasoned with her. They drank wine together. Marival sulked at the day's heat. Marival scorned Sabara's counsel and her demand for peace to be made. It is actually doubtful if peace could have been made by then, and maybe Sabara knew as much, her debate with Marival merely the excuse for what came next.

"I would say," said Cyrion gently, "one of the lady's many rings was ready-primed, either from Naldinus' store or by her own knowledge of drugs and magic. Whatever the ring carried, she caused to spill in Marival's cup. Some slow-acting powder, most likely to induce sleep and to kill in the sleep. I do not think Sabara's hygienic mind would let her stoop to inflicting anything messy or agonizing. It was a legal execution to Sabara. She was hangman, not torturer."

Sabara's fortitude had deserted her. She sank in a chair, hiding her eyes, and whispered. "You do accuse me. You do."

"I state facts," said Cyrion. "Radri poisoned Marival. So did you. And now I am going on."

"Jolan saw Marival at some point before dinner. He was suffering beneath his new knowledge of her, her carnal frolicking, her predatory demands to be married to a rich nobleman. Jolan was in love with Marival, and writhed at his incestuous desires, all the more so since they had never been gratified, while those of so many men apparently had. At the interview, Jolan eventually refused to make a match between his elder sister and any lord of the city. His motive, he probably declared, was that her unchaste state, learned on the wedding night, would bring humiliation and dishonor to her house. Marival, whose temper was on short leash, accordingly gave Jolan the verbal lashing of his life. In those moments, worship turned to antipathy. He was adept enough to conjure some sorcerous blight to blast her, he did not need to resort to poison at the dinner table. Indeed, by dinner time, the spell was already cast, was it not, Lord Jolan?"

"Yes," Jolan said. Dry-eyed, he stared into the rug. "Just as you say. As I hazard you have been correct with all of us. Three stinking murderers. It is almost a vile and horrible joke."

"It gets," said Cyrion, "better still."

"During the meal, Marival gasped, caught at her throat and side and presently lost consciousness. Each of the trio, concealing their guilty joy and horror from each other, saw Marival to her bed. There, as her state worsened, each of you, thinking you alone had been responsible, trembled and palpitated, awaiting the end. But the end did not come at once, and at last you stole away to nurse your terrors and your righteousness. You left Marival to the ministrations of Naldinus." Cyrion looked up, and at the priest. The man's hollow and aesthetic eyes winced and hooded over. "Naldinus," said Cyrion, "priest—scholar—magician—physician—innovator. Celibate Naldinus. Disciplined Naldinus, whose creed does not permit him to lie with living feminine flesh.

"Naldinus," sayd Cyrion, "knew the mood of the house. He needed no scholarship in medicine to deduce what ailed Marival, and it is conceivable—you must not be modest, sir—that he thought he might have saved her. But Naldinus, alone in the bedchamber with this half-dead lady, had become possessed by two overwhelming concepts. The first he put into practice swiftly, administering the potion by some insidious method known to the physician. It was not, you understand, a restorative. It was a seal to what had gone before, something that made absolutely sure that Marival would never open her eyes again upon this world. It was also the first important stage of the embalming procedure. His best experiment yet. And when she was securely dead, my friends, Naldinus gave rein to the second concept. He did with

Marival that which he had always wanted to do, but which his office had not permitted him, while she lived."

Radri and Jolan had both risen with appropriate spasmodic cries. Sabara lay eclipsed in her chair, unmoving. Naldinus glided backward until his shoulders rested on the wall of the tomb.

"I'll gut you," said Radri, his bluster frighteningly gone to a hiss, "I'll stuff your entrails through your putrid mouth—"

"I believe," said Cyrion, in a soft chill tone that somehow stopped the men in their tracks, "that you are forgetting the uselessness of such an act. I would remind you, gentlemen and lady, that you have all committed a heinous crime against the woman on the bed. None of you has any right to take arms against any other. Nor have you had, as yet, your delivering omen, the omen you were promised, I can only conclude, by the unquiet ghost of Marival."

Radri turned on Cyrion with frustrated anger.

"You have it there—no omen. Indeed, all this is probably a bag of lies, spun by you to deflect our wrath. I never admitted your charge. Nor did the priest there, nor Sabara. And if Jolan did, well, he is mad. How dared you offer us such a preposterous dish of dung! We *all four* poisoned Marival! How did you arrive at *that*?"

"Your equal appearances of and motives for culpability," said Cyrion lightly. "Allied to your avowal that over forty judges (although I think there have been rather more) had been employed by you to unearth the truth. Even out of forty, by the laws of chance alone, one at least should have hit on the identity of the assassin. Which led me to assume you had all, at one time or another, been accused. Since your omen had still failed you, I came to the conclusion you had collectively had fingers in the pie."

"But since the omen still fails," grated Jolan suddenly, "you also are in error. Each of us is guilty of the attempt, but who is *responsible* for my sister's death?"

"All of you, by intent," said Cyrion. "None of you, in fact."

There was an outcry. Even Sabara roused herself to stare at him. Even the priest crept half a step forward once more.

"Egomania, I am afraid," said Cyrion, "has been the undoing of you. You have suffered for uncountable years, from the lingering unsatisfied malice of Marival. She fastened on your guilt and drove you to excesses, and all because you saw nothing in your world capable of murder, save yourselves. But there was another killer in the house that day. I would guess Naldinus guesses too, of the four of you, and perhaps he guessed that night, though if he did, his resultant actions were ridiculously foolhardy. I make no indictment there. Nevertheless, if he had examined Marival as she wished, the day before her death, he would have had some inkling. No, she was not in pursuit of your virtue that time, priest, it had verity, her aching head, her pounding heart beneath her breast. And the next day, her short temper, her complaint of the heat. . . . My poor babies, as each of you poisoned her, she was already dying. Marival had the plague. It was plague that struck her down at dinner. It was plague which, left to itself, would have finished her."

"But I closed the house!" Jolan cried, with inappropriate and ludicrous indignation.

"And before you closed it, you provisioned it. A sick baker, or butcher, or vintner, or even a seller of lamp oil."

"Gods!" Jolan cried, like a great and terrible choking. "Gods! Gods!"

And then the priest shrilled and jumped all the way from the bed to Sabara's chair.

For the lovely embalmed woman was crumbling, turning into snow and into ash and into a fine white pollen that melted and was no more. In a few seconds nothing remained of that luminous body save a faint imprint in the embroidered sheet.

"The omen?" Cyrion asked. "Or would it be a faulty embalming?"

Dawn was breaking, the amorous shade of Sabara's hair, as Cyrion walked out on to the street. His leave-taking of the eccentric family had been swift as the deliberations before had been lengthy, which had not surprised him. As for the promised reward, he had been handed a key. He would find a chest on the north side of the Remusan temple. . . . Another might have thought he was being fobbed off, but Cyrion knew quite well that he was not.

Marival had set her ghostly curse on them. Its effects were more apparent than they knew, even through their sorcerous disguises. In the wake of her embalment, unease, next suspicion, accusation—and, unavoidable, nemesis. And when she had hunted them to the brink and beyond, Marival had cast the last despair upon them, and only one who solved their plight, and its deception, could set them free.

Just before the magic door had reappeared to let him out, Cyrion's concluding sight of the family had shown Naldinus huddled on the floor, and Radri and Jolan leaning on each other for support—they would not have long for that renewal of comradeship, just till sun-up. But they—even the priest—had seemed glad, relieved, as well they might, that it was over. Jolan's voice was so harsh beneath the tall collar that probably he had been throttled, and no doubt by Radri. Radri had rubbed his chest: the memory of a stabbing at Jolan's dying hand? Sabara's voice had been whole and beautiful, so most likely it was the veins of her wrists she had cut, the marks hidden under the gold bracelets. She would have done it in a bath of hot water, the traditional female suicide of Remusa. For they were all Remusans. Despite their changed names, their sorcerous overlay—which translated their apparel, their furnishings where essential, into the current mode—despite their sorcerous ability, being dead, to speak one of the new tongues of the land they were still forced to frequent, once a year, on the deathnight of Marival. Marival, more dead than they, but free as they were not.

The child sun flew abruptly over the pillars of the forum on its young wings. Cyrion turned, and the house was gone, and the garden, and the marble tomb. He had anticipated nothing else.

Naldinus had died of the plague, some lingering germ of it, having seen the others go before him. That had a certain justice. And wherever they were now, they were no longer in the earthly hell. Unable to confess, they had pleaded to be given peace, pleaded with tears, cries and ghoulish murders.

Only Sabara had watched Cyrion depart. Sabara—her name alone was Remusan, unchanged. There was some nuance beyond words in her eyes. But there were only minutes then before sunrise, and now no time at all.

A peculiar unevenness ran over the waste ground that led off the street to the steps of the Remusan fane. It seemed to mark some ancient boundary, not illogically, the wall of a house. The bones had been found here, the bones of more than forty—many, many more—who had failed four angry guilt-ridden mad ghosts.

On the temple's north side grew a slim green tree. The earth about its roots was colossally displaced, as if by an earth tremor that had strangely vandalized no other spot. Among the earth lay a large box of gilded iron, in portions gone to rust.

The key fitted the lock, which broke on the twist, yet somehow sprang open. Cyrion pushed back the lid.

Within, two gold collars, one with a pendant portrait of a black-haired woman, surrounded by sapphires and rubies; several pearl talismans; a richly jeweled dagger; five cups of hammered silver (yes, who would not have detected that rich Remusan wine of which poets sang, and to which sunset oceans and blood and women's lips had been compared?); a heap of glittering flawless rings; two bracelets of gold. Only Marival had not left him her jewels. Great antiquity had turned everything a little dim, had given it a fine green tarnish, more fabulous than the metal, like treasure redeemed from the sea. In weight alone, it would be stupendously valuable. In antique worth, it would be next to priceless.

Cyrion left the casket open, for the lucky ones to find, whoever they were, when they came by. He took with him a solitary thing. A single slender bracelet of greenish gold, which for twelve centuries or more, though only on one night of the year, had clasped Sabara's wrist.

3RD INTERLOGUE

The noon dinner was being served at the Honey Garden. The succulent kid was coming in with loaves of golden bread and platters of vegetables fried crisply in oil and pepper. The delirious smells had roused even the soldier from the stupor into which the scholar's complex narration had thrown him. Roilant, however, had remained alert throughout.

"That is really—very *clever*," he said, as the main dish was placed on his table.

"Thank you," said the slave modestly.

Roilant did not correct this mistake. He turned to the scholar, searching his face.

"I see the labyrinthine twists would appeal to a scholarly mind. Do you think it to be true?"

"Yes. I have myself seen ghosts and similar phenomena, and I am an ordinary man. Cyrion, one has to suppose, is one who naturally attracts bizarre, uncanny events, as some persons attract misfortune. And Teboras, or Teborius, as it was once known, is a haunted place, the Remusan ruins everywhere, like ghosts themselves of that fallen Empire's greatness."

"And the lovely Sabara. It seems he had a weakness for her."

"It seems he did. If he has any weaknesses."

"I would assume he is subject to the human affections."

"But masters them with unusual control. One further thing," said the scholar. He paused for a moment to watch with interest as the drunk blond soldier tore the kid in pieces, added vegetables and half a loaf to his plate, and began heartily to eat. "The slave Esur told you, I think, the tale of the desert city and the demon beast. You will have noted, perhaps, that, offered treasures from the city hoard, Cyrion ultimately left them quite carelessly behind him."

Roilant considered this.

"So he did. While at the end of the story of the ghosts—"

"Confronted by a priceless antique cache, he leaves this also behind, keeping only the bracelet from, one imagines, some regard for the young woman it belonged to, rather than cupidity."

"Yet he is reckoned to be wealthy. Surely the wealth must be the fruit of his adventures. He cannot always have abandoned his rewards so lightly."

"Or else he has never needed to take payment. There is one rumor of Cyrion, you know, which has him as the son of a Western king, stolen for ransom in infancy, and at last left by the thieves in the desert, where the nomadic races found and cared for him."

"Hence his traveling garb."

"And his occasional reference to the proverbs and psychic disciplines of the nomads, who are a strange, savage, yet curiously wise people. According to another rumor, Cyrion's wealth is stored in fabulous stashes all about the lands from here to the Auxian Sea. He has only to visit certain places, and produce credentials, in order to receive unlimited funds."

"And hence also the fine city clothing and penchant for good inns."

Someone, who had entered quietly, suddenly shouted from the door-curtain.

"Foy! In the name of—*Foy*!"

Everyone looked inquiringly about for Foy. (Save the sage, who was busy breaking his fast on a plate of fried lentils and olives.)

Getting no response, the latest arrival, an extremely short young man, came striding across the room, his ringmail shining dully, as did the light steel cap on his head. He was indeed very unhigh for a soldier, as if to make up for lack of inches, he had the frequent bluster of his ilk. Also a surprising amount of burnished brown moustache, which somehow seemed to conceal most of his face. It did not, nevertheless, conceal his obvious annoyance as he marched up to Roilant's table and positioned himself beside the hungry blond drunk.

"Foy. You are due in barracks in half of one hour. I have

been searching every inn and wine-shop in Heruzala for you."

"Oh, little mother," said Foy, the blond soldier, "let me repay your trouble. Sit down, dear soul, and join in the repast this generous gentleman with the orange hair is buying me. You will not objuice, obhic—" Foy peered at Roilant solicitously. Roilant made a gesture which implied he was past objecting, however it was mispronounced.

"Foy. Half of one hour. Come. Leave that."

"Leave? How can I be so rude? Besides, I have not yet told my story, my only entitlement to sit here."

"Story? What damnable story?"

"We are recounting tales of—" the blond soldier made a huge effort "—Shyrion."

The soldier with the brown moustaches looked at Roilant and the scholar and nodded.

"Excuse me, sirs. If that was the bargain, I am afraid he must renege. As for Cyrion, you might well see him yourself if you remain in the city."

Roilant let go his knife in his dish.

"He is in the city for sure?"

"In Heruzala? Yes. I noted him an hour ago, on Sweet Street."

Roilant rose to his feet.

The moustached soldier said, "but I doubt if you would catch him there now. He was evidently on his way elsewhere when he passed me."

Roilant wilted. It took the scholar to say:

"You know this man to recognise him."

"And to exchange the time of day. From the things that get told, I would prefer not to know him any better. A very chancy profession, the free-lance sword. Now, Foy, in the name of *ouwph*," concluded the moustached soldier, and grew shorter still by dropping to a vacant seat on the bench beside Foy. Through a mouthful of roast kid, Foy was heard to say, very quietly, lucidly and distinctly: "Shut your mouth, idiot, and pay heed. I did that for a reason. If you look where I speak of I shall do it again. The holy-man there, with the rings, and oil all over his robe. I would swear he is the very wretch who calls himself a prophet and has been going about inciting riot and disorder, inventing infamies against our dear King Malban. We have tried to apprehend him, you recall, thrice, and missed the devil. Even the Knights of the Angel could not take him, and you know they rarely fail. I came in here and saw him by chance. Now I am in pursuit, or will be once he stirs. Stay and be prepared to follow him with me and detain him at the first hint of strife. Or go back to the garrison and tell them why I have not."

The moustached soldier grunted, rubbing his calf, apparently inclined to stay.

Roilant stared at the blond soldier.

"You are not drunk," said Roilant in hushed tones.

"Who ish not?" demanded Foy, resuming his character-acting.

Roilant sat down. "This is absurd."

"Not at all," said the scholar. "You now have proof Cyrion is in the vicinity and may come here. As for the other matter," said the scholar, lowering his voice, "I was myself unsure of the sage. A very curious old man."

The moustached soldier had recovered from whatever blow Foy had inflicted, and without a word had decided to join in the party, helping himself to meat and wine."

"I have always been interested by what the true Remusan names of the ghosts may have been, stripped of Western disguise," said the scholar. "Naldinus and Sabara, one would assume, are unaltered. But Jolan I take to be Jolius, and Radri—Radrix. Marival, though, provides conjecture. I suspect two names, married. Perhaps Marea Valia."

"I had a cousin called Valia," said Roilant, rather unexpectedly. "She vanished in childhood. Which left only her sister, Eliset."

The moustached soldier had cheered up. Whether he wished to imitate his fellow's acting, or whether he was genuinely over-susceptible to liquor, one could not have sworn.

"Cyrion now," he said to Roilant, glad to help, "there really is a story I know."

Roilant heaved a sigh.

"Go on."

"Not that Cyrion told it me. A genius with a knife, by the way. Not that that comes in the story. There was this sorcerer."

"Another sorcerer," said Roilant painfully.

"Called Juved. Juved the Sorcerer, who had rather overreached himself in the matter of magic. . . .

CYRION IN BRONZE

Nearer to heaven than the trees, the tower rose from the green cloud of the oasis.

Below, lay a round of still water, oleanders, reeds, the columns of palms with their tattered lattices of fronds, which the westering sun had torn with thin red shafts. Beyond, on all sides, the dry dunes of the desert, copper-colored on their western slopes.

The man in the tower did not look at these things. He looked into a crystal mounted on a stand of brass. The crystal showed him an area of desert one mile from the oasis. Over the blank sand of it another man was walking, moving west in the same direction as the day. Toward the tower.

The traveler was young, tall and slim, clad in the black loose garment of the nomads. A sword sheathed in red leather rested at his side. But the sun fired his flaxen hair and his quite marvelous face, prompting the watcher in the tower to unease. Prophets had come from the desert, radiant, beautiful and terrible. Prophets, and demons.

Something stirred beneath the tower, close to the barred and bolted door. Juved, the watcher, took no note of it, having seen the stirring often, knowing its nature well.

Presently, the young man would come from the desert into the oasis, and the stirring would increase. There would be a flurry of reaction, a cry of surprise. Steel would leap from the red scabbard, catching the sun's red rays. Red blood would soak into the dust. There would then, for a little while, be peace for Juved.

The last watering place had been poisoned, fouled by salt. Vandalization of the desert's sparse hospitality was rare. Few men would risk so base a crime. Among the nomads, the penalty for such a deed was grim.

Cyrion, finding the polluted water, had scratched the appropriate warning sign on the well, and journeyed on. By certain talents developed among the desert peoples, he was able to locate a second oasis, but with a bitter taste of salt in his mouth, and a look behind his long-lashed eyes that could have been anger. It was his second day without water, a matter between himself and death.

Reaching the second oasis, he paused at the edge of the oleanders for a swift scan of the prospect. He glanced at water, trees, tower. If he missed anything was not evident.

He came to the brink of the small round pool, kneeled there and lowered his head, scooping the liquid into his mouth with his heavily ringed left hand.

Behind him, there was a stirring between the trunks of the palms.

Something large, hulking and bizarrely blanched, flickered in a soundless coalescence from shade to light.

Cyrion continued to drink. If the scooping actions of his hand were lighter, his stance subtly altered, it was debatable.

A bar of shadow fell across the pool. Instantly Cyrion was six feet away from the spot where he had kneeled. While directly upon that spot something descended. Missing Cyrion, the creature screamed with rage, flinging itself upright, careering monstrously to confront the man it had sought to catch between two vast pallid hands, the pointed nails of which extended five inches from the fingertips.

Cyrion, escaped prey, stood immobile, the sword free of its sheath and poised, almost delicately, in his right hand. His face betrayed only the mildest surprise at what was before him, a being surely minted in hell.

It somewhat resembled a man, save it was too high from the earth for any man, eight feet or more, and besides, too skinny to live, which plainly it did. In color, it was a fearful molten white, a pallor unlikely in such a landscape and under such a sun. Whitish hair flapped flaglike from its skull. Its eyes—for eyes it had—flamed with a willful blood-lust. It had no weapon, apart from its claws, which were weapon enough.

Having hesitated, as if purposely to alarm its adversary by sight of itself, it now launched itself again, straight at Cyrion.

And Cyrion, again, was missing from the point of impact. The fiend instead embraced a palm, and uttered another scream of fury. The beautiful sword blazed and completed a stroke which should have cut the monster virtually in half. But the sword, gliding effortlessly through the molten flesh, met neither tissue nor bone, drew no ichor and effected no wound.

Cyrion darted from range as the horror turned.

Black claws skimmed the air a thumb's breadth wide of Cyrion's throat. And a second time the sword dazzled and bit deeply, now in the belly of the monster, withdrawing unbloodied, the white flesh unscathed. So near, naked and looming, it was obvious the beast lacked a navel, while on its bald loins were other omissions. Above, its lips seemed concave, its nose similarly indented, with protrudent nostrils; the fiery eyes were pits. An inverted parody of a man—Even the claws curved in the wrong manner, upward rather than down.

Once more Cyrion vacated his ground, but on this occasion the erroneous hooks ripped through his sleeve, and the sword, skidding on an impenetrable wrist, struck on one of these hooks with a noise to cheer devils. The monster, however, squealed and jumped violently backward.

As if in mimicry, Cyrion himself spun about, and ran. As the beast, recovering itself, erupted after, Cyrion abruptly whirled and brought the sword lashing up to meet both the descending ab-human hands in a single pyrotechnic twisting motion. The noise now was of scythed steel. Ten black shards shot away through the roseate atmosphere, followed and propelled by ten vehement jets of slimy white fluid.

Shrieking in agony, the fiend crashed to its peculiar knees, its head lolling. Now but five feet from the earth, its banner of hair flapped forward, accessible. The hair was immediately in Cyrion's ringed left hand and sheered by the sworded right one. As the nails had done, the hair bled profusely.

Shuddering and moaning, the thing tumbled on the bank among the reeds, its white ichor staining the sand-drifted soil. Twitching evilly, it seemed to sink in an ante-mortem coma.

The moans faded, but a fresh outcry arose, this time from the tower.

There was the yammer of drawn bolts and lifted bars, and out on to the margin of the water stumbled a man. Of short stature, plump, dark of skin and black-haired, the newcomer was dressed in a robe sewn with scarabs and similar thaumaturgical devices.

"Stranger," he called to Cyrion, "you have accomplished an impossible feat."

Cyrion wiped his sword upon the reeds.

"You are too kind," he replied modestly.

"Indeed," the man from the tower averred, "I take your jest. But how did you find the weakness of the monster?"

"Patently," said Cyrion, "it was an invert of the human. What could be hurt in a man was impervious in it. Therefore, what, in a man, may be severed without harm, the extensions of nails and hair, in this creature proved fatal. It is dying, but not yet dead."

"Quite so," said the man. "But you have done me a service. For three years, that vileness has penned me in this tower. I am no man of the sword, but a philosopher. I have prayed God for such as you. My name is Juved. Please enter my refuge, share a meal with me. Let me show you the treasures I have amassed. Select whatever you wish. I am in your debt."

Juved led Cyrion up a stone stair into a spacious chamber.

Instruments of magecraft were everywhere apparent, polished skulls, star charts, a long eastern window from which personally to observe the heavens, a crystal of clairvoyance mounted in brass. Further apparatus stood on chests, stands and a table. A second table was laid with cold meats, confectionery, fruit, even a jar of wine, silver drinking cups and golden cellars of spices. In the southern wall, a further door stood ajar on a gloomy sleeping chamber, here and there agleam with vague objects.

Juved seemed fatigued either by excitement or by climbing down and up the stairs. He half toppled into a carved chair and waved Cyrion toward the food and wine.

"I am impressed," said Cyrion, "by your dinner. Three years did you say you have been imprisoned here?"

"Dear sir," said Juved, "I do not boast, but I am a magician. I can obtain such items. Only over that ghastly thing outside did I have no power."

Cyrion sampled a portion of bread and meat. Idly, he investigated the spices: ginger, nutmeg, pepper, salt and cinnamon. When he approached the jar of wine, Juved said:

"And for myself, if you will. I am exhausted dear sir, and must sit here." Cyrion poured a cup of wine and handed it to his host. Juved's hand trembled, and he laughed self-deprecatingly. "Forgive my feebleness. Pray look into the adjoining room. Choose whatever you wish."

Cyrion pushed wide the ajar door. A bed occupied some space, the rest of the chamber held occult figurines, talismans, statuettes of animals and inscribed tablets. All were of precious materials, gold and silver, onyx, ivory and jade. But against the eastern wall, hidden almost behind the door itself, a slender oval hung from a peg. Yet faintly glowing, this oval had been veiled by a piece of black gauze, which oddly, even as Cyrion turned to regard it, slipped from the peg to the floor.

What was revealed was a mirror of limpidly burnished, flawless bronze, that reflected Cyrion perfectly, almost with the clarity of looking glass.

"So you have found Zilumi's mirror," called Juved. His voice was fresher. He beamed. Unable to see the mirror itself from the outer room, he was able to perceive Cyrion, and presumably therefore able to gauge the nature of his interest in the east wall. "Is it not fair?"

"The nomads have a saying," said Cyrion, " 'It is difficult to see through a veil.' "

Juved seemed disturbed.

"But has the veil not fallen from the mirror? Generally it does whenever one enters the room—due to a draught, no doubt."

"The veil fell," Cyrion said. He continued to stand, as if in thought or vanity, before the arresting reflection of himself. But he had grown unaccountably pale.

"You will recall, of course, the story of Zilumi," elaborated Juved, merry again. "How her stepfather, King Hraud, had imprisoned the prophet Hokannen in his dungeons, and Zilumi, having seen the prophet, was stricken by love of him. She was a sorceress and part-demon, golden eyed, with hair the color of the bronze mirror itself. Hraud in his turn, desired her, and one night begged her to dance for him certain of the erotic dances the demons had taught her. Drunk, he promised her jewels and riches in exchange, and growing drunker and more lustful as she grew more stubborn in refusing, he finally swore on the name of God and before all his court, that he would give her, for a solitary dance, whatever she asked of him. Then she did dance. The dance being such, they say, that unlit candles came alight of their own volition. When it was done, Zilumi reminded Hraud of his promise. He laughed and inquired what she would have. "Give me," said Zilumi, "the head of Hokannen, severed from his body." Hraud was shocked and horrified, for though he had imprisoned the prophet and meant him to rot in jail, he feared to kill him outright. But Zilumi insisted: "You swore an oath before God and your court." Hraud offered her alternatives, coffers of wealth, even his kingdom. But Zilumi was adamant. "The head of Hokannen and nothing else." At last, sweating mightily, Hraud agreed and was about to signal to the executioner, when Zilumi again spoke. "It is clear to all," said she, "that if you give me his severed head, you give me the life of Hokannen." Hraud remorsefully agreed. "Then," said Zilumi, "since you have shown his life belongs to me, I will not have him slain, but freed." Thus entrapped, Hraud could only obey. The prophet was accordingly sprung. Zilumi herself, forsaking her life of luxury and witchcraft, followed Hokannen into the desert, where, to demonstrate her heart's change, she lopped her hair and left her fine clothes lying on the sands, and even her magic instruments she left, this mirror among them, through which she had worked the worst enchantments of all."

Cyrion had not moved.

"I know the tale. Many claim to own remnants of Zilumi's possessions."

"But this mirror," said Juved softly, "this mirror will prove to you that it is a piece of wickedness."

The watcher from the tower had by now resumed sufficient equilibrium to advance to the doorway. Reaching in and grasping Cyrion's arm, he guided the young man from the bedroom, and back into the outer chamber.

"Did you feel the soul sucked from you, most elegant swordsman?"

Cyrion's color was reestablished. Blithely, he said:

"What gives you to suppose I have a soul?"

A solicitous frown replaced the smile on Juved's countenance.

"It grieves me to destroy you in this way," he said. "But ego has triumphed. I wish to live. And though I dislike the wastage of your own vitality, what must be, must be. The wealth of sorcerous knowledge I can impart to the world, compared to your own transient beauty and skill, should recompense. God will forgive me."

Juved had become positively energetic. His smile was gleeful, beneficent.

"I have told you one story, of Zilumi and Hraud and Hokannen. Shall I tell you the story of Juved and the mirror?"

Cyrion walked to the window. What thoughts were passing through his mind it was hard to deduce. But he gazed from the window as if something had compelled him there, some unseen gesture, some unheard voice summoning from the oasis. Even the eastern sky shone now like a topaz furled in fire. Among the sun-dyed trees, beside the water which the sunset had turned to wine, something was standing. Indistinct and small, a dwarfish thing, not quite discernible. A shadow? A *white* shadow? And where the monster had lain in its death-coma the ground was empty. . . .

"I gained the bronze mirror of Zilumi, no matter how," said Juved, "intending to use it in particular sorcerous experiments. It was light to carry, uncannily so, and flawless, as you have seen. But, unhappily, it had had a terrible safeguard placed on it, probably by the witch-princess herself in her days of magery, that she alone might profit from its powers. Since that era, it had been interred in a casket from which only fierce spells could release it. Having affected the release, I was the first to look into the bronze. I felt at once a faintness, a drawing of my spirit, as if my soul, or some comparable intrinsic element, were being drawn mercilessly from my body. Once the tension eased, I frantically researched its cause. This tower, to which I had traveled for seclusion during my experiments, I had already imbued with talismanic properties. No dangerous essence could manifest within its walls. But, on spying from the window I beheld—guess what I beheld, handsome swordsman!"

"I would not dream of anticipating," said Cyrion politely, his eyes yet riveted on the oasis below.

"Perhaps you are wise," said Juved. "I will reveal what I saw. Some eight feet tall, a man-thing white as molten steel, skin and gristle, black clawed—it lurked beneath, ranting and slavering. The miror, you see, took from me some piece of my psychic fiber, turning it against me, inverting, and creating the exact opposite of myself—gigantic and thin, where I am short and rounded, white for my olive complexion, primitive, barbaric and ferocious, where I am urbane and timid.

"But I am not a fool. I barred the doors of the tower as an extra precaution, and reading from my scrolls and parchments, I defined the precise nature of the thing below. Thus I learned that its paramount longing was to murder me and drink my blood, that my death accomplished, the creature itself would fade and be no more. I learned that I could not, even had I the courage, attack and kill the being, for, though I might discover some weakness whereby its invulnerability could be overcome, if it perished, then so must I, bound in spirit as we were, dual though opposed. Two methods I could utilize to save myself. The first of these I accordingly adopted. This was that I should sorcerously entice others to this spot, as many as I might throughout each month of the calendar. These innocents the monster would rush upon and butcher, draining them of blood, subsequently devouring flesh, organs and bones. Its grisly appetite temporarily appeased, it would then leave me in peace, even permitting me to journey some way from the oasis, though never itself lagging far behind me. Most recently, I visited a neighboring well and fouled it with salt, which has been useful in bringing extra victims to this water. As for the second method of protection from the fiend, I had never thought to try it, partly because it required I should bring some person other than myself into the tower, which meant an imprudent relaxing of the talismanic guards. Besides, the monster would set on whoever arrived. They never reached my door, even had I hoped to invite them inside.

"And then, dear sir, your advent. You solved the problem of the monster's vulnerable point, and sent it to the brink of death—which death, of course, soul-bound as it and I were, would also have been mine. Hence my rush to your side, my desire to act as host, my conducting you to the room where the bronze mirror stands. For the second method of escape is this: Should another look into the mirror after me, his soul is forfeit in exchange for mine: His psychic fiber is sucked in and mine released: My inversion fades and his is formed. And what will it be in your case, heroic stranger? Squat for your tallness, gross for your slenderness, white for your tan, black for your flaxen, hideous for your beauty. Gaze from the window. Tell me, is it so?"

"You may judge for yourself," said Cyrion.

"Rest assured, I have. But I think you are pondering retaliation, gentle sir. I had better elaborate upon my explanation. Firstly, it may occur to you that, should you be able to coerce me into looking once more into the bronze, the exchange will again be effected, your soul freed and mine enslaved once more. This would be so. However, I have discovered and prepared spells during my sojourn here against just such an unlikely event as you have brought about in slaughtering my invert. Should I confront the bronze mirror a second time, I have only to rehearse a select phrase of lore to immunize myself against its enchantment. Quite safely I may stand before the mirror, providing this phrase is intoned—or even mentally reviewed—to mutilate my tongue will not help you. And there is no way that I can be made to look into the bronze, believe me, without my knowing I do so. For, should it be enough hidden that I might mistake it, muffled, say, behind a curtain or thick veil, my reflection will not strike the surface and the magic suction cannot take effect in any event. You may think that you can circumvent my spells in another fashion, by rendering me unconscious and thus lugging me before the bronze. But this will also be valueless. Asleep or unconscious, a man's psychic fabric is detached from his body and may not be absorbed by the mirror. Once awareness returned, I should activate the phrase of lore, and so annul the influence. This being the case, I advise you to consign yourself to your fate. And also to your death.

"You cannot, as I did, substitute another's blood and life for yours. I am the only alternate victim to hand. And though powerless against the emanation the mirror evolved from my own body, against another emanation I am not powerless and have shielded myself by my magic. I have, moreover, lifted the talismanic guards from the tower, so that presently your invert may fathom entry and destroy you. I feel that too great quantities of hapless lives have been lost. You have given me the opportunity of freedom, and your death shall be the last. Therefore, the swifter, the kinder. You may sacrificially offer yourself to your invert monster or you may slay it. In either instance, the results will be identical.

Both you and it will die. I am sorry, but I am obdurate. Console yourself that your demise enables a masterly philosopher to persist."

"Such an honor is insupportable," said Cyrion.

A fraction of a second after these words, light as a springing cat he was gone through the door and down the stairs.

Squeamishly, Juved did not any longer, by crystal or window, watch the tidal sand, the darkening oasis.

It waited, lurid as a beacon in the accumulating night, the alter ego of Cyrion, born from Zilumi's mirror of bronze.

It was as Juved had prophesied.

Squat for Cyrion's stature, gross for his slimness, grotesque for his fineness, obscene for his looks. On its fungus-white revulsion of a head, black wire, the antithesis of Cyrion's hair. And on its weirdly taloned right paw a parody of rings, and in the left a kind of sword, wider at its tip than at its base, the shade of putrefaction.

And it tittered, simpered, invited. Its stumps of teeth grinned, and it sailed toward him through the dark like a luminescent ball of filth.

But it was, of course, clumsy for his fluidity, awkward for his brilliance.

Easily, meteoric, Cyrion dipped aside, reached and caught the black wire, and severed it. The thing sprawled and the white blood flowed phosphorescently. Twice more the steel sword dealt a blow, and all the claws lay among the night-breathing oleanders. In death, it wailed. And Cyrion felt its death. Its death, which would become his own. But you could not know he felt it, as he must. His ebbing strength was in parentheses; ignored.

He ran into the tower. The talismans having been removed, nothing barred his re-admittance. His feet connected almost noiselessly with the stone, three or four steps disposed of by each ascending foot. What sound he made was masked by the mewling of the thing below.

Juved did not expect him, or, if he did, did not expect him in the form he chose. Like wildfire, Cyrion arrowed through the room. For a moment, the magus stood gaping. In another, the heavy crystal of clairvoyance, which Cyrion had secured in passing, met the magus' forehead with a blinding concussion.

Juved roused in nauseous discomfort and confusion. Though he retained a complete recollection of all that had gone before, the mirror, the trick, Cyrion and the crystal, these memories were negated by the atrocious agony in his skull and the appalling amount of salt which had been systematically rubbed into his lips, tongue and gums. Staggering to his knees, gagging and spitting, Juved seized the wine cup on the table, gulped and swallowed a mouthful before he could check himself. It was unfortunate he could not, for the wine also was doctored. The entire contents of the spice cellars had been poured into the jar and the cup, not merely the salt, on this occasion, but the cinnamon and pepper, the nutmeg and the ginger, too. Nausea immediately claimed its dues.

Relieved but shaken, eyes awash and throat parched as bone, Juved picked his way carefully down the stair of the tower. Cyrion's childish revenge baffled Juved. He was irritated that a young man of such singular appearance should not have accepted death nobly, or at least resignedly. But this prank with violence and spice—Juved retched profoundly and tottered hurriedly the rest of the distance into the cool and sky-bathed serenity of the oasis.

The moon hung above the palms, clear-etched as engraved ivory, flooding the water of the pool with a miraculous sheen.

Despite Cyrion's prank, Juved had done well and cunningly. There was nothing left to fear. A brief sickness beside a savage death—what was that?

Pleased with his philosophy, Juved knelt by the pool and lowered himself toward it. From a dim pallor among the oleanders he scrupulously averted his eyes. Soon, the horrid thing would die entirely and vanish. Cyrion's body was luckily absent. At least the swordsman had had the decency to drag himself into the desert in order to expire.

Gratefully, Juved tested the pure liquid of the pool. Despite a sudden floating sensation, some backlash of his sickness, he drank with vast calm and an accruing store of complaisance. Until an elongated shadow blotted out the moonlight on the water.

Then, with an incredulous scream, Juved writhed about to greet the towering height and burning pits and rending claws of the inverted thing which was his, that which had first evolved from the mirror.

Just beyond the oleanders, Cyrion lay on the night-black dunes, and let his life come back to him like the blown sand.

He had done much in the tower before he had been at liberty to fall down here. As the dying monster took his life away with it, surrendering perforce, he had understood that logically he should win this game with death. But with death, there is no positive gate, no warranty, no honor. So he lay, the moon white on his eyes, and waited to end or to continue.

But life is life, and coming back it brought its own balm.

Soon he could rise, and walk to the margin of the pool, keeping away from the edge of the water, though nothing lay there, no remains either of magus or monster.

Meticulously, Cyrion scratched the warning sign on the trunks of the palms, to show the water of the oasis was fouled.

After this, from an evaluatedly adequate distance, he kicked and thrust a landslide of sand and soil into the pool. It was a wearying task, but he did not abandon it until the oasis was swamped, muddied, and its floor raised by several degrees. By then, he had buried and erased what earlier had been simply camouflaged, its reflective quality unobscured by nighttime water. And settling sand hid the bronze mirror he had thrown into the pool half an hour before Juved had leaned over there to drink.

4TH INTERLOGUE

A round of limited but enthusiastic applause greeted the ending of the story, during the course of which one of the merchants and his lady had approached to listen.

"Very quaint. Very cunning," exclaimed the merchant, clapping the merry moustached soldier on his hiccupping shoulder. The merchant, by contrast, was a big man, his head wound in a cloth of soft green muslin stitched with opals. Rings fired light from his hands. It was small wonder his dainty companion clung to him with such determination. Though she also spared a smile for both soldiers, tall or short, and a wink of one silver-lidded eye for Roilant.

The scholar had apparently enjoyed the story also, and was vowing he would remember it for the future. The blond soldier leaned boss-eyed on the blue-washed wall, beaming on everyone, particularly the awful sage in the embrasure—now slobbering his way through three sherbets. The fast, it seemed, had not merely been broken, but smashed.

Roilant had not enjoyed the story. This was plain. If any of what he was hearing was true, it only increased his need to locate the miraculous Cyrion. And where was Cyrion to be found?

"You say you saw him on Sweet Lane?"

"Yeah," said the moustached soldier. "No. Sweesh Streesh." He elaborated upon visiting a barber there in order to have the lustrous facial hair trimmed: "Fool in barracksh no more shkill than 'n ostrish with sheersh." While seated under the awning, he had perceived Cyrion walk by dressed like a prince."

At this juncture, the caravaneer, who had come dustily

over to speak to the bejeweled merchant, said, in concern, "you mean the Cyrian, Cyrion? He of the white hair and the nomadic persuasion? If so, I regret it was not *that* Cyrion you saw on Sweet Street. I spoke to him only yesterday, some ten miles from Heruzala. He was on the road to Bakrad."

"Bakrad!" Roilant displayed horror.

"You are in error, shir," said the short soldier. "I know Scyrion as I know my brothersh. And I shaw him on Shweet Sheep shmorning."

The caravaneer shrugged with complacent emphasis.

"As you wish. I know who I met."

"And I know who *I*—pardon me—met."

"You know Cyrion well?" Roilant asked the caravaneer.

"He once did me a service. Yes. I know him."

"How *far* on the road to Bakrad?"

"Not far. By now, he will be considerably farther."

Roilant cursed softly. He took on the childish wretchedness of the defeated adult.

"If this is urgent, you might send a pigeon from the post here. There are stations all along that road."

"Time is—short," said Roilant vaguely, and was rewarded by a suspicious glare from the moustached soldier, who tended always to react to one word in this way.

He, and the defeated Roilant did not, therefore, turn at the uproar that next broke out behind them. Its source, as formerly, was the sage.

The charming brunette who had passed Roilant on the way out previously, was now returning, floating down the room in a mist of gauzes, pearls gleaming, the little maid stepping delicately after, carrying flowers. The sage, at this rather mesmerizing entrance, had arisen in a splutter of sherbet.

"The Whore of the City, she walks in scarlet and gems, and the holy stones are stained by her iniquity."

Instead of embarrassment or dismay, the lady evinced a curious amusement, and turning lazily, said in her pantheress's voice, "be quiet, you silly old man. I am neither wearing scarlet nor staining anything, unlike yourself. I shall strongly suggest to the innkeeper that his inn be disinfected, and fumigated by strong incense as soon as you have left."

The silver-lidded young woman giggled. All three merchants gave a resounding cheer. The sage, a terrible shade of puce, flung up his unappealing sleeves and, uttering bubbling noises, swept from the room.

The general acclaim increased. The handsome brunette was toasted and promised cages of doves and phials of rare perfumes. The scholar meanwhile got up and hurried to retrieve his parchment. He stood over it some while, having found lentils spilled on it.

Amidst the clamor, the blond soldier, Foy, jumped up.

"Come on, Whiskers. He is off and we must follow."

"Whah?" inquired Whiskers, whose drunkenness was now revealed to be unfortunately valid.

"The troublemaker, the mad prophet. Come, fool!" And dragging the whiskery soldier to his uncertain feet, aided by the latter's lack of stature, Foy drove him toward the exit.

Reaching the door curtain, Foy paused, as Whiskers tried valiantly to regain a warriorlike stance, and succeeded in upsetting a small stool.

"My thanks for the feast, and my sorrows I am unable to fulfill my part of the bargain after all, but duty calls with her brazen voice. Ask them if anyone knows the tale of the murder at Klove fortress. That is a good one."

As Whiskers floundered out through the curtain, Foy strode after him. There came a faint sound, hidden, of the Qirri statue being subjected to a short man's loving embrace, and Foy's exasperated: "We shall lose the old fiend again." Followed by an elephantine stampede up the three steps and the bang of the street door.

Roilant said dully, "I wish to hear *no more stories*."

"Poor young sir," sympathized the silver harlot, and was, for her pains, promptly removed to the other table by her merchant.

"You should not despair," said the Scholar, who had come back and was carefully dabbing the parchment. "It has always been this way with Cyrion. One man sees him here, another there. Come, sir," to the caravaneer, "can you swear that the man you met on the Bakrad road was Cyrion for sure?"

The caravaneer looked affronted, then thoughtful. At length:

"To be honest, he went by in a whirl of dust. We shouted greetings. He seemed to know me, but in my trade, many do. I took him for Cyrion. But he was mounted, riding, and that is rare for Cyrion, now I ponder it—Incidentally, I know about the assassin at Klove, if you should wish—"

Roilant made a noise not uncourteous, but decidedly unencouraging.

"However," said the scholar, "if you will forgive me, I have not heard this tale. I believe it is my turn to purchase the wine." And to the caravaneer, "Be seated. Tell me about Klove. The young gentleman will indulge me."

Roilant looked betrayed, but did not shift his seat.

As they had been speaking, the innkeeper had come back, and realized the sage had failed to settle his account. This led to outcry. A fat priest had also come sailing in, the slaves were darting about and fresh dinners being served or slopped, the whole room in a new frenzy of activity Roilant seemed currently too weary to negotiate. Although a half-formed desire on his part to leave was detectable.

The caravaneer sat down. "Well, now. Klove. It is the utter truth. A very odd affair."

"You do astonish me," said Roilant with a feeble attempt at sarcasm, which was ignored.

Pouring himself wine, the caravaneer began to speak, and presently all three merchants and their ladies returned to Roilant's table in a body.

Across the room, the brunette seemed to be listening, too, as she neatly skewered roast kid and apples with her rather large, but elegant, hands. . . .

THE MURDEROUS DOVE

Three black specks in the white-blue fluid of the sky, the vultures were slowly swirling. Giving their usual infallible signal of a death, somewhere in the desert below.

The second signal was more obvious still.

Going over the last rim of the dunes, you beheld at once the waterhole, and through the eternal smoking of the desert dust, another more ominous smoke going up beyond.

Cyrion paused on the slope, dark on the desert's pallor, the wide hood of his nomad's garment pulled over his fair head to keep off the sun. Nothing stirred on the grassy lip of the water hole, nor by the solitary raddled tree. The little dwelling was a blackened collapse, veiled only by its smoke, now the fire had died. Between the ruin and the tree something else had died. A man lay sprawled there on his face, and all about him a scatter of small, oddly similar shapes, grey and white and red, which Cyrion recognized presently as ten or so dead pigeons.

The clue to the scene resided in the circling but undescending vultures. There was a fine meal waiting for them on the ground. If they kept aloft, they would have a reason. Apparently, from their aerial advantage, they had seen and yet saw a live and potentially dangerous presence the far side of the smoke.

Cyrion had a choice. He could retreat. Though it was not much of a choice, since his water was gone, and he had been all morning heading toward this watering place.

With a practiced gentleness, he drew the sword from its red leather sheath. Then walked down the dunes toward the water hole, as if ignoring the burnt ruin.

Planting the steel carelessly in the sand, Cyrion began to

draw up the leather bag from the well's floor, the rope passing through ringed left hand and bare right one.

The movement, when it came, was surprisingly fluent and complete. The space between ruin and water was empty but for corpses, then suddenly no longer so.

Cyrion glanced up.

The arrival was a stranger, but he was nevertheless unmistakable. He was seated on a white gelding, trapped in white leather and silver, and clad himself in steel ringmail, a snow-white tabard over it, a helm of blanched steel, with the nasal crosspiece stretched horizontally under the eyes, good as a mask, and a comb of white plumes above. On his back rested a silvered shield with a device—a white dove. By the dove alone, anyone would know him. He was one of the Knights of the Angel, sometimes called "Doves," otherwise known as the White Riders.

Cyrion went on drawing up the water bag from the well. He smiled.

"Can I offer you a drink, my friend?"

The knight sat on like a block of impossible ice in the heat. Nothing of him moved now, not even the horse twitched its ears.

"After all," said Cyrion disarmingly, "it is thirsty work, stabbing a man in the back and burning his home. Not to mention the pigeons."

The knight spoke.

"How are you named?"

Some, asked this question by a White Rider, might have been tempted to lie. Cyrion was not tempted.

"Cyrion."

"And is that your name or your birthplace? Are you from Cyroam?"

"Maybe," Cyrion hesitated delicately, "not."

"You clothe yourself as a nomad, but are pale-skinned." Cyrion did not answer this time. "Where are you bound?"

"Nowhere in particular."

"You will know of the Fortress of Klove, half a day's journey northeastward."

"Surely," said Cyrion, "that is where you are bound, not I."

Klove was a possession of the Knights of the Angel. They

had several such castle-fortresses in the desert, besides their stronghold in the city of Heruzala, to the southwest.

The knight still did not move. His immobility was menacing. He said:

"Yes, I am bound there. From Holy Heruzala to Klove. If you have found any trouble here, seek recompense at the fortress. Speak of me at the gate. They will greet you kindly if you bring a complaint concerning me."

The words made no sense, delivered flat as they were. The next event made less sense—or perhaps more.

From utter stasis, the knight's whole body exploded into vivacity. Cyrion might have been expecting the long sword, but it was not the sword which was used. Instead, a small lethal weight of jagged marble shot from the knight's mailed hand.

Cyrion flung himself sideways. But seemed to falter, was not entirely swift enough. The weight dashed past him, carrying the nomad's hood with it, parting the bright hair beneath. And Cyrion dropped soundlessly before the trained, stone-still forefeet of the white horse.

The Fortress of Klove lay one hundred and fifty miles from Heruzala and some distance inside the perimeter of the desert. Yet the rocky hill where the castle stood was patched by grass between the sallow boulders. In the valley beneath, an oasis, acid green, watered the fortress above and the rambling village that served the fortress. Sheep and goats grazed bleatingly along the banks of the pool. Women came and went with their jars. The men labored in forge, tannery and other industries considered necessary to the upkeep of the fortress. The White Knights had no truck with such work. A century before, God's Angel had appeared to a lord in some faroff western land. That had been sufficient. The Knights were founded. They were priestly, sworn to celibacy, conscientious in the matter of prayer, fasting at set periods of the calendar. At other times, they rode to battle. Their wars were against all brigands, all armies belonging to rival kingdoms threatening Heruzala and any militants within Heruzala herself. Coming of the fair-pigmented western race, their whiteness did not limit itself to dress. The swarthy nomads of the desert and olive-skinned coastal peoples had their own names for the Doves. Their racial brothers were also wary of them. They were known to practice bizarre and esoteric rituals, basic to their code and worship of God. And they were said to carry out secondary secret wars. In uncanny ceremonies, the story went, they could make themselves blind to fear and impervious to pain. Controlled, efficient and thinking madmen, they would then seek out some condemned victim, one who had infringed upon their honor or harmed their purse, and slay him, cutting down obstacles or brutally diverting them, merciless and unstoppable—demoniac assassins.

Nothing, beyond stories, had ever been laid squarely against the Knights of the Angel. The young king in Heruzala found them, presumably, useful. Or else, he feared them too. Certainly, he paid great sums into their coffers. Their fortresses stood like yellow markers all about Heruzala's hem of the desert, and as far as Daskiriom in the north.

At Klove, poppy-red in the swift desert sunset, the fires were burning up outside the baked mud dwellings, while, high on its rock, the castle-fortress blazed like a hot coal in the going of the light. A few birds were circling about there over the towers, plump, tame messenger pigeons.

Where the last dwellings abutted on the sands, a woman, bending to stir the pot on her fire, poised, staring. From the close western desert, where night was already rising like an indigo mountain, came a man. He had no horse, and walking, he stumbled often. He wore the robe of the nomad, but the brief afterglow was on his face, which was white, framed by pale hair, and streaked down the right side with the dark wetness of blood. As she watched, he unsteadily entered the village, and made at once toward her. Alarmed, the woman rose, shouting as she did so, to her own man inside the house.

The stranger stopped a couple of yards from her, swaying mildly.

"I need your help," said the stranger. "Am I to get it?"

"What is this?" demanded the woman's husband emerging at her side.

The stranger subsided to the ground, rather as a child will fall, unsure of its legs.

"You want the tale first, do you?" he asked. "Hear then. By the water hole with the tree, I met a White Rider. He brained me with a bit of marble, having told me beforehand that I should be loved here for his misdeed."

The woman gasped. The husband carried a leather bottle

of water to the stranger and held it to his mouth. When the stranger had drunk, the husband said urgently:

"What of the hut by the water hole?"

"Burned, and the inhabitant slain. Not to mention his pigeons."

The husband sucked in his breath as the woman had done.

"That answers much," said he. "Sir stranger," he added to the prone man, "you must come with me."

"My name is Cyrion," said the stranger. "Come where?"

"The fortress. And quick."

"Is it true then? He told me I should be well received in Klove for maligning him—whoever he may be—"

"Oh, we know of him," said the husband, dragging the stranger to his feet, and starting to support him up the track toward the high fortress.

On the way, many left off their business to gaze at them. Some called ambiguous questions to their fellow villager, who answered as ambiguously. A couple ran to help, but were sent back. The track up the rock hill was steep and could have proved difficult, if the invalid had not recovered himself somewhat.

They reached the loom of the outer gatehouse. The white tabarded sentries, who had reviewed the ascent like figures built of the same stuff as the wall, now shifted. One called down the twenty feet of gate tower:

"What do you want?"

"This man," the villager of Klove shouted back, "he brings news—the news Grand Master Hulem has been waiting for."

Another of the white tabards on the battlement reacted. He said something to the first, who in turn bawled down to the village man:

"Hold there. He shall come in."

"You are called Cyrion?" inquired the Master Minor of Klove Fortress. "Is that because you hail from Cyroam?"

"Maybe not."

In the square stone hall, lit by its torches, and warmed by its tall hearth against the chill desert night, its table piled with meat, fruit and wine, and its interstices with white knights rigid by their rigid lances, an injured stranger had received noble treatment. He might have expected something austere or frankly rough, but the soldierly hands which had probed the wound on his forehead and bandaged it had been nearly tender. The meal which followed was good, not to say extravagant. Only the thicket of guards, every one of them with ears, showed the nature of cautious sufferance rather than hospitality. While Grand Master Hulem, so reputedly eager for news, had not been manifested. Only the Master Minor, who had just entered, and who seemed inclined more to polite chat than interrogation.

However, the guest knew better than to betray impatience or amusement in this notorious sanctum.

The Master Minor himself was sandy of hair and complexion. Now his sandy eyes fossilized to flints, and he said: "Tell me the whole of your encounter with this knight. Everything, if you please, Man-Called-Cyrion."

The man called Cyrion obeyed. He told of the burnt hut, the sliced pigeons, the human corpse; of the White Knight, his words, his action with the weight of marble. He told of coming to his senses and struggling in this direction, to Klove, to ask recompense as the knight had suggested. When he was done, Master Minor Sandy-Locks stood awhile, pensively. Then he said: "This affair is between the Dove Lodge of Heruzala and our own Lodge, here. It need be of no interest to you. Yet, we are grateful, for indirectly you have brought us tidings." He waved brusquely. A knight stepped forward and placed at the elbow of the bringer of tidings a bag which clinked.

The bringer of tidings looked at it. Then, with his ringed left hand, he composedly slid it aside.

"I understood," he murmured, "I was to deliver my news to Grand Master Hulem."

"Really? And why should you understand that?"

"The man from the village was specific—that my news was what Hulem wished to hear."

At that, a startling snort, not quite laughter, escaped the Master Minor. The flaxen face lifted. It asked:

"Is it then news he does *not* wish to hear?"

"Whatever, my fellow, it is no concern of yours," rapped the Master Minor. "You have been tended, and paid. Tonight you may sleep on a pallet here. Tomorrow, you shall have an ass to ride and go on your journey."

He turned, only to be recalled by the soft voice again speaking, behind him.

"Sir Master," it said, "I have been wondering if the knight I met had burnt the hut by the water hole and killed the man and his messenger birds—to prevent news of his coming reaching you. And I wonder, too, why, since he told me he would travel here, he has not already arrived, for he was well-horsed. Now, do you think he has come, unseen? There was some commotion, I remember, when I was brought into your castle—under cover of that, possibly—" The sentence was allowed to trail. Strange, the effect it had upon the Master Minor. "Perhaps," resumed the blond man, "I should speak to the Grand Master after all. Perhaps he would wish to get the details from my lips."

The Master Minor snapped his brows together.

"We shall see. For now, you shall go to your allotted cell. I may interview you more fully tomorrow."

Minutes in the wake of this exchange, thirty Knights of the Angel, armed to the hilt, mounted and bearing torches, swept from the castle-fortress of Klove, descending on the village below. For a while they galloped up and down the mud streets, then out along the banks of the oasis and into the surrounding strip of desert. Near midnight, they returned to Klove, leading a riderless white gelding. Other than the gelding, they had found no evidence of an alien knight. Indeed, no other stranger at all, saving an old eccentric being, one of the roaming holy men of the desert who, from time to time, percolated into the village and out again.

The holy-man sat bowed in his bent-over fashion before one of the outdoor fires of the village. Despite the deformity of his posture, he looked to have been powerful in his youth. Maybe he had been fastidious then, too. Now, like most of the holy-men, he was filthy, his hair matted grey-white and, though recently pruned, dangling over his forehead. His aged face, in the dusky jumping firelight, was a mass of shallow movable linear cuts, caked with grime. His messy robe had a rent down the back, and he hid his dirty hands in his long sleeves, muttering to himself. When the knights came by, questioning him cursorily, he was roused to driveling anger. After they had gone, and the noise of their rampage had faded, he sat down again by the fire. There, in answer to the entreaty of the people who had gradually crowded up to him, he agreed to expound his philosophy. The philosophy turned out to be a mesmeric rendering of the exotic parables of the desert, the myths of that ancient lion-haunted land. And as the old man spoke, his vile graveled voice assumed a hypnotic rhythm.

When the knights returned, leading the white horse to the fortress, the people at the fire looked after them and whispered and the old holy-man broke off his monologue. As the last torch vanished in at the gate, he began barking at his audience, demanding what was afoot in Klove. Respecting his vocation, needing, besides, to be relieved of their fear, they informed him.

Klove was at war, in a manner of speaking. At war, Dove Lodge with Dove Lodge, with the White Knights of Heruzala. As usual, it was a secret thing, but the gist was an act of pity, carried out by Grand Master Hulem of Klove, in pardoning a thief a month before, when he had begged for life. Of this, Heruzala had somehow got word. The act, deemed fatal weakness by the Grand Master at Heruzala, was to be rectified by Hulem's own death, under the sword of a chosen knight from the city Lodge.

These assassin-knights, having magically primed themselves to their task, were like cunning automata, and could not be deflected. Once his doom had been pronounced, the unfortunate Hulem had sat morbidly in Klove Fortress, awaiting the avenger with barred gates. And outside, the village of Klove waited too, in terror of ruthless, indiscriminate vengeance on themselves. The pigeon posts of the region, loyal to Hulem, had taken oath to warn him, sending birds ringed in a particular way as a sign the assassin approached. But not a single bird had arrived. On the testimony of the man who had entered the village earlier, it seemed all the posts might have been destroyed. Luckily, however, through this same stranger called Cyrion, Klove knew danger stalked near. There was a plan in the Fortress to deal with the assassin: Since such a man, primed by the Ritual would be, until his kill was accomplished, impervious to pain and temporarily to wounding, and thus to lance sword or arrow, they planned to let loose on him a cauldron of boiling pitch from the gate towers. Even a primed knight could not survive such an onslaught.

The aged holy-man seemed half smiling.

"Suppose," he offered, "the cunning assassin guesses such a measure will probably be employed. Would he not guard against it by some means?"

"But," the people protested, "he must come, and therefore will be seen. Who could miss such a man, in mail of steel and white tabard, even without his horse?"

"Who indeed," echoed the holy-man. His chin tucked in his torn robe, he was most definitely smiling now.

Soon after, the holy man threw a fit. It was quite a notable one. He sprawled upon the street, pummeling the air and salivating profusely. The people drew off respectfully, watching in dismayed approval this demonstration of Divine Possession. Presently the fit ended, and the holy-man sat up.

"I must go to the fortress," said the holy-man in tones that brooked no denial. "Heaven has granted me foreknowledge of the fate of Grand Master Hulem."

The village of Klove, giddy and light-headed through lack of sleep, general anxiety and story-telling, decided the will of Heaven should be obeyed.

Under the black cold sky of a desert midnight, thick patched by its stars, the village conducted the holy-man to the gates of the castle-fortress.

Some altercation between villagers and sentries followed.

The holy-man sat upon the ground in an attitude of disdain, filthy, lofty and silent.

In the midst of the shouting, the Master Minor appeared on the battlements, and pushing through men and torches, leaned down to peer at the sage. Master Minor Sandy-Locks was yet fully clothed; his nervous vigilance had kept him also from sleep on his hard knight's pallet.

"The old fellow has had a vision, you say?" demanded the Master Minor. One would not have thought him a man inclined to be tolerant of wandering epileptics, but probably he had reached the position of clutching at any straw.

To the query, in any event, the holy-man was prompted to reply.

"I have learned the fate of the Grand Master," bellowed the sage from surprisingly ample lungs.

"Have you so?" The Master Minor had turned to the captain of sentries. Unheard by the crowd below, he said: "Dear Heaven, could it be this ancient has been sent to guide us? We are taught, surely, never to reject a sign, no matter how humble. I am put in mind of the fact that God Himself marks even the sparrow's fall—" The captain nodded. An order rang out; the gates of Klove Fortress opened and the steel teeth of the portcullis were raised.

The sage marched through, and was enveloped by knights. The villagers were turned away, yelping with frustration.

Closely guarded, and ignoring the guard, the loathsome holy-man was conducted across the outer ward of the fortress, through the inner gate and up steps, and finally sent alone into the private chamber of the Master Minor.

No doubt, to a holy-man, used to unluxurious subsistence amid the caves and oases of the desert, the chamber was impressive. Indeed, it did not quite match the unworldly cells of the lower ranks. Tapestries and carpets were hung from the walls. On a stand, a great religious book lay spread, beautifully ornamented by colored pictures and jeweled clasps, glinting in the firelight from the carven hearth, as did the swords and shields on their rack.

The Master Minor drank wine from a chased silver cup, and regarded the night's second impromptu guest.

"Well, sir. You may recount your vision, now."

The holy-man was undaunted. He hawked vociferously and spat in the rushes.

"I will recount to the Grand Master."

"I act for the Grand Master."

"And I act for God."

"Do you, in truth?" The Master Minor's face had taken on a deeply observant look. "You would claim you are God's mouthpiece?"

"Mouthpiece, and sword."

The Master Minor checked. His cheeks paled.

"You had better explain."

"The sword of ill news to Hulem. We are alone. I have considered, and will entrust you with my vision. Your Grand Master will die tonight, and none can prevent it. But for you, there is glory. Your star ascends as Hulem's declines."

"These are strong words," the Master Minor said. His

voice trembled a little but he controlled it quickly. "You had better visit the Grand Master after all—I have not the authority to deal with you."

He moved abruptly, drew aside a hanging, and tapped a portion of the wall behind it. The wall swung back, revealing a narrow stair.

"This way links my apartment to that of Grand Master Hulem. It is the swiftest route."

"Should you not," murmured the sage caressingly, "search my body first, for lethal weapons? I might hide an assortment beneath this garment."

The Master Minor cringed. Conceivably at the thought of close contact with the holy-man's vilely dirty robe.

"I have seen many of your persuasion. They do not go armed."

"No, that is positive. They do not."

The Master Minor went up the stair, the sage slinking after. A solid door blocked the stairhead. Sandy-Locks smote it with his fist three times, and called through the panels: "Grand Master, it is the Master Minor."

An iron throat replied with a single word: "Wait." Seconds later, a bar was lifted within, and the heavy door swung open.

What occurred next was whirling and savage, and might be examined only in retrospect.

It seemed that the Master Minor attempted to throw himself aside, at the same moment hurling the sage forward into the area beyond the door. That was the attempt. What actually happened was that the sage, unexpectedly agile and strong, seized upon the person of the Master Minor, and catapulted the sandy figure forward into the room, leaping through himself in the man's crashing wake, and kicking the door shut as he came. The sage's next unanticipated deed was to pounce catlike on the sprawling Sandy-Locks, and render him unconscious by a neat blow to the side of the jaw.

The sage then arose to face the Grand Master of Klove Fortress.

Hulem stood, not unreasonably dumbfounded; perhaps more than a little afraid. The long white robe with its gold collar of doves did not conceal the mail beneath, and a sword lay across the table—sound evidence of a readiness for discord. But the stern face and chill eyes showed courage and rage.

The holy-man flowed gracefully into a deep bow. With a friendly smile, he added, "You have no need to bother trying to reach your sword. If I were who you suspect I am, your blade would hardly stop me. Besides, I should already have set on you, should I not?"

Hulem went on staring at this elderly wreck who had suddenly begun to speak in a young man's pleasing voice.

"You are not, then, the one sent from Heruzala to slay me?" Hulem said, steady as a rock.

"*He* thought so," said the old-young holy-man, indicating the senseless Master Minor, "and once he was fairly certain of it, and had no witnesses to note his misdeeds, he could not wait to lead me to you. A viper in your bosom, sir?"

"Someone, I know, betrayed my clemency with the thief to Heruzala. I had not reckoned the barb to be this close to me. But if my Master Minor is the viper, who are you? And where; for the matter of that, is the assassin knight?"

The sage told him.

When the white knight emerged from the cover of the burnt hut at the water hole, Cyrion already had some inkling of his motives. To kill pigeons tame enough to fly toward the sword rather than away from it, indicated a desire to stop the messages of a pigeon post from getting to their destination. To kill the pigeon keeper and burn the hut showed a thoroughness that intended no word of mouth to carry, either. Cyrion, arriving to drink at the well, was simply another tale-bearer for the knight to kill. Thus, when the knight threw the weight of jagged marble, Cyrion had been ready to dodge anything that came at him, for it would be death. In the split second of the missile's flight, Cyrion had been hard put to it to get back into the line of fire, for he perceived the missile was not, after all, meant to slay him, and he was slinging himself too wide. He managed to regain ground enough that the marble parted his hair and nicked his temple. Acquaintance with the nomads had lessoned Cyrion long ago in the utter loosening of sinews and low faint breathing that gave the impression of unconsciousness. He now put the lesson into effect, dropped on the sand, and awaited events with interest.

Most interesting they were, too.

The knight dismounted, and stripped Cyrion methodically naked, taking even sword belt and rings. The knight then divested himself of his mail, tabard, helm, shield and sword, in short of everything, and donned Cyrion's garb instead—with this difference, that the sword in its red leather sheath was buckled on beneath the nomad's robe, concealed.

These things Cyrion watched, as the situation gave him opportunity, under his lids. He was not astounded when the knight covered him against the sun with his white tabard, nor when the knight retrieved the jagged marble from Cyrion's side, and scored his own forehead with it till the blood coursed scarlet.

The man, of the light-pigmented western race, as were all the Knights of the Angel, was nearly as blond as Cyrion himself. The blood looked dramatic as it dyed his face, but he obviously felt no pain from the vicious wound he had given himself. The absence of pain, joined to his demeanor, proved him to be what Cyrion had reasoned he might be—one of the infamous, magically primed assassins—and on his way, by his own admission, to Klove.

When he had ridden from sight, in Cyrion's gear, but on his own white horse, Cyrion "revived."

He already had the theme of what went on.

An assassin knight was feared in Klove and provisions had been made for defense against him. The knight, finding a man fair like himself, had decided, with his assassin's cunning, to let him live, substituting one for the other.

Rousing, naked and sick in the broiling desert, it was predictable what any man would do. To commence, he would put on the only protective clothing available to him, the mail and tabard of the knight, left so conveniently to hand. And thereafter he would pursue his attacker to Klove and create an uproar. Whereupon he would be mistaken for that same attacker, and slain by some reliable method, such as boiling pitch from the battlements. The perfect scapegoat. With a head start, the true assassin would already have entered Klove. Taking his scapegoat's name and pretending to his grievance—assault by a mad knight—he would get access to the fortress as a bearer of news. The cut on his forehead, which he would make out troubled him a good deal, would be an additional assurance that he was no sorcerously set up assassin, impervious to hurt. Eventually, when the scapegoat knight had arrived and had been eliminated, the assassin's intended victim would accordingly emerge from cover, straight into the arms of death.

Having this theme, Cyrion could have made off in the opposite direction to Klove, but he had no mind to leave the fruit unplucked. The clever knight-assassin had also forgotten something. His were not the only garments available to Cyrion. There was also the robe of the dead pigeon keeper.

Soon Cyrion had washed the robe clean of blood using the water of the well, then dirtied it with mud, sand and the smitch of the burnt hut. The rent in the back remained where the sword had run through, but was simply a further demonstration of pious sluttishness. Next Cyrion worked upon his skin and hair, with the grease from the dead birds and the hut's white ash and black. Shortly, the sun had baked his face to a bandaging of wrinkles and his hair to bleached greyish rags.

In the guise of a holy-man rather than a white knight, Cyrion penetrated Klove and won its heart with stories. All the while, he could visualize the false Cyrion awaiting the real, with nail-gnawing impatience.

To breach the fort was easy. An overacted fit, a statement of prophecy. To attain the Grand Master might have been much harder if Cyrion had not uncovered a sandy-haired worm on the way.

The sage had already put to use the Grand Master's silver ewer and basin. The Grand Master sat stunned, confronted by this unlikely, metamorphosing creature, which now stood and coolly contemplated him, looking much as the Angel must have, who had begun the Order of the Dove.

"Your activities are incredible—your story, more so."

"Then believe it," recommended Cyrion.

"I am forced to. You, a stranger, appear to be the only man I am able to trust."

"Oh, better than that, I think. Your Master Minor was afraid to work his treachery in the open before the rest of your men. So you can presume them loyal to you."

"And the assassin is in the fortress, claiming your identity. No chance of hot pitch now, I would say. Generally, I do not entreat advice, but this once, I shall. Tell me what I should do?"

"What your would-be murderer hopes for. Have someone go to him and say the knight arrived and died at the gate, and that now you would speak to—Cyrion—and thank him. Grant him the audience he craves."

"But he will kill me. They are unstoppable, invulnerable till the murder is done."

"I know that. Invulnerable, unstoppable, cunning—and lax in the matter of details. I will outline your plan."

Less than half an hour later, the fake Cyrion, having received his invitation with apparent equanimity, was conducted to the chamber of the Grand Master of Klove, and the door shut on the two of them.

The assassin did not pause. One glimpse of the upright figure, helmed and robed in its chair, was sufficient. Speechless and fiendish, the man who had become only a machine for destruction raced forward, the sword unsheathed from under the robe as he ran. Lifting the blade in both hands, he executed one soaring deadly terrible stroke that sheared the throat-cords and the windpipe of the seated figure and almost the entire head from the body.

Then, dropping the sword, the assassin sank to his knees, eyes like glass, his tongue lolling, an idiot, his goal attained, his invulnerability gone.

As he knelt there, another stole upon him from behind, and decapitated him.

The Grand Master, holding a red sword, stood over the body of his headless adversary. No tremor disturbed Hulem's features. Not even when he gazed upward at the bloody corpse which sat in his robes and his chair. Above the rent neck and under the masking helm with its crest of pure gold, the Master Minor's sandy face was blank. He had never regained his senses which in a way was a pity, for he had got what he wanted, for a little while though not in the mode he had foreseen. For ten minutes he had been Grand Master of Klove.

Presently Hulem spoke.

"I have won the first battle, at least. Though I am still at war with the Dove Lodge of Heruzala."

Cyrion glanced at him.

"Debatably. I judge this was a test they set you. They said it was to punish you for your weakness. Send them these two heads in a pretty box. The message to read: 'This is how the weak man greets his enemies.' "

5TH INTERLOGUE

The brunette had finished her meal by the time the story of the Angel Knights was over. While the rest of the room's occupants had gravitated to Roilant's table, including at least even the portly priest, she retained her distance with the little maid, both of them nicely framed by the sheaves of hyacinths and tigerish lilies they had carried in with them.

The wine the scholar had bought had been drunk, and the merchants had ordered another brace of flagons. There was some discussion going on, relating to the abilities of Cyrion, not only a swordsman and solver of mysteries, by Lucefael, but also a master of impromptu disguise.

Roilant, who had sat brooding throughout the tale, did not join in this discussion. Something was obviously bothering him. He appeared to be unsure of what it was.

The wine came and was set down, plus one black flask that had not been ordered.

"What is this?"

The innkeeper hurried over.

"*This* is our very best vintage. It is for the red-haired gentleman."

"I did not order it," protested Roilant uneasily.

"No. Just now a child came to the door of the kitchen with money and the message this fine wine was to be served you."

The table gave evidence of admiration.

"Who sent the child?" inquired the scholar.

"He said a blond man had stopped him in the alley and sent him."

"A blond fool to trust a child of the streets with cash," said one of the harlots, knowingly—perhaps some recollection of her own childhood.

"It seems the child *was* to be trusted, however."

"But," said the scholar, "is any explanation to be given this gentleman with his wine?"

"None that I know of," said their host of the Honey Garden.

Roilant watched the flask as if it might talk to him, and said nothing himself.

It was the jeweled merchant who announced: "Can it be *he* heard you were looking for him and sent you this as a recompense? Or a jest?"

"That sounds the sort of trick he might care to play," intoned the priest comfortably. "From what I hear, he is a young man of sparkling if not always kindly wit."

Roilant took the innkeeper's arm.

"Is the child in the kitchen?"

"No, it ran off. Having stolen a pie standing by the door. This has been a trying morning, sir. That elderly prophet who did not pay his bill. The wretched soldiers of the King who *never* pay for anything and cause havoc wherever they go. Now thieving children. And the accursed slaves complaining—" The innkeeper bundled away.

Roilant sat like a stone while his friends examined the black wine flask, and eventually prized it open for him, pouring drinks for one and all as a result. Roilant seemed not to notice. Very gradually a look of awful suspicion was coming over his plump face. He glanced toward the empty embrasure once, twice, glared into space. . . .

Surely it was not possible—was it?

"The sage," he finally got out.

"The stenchful beast," said the violet-lidded harlot. "To call us heifers."

"But," said Roilant. He turned desperately to the caravaneer who had told the yarn of the assassin knight. "If Cyrion formerly disguised himself as just such a wandering holy-man, do you suppose it conceivable—?"

The notion struck them all at once. There were oaths, courteously stifled out of deference for the throat-clearing of the priest, and wild comments.

The voice of the scholar came behind the rest.

"The two soldiers seemed to know him, however, to be

what he was, sage and troublemaker. I myself," continued the scholar, "had the dubious pleasure of a long debate with him. His erudition was faulty but, in essence, profound. I think, too, in such proximity, I might have seen some clue he was not what he seemed."

"Not decidedly," said the priest. "Cyrion is a prince of disguise, and a peerless actor. Although I cannot guess any good reason for it, he might still have been quite easily among us and fooled each. Thereafter sending this wine to tantalize our noble young sponsor here."

The lively chat stayed on the subject for some minutes, until the noble young sponsor stood up and was pulled down again.

"No, no. Stay with us. You will never catch him now."

They held the wine flask that had been bought for him over his cup and urged him to drink. With an expression of defeat, Roilant drank.

"In fact," said the fat priest benignly, "the prank might not be limited to the sage. Cyrion could still be here, seated among us. Almost anyone in the room could be he, disguised."

"Saving, of course, the ladies," said the jeweled merchant.

The priest did not quibble at the term. He had apparently already decided to pretend the "ladies" were ladies, for the sake of camaraderie. He did quibble at an exclusive gender. "Even there, we cannot be entirely certain." There were suitable, tipsy cries. "When I was with the brothers at Andriok, I happened to hear of a very peculiar event. It concerned the eternal battle of Good with Evil, in which innocence and piety had been strangely perverted to assist the powers of the Fiend. Cyrion's name is mingled in the tale."

The circle settled itself for further entertainment.

Roilant drained the flask and reached for one of the neighboring flagons determinedly.

"Once upon a time," said the priest, folding his chins, "there was a rich man who had one beautiful daughter. . . ."

PERFIDIOUS AMBER

"It is true they say the ring is cursed," the young man said quietly. "But for myself, I discount such things. I do not believe in demons."

"The more unsanguine for you, should you ever meet one," said Cyrion, with a melancholy smile.

"Well, then, what should I do? My family fortune was lost to me in stupid excesses of my adolescence. Scurrilous acquaintances led me astray. Bitterly regretting these faults, I strove to rebuild my vanished wealth. In the midst of this struggle, walking one morning through the city, I beheld an angel carried in a litter, the most lovely maiden in Andriok: Berdice, Sarmur the silk merchant's daughter. Sarmur is rich, I, at that time, penniless. But, for the sake of my lineage, he permitted me to wed his child, and settled on her an excellent dowry. What can I offer in return? Nothing? Naturally, I thought of this ring, the one possession I never squandered. My family has held it, generation to generation. Should it lie in a box, or jewel the hand of my exquisite wife?"

Blond, handsome and apparently just a touch politely bored, Cyrion observed the ring in question.

It lay in a nest of azure velvet, that made it, by contrast, all the bloodier and more rich; an amber intaglio, set in heavy gold, its surface engraved with the design of a lily, a swallow in flight, and a rayed sunburst. Certainly, it was splendid. Certainly, Cyrion had heard of it. It had a nickname: *Farewell.*

"What do you say, Cyrion? How do you advise me? I admit the *legend* of the curse, but no one has died because of it for a hundred years."

"Neither has anyone worn it during that time."

The young man sighed. He had a strong, attractive face, augmented by bright blue eyes, betrayed by a dissipated mouth. Volf, he was called. He came from the west, though his bride and his ring were eastern in their origins. He had met Cyrion at an expensive tavern on the Street of Heaven. The meeting had been casual, but Volf had seemed to recognize Cyrion's person and cognomen. It was possible he had sought Cyrion out purposely for council for, here and there, Cyrion had a reputation for ruthless wisdom.

"I am interested by the engraving," said Cyrion.

"Oh, yes. The lily, symbol of the soul; the flying swallow, symbol of freedom; the sun, symbol of the sky."

"I see you have pondered the matter," said Cyrion blandly. "But now, tell me what you know about the curse itself."

Volf grinned. "What I know proves the legend to be merely that, a tale to scare off thieves, no more. Allegedly, an eastern queen had the ring made as a token of her passion for her husband. But, in order to attain the best, she required a demon to fashion it. Hence the symbols, each connected with the power of Good—lily, swallow, sun—which she had the demon incise in the amber to negate any evil it might be planning. The demon paid no heed to these symbols, however. The queen gave the ring to her husband as he rode out to battle, hoping it would guard him. But no sooner had he raised his sword and spurred his horse to meet the enemy, than the king fell dead from the saddle. There was no wound upon him, but his countenance was fixed in a grimace of extreme horror.

"The battle was lost, and the ring passed to the conqueror, who dismissed the event. He wore the ring successfully for three years, though he was an irreligious scoundrel. Then one day he went hunting lions in the desert. No one was near him, but suddenly his horse stumbled. Next moment he was dead. Again no visible assailant, no wound, and a grimace of horror. But this is patently absurd. It offends our reason. Must I go on?"

"If it tires you, there is no need." Cyrion rose.

"No, no. Wait. I rely upon your advice, dear sir. I will continue. The ring was inherited by the son of the conqueror, but the son was afraid to wear it. A century later, the ring was stolen from his treasury by a mage, intrigued by its magic properties. He wore it without harm for some months.

Then an earthquake destroyed his house and he perished. The ring was extracted from the ruin by bandits. The leader of these wore the ring only a day. He was captured by warriors of the prince of those parts, but dropped lifeless on the way to his execution. The ring was appropriated by one of the warriors, who gifted it to his pregnant wife. During childbirth she died—her face fixed in horror, of course, and the child was stillborn. Thereafter, the ring was buried with her, and came into my family as loot from the rifled tomb. Three of my ancestors reputedly died through it, but I would credit their deaths to mischance. One met his end by falling from a wall when the parapet gave way. One died during a storm at sea. One died of a fit during an eclipse of the sun. Since then the ring has gone unworn."

"And have you never worn it?" Cyrion inquired innocently.

"I never thought to, in my penury. But I am not afraid to do so. Mark." Volf drew the amber ring from its velvet and slid it onto the small finger of his left hand. He laughed, decidedly without nervousness. "If a malign fate resides in the ring, let it mow me down. But I do not believe in it. Men have always been prone to death. The termini of my forebears are explicable without recourse to a curse. Even the deaths recounted in the legend are explicable."

"Nevertheless," said Cyrion, "death and the ring go hand in hand."

"But without a pattern—men who die after three years, three months, a day, or less! And such variable deaths. Some without apparent cause, some by earthquake, water—and one a woman in labor. No. Coincidence, Cyrion. If not, I, too, will die. I mean to wear this ring one day and no longer. If we are to credit that all who wear the intaglio are slain by it, the demon has no choice but to kill me during this period. Do you agree?"

"It seems," said Cyrion, "feasible."

"At midnight tonight," said Volf, his eyes shining, "I will remove the ring. At that hour I will give it to my wife. Will you visit us tonight? Eat with us, and remain till midnight. I do not reckon on any danger, but even so, they say you have mastered demons, or what passed for such. In your company, Berdice will be doubly protected."

Cyrion moved toward the door.

"Until tonight, then. Providing you are happy to linger alone with the demon of the ring."

"More than happy," said Volf, and laughed again. Cyrion took his leave.

The house of Volf, a portion of the dowry Sarmur's daughter had brought him, was an opulent one. Gates of wrought iron led from the street into a courtyard of flowers and fountains. Two storeys of white and pink washed stone followed, palm-wood pillars and suitable silken hangings.

Nowhere was there more silk than in the apartment of Berdice herself. Hangings fine as smoke and heavy as syrup gleamed on their rings, draped by silken ropes, blue, green and purple. Mirrors of real glass stood in silver frames. Rainbow birds twittered in ornate wicker cages. In the middle of the bower, Berdice herself, twittering too.

Undoubtedly, she was beautiful. Jet-black hair poured unbound to her tiny waist. A flawless complexion of most delicate olive flushed into faint rose at her cheeks and lips. Gazelle eyes, dainty hands, full breasts, gave further evidence of perfection. Beauty, and to spare, she had. She had also, from the age of thirteen, been paralyzed from the tiny waist downward.

Regardless of the disposition of Berdice, her physical attributes and her wealth, the affliction had proved a bar in the matter of husbands. Then handsome Volf, poor, but of honorable name and useful western blood, had been smitten by Berdice, and, finding out the truth, had simply wept on Sarmur's shoulder, saying it made her but the dearer to him, that eventually his adoration might cure her of her trouble, that even if it did not, she was the only woman he could ever love.

Luckily, Berdice was empty-headed. It had helped her to brush aside her grievances. She twittered and twittered. She hardly ever stopped. It could have been irritating, despite her grace and her bravery. It *was* irritating.

Now there was a brief pause. A maid had entered and said: "There is a woman at the gate. She asks to read your hand. I never saw anyone like her before, nor so grand. Shall I tell her to be off?"

"Tell her to come in right away," twittered Berdice.

She liked to be occupied during the long hours when her

husband was absent, at a tavern or similar resort. All manner of charlatans came and went through the house. Now one came who was not like the others.

She was a very tall woman, with imperious chiseled features. These she had plastered skillfully but heavily with paint and powder, which did not hide that her face was far too masculine for beauty, though somehow she was still as beautiful as Berdice, and probably more so. Her head was bound by a black scarf stitched with pearls, her figure swathed in a sacklike robe. Enameled bracelets clanked on her wrists. Her large but well-shaped hands blazed with rings. She bowed herself almost to the ground before Sarmur's daughter, with the flamboyant courtesy of one who secretly rules the kingdom.

"Ethereal mistress," she whispered in a hoarse yet strangely musical voice, "will you allow me to unlock for you the occult lore of the universe?"

"Pwobably," said Berdice. "But what is your pwice?"

"I will inform you presently, maiden mistress." The tall charlatan seated herself at Berdice's feet, and took up the girl's hand in a thrilling, ringed clasp. "You suffer," pronounced the charlatan.

"No." Berdice looked surprised.

"Yes," said the charlatan. "You are unable to walk."

"How clever," said Berdice. For a moment her gazelle eyes were naked and wretched. Then they glazed, and she twittered again: "How ever did you know?"

Most of Andriok knew about Sarmur's daughter.

"My talent for divination," murmured the charlatan modestly. "But," she hissed, "what can have instigated this tragedy? An accident—"

"It was a—*cat*," Berdice blurted, blanching.

"I see in your hand a cat," swiftly interrupted the charlatan. "You are afraid of cats. The cat frightened you."

"I was asleep," Berdice confided. "I woke to discover the—cat—sleeping across my lap. I scweamed and scweamed, but it only stared with its evil fiery stare. Then it bit me and wan away. Since then I have not walked. I never could bear—*cats*." Berdice shivered and closed her eyes. "God deliver me," she moaned.

"Does your husband know your fear?" asked the charlatan.

"Oh, yes," said Berdice. She cheered up. She twittered: "What will happen tomowwow?"

"Night will come before day," said the charlatan. "Understand, maiden, I have read your stars. You are in danger's jaws, at the brink of your grave."

The maids, but not Berdice, uttered outraged shrieks. The charlatan silenced them with one glare of her brilliant, kohl-caked eyes. "Send out these bats," commanded the charlatan.

The bats were sent out.

"I speak to save your life," said the charlatan to Berdice.

"God deliver me," said Berdice again.

"Here are amulets to protect you," said the charlatan. "Wear them, and do not reveal their source or their nature. By their efficacy you will live."

Berdice looked at the amulets and tried to twitter. The twitter faded.

"But—" said Berdice.

"Do as you are told," said the charlatan, "or I cannot be responsible."

Kissing Berdice on the forehead, and adorning it thus with the likeness of two carmined lips, the charlatan rose.

"Am I to pay you?" gasped Berdice.

"I will take this," and plucking carelessly undone the purple silken cord from one of the drapes, the charlatan stalked from the chamber, ignoring the resultant gallon of loosed silk which plummeted upon Berdice's head.

Night clothed Andriok soberly. Andriok retaliated by gaudily bejeweling itself with lights. Volf's house was no exception. Scented resins flared and perfumed the air, golden filigree lamps smoldered.

Volf welcomed Cyrion like a long-lost brother he had not seen in ten years but for whose company he had continuously pined. In the satin of Askandris, and the silver of Daskiriom, not to mention his own impeccable glamour, Cyrion was fair set to outshine the house.

Entering the dining chamber, Volf displayed his left hand. On the small finger, the amber intaglio lay like a great bead of rufus honey.

"Again, mark, my Cyrion. It and I are yet together, and I thrive. Only two hours remain to midnight."

"My congratulations," said Cyrion. "This far."

"Pardon me," said Volf. "I assume, from your appearance, you never lacked for money. I have now only what my wife has brought me. And I am sick with wanting to give her something of my own."

Just then, two servants came in, carrying Volf's wife in an ornate chair, which they put beside the open window. She was prettily (if over) dressed. A gown embroidered with good omens, gold coins—oddly impressed—at her throat, bracelets hung with small medalions of jade and malachite, sapphire earrings in the shape of charms, a girdle of striped silk pinned with a lucky golden snake, a rose in her hair pinned with another, and a pair of thin silk gloves, rather stiff.

"Here is my light of love, Berdice, my beloved wife," enthused Volf.

"Madam," said Cyrion, bowing. "You seem to be in fear of something. I trust it is not of me?"

Berdice, who had been rather pale, regained her color violently. Her eyes widened in alarm on Cyrion.

"My dove must fear nothing," said Volf. "At midnight I shall give her this amber ring, which will thereafter safeguard her from all ills. You see, Cyrion. I believe in Fortune's smiling face, if not her frown."

Berdice viewed the ring and paled once more.

"This is the wing they call *'Farewell.'* Oh, Volf—It will harm you!"

Volf laughed loudly, and explained his scheme.

Berdice recoiled.

"God deliver me!" she wailed.

At that, Volf laughed even more loudly.

"Have faith in me, beloved," he sang. "Let us prove to the world that superstition is idiocy and all the demons are dust. Besides, we have Cyrion here to ensure our health. Cyrion is a hero of unsurpassable wit and gallantry."

"You will cause me to blush," opined Cyrion.

Berdice gazed at him in confused suspicion.

Dinner was served.

They ate the several courses, Berdice mute, Volf voluble. Through the open window, framing Berdice in spangles, stars shone. The scents of night-blooming flowers also wandered in from that direction, and the trilling of a sulky nightingale. In a corner of the room, meanwhile, a gilded clepsydra dripped away the minutes, quarters, a half hour, an hour. And then began to waste a fresh hour, by minutes, quarters, halves. . . .

It was almost midnight.

Suddenly Berdice started frantically to twitter.

"This afternoon, Volf—such a peculiar thing. A huge tall woman, a palm-weader and astwologer, she said. She burst into my apartment and told me I should die—"

Volf jumped, and dropped his wine cup. The wine spilled across the napkins, the mosaic table, sinking in its crevices.

"But the silliest item of all," piercingly twittered Berdice, with a maniacal glance at Cyrion, "is that I wealize the woman to have been—"

"Forgive me, madam," smoothly interposed Cyrion. "But I fancy your water-clock is slow. Is that not the midnight bell from the citadel?"

Volf and his wife froze. Sure enough, the bell was being rung.

As the bell finished, Volf leapt up and clasped Berdice's gloved right hand.

"My darling, I wear the ring and live. And now—he drew the amber from his finger—"I no longer wear the ring. The demons are defeated. These demons who never existed. Here, my angel. The ring is innocuous. Take it, with my heart." And with these words, Volf slid the amber intaglio on to her index finger. Then, raising his arms aloft in an ecstasy, Volf roared: "Heaven be praised!"

Somewhere in the dark courtyard outside, there was a muffled oath, and a scuffling.

Something hurtled through the window.

It flailed and revolved and kicked and spat and yowled.

In the midst of flailing, revolting, kicking, spitting, yowling, it landed in the lap of Berdice, and to the symphony of noises was added a sound of ripping claws and a single awful scream.

"A—*cat*!" cried Berdice in maddened terror. "A—*cat*—a—*cat*! Oh—God deliver me!"

"Berdice!" Volf shouted, ecstasy replaced by agony. He flung himself on her and gathered her limp form into his arms. He wept uncontrollably. "Cyrion, even you could not save her. I was a fool. The curse is true. The demon of the ring has struck her down, and it is my fault. I am to blame, in my stupidity. You warned me. Demons exist. Now I am left with nothing."

"Not quite," said Cyrion mildly. "Her fortune will be yours upon her death."

Volf shot him a livid, tear-splattered glare.

"What use are riches to me, when my love is slain? I am a broken man."

Cyrion in turn was nursing the cat. Initially furious at its propelled entry through the window, it had now relapsed into a purring drapery for his shoulder. Thoughtfully, Cyrion spoke. "Your grief is premature, Volf. Your wife is not dead."

"Foul mockery. She is."

"No. She has fainted, and will presently revive. Much to your chagrin, dear Volf."

Volf tremblingly peered into Berdice's face, and gasped.

"You are correct—she lives. But—"

The cat kissed Cyrion on the lips.

"Your scurrilous acquaintance, by the way," said Cyrion, "the man you paid to throw a cat in upon your wife, has probably already been apprehended. I gave a warning to the night-watch, earlier this evening."

Volf set Berdice back in her chair, and straightened. His look was currently one of wary incredulity.

"What are you saying?"

"What am I saying?" Cyrion asked the cat.

"You impugn I paid a man to shock my wife to her death?"

"Frankly, my dear," Cyrion reproved him, "if you were clever enough to solve the secret of the intaglio, you should have been capable of a better plot than this."

"Explain yourself."

"Shall I? Why not. It will fill the time until the watch proceed to your gate.

"To begin with, despite your protestations, Berdice was a burden you never intended to shoulder very long. Having married her, you would next get rid of her, so inheriting all her wealth, not to mention her father's, after his demise. Your only problem was method, some tool which would leave you, ostensibly, blameless. It was easy. Sarmur and his daughter are both highly superstitious, while you have been at pains to show yourself an unbeliever in all things intangible. Hence, the amber intaglio, which you knew could kill anyone, given the relevant circumstance.

"The legend of the ring is precise, for it was written up in the woman's tomb, was it not, from which your family pilfered it? The deaths among your forebears are also well documented. Though there appeared to be no pattern, nevertheless, unfailingly, deaths occurred. How long did it take you to answer the riddle? Let me reiterate the fatalities. A king spurring toward a battle. A conqueror on a stumbling horse. A mage in an earthquake. A bandit en route to the gallows. A woman in childbirth. And in your own family, a man falling from a wall, a man in a storm at sea, a man throwing a fit during an eclipse of the sun. And what is the common denominator? How long did you say it took you to unravel the mystery?"

Volf snarled: *"Two years."*

Cyrion diluted a smile. It had taken him two minutes, a little less.

"Danger is the key," said Cyrion. "Danger and its complement, fear. And one further thing, dependent upon danger and fear."

Cyrion was silent.

"Say the rest."

"Must I?"

"I want to hear . . . if you have it right. You owe me that."

"I owe you nothing. It shall be a gift. That further thing, then. I remember how swiftly you named the symbols engraved in the amber—a lily was the soul, a swallow was freedom, the sun was the sky. But, like most symbols of picture-writing, the meaning can be accepted as slightly more exact. The soul-lily may also represent the ego, thus 'I' or 'me.' The swallow does not only signify freedom, but freedom from bondage—deliverance. As for the sun, it is the ancient cipher, not only for the sky, but for God. So the lily, the swallow, the sun offer us, you agree, a sentence of picture-writing to be translated as *God deliver me.* An established religious phrase in most languages, then or now. The king riding to battle whispering a last prayer. The man on the stumbling horse calling out in alarm. The mage, feeling the house shake with the earth-tremor—who could guess him slain before the walls buried him? The bandit uttering the traditional orison on the road to the gallows. The woman in the pain of childbirth, shrieking. And your ancestor tumbling from the broken parapet, dead before he hit the ground. The second dead before the water closed over his head, and long before he was pulled to safety. The third, appalled by the darkness of eclipse—*God deliver me* they each cried. And the ring killed them instantly, as its engraving warns it will. Those words, spoken by the wearer, activate a device under the stone. A hair-fine sliver darts into the skin of the finger. Poison runs. A demon poison, so virulent it can dispatch in seconds. The victim sinks prostrate, with a look of horror and no visible wound.

"Knowing all this, you could wear the ring and avoid death. But when a cat descended on your cat-fearing wife, you knew she would exclaim the fatal phrase and die immediately. And I, with what you foolishly deduce to be an heroic reputation, was to attend the scene as your witness to inescapable Fate."

"But Berdice has not died," Volf said. He looked drained, no longer angry or malevolent. His weak mouth wobbled, and his feigned tears for his wife had altered to genuine tears spilled for himself.

"Luckily for the lady," said Cyrion, "a witch-woman happened to visit her this afternoon, and persuaded her to wear two amulets. These." He pointed to the silken gloves on Berdice's hands, the fingers of which gloves were all internally lined with thin but impregnable jointed steel of Daskiriom—unpierceable by any venomous sliver, no matter how fine.

Berdice was stirring. Cyrion gently divested himself of the cat, leaned over the girl and took her by the elbows. He pulled her suddenly to her feet.

"The shock of the second cat has cured you," said Cyrion sternly. "Now you can walk. Do so."

Berdice gaped at him, then took a faltering step.

She screamed, and took another.

Still screaming and still walking, she permitted Cyrion to aid her from the room. On the threshold he placed in her grasp a purple silken cord, but she barely noticed. She seemed to have forgotten Volf, too, which forgetfulness would presently stand her in good stead.

When Cyrion returned to the dining chamber, the watch were already hammering at the gate.

Volf huddled in a chair.

Cyrion set beside him, on the mosaic, the ring.

"To hang is a prolonged and unpleasing business," Cyrion murmured, fastidiously.

When they reached the dining chamber, the watch found one man alone in it, and he was quite dead. Volf lay across the table, with the amber intaglio on his hand, a look of horror on his face, and no visible wound.

6TH INTERLOGUE

Mild uproar followed the priest's offering.

Most of the occupants of the table were by now somewhat sozzled. Even the scholar had mellowed, his long-lidded eyes half-closed, a slight smile playing about his well-formed lips. The plump young man of the ginger hair, though flushed with wine, was neither drunk nor in the spirit of the thing. Indeed, he seemed oppressed. From the moment the fortune-teller had appeared in the narrative, he had begun to fidget and to gaze about him, like one fearful of going mad.

When, near the story's end, the pantherine brunette had arisen, with her gauzes, pearls and maid, from her distant table, and gone up the stair at the back of the room (having herself determined the ending of the tale, it would seem), Roilant had been dumbly and inactively beside himself.

Now the romance was concluded, he got up and—waving protesting hands aside—excused himself on the grounds of insistent nature. On these grounds, he was allowed to absent himself, and one of the merchants went rolling out with him through the curtain, eulogizing the while on the hapless Berdice. "A jewel, a bird. What I would give for such a lovely, simple-minded wife."

"I commiserate with her lot," said Roilant. His tone seemed unduly somber. Then, beside the Qirri statue, Roilant, sweating, said: "The woman who left the room a few minutes ago. Did you see her?"

"A lovely package. But, I am sure, not at all simple."

"But tall, and large-boned."

"Truly, a desirable and voluptuous being."

"You miss my point. She might have been, might she not, a *man*?"

The merchant began to laugh. He laughed until he was forced to lean upon the brass Qirri. He held his aching sides and gurgled. Presently, under threat from his bladder, he retreated down the passage, still squeaking with airless mirth. Its instigator was left to feel both ridiculous and nervous. If the woman *were* Cyrion, should he, Roilant, go after her? If she were not Cyrion, how would it look if he went galloping up the inn stair in chase?

Besides—a horrible confusion grasped him—what the priest had said was true. So many of them might be Cyrion in disguise. The caravaneer, obscured by an untidyness and dust belied by his composure. The handsome scholar—were his lines the result of late middle-age, or of brushwork? Or the three merchants, the third of whom, now Roilant thought of it, had a face far too lean to suit his bulk. Padding? The priest himself, presumably, was unlikely to be a candidate. He really was a very fat man, with no pretense to glamour. Yet even that might be some form of incredibly complex camouflage.

Then there were the slaves. Roilant had scarcely looked at any of them, yet they were well-dressed by the inn, and had been everywhere about him. Esur, now. Perhaps white-toothed Esur was Cyrion, and the inn-keeper in on the game.

Roilant began to pace. He was still pacing, when the second merchant returned from the latrines and burst into a jolly squawk at sight of him.

Roilant swore back, then contritely apologized. The merchant patted him fondly on the shoulder. As this went on, the street door opened and down the steps came floundering Whiskers, the abbreviated soldier of the brown moustache.

"Did you arrest that old monster of a holy-man?" asked the merchant.

Whiskers hiccupped and nodded vigorously. He tumbled past them and back into the main room in a riot of mismanaged curtain, from which both Roilant and the merchant were forced to shy away. For someone seriously stunted in his growth, Whiskers seemed capable of causing the maximum of impact.

Roilant looked at the gong in the hands of the Qirri, longing to bang it ferociously and yell: "Fire!" In the scramble, the devilish Cyrion might be unmasked. It was just the kind of trick Cyrion himself would resort to. But Roilant? Never. Hating his own timidity, his own lack of amour propre, Roilant said, "I must settle my account and get on. I have business to see to in the city."

"Let it wait. The afternoon is young."

Roilant found he was being led back into the main chamber.

The scene was substantially as before. The returning Whiskers, despite welcoming shouts, had not joined the common table. He sprawled where the black-haired woman had sat, his head on his arms, preparing, rather noisily, to sleep off his wine. The snores which rattled from under the moustache grew in volume, until conversationalists were forced to shout, then abated suddenly.

"How exasperating," said the jeweled merchant. "I had anticipated news of the sage's capture and, hopefully, torture, at the hands of Malban's garrison."

Esur entered the room, gazed at them all with impartial dislike, and began to clear the wreckage of their dinners. Two other slaves followed. Roilant examined them all. Slim, youthful and dark. Which could mean very little. A unified gasp recalled him. He turned and beheld what everyone at his table beheld, with fascination, disbelief and awe. On the back stair, poised and frankly amused, was a young gallant of medium height, sturdily built and fashionably clad, vividly handsome and girded with a sword. The sword, however, was sheathed in white vellum, the left hand was naked of rings, and the shoulder-length hair was the color of midnight. One step farther up stood a slender page-boy, with a tiger lily and a hyacinth tucked behind one translucent ear.

There could be no more than a second's doubt. These apparitions were none other than the elegant lady and her maid of the prior twenty minutes.

The question now was blatant, and astonishingly unanswerable. Had they been a boy and a gentleman in the roles of a girl and lady? Or were they girl and lady in the roles of boy and gentleman? Which? Either? *Both?*

Gazed on by many wide eyes, they completed their progress down the stair. As the gallant passed Roilant, a bow was swept with the utmost formal magnificence. "Good day," said a voice, once a seductive contralto now a flawless tenor. Man and page moved through the curtain and were gone.

"Damn my drawsers," exploded the priest, and blushed like a rose, trying to excuse himself while being congratulated and clapped on the back.

The plump one plumped into his erstwhile seat. Nothing was what it seemed at this unnatural inn. Was he still Roilant? Unfortunately, yes. Esur had crept up to him, carrying a platter of picked bones defensively. Esur breathed: "I have recalled another story of Cyrion—"

"Go away," said Roilant.

Esur snarled and did so.

Steep shafts of golden light fell through the windows. The caged bird cooed and hopped, and the drowsy snores of the soldier had resumed, and now came rhythmically as thunderclaps.

The party, having run out of fables, or the wish to deal in them, drifted apart with moist-eyed regrets. The three merchants went aloft to their apartments, winking silver and violet hanging on their arms. The caravaneer, whose dinner was to be paid for by the jewelled merchant, swung out, yawning and stretching, into the richness of the afternoon. The scholar, too, removed to pack his bags of scrolls and books. He must join a caravan at dawn tomorrow, bound for the kingdom of Kyros, and the city of Askandris. The slaves muddled out, snapping at each other and dropping plates.

Quite quickly only the loud Whiskers, the disheartened Roilant remained.

The innkeeper bustled through.

"Your inn," said Roilant, who had been finishing the wine, "is a madhouse."

"You tell me nothing I am not familiar with."

Roilant stared at the large eyes, wondered if the balding pate might be faked—

"However, good sir," said the innkeeper, in a voice that could be assumed, "I have recollected the man you were asking after. You were in error with the name."

"I—was?"

"Quite so. He is called Cyrion."

Roilant fastened his eyes closed. Coldly, he said, "Remiss of me." And resisted the temptation to anoint the man with the last of the wine.

"Which being the case," proceeded the innkeeper, unaware of his escape, "I feel you should be warned. This adventurer is ruthless. As an enemy, he is terrible, so I hear. Confidentially—"

"Confidentially, you know a story about him which illustrates this failing."

"No," the innkeeper amazed him by saying. Then spoilt it. "There is an old man who begs, and he is at the kitchen door now. He sometimes comes here, and I give him food, for the luck of the house. He is partly blind, but lucid. He has spent time with the nomads, and says he has a strain of their blood in his withered veins. If you like—"

Roilant was about to refuse. From upstairs, a flight of bright lascivious laughter broke like a chain of beads. Somehow, it alerted him.

Carefully, Roilant said, "very well. Let him come in. I will pay."

The innkeeper nodded, and went out again.

Roilant waited, impatient and anxious, jumping nearly out of his skin when the recumbent Whiskers once more reached a crescendo of noise. In the silence which succeeded, there came the rather sinister sound of a tapping stick. Then a tall old man in a black garment glided in at the curtains, his staff feeling its way before him. The nomadic hood was pulled low across his eyes, which were lightly bandaged over. The face was inscrutable, cut fine, quilted by age and desert sun.

Roilant held himself in check until the old man had lowered his frame into a chair. Then Roilant went forward and stood over him, breathing fast.

"I have gold," said Roilant. "For that gold, I want truth. I tell you now, my life is in the utmost peril. The reason I came here seeking—seeking Cyrion, is to employ him on whatever terms he stipulates, for my safety. Do you hear?"

"I hear," said the exaggeratedly ancient voice.

"So now," barked Roilant, "stop this sham and reveal yourself."

"I am revealed."

"No. You are *not*. You are Cyrion."

The beggar laughed. His teeth were few and the inside of his mouth aged and shriveled as the rest of him.

"Cyrion? God did not bless me so. I am myself, the father of Esur, who one day will buy his freedom and grow wealthy. But I. I was freed and cast out as useless, and found my boy, who was torn from my side at Heshbel years ago, only after a lengthy, arduous search. And I am free and penniless, he a slave, and opulent. Yet how is a slave to support his poor old sire? I am fed here from kindness, a blessing on the inn. But I have never even touched a gold coin—"

Between embarrassment, anger and pity, the mistaken nobleman almost choked. He promised and produced two coins. Then sat down to listen as his penance, but for the very last, to a tale of Cyrion. . . .

A LYNX WITH LIONS

At midday, beaten almost flat by the hammer of the sun, the desert lay in the perfect imitation of one near death. A deception. Life lurked and thrived in its own way just beneath the skin of the desert. Husks, buried shards, lost treasures, veins of water, and magic. While at dusk, the dying thing would rise and shake itself, and stretch to receive the cold balm of the stars.

Karuil-Ysem turned a black-hooded head, and seemed to listen more attentively to what the scout was saying. The black eyes of Karuil-Ysem, old, cruel, and intransigently wise, half closed. It was a sign reminiscent of the prostration of the desert, a deception of lifelessness and quiescence.

"And you say he has followed us since yesterday's sunrise?"

"Just so, Karuil."

"And on foot, and alone. And garbed as our people are garbed for the desert."

"And so, Karuil."

"And he is white-haired?"

"Or very fair. A Westerner. Neither of the cities, nor of our own people. Yet he walks the sands with the sure step of the nomads, as careless and as cunning. He wears a sword, yet this morning a viper came from the stones by his hand, where he had lain sleeping. It rose up to strike him, but he struck first. He threw a knife that parted its head from its body before it or I caught breath. He found the hidden watering-place, also, that only our people know of. Who can it be, Father, who understands our ways yet is neither ours nor our land's?"

Karuil, slowly blinking his eagle's eyes at the King's title:

'Father,' as he always did now, as if surprised still to be so addressed, turned his head back again, to regard the recent erection of black tents among the pillared trees of the oasis. Life moved sluggishly there, paying homage to the desert's temporary death.

"I believe I know who he is," said Karuil-Ysem. "I shall return with you. Let us see if I am wise, still, or have become a fool."

The scout kicked his horse so it leapt about and raced away, the reddish sand splashing up from its unshod feet. Karuil's horse moved no less willingly. They were gone.

Some of the nomads, tall men, all dressed alike in the long black robe, the hoods mostly up against the sun, sat under the soaked-out shadows of the palms, watching Karuil and the scout vanish.

"What causes that?" one asked.

The son of Karuil-Ysem, Ysemid, made the nomadic gesture equivalent to a wink.

"Someone has been following us, the scouts say. One of the Angel knights, perhaps, a Dove who has mislaid his nest."

"Who pursues the Lions of the Desert should be more careful of his meat," quoted another man.

Ysemid acknowledged this. He was handsome, young and proud, one ear pierced by a knob of sapphire. Across the shadow-patched sand, more of his riches were observable. One of his three beautiful wives, black-clad but with girdle, wrists, ears and forehead dripping with jewelry, the veil which covered her lips and chin sewn with sequins of polished gold, was bringing him a drink in a cup of fluted glass, on a tray of chased silver.

"My father, the Father," said Ysemid, "will give us the carcass if it is an emeny. If not, we shall see."

On a rise among the dunes, Karuil and the scout sat their horses, seeing for themselves.

The pursuer, now in sight, climbed steadily and unerringly toward them. He had probably seen them also, but as yet gave no sign of it.

"Behold how he treads, Father. He knows the sand."

"So he does."

"And the hair."

"Just so."

A minute more and the object of their scrutiny lifted his

white-blond head. Without pausing, he looked straight at them. Coming on in this way, he was soon near enough that they could discern the features of a face lightly tanned but otherwise entirely remarkable.

"A Jewel of God," declared the scout, with contemptuous awe. The term denoted great beauty and was usually employed in scorn. The nomads, relentless travelers, ruthless warriors, and holding to a rigid and sometimes bloody code indigenous to themselves, tended to believe the truly beautiful were also the truly useless.

"A Jewel," the old man agreed. "But set in steel. Yes, it is the one I reckoned it must be."

Karuil-Ysem swung himself from the back of his horse—he was surprisingly limber. He stood, in obvious waiting as the un-stranger, his glamorous face composed and expressionless, came up the last of the rising ground.

When the young man was twenty paces off, Karuil said, still in the nomadic tongue, "the desert flowers at the footstep of the desired guest."

At this the arrival halted, and replied, in the same tongue, faultlessly: "and water springs from the rock at the re-finding of a friend."

His voice was beautiful as the rest of him, and the scout listened with offended amazement. Which increased, as with no great show Karuil opened his arms, and the blond Westerner completed the distance and walked into them. Embrace was calmly and strongly given and returned.

"Welcome, Cyrion," said Karuil.

"Your welcome is welcome," answered the Jewel of God who was called Cyrion.

"How did you happen on us?" inquired Karuil.

"In the usual manner. By following those signs the People of Karuil leave, for those who seek them in brotherhood."

"My scout is astonished."

Cyrion glanced at the scout, and smiled at him with appalling charm. "There are many roads to wisdom, of which astonishment is one," said Cyrion, demurely quoting a nomadic proverb.

Karuil laughed. It was rare, that dry crackle of amusement.

"Cyrion has spent time among us. He is also a swordsman and adventurer famous in the coastal cities and in yellow-walled Heruzala itself, which is now the Westerners' playground."

"And does he also," asked the scout, "heed the teachings of the Prophet Hesuf, as we do, and as the Westerners pretend to do?"

"I note astuteness and virtue in the teachings of Hesuf," said Cyrion, amiably. "Like yourself, perhaps, I sometimes stumble over that particular one which says I should enjoy being struck twice in the face."

The scout's eyes widened, then he grinned.

"You will go back with us to the tents?" Karuil asked.

"My intention, if allowed."

"It is allowed."

Karuil did not re-mount, and Cyrion himself took the tasselled reins of the desert king's horse, leading it. The scout trotted on a little ahead of them.

For a while there was silence, separated only by the hushed, blistering shifts, as the sand eased itself. Finally, as they descended from the last upgrade, and the oasis came in view, Karuil said: "And you live well, Cyrion?"

"Not so well as I have."

"Some reversal in fortunes."

"A reversal," the musical voice hesitated, "of a kind. I have come back into the desert in sore need of the disciplines I once learned here, things which fail me from lack of practice."

"The muscles of the spirit—you were adept. What is your need?"

Again, a pause. The man who rode ahead was not so far off he could not overhear, through the still, roasted air.

"My scout is to be trusted," said Karuil. "But yet. We will speak in my tent."

Cyrion murmured, "Father, I have no cause to mistrust any of your People. Better I tell you now. I fear it will become necessary in any case, very shortly." Again, a hesitation. Then, coolly and firmly: "There is an affliction of the brain and eyes, in itself unfatal and spasmodic. It begins with a slight disturbance of the vision, progresses to a period of blindness, and ends with a pain that inhabits half the skull for any number of hours, like a roosting axe-blade. The causes are numerous and unknown. Drugs will generally relieve the pain, and to those of a quiet disposition, the ailment is negotiable if unpleasing. However, you can judge, Father, its dangers to a man known to have lived by use of a sword."

Karuil stood immobile. Below, the drinking cup of the oasis glittered its water. The scout had reined in his horse nearby. He looked away, down into the encampment, frankly listening to what was said at his back.

"You?" said Karuil-Ysem to Cyrion.

"Very unluckily, I. You never heard of such a disability? The Cassian emperors of Remusa were afflicted by it. Noble company, it would seem. But you tell my predicament."

"The cause?"

Cyrion shrugged, smiling, as if he spoke of nothing much. "I have no idea. A blow to the head, maybe, of which I have been gifted a few. Or some form of witchcraft—I have also come in the way of one or two of these. . . . My dissolute life. Whatever opened the door, the guest has come in. And while I can wield a blade through most sorts of pain, it may prove difficult to fight a man I cannot see."

The tent of Karuil-Ysem was set by itself, very close to the water, in a green net of shade. Inside, an incense lamp of bronze latticework depended low from a complex arrangement of chains stretched between the tent poles. The complexity of these chains resulted from the fact that they must avoid forming a cross. Hundreds of years before, the Prophet Hesuf had almost died on such an instrument, before being saved by popular outcry. For this reason, anything resembling a cross was abhorrent to the nomads. Their dislike they demonstrated even in the matter of their swords, the blades of which, in order to escape the accursed shape, were curved like a new moon.

Karuil-Ysem sat under the lamp, among the silk pillows, facing the opened entrance of the tent where the sun fell, Cyrion beside him. They had been served wine and date-juice, and a variety of candies. These sweets and the wine, Karuil remarked, were the product of his son's generosity. Ysemid spent much profitable time now in the cities. Across the glimmer of the water, Ysemid's tent was visible. As the heat of noon died down, black-robed men were indulging in violent horse races there, dust and cries splintering up into the bleached sky.

After the courtesies of eating and drinking the fare of

Daskiriom and Heshbel, Cyrion sat at apparent indolent ease, his chin resting on his ringed left hand, as Kuruil, with unexpected appetite, quaffed and chewed on.

At length, Cyrion said, casually, "I take it, we shall no longer be overheard, here?"

"No," said Karuil, selecting a pastry.

"While your busy scout is already spreading the news of my sad affliction."

Karuil blinked. The snake-skin lids hovered. It was a signal of decided attention.

"The scout? I told you he would say nothing."

"Then what was the purpose of your invitation to speak in front of him?"

Karuil set down the pastry. The old face grew wickedly intent. Very slowly, his long teeth appeared. "What I told you, and what is true, may not be one and the same."

"You do delight me. The thought of engineering more rumors seemed unexciting, not to say heavy-handed."

"You also then play with truth. Your illness is a lie."

Cyrion looked at Karuil for some moments, then glanced toward the seethe of dust and action sixty feet off, over the water.

"The illness," said Cyrion quietly, "was a useful coincidence. I was instructed, was I not, to arrive armed with an excuse?"

"Then it is a fact—this blindness—"

"The thing is normally occasional. What disciplines I learnt among your people I have not forgotten, and do not need to re-learn. You may imagine, if I was sick I would have tried them. Perhaps they would not be of help."

"Then," said Karuil, "you are here solely—" there was a distended pause. At last—"because I sent for you."

"Which is rather odd of me, I see, since you appear to trust me very little."

"That I should send for you at all demonstrates I trust no other so well. How did you come on my message?"

"In one of the places that I frequent and that you left it. How else? If I deciphered it correctly, you meant me to understand you were in danger."

Karuil, who had taken up the pastry again, set it down. His eyes sank into their deceptive dozing position.

"Ah. I thought you would interpret it in this way."

"I was mistaken."

"No. He is my enemy." Now the words came swiftly, with an edge to them, sere and bitter. "He cleaves to city ways. He revels in their decadence and luxury. He hangs his women with gold and his tent with gems, and sends this much of the bakeries to draw my strong teeth—" Karuil struck out suddenly, and sent the sweetmeats rolling like colored dice. "Ysemid would make a dotard of me. Like an old lion, he thinks to lull me, then spring the trap."

Cyrion waited a moment before saying, "among the People, patricide is the worst of all crimes, and receives the worst punishment. Will Ysemid risk that?"

"I do not know. Yes, I believe he will. Oh, not yet. But soon. He has those among us who love him, those who admire his dreams. He would pitch the tents beside the city walls and make a bazaar and show of us, and loll on his bed with his women while the bones of our sons turn to sticks and our daughters are made into whores—" Karuil broke off. His voice had not risen. The phrases were a fury, the rest of him stayed still as an eagle watching from a high rock. "Only I," he said, "stand in the beast's way. Yes. He will kill me. So I sent for you. You, that once lived among my people, and were like my son to me. You remember this?"

Softly, Cyrion answered, "I remember. Without Karuil-Ysem, I should be far less than I am. What would you have me do, Father of your People?"

"For the moment, nothing. Linger here, and wait, as I do."

The old man drank Ysemid's wine, savoring it as if it were the blood of a foe, which like the demons, the nomads of ancient days had sometimes swallowed.

"Then," said Cyrion, "I will wait."

"They shall prepare you a tent. You shall be one of us again. But this affliction of your eyes, it troubles me."

"No. It is me that it troubles. When you require it, I shall be at your command."

A shadow fell across the threshold. Both Cyrian and Karuil-Ysem fixed their gaze on it. Abruptly, the man that the shadow had preceded stalked from around the tent. It was unlikely, even had he been listening, that he would have heard much. Their voices had been low, and the noise across the water, only now dying down, would have masked a good deal.

The man bowed in the nomadic way to Karuil. At Cyrion he stared.

"The Prince Ysemid begs you, Father, to grant him also the happiness of greeting your guest."

Cyrion rose, and observed the hanging lamp, now level with his forehead, as Karuil said to him: "Yes, go to my son, Cyrion. The young lion must have his way."

Cyrion politely agreed.

As he walked with Ysemid's messenger around the oasis, the man tried to conduct a stilted, partly scathing interrogation.

"The Prince wonders what you can be, clad in our attire, yet of the pale foreign blood. It is said you lived among us. Why do we not recall you?"

"Either we did not meet at the time, or I am humiliatingly unmemorable."

"Hah! To live with us—did your own mother, revolted by you, slough you in the desert and run away?"

"Mothers are notoriously partial. They will put up with almost anything. Such a small number of us would otherwise survive."

They moved among the flock of black shelters. Lazy fires had been lit where meat already broiled. Where the water gathered in a pool, women idled over their pitchers, gossiping. At the approach of the two men they glanced, and giggled. On Cyrion, their eyes grew large, and often melting. Kept close among the tents they had not frequently seen a Westerner. He, with his hair like the sky of earliest sunrise, his fair complexion, his eyes gilded by lashes longer than their own, was like a being from another world.

On the far side of the oasis the races had finished. Ysemid sat before his tent on a carpet, sipping from a glass cup. About him, his favorites sat or stood, joking and drinking. The three beautiful wives were in glinting evidence. As the sun touched their faces, one saw their black face-veils were thin as smoke, in violation of tradition.

Noting Cyrion, Ysemid rose, lifting his arms in a gesture of welcome and pleasure. The scout was nowhere to be seen, but no doubt had been here, before returning to his watch beyond the camp.

"Behold," announced Ysemid, "the white cat is a friend, or

surely my father the Father would have slain him. Come, friend of Karuil's People."

Cyrion went forward and suffered himself to be embraced. Ysemid's entourage in their turn fell to patting him and smoothing his blond hair. Earrings and teeth flashed and the slanting sun hit the scene with blows of tilted, steady light.

Ysemid pressed on Cyrion a cup of wine. Cyrion graciously sampled it and set it aside. Another of the men graciously pressed it on him again.

"It is not to your liking?" Ysemid was concerned.

"A little stony. The wine of Andriok is better since you are prepared to pay such prices for it."

"A merchant! He knows and prices my wine. What else wonderful can you do, friend of the People of Karuil?"

Cyrion smiled dazzlingly.

"You should not overvalue me."

"But I divine genius. Come," said Ysemid once more, throwing an arm over Cyrion's shoulders, "we have brought horses out of Heshbel. Come and see. Tell us how they seem to you."

In a surge, the laughing young men thrust forward, Cyrion borne with them. As he passed, two of Ysemid's wives modestly lowered their eyes. The third looked after him with a strange deliberation.

In Ysemid's ear, the knob of sapphire sparkled, fired. Again and again the shattered brilliancies of the sun shot from it. It seemed both to attract and repel the eyes of Cyrion.

The horses stood in the shade of five palm trees, all but one stallion which, held by several boys, plunged and stamped, tossing his head.

"Now what," said Ysemid, "do you suppose is wrong with this animal? He has unseated two of my best horsemen. No sooner up—than down."

Cyrion said nothing amid the laughter of the entourage. The horse shook his head as if to loosen it from his body.

"Perhaps," said Ysemid, "you, illustrious guest of my father, would care to test your ability."

"No," said Cyrion, "I regret I should not."

All the gladsome faces, as if rubbed by a single cloth, were cleaned of their merriment.

"But am I to think you afraid?"

"Think me rather aware the horse is ungelded and there are nubile mares in the vicinity."

Ysemid cried out joyfully.

"Did I not commend him as a genius? Wine, horses. . . .

The voice of a boy piped through from beyond the crowd.

"A dwelling has been set for the stranger, under the stunted palm tree, a short distance from the tents."

Cyrion offered Ysemid the proud obeisance of the East, and asked leave to depart for the tent.

All fondness, Ysemid waved him off.

"Go, blessed Jewel of God."

He doubtless noticed the Westerner walked slowly, going back around the oasis. He did not seem inclined to look about, and reaching the segregated tent Karuil had allotted him, went directly inside, letting down the flap behind him.

Ysemid spat on the sand, a rare act among those who learned early to respect water.

The red flower of sunset opened, bloomed and faded. In the black night the clustered stars of the desert blazed. When the stars of the fires died in the nomadic encampment, Ysemid walked from his tent, stretching himself, smiling as, within, the sleepy voice of a woman murmured. Presently Ysemid moved silently through the camp and around the water, responding, en route, to two brief challenges, with a muffled jest that caused the camp's sentries to chuckle. Just before he came to the tent of Karuil, the prince palmed up a handful of glisten from the oasis, and drank it.

At the entrance, where the flap hung closed, the young man stopped and called, very low, "My father?"

After a moment, from inside the tent, the old voice stirred in answer.

"What is it?"

"Do I disturb you? It is your son, Ysemid. Something weighs on my mind. May I come in?"

"Old men sleep shallowly. Enter."

Ysemid slipped inside the tent.

What greeted his eyes was perhaps a very curious sight. Seated on the pillows under the dully burning bronze lamp, Karuil-Ysem, Father of his People, sat ravenously devouring sweet jellies, gulping sherbets and redolent wines. Many trays and many cups stood about him, the clawlike fingers reaching for them eagerly, nor did the meal cease at the arrival of his son.

Smiling still, and still very low, Ysemid said:

"What a disgusting creature, the pig."

Karuil, even now not hesitating at his feast, replied: "Bondage and hire. I take my wages."

"You are owed no wages, foulness, being a slave."

"And how much longer must I be your slave?"

"Till I am done with you."

"Till you are sure?" The old eyes glittered like knife points. "But can you ever be sure, dear son? Having played with us, how shall you ever be forgotten?"

"You forget already. You forget I have a security."

"One day, your security may be lost."

"I think not. And now. Tell me what the Westerner said to you in this tent."

Karuil-Ysem crushed a powdered slab of lakoum into his mouth and ate it, while the young man scowled and fretted. Eventually, Karuil was done and rejoined, "He said what you expected, having been sent for as you expected. He said he knew me endangered by you and that he would aid me against you. So I bade him bide for my word. But there is another thing."

"Which is?"

Karuil raised nougatine to his lips, and Ysemid, with an oath, strode forward. Karuil lowered the sweet, beaming twistedly up at him. "Which is that the declared sickness is a true sickness, for he admitted it to me."

Ysemid, distracted from annoyance, nodded.

"So I thought it, though it sounds so curious. He crept to his tent. It is on him now. One I sent before me found this Cyrion sleeping like the dead—or the drugged. Nevertheless, this white house cat, I never feared him."

"Did you not, pretty son?"

Ysemid moved abruptly. He slashed the old man violently across the face, so he was flung back among the sweets and the cushions. Lying there, Karuil hissed, "be careful of me. I am brittle and may break. That would not suit your plan."

"And you, vileness, you be wary. The sweetmeats may do as much harm as my fist."

"It is only for a little while," the felled king said. "I crave the novelty. I am your slave. You must allow me something."

"You shall have what you truly crave, very soon."

Karuil maneuvered himself upright. The movement was oddly fluid and serpentine.

"Do you mean freedom? Yes, I crave that. As does my sister. To bind such as we, O brat, is to build fire in a vessel of dry reeds."

"Is it? We shall see."

Ysemid returned to the door-flap of the tent. Emerging, he looked upward at the stars, then back again at the weird figure on the pillows. Loudly: "The blessing of God upon you, my father."

With a terrible grimace, Karuil responded: "And the light of heaven gild *you*, Ysemid."

Ysemid did not move directly toward his own tent. He strolled to the edge of the oasis where the nomadic shelters ended under the palms. One final tree, warped and dying, rose on the outskirt, with one final tent beneath. Quietly, Ysemid approached, raised the flap, and looked within. Starlight vaguely revealed the sleeping man, huddled in his nomad's black, a strand of white-blond hair frayed out like silk from under the hood, across a handful of shining rings. And, under that, the sheathed sword set handy. But Cyrion, it seemed, slept like the moon tonight. It would be easy to kill him so, but his death would not, in these circumstances, look well. There were more attractive ways.

Ysemid let fall the flap and went away. From the shade woven between two nearby palms, Cyrion watched him go.

Cyrion, with fire-soot rubbed in his hair—one skein of which he had previously lopped—dressed in the western garb of black silk he had affected beneath his nomad's robe, was barely to be seen in the moonless dark. Even the rings did not gleam on his left hand; for once he had removed them, and left them on five pared reeds, under the lopped hair, over the sword, beside the bolster-packed bundle of the robe. Only the knife had come out with him. These elaborate precautions had proved, however, an enchanting success. About an hour before, one of Ysemid's courtiers, coming to visit Cyrion, had been completely convinced, as Cyrion witnessed. The muffled sleeper's groan Cyrian had also generously supplied may, of course, have aided in the matter.

Across the water of the oasis, Ysemid might be heard cracking another joke with one of the watchmen. Cyrion, a vagrant shadow, moved soundlessly between trees and tents, gained that of Karuil-Ysem, and entered it without preliminary.

The Father was gormandizing, as he had been previously to judge by the earlier—overheard—conversation. Now the old man stared, wine cup in one hand, candy in the other.

"Night's benisons," said Cyrion. "Still hungry?"

Karuil gathered himself slowly.

"I heard you lay sick."

"It is sometimes possible to delay an attack, or forestall it. For the time being I am in no pain, and can see very clearly."

"Why are you here?"

"I saw Ysemid come to your tent."

"You feared for me?"

Cyrion was mildly astonished. "What other reason would I have?"

Karuil lapsed back on his cushions, putting down as he did so the wine cup, and reaching for a cup of sherbet. Cyrion stepped forward, took the cup and courteously extended it. As he leaned close to Karuil, something happened that seemed to have to do with Cyrion's left hand. There was a dull lightning that ran from Karuil's throat to his sash. At the same instant the cup went flying in a spray of heavily scented juice, and Cyrion too, springing back, the knife bright in his grasp.

Karuil sat gaping. His robe gaped with him. Slashed from collarbone to waist by Cyrion's blade, it hung open to display the gnarled and swarthy chest of a very strong and very old man. That, and one other thing. Above the heart were two black holes, jagged, deep, and utterly bloodless. Mortal wounds that had been cold a month or more.

If Cyrion was paler than he had been was hard to tell. But very softly he commented on God in a way a priest might not have cared for.

Then the dead-live thing came at him, bounding with an agility it should not possess, and in its right hand, still sticky from sweets, Karuil's curved sword.

Cyrion was armed only with a knife. He ducked and came up with a bolster added to the itinerary. It met the first swooping advance of the sword and suffered from it. The second blow was more demanding yet, and cleaved the bolster almost in two.

As the larger blade stuck, clotted in silk, Cyrion lashed for Karuil's face with the knife. The sword dragged free, and Karuil jumped away—some reflex, the knife-play was a feint merely. Plainly, Karuil could not be wounded, or slain—both had already happened, and here he was, bouncing like a locust. But this, this was not Karuil.

The eyes of what had been a man flared, full of hate and a furious confusion. Cyrion was not meant to die quite yet, and the hour of his death was to be of Ysemid's choosing, so much Cyrion had gathered. Ysemid who was this thing's master—

Cyrion slid past the third sweep of the sword, casting the remains of the bolster. The pile of cushions was the last stage of his journey. Having achieved their eminence, gracefully avoiding as he did so the low-hung lamp, he turned again and made to the corpse-creature an unmistakable motion of encouragement. With a feverish growl, it plunged forward, the sword spurling in a web of torn silk. Cyrion watched it come. Then he moved like fire.

His hands found the bronze lamp and hurled it the length of its chain. A second more, and Cyrion dropped flat on the pillows. He seemed to have been smitten there, but the blow had not touched him and indeed was what he eluded. It passed over him instantly with a rasp of parted air, the sickle blade rushing through the empty space that should have been occupied by his body. Then came another noise: the inexorable muffled clang of bulky metal contacting, at speed, a human skull.

With a nasal grunt, the creature which had been Karuil was thrown backward and went down. Cyrion in his turn was off the pillows, and leapt after it. In less than a moment, he had prized the great sword from the scrabbling long-nailed fingers. In half a breath more, the sword swung upward and waited, shivering with light, as a woman's voice said, quiet and harsh as a scraped bone: "*No.* Do *not*—"

Cyrion did not lower the sword or look about. He looked only at the glaring and now terrified eyes that still lived in Karuil's dead face on the floor below him. The lamp had singed the hair of the brows. If the flesh above them had lived, it might have been bruised.

Just beyond Karuil, a drop of oil had fallen from the lamp and burned sulkily. Not glancing, Cryion put out his foot and quenched it. Conversationally, he said, "Decapitation. One of the few deaths a demon truly fears."

"Yes," whispered the voice in the doorway of the tent. "We are demons, my brother and I. Remember, if you know of our kind, our powers are greater by night and in dark places. Kill him, and you have me to reckon with."

"Well," Cyrion answered gently, "it seems your brother has slaughtered one I valued somewhat. This man whose body he now uses like a glove. Perhaps I am not amenable to reason."

"Neither he nor I slew Karuil-Ysem. It was his son did that for him, with a dagger, many days and nights before you came here. It seems he sent for you, but you arrived too late. Hear the story, before you judge it."

For a moment longer, Cyrion did not move. Then he lowered the sword. Stepping away from the body of Karuil, he planted the blade in a cushion, and standing by it took up the knife he had dropped and sheathed it. Only then did he gaze across the tent.

The young woman who stood there, just within the closed flap of the tent, had entered as silently as he, despite the costly sequins sewn so thickly on her garments, and the jewels roped at her girdle. Her unveiled face was seen to be very beautiful, and where the veiling had slipped from her hair, its color was the fierce peach-golden common among female demons. Her long nails were painted with gilt, however. She was Ysemid's third wife.

Karuil-who-was-not was now attempting to crawl to her. The corpse appeared to be in sudden agony, and with a sharp intake of her breath, the woman kneeled to help him.

"Yes," Cyrion observed. "And old man's body can be forced to the flexibility of youth, but will suffer for it. I am fascinated so much feeling remains in the nerves, and so much information in the brain. The sense of taste, also. For one who normally feeds on the exclusive diet of raw flesh and blood, the experience of second-hand sweetmeats must be novel."

The demon woman held the living corpse against her breast.

"I have heard tell of one who has your name," she said to Cyrion, with loathing.

"And I have heard of you," he returned graciously. "Or, of your kind."

"Yes. The nomads know us, and believe in our magic."

"And I was lessoned by nomads."

"You knew at once."

"Not at once." Cyrion seemed to look beyond her, into a void. But she did not make the mistake of thinking him unwary. "I suspected. Only a demon, it is said, has the spells to inhabit the dead and cause the flesh to animate."

"His own people reckon Karuil to be alive."

"They should note, when he embraces them, that he has no heartbeat."

"This was your warning?"

"This and other things. The borrowed brain yielded the memory to your brother that once I was, spiritually, the son of Karuil-Ysem—but the memory did not stretch to the correct area of occasion. Information was patchy, a threadbare traitor. This gave you away. There were other things. For one, Karuil had no liking for sugar and little for wine. With age, he might develop such greeds. But to trust the man he feared most to supply them? The Father of his People would not have been such a dolt."

"You owed Karuil filial love and desire vengeance," said the woman, staring at Cyrion through her rosy golden hair.

Cyrion stared back at her, bland again, innocent.

"Did I? Do I?"

She said, "your vengeance and ours may be one. He has made slaves of us, this *Ysemid*." As she spoke the name, her painted claws raked at the floor.

"You mentioned a story. Tell it."

"Listen then. There is an ancient place far off in the desert, a ruined shrine. He came there, Ysemid. He was hunting, and seemed to have followed some beast to the well in the courtyard, but it was gone. Instead of going on himself, he drew water and drank. It was midday. My brother slept. I saw Ysemid, and I was roused by his handsomeness both to lust and to hunger. I put on myself the illusion of human rags, and went out to him, as a beggar, some pariah waif of the shrine. We spoke awhile, and then he offered me food if I would lie with him. I knew he had no food and sought to trick me, but I agreed gladly, for it served all my plan. We lay down together under the wall. . . ." The demoness bared her teeth in her rage. "I must inform you, he was not dressed in the clothing of the nomads, who are wary of us and wise. If he had been so, I should have shunned him. But he wore city garb—I thought him some merchant's son, easy prey. And when the sun should set and my brother wake—"

The sharp teeth were ground together. In her arms, the corpse which held her brother whispered its hate.

"Ysemid had an amulet," she said. "It was woven over by magic, for I had seen it, and thought it no more than a jewel. I remember, I meant to keep it as a plaything, when we were done with him. Then, when he stretched himself upon me, the thing touched my shoulder and—*burned.* At once he pulled away, and then he laughed as if vastly amused. He spoke at last in the nomadic tongue. He said: "You are as I believed you to be." And he touched the amulet and uttered the words, and I was bound. Presently he had discovered my brother and bound him, also. I suppose now Ysemid had come hunting us rather than any animal. He required our kind. You comprehend the power of such an amulet? We might not move against him, and must obey him in all ways. Quickly, we learned his purpose."

A day after, the People of Karuil encamped some miles from the ruin. A genuine hunt was mounted, and Ysemid persuaded his father to ride with him. When dusk fell, the party sheltered at the shrine, and Ysemid took his father aside into the inner court, saying they should talk together for once. There had been many arguments between them. Among the nomads, the authority of any father was absolute, and of a king—paramount. Ysemid yearned to adopt urbane ways, and to make profit in the cities, using the wealth of the desert people as ballast. This Karuil would not allow, nor was he ever likely to alter his mind. Ysemid's options were limited. Either to fly with nothing—to rob the People would be to incite a dedicated pursuit with, even for a prince, stoning at the end of it—or to submit and live in the manner of his forebears until Karuil eventually died. And Karuil showed no sign of impending death. He was mighty and in excellent health, and might continue hale for a decade or more. To kill him was Ysemid's only hope, but to kill was to risk a hideous death penalty. Even those who followed Ysemid, his courtiers, would not have countenanced patricide.

It would appear Karuil-Ysem had guessed some circumvention of justice was devised, or why else had he sent for Cyrion? He did, nevertheless, walk into the inner court of the shrine alone with his son, and there Ysemid stabbed him, twice, to be sure. And there the demon, bound like his sister, had been required to use his magic, squeezing his own form, by fantastic demonic means, inside the fresh corpse of Karuil, before it should stiffen. They had begged, the demoness said, that rather than use this vile method, they might employ their spells of illusion to perpetrate the fraud. But Ysemid would have none of it. Illusion held too long might weaken, and was besides susceptible to revelation in countless ways.

In the morning, it seemed the king had softened to his heir, and come to admit his view of things. Ysemid had performed his seduction of the People well, and rather than be suspiciously amazed, they were only glad at the change of heart, looking forward to the benefits of fat living, thinking their traditions could not be radically harmed or their strengths diffused. Like an omen to all this impending fortune, Ysemid had found a lovely beggar girl blooming like a golden rose in the shrine. He soon made her his wife.

Since that time, more than a month ago, the People of Karuil trod nearer and nearer to the cities. Ysemid lived more and more with city ways. There was chat of a palace close to Heshbel. Karuil, abruptly in this mild dotage of his, seemed resigned to the notion.

"And when all is as he wishes," said the demoness, licking her lips, "Ysemid will permit my brother to feign a peaceful death, and then escape the body before burial. Although we must set another spell on the flesh to prevent its instant disintegration. Me, he will divorce. But until that hour we must serve him. My brother samples sweets, by means of the human palate, which in his own form would choke him. But I, with whom Ysemid lay nightly—now consigned to another tent since he tires of me, as of a *mortal—I* yearn for the taste of his rent flesh and his smoking blood."

There was a silence. After which Cyrion asked, "The amulet is the sapphire in his ear?"

"*Yes*," she breathed.

"Could you not," he said, with apparent idleness, "have stolen it from him, on those nights when Ysemid slept by you?"

"It burns my kind and would char my fingers to the bone.

Yet, if it had been possible, do you think I would have left it to him? But the gem is clasped through his ear and secured by three golden wires. I would have to wrench it out, and he would feel the wound at once. And if I had the amulet, still it would convey his sorcery, and I should be powerless as ever. Do you know nothing of the lore of such things?"

"You," said Cyrion, "tell me."

But this time it was the male demon, trapped in Karuil's body, who answered. In the dry borrowed voice, he said: "Unless Ysemid's own hand removes the jewel, and with his own hand the jewel is given into our keeping, the safeguards will not break, and we remain his slaves, and must follow every commandment he sets on us. Which he enjoys, being vicious. He loves to play, cat with rat. It is this way with certain men, uncleanly brutishness."

"Unlike your own clean and wholesome peccadilloes? From what you say, I can hardly see any way to come at him."

"You might coerce him to abandon the jewel to us," the demon woman insisted.

"I doubt that. Ysemid is of the people, despite his ambitions. If he is a sadist, he will be sensible to such matters. He will therefore prefer any torture I could inflict on him to the games your race would play. On the other hand, if I reveal his acts, either of you will be compelled to support his lies."

"This people understands such magics as his, and ours, exist."

"They also understand I am a foreigner, and that foreigners always lie."

The demon Karuil sat up.

"Go back, my sister. Ysemid may go to your tent and miss you."

She made a sound of derision, but still rose, her finery clinking now. It was likely the camp's guards had heard her pass them, though not seen. Being what she was, she could become less visible than the night itself.

"I will go back. And you," she said to Cyrion, "angel-hair with your sick beautiful eyes. You had best run away."

Cyrion drew the curved sword from the pillow and threw it down by the two of them.

"Oh, and I may."

The dawn, inverse of sunset, flowed from the east, set fire to the water of the oasis, and turned to electrum the sootless hair of Cyrion, as he was flung face-downward on the sand.

One of Ysemid's courtiers planted his foot on Cyrion's spine and dug in his heel. Another relieved the fallen man of his weapon belt. Yet others stood about smiling, a grim smile that had nothing whatever to do with jocularity.

"Turn him on his back." The authoritative tones of Ysemid himself. And Cyrion was wrenched up by electrum hair and black-robed arms and duly turned. He landed with a splash of dust, and Ysemid said: "Now strip him of the nomad's garment, the lion-skin he seeks to hide in, this jackal. Search for evidence of his crime."

Cyrion lay loosely as a doll, and quite expressionless, as these instructions were ungently carried out. Soon, the nomadic robe was gone, and the silk tunic after it, leaving him in the fashionable fitted breeches and soft leather boots of the Westerner—at which Ysemid's men ritualistically jeered.

"Oh, come now," said Cyrion, "when your lord lives at Heshbel, you also—"

—And was silenced by a blow across the head.

Aside from the burnished, lethal little knife, the clothing search had revealed a stoppered vial. This Ysemid showed about; to his favorites, to those who, hearing the commotion, had gathered by Cyrion's tent.

"You see this thing? This has been part of the witchcraft." He leaned down to Cyrion. "Its function?"

Cyrion looked at him, and not liking this look, Ysemid struck him again.

"*Answer*, jackal."

"The vial contains a drug."

"Which you would use in your death wishing."

"Which I would use to numb pain."

"Ah, yes. This aching of the head and blindness you pretend to. *Devil.*" Ysemid struck Cyrion more determinedly, and Cyrion closed his eyes, apparently bored.

Ysemid sprang upright. He held up the vial again. In his other hand was something else. Slowly, he displayed both objects, and a hush settled, dense as sand upon sand.

"You see?" Ysemid asked the People. "A little image made of wood, with the symbol upon it, graven *here*, that is the Father my father's name. We know the use to which such toys are put. This dung of the Arch-Demon, this spew of the Fiend, has come to us, aping friendship, seeking to settle some score with Karuil, our King. And if I had not found this item of witchcraft in the stranger's tent, who knows but Karuil might have died, and left us—fatherless."

Then, and only then, the soft, smooth growling. Cyrion did not look for it. Probably he knew how they would seem, like the lions for which they were so often called, black lions with eyes of black flame.

It was an unwieldy plot, but would serve. Cyrion was the alien, and aliens notoriously fared ill. Besides, here came the ultimate proof.

The name was murmured: *Karuil, Karuil.* Then the hush of impending murder descended once more. And in the hush, Karuil-Ysem's voice clear as the bite of a dagger.

"I have trusted a serpent, and almost, I have died of its venom. My son has saved my life. Take this viper and slay it, in the way we keep for the practitioner of evil magic." And, after this, the law-giving of Karuil-Ysem, real as when he had been alive: "I command it."

On the sand, Cyrion softly laughed. This time the blow they awarded him brought a respite of darkness.

The night of unconsciousness, however, also found a hurtful dawn. Thereafter the light came back and showed small mercy.

It was the custom of the nomads to tether a condemned felon at the center of the campment for a day, and at dusk hygienically to take him a quarter of a mile from the tents to a death which, by then, he often wished for.

Cyrion, conscious or not, hung from his ropes and the post to which they bound him. All about, the tents, and the cool inks of the palm-shade, and cradled among them the glowing water, like spilled sky. But here, a patch of open sand, by noon white-hot, and a patch of sky above where the sun endlessly beat like a fiery dying heart. Now and then, of course, a shadow fell, refreshment, the prelude to unrefreshment. A stone was hurled—the blood soon dried in the heat—someone shouted, a pin scratched down his side, another was thrust under one of the nails of his ringed left hand—they would disdain to steal from him—a rain of kicks and slaps, dust tossed in his eyes, or rubbed between his lips. The nomads, who dwelled in a hard country, learned the trade of punishment well. That there was no worse Cyrion owed solely to the fact that he must be kept just sensible for death. So much he knew. Indeed, he guessed each act before it was performed against him. Some he foretold that had not yet come—

The thin rim of the cup, pushed out of the sick and pulsing haze against his lip, that alone surprised him.

"Drink," said a woman, close to his ear. "Quickly. Before they see what I do."

Cyrion wasted no time in inane queries. He drank the water, which she had known enough to warm before she gave it to him. Then he opened his eyes, straightened somewhat, and looked down at her through the long, long lashes mazed by thrown sand.

The demoness stood, exquisitely veiled, before him.

"Thank you," he said. "And now. Do you passionately release me?"

"If I did, he would kill me, too. He has you as he desires to have you. *Fool!*"

"Why then," Cyrion murmured, "waste the water?"

"Oh beautiful flower," she mocked him, "to see you grow and burst your bonds." Cyrion's mouth curved faintly, and she said. "You have powers. Your skin is fair, but does not blister—"

"No. I have enough of the nomadic arts to save myself that inconvenience."

"The power of Will." She muttered, "break *free*. *Kill* Ysemid."

"And be myself immediately killed by his loving court? That will happen at sunset, anyway."

"Dog of a coward."

"Gloriously lovely—" Cyrion paused—"astoundingly winsome—drinker of—"

"I will curse you," she interrupted. "We shall find your grave, and defile it."

"Alas."

"Die then," she said, and moved to go.

"One thing," he said, and she halted. "Will your brother, the King Karuil-Ysem, oversee my death?"

"He must. It is their law. You know this."

"Then," Cyrion sighed, slipping down again in his bonds, his head dropping forward, "follow him.."

At once she was sizzlingly alert. She gripped his arm, pressing her claws into the naked flawless skin and the firm muscle beneath.

"Why? What is it?"

"For God's delightful sake," Cyrion whispered, "scratch or strike me. Five men are watching you."

She snarled her fury. "I shall see you die in your blood then, even if I may not drink it. That will appease my famishment."

To her increased rage he did not flinch as her nails scored over his breast. Then, concealing the glass cup, she ran.

When the first coolness sank down from the red-hot sunset sky, the bound man glanced up once, then lowered his gilded head again. The blessing of the cool was also the chime of the bell which sounded for his death.

With the shadows, came his executioners.

They dragged him, still roped, from the post, and hauled him after them, out of the encampment. The women, who had watched him with melting eyes before, now watched with hard flints, resembling those they had cast at him earlier. Though allowed to torment him, they were not allowed to see him die. No great odds. It was likely they could imagine how it would be. A fate decreed by custom, and somewhat nasty.

Most of the men went from the camp. They moved like a sinuous black herd, following their shepherd. Karuil-Ysem rode his horse, Ysemid striding by him, a proud son, reveling that he had rescued his king and his father from the assassin.

The first stars were embarking on the red air, when they reached the chosen spot. It was the same as any other, merely the sand under the sunset.

The men formed a broad circle, to the center of which Cyrion was conducted. Mostly, he walked. Sometimes he fell, and was helped to his feet by the fists and footwear of his captors. The post had also been brought and was rammed into the new sand, and the bonds again secured to it. Karuil sat his horse, looking on.

A wind blew over the desert. The sun was almost gone, and soon it would be night. And then night forever. But not quite yet.

Ysemid called, and torches were lit and placed along the circle. They would need to see what they did next, and the light was excellent.

Ysemid moved close. He stood looking at Cyrion's bowed head, and the sculpted torso that, despite all psychic art, had begun at last to flush along its pale gold with sunburn.

"Well," Ysemid said. His voice was quiet, private, for Cyrion only. "I trust you hear me, dainty house cat."

"I," Cyrion said, "hear you."

"Good, my house cat. Good."

"Have you never been told the story," Cyrion said—his own voice was a crumble of itself, yet audible, interesting; Ysemid listened attentively—"the story of the lynx who found himself among lions."

"Am I to be told it, little lynx? Soon told, I would think."

"Soon told. It seems the lynx explained to the lions that he was both a rare and a succulent animal, and that only the best of them was fit to devour him. At which the lions fell to disputing which was the best of them, and then to trial and combat. Being confident and ferocious, none of them survived. The moral of the story is, that the lynx was not eaten."

"But the moral of your story is that we shall not fight over you, but simply kill you."

Ysemid pressed closer still. In his ear the sapphire was like a drop spilled from the dusk.

"Do you see, fabulous swordsman?" said Ysemid. "Look at me and see me. I recall, my father spoke of you, not often, but tellingly. Look and see how we match with each other, now." And, growing impatient, Ysemid caught at Cyrion's jaw, and pulled his face up to confront him. There was something wrong, Ysemid beheld it at once. The face did not express its despair in the anticipated way, and the eyes—what was the matter with the eyes?—"*Look* at me," Ysemid repeated.

"I regret," Cyrion said, "I cannot."

Ysemid stared. Then he swore, with disbelieving pleasure.

"It is the truth then. This sickness of the vision—you have it now."

"I have it now."

"And how long will the affliction last?"

"An hour, perhaps a little longer."

"You may die blind, then."

"I hardly think it matters. And if you ever research the disease, you will learn that with the headache one sometimes wishes to be dead. You will be doing me a service."

"There is another service," Ysemid said. If Cyrion had been able to see him, he would have perceived that the prince shone now with a radiant joy. The sadistic, rather predictable game that had burgeoned in his mind was irresistible to him. "I have been told of your prowess as a swordsman. Over and over, told of it. And the scout reported to me your words as you were brought into the camp. What were they? It may prove difficult to fight a man I cannot see."

Eventually Cyrion said tonelessly, "By the codes of your own people, whatever else you do to me, you would spare me that."

"*My* people, cat-lynx-jackal. *Mine*. Not yours. And my father, not your father. And my wish, not your wish." Ysemid straightened. "I shall tell them you boasted to me that, unbound and armed, you could slay me. I shall tell them I must accept such a challenge. My valor is in question, and I must bring you to humiliation before you are slain in the proper manner. They will agree, and then witness how I out-fight you, while you stumble up and down—like one blind."

"Any man standing in that ring is close enough to see, once it begins, I cannot fight for that very reason."

"Then I will send them farther off. I shall say you expect treachery. That you must be shown I can beat you unaided."

Quickly, Cyrion said, "And Karuil-Ysem also. Send him back with the others."

Ysemid frowned. He studied Cyrion's vacant face, its hateful glamour that even now was like a mask, the searching, hopeless eyes.

"Why? What have you fathomed? There is some trick you think you may play—" Ysemid nodded. "No. The old man shall come forward and watch. But only he. You will find, he will not try to help you. Or did you know that, and fear something else? You have only Ysemid to fear. Poor sick-eyes swordsman."

Ysemid turned and went to the human ring, shouting out at it. Cyrion must have heard some of the words, and the uncertain response, shortly swelling to assent. Then there were sounds, if not the sight, of the ring widening, drawing away. When the sounds stopped, one might judge the distance that had been added. If any in the surrounding ring had yearned to come to the rescue of a man in the circle's center, it was doubtful they would reach him in time. But who would want such a thing? Only Karuil had dismounted and moved nearer, leaning on the shoulder of a young boy. Karuil who was a demon.

A knife cut through ropes, and Cyrion, losing their support, staggered forward. With a congratulatory curse, Ysemid steadied him, then pushed him away again. Something was insinuated into Cyrion's right hand. Familiar—a cross-hilted western sword.

As Cyrion raised it, awkwardly for perhaps the first time in its years with him, Ysemid came at him. The advance was leisurely, dancing, almost cloddish with its parody. The noise the sand made under this would give a clue even to one blinded—Cyrion swerved. His arm flung up and retracted, his sword glancing by under the other, clumsily. Like a drunkard, he finished the move by lunging aside. He fumbled at the darkening torch-fretted air with his free hand, trying to balance himself.

And now Ysemid entered swiftly. The sand responded with only the barest hiss at the upsurge. Cyrion heeded it, and spun away, almost falling. Ysemid's playful sword was cheated of him, by an inch. As Cyrion continued to give ground, uncertainly twisting his head to catch any sound from the sand which was his only friend, Ysemid began to stamp and kick about in it, silently laughing at Cyrion's bewildered dismay.

Suddenly, Cryion came lurching after him. Ysemid sidestepped neatly, swirling his sword, then, enraged at such temerity, swung back to cut at Cyrion's left side. The blow should have hit home. Only Cyrion's present ungracefulness saved him, sending him into a sprawl before the blade reached him. Trying to rise, he almost put his hand on the curved steel, which would have sliced it to the bone. Some fluke saved him also from this, a shift of sand giving way, throwing him on his elbow, as the nomad's sword glided upward. The laugh was not quite silent now.

Finding himself with space to rise, seeming to mistrust it, Cyrion dove to his feet. Ysemid gazed at him, at the blond face now wide open and maddened, trying to read everything from the night which useless eyes would deny him. Ysemid's ecstasy was evident to any who could see. Then he lashed forward, deliberately missing the devastated figure before him, whirling the curved sword into a wheel of torchlight and metallic singing. Ludicrously, without cause, Cyrion ducked. Something in Ysemid overbrimmed. With a cry of pure orgasmic evil, Karuil's heir threw himself forward, knocking Cyrion once more to the sand. Even the cat will eventually sink its teeth in the spine of the mouse.

Kneeling over him, Ysemid had Cyrion by the hair, a left-handed grip, while the right hand, shortening its grasp on the blade, gathered itself for the initial wound of the death sentence: Castration.

Somewhere in the fume of sand between the two men, there lit two coals of icy fire, two stars—the torchglare on two brilliant eyes. And then a blade almost as bright came up with a wave of sand. A sword of fire, and it burned.

Ysemid found he had not completed the emasculating stroke. Stupidly perplexed, he peered down to seek the reason for failure. And saw his own hand, severed just above the wrist and lying, bleeding and lost, under the edge of Cyrion's sword.

Before the scream could find its way through Ysemid's face, a ringed fist hammered upward into his jaw. Ysemid's teeth met in his tongue like an agonizing vise. He slumped over into a roaring tawny darkness.

The next pain began far away, the awful pain in his earlobe—

Cyrion, having taken Ysemid's severed hand in his own, had clamped its fingers, tong-like, on the sapphire and ripped the amulet free. With a wicked twist, utilizing the gold wires that had formerly held the jewel in Ysemid's ear, Cyrion bound it to the disinherited fingers. The operation had needed seconds. Now, gaining his feet without effort, Cyrion flung the bloody hand and its gem into the sand before Karuil-Ysem. Who bowed towards it, predatory, and next quite motionless.

From all sides the men of the People were running forward. Their wailing and the grin of their blades filled the night.

Cyrion, his voice dry and eroded, shouted at Karuil.

"Plucked from him by his own hand, and given you by his own hand. Pick it up, damn you, and use it."

But it was the boy on whom Karuil had leaned who crouched and caught up the hand and its prize. As the boy straightened, gold snaked under his hood. Face unpainted, and in purloined or illusory male attire, the demoness raised the piece of carcass to her lips, then paused.

"You are not blind then," she remarked to Cyrion.

"No. I shall be dead, however, in a few more moments."

"And we must save you by revealing the truth here and now?"

Cyrion shrugged. His eyes were clear and still. "Honor among slaves. If you would be so kind."

"For your beauty, then," she said. And beside her, Karuil-Ysem opened his mouth in a strangely terrifying yawn.

The first of the nomads were a handful of paces away when they checked. Through the yelling and the howl for retribution a high thin chord seemed to vibrate, and then all sound died. They stood in the attitude of those who grasped the night ways of the earth, respected and abhored them. There was no fear, only the revulsion of total knowledge.

Karuil-Ysem, the Father of his People, had begun to split, as the robe had split from him under Cyrion's searching knife. Now skin and sinew parted, and the cloth of the garment fell intact from the bisecting cage of bones beneath. There was no bleeding. Within the dividing bag of the corpse there came a battling motion, a moan of anguish, and then the chrysalis of death was discarded absolutely. A naked and well-made man, physically even younger than Cyrion, bowed to the ground, holding his own body in his arms, his hair black as the sky now was, and showering about him.

Cyrion spoke briefly to the People of Karuil-Ysem, as the demoness embraced her brother, and clutched the bloody hand of the tyrant between them both, where both could see the spark of the vanquished jewel, and scent the warm gore. The story Cyrion told now was credited, and when he had finished, which was swiftly, the men were like statues about him, waiting, avoiding the demons with eyes and speech, prepared to listen only to the inevitable concluding words.

But Cyrion had waited also, for the stirring behind him in the sand, the tiny crying notes which informed them that Ysemid regained his senses.

"He bound demons," Cyrion said. "We know their

pleasure. Perhaps a more fitting death than the lawful sentence, for this patricide. Leave him to them."

There was no given answer. Except the gradual turning away, even of Ysemid's court, those who had loved him, in tens and in scores, and then as if the whole night turned its back to depart, bearing the torches with it. The king's body they abandoned. There had been no choice. It had become one with the dust.

Cyrion heard the muttering of the demons over the hand and the gem and the honey to come. He too had turned. From the sand he drew the robe of Karuil-Ysem, and brushed from it, with quiet, unhurried strokes, the odorless sterile powder that had been a man.

Presently Cyrion put on the robe, and drew it closed under the belt of red leather in which his sword was now sheathed. He did not seem to pay attention, as he did this, to the weeping groans and entreaties, the shrilling upsoaring pipe of terror, nor to the climaxing shrieks of the condemned.

Under the ruthless cold of the gathering stars, Cyrion walked away.

He was a mile off before the shrieking ceased to be audible. That the shrieks were done did not, in any case, mean death had yet arrived.

Later, the infant moon arose, and seemed to embroider, over and over in the sand, the symbols of Karuil-Ysem's last message. Cyrion's clear-visioned eyes and brain, which no ailment of any sort had ever affected, yet followed these moon-mirages, sought them, lingered on them. Karuil had written thus:

This comes to you by the hand of another people than mine, or yours, yet the man is my messenger. If you recall me, attend. I am threatened. There are troubles in me which are not the troubles of age. I have fallen prey to a hellish phantom which destroys my sight for an hour at a time, and ends in an enduring and grievous pain, covering half the head. My disciplines remain, and I evince no sign of this disease, but I think that one works on me, through a doll or some other witchcraft, to strike me with a bane unknown to me, and for which there is no cause, and no cure, unless you find one and bring it me. It is a fact, I suspect who is my enemy. He has given me to wonder by his sudden concern for my health, and, if it is true he practices on me, by his own randomness of skill, for it seems he looks for my ills, but does not know what form they should take.

I have a plan to be certain, and to bring him out.

You will, if you remember me, remember the sapphire amulet I had always about me beneath the breast of my robe, which could exert such sway over demons and similar spirits. You knew of this talisman, you and one other, a favorite wife who died, but who, I think now, passed on the knowledge. I mean purposely to lose this gem, and leave it where he may come on it, for only he is educated in how it may be used to set demons against me. Only he. I doubt if he will display it while I live, but should he find some way to kill or bind me, then he may flaunt it, a secret jest. So you will know.

I must inform you that if it is he who so hates me, then in my bitterness I will resign my life to him, and to God. Yet if it is to be so, and you ever in your soul, though not in blood, my son—AVENGE ME.

7TH INTERLOGUE

"A ghoulish account," said Roilant, at last.

"But an account of justice."

"You, of course, will avow it is true."

"I do not know if it is true."

"And what of Cyrion's relationship to the nomads?"

"The story does not explain this. Only that the guesswork of the wicked son was wrong."

"Quite."

Roilant rose moodily to his feet. The elderly beggar, father of Esur, remained seated, smiling down at the two gold coins which allegedly he could not see. The whiskery soldier had again ceased to snore, having re-started during the most suspenseful part of the chronicle. Some angle of his position gave the impression that his legs were much longer than they were. Probably this was something he unconsciously arranged even when intoxicated. Such were the ways of mankind, always trying to deceive others, or themselves.

Roilant caught himself, with exasperation, slipping into vacuous philosophy, a sure sign his opinion of life was at its very lowest.

Leaving a superfluous coin for the beggar, (Roilant's fortune would soon be lost to him in any case; why grudge a coin?), the plump young man went to the curtain. Finding the innkeeper supervising the polishing of the Qirri statue by a grumbling slave, Roilant settled his account.

"If Cyrion comes by tomorrow," said Roilant, "you may tell him to go hang."

"I doubt if I would tell him, or if he would oblige," said the innkeeper, pocketing the money with a bow.

Roilant walked up the three steps, once more tripping on them, though less dramatically than before, and out of the door.

The street lay drowsing in the midst of the afternoon. From various points in the biscuity walls, awnings cast their shadow, and not a fringe or tassel moved. Out of a narrow latticed window across the way, came a sad melody on an eastern lyre, and from a nearby garden, the scream of a peacock. A march of buildings rose in the distance to the flaxen fortress of Heruzala, where Malban's banners, plum and gold, hung lifeless as dead flowers against the cloudless sky. Not a breeze anywhere, and, all that was to be expected, the hot sunset wind blowing off the desert, hours from now. While in Cassireia, fragrant coolness might be wafting inland from the sea, spinning a web about the wooded hills. . . .

Roilant stood tranced a moment, irresistably picturing the scene he had approached only three times in his life, but which had taken on for him, in the past weeks, such ominous importance. The sweep of the orchard trees, the dark plumes of cypress rising between. Presently the ruined outer wall of a Remusan fort—all that remained, save the renovated bath-house farther on. Beyond the wall, the green slope, and the mansion. It was built in the eastern manner, and one met, as the leaves of the gate parted, the painted outer courtyard, stemmed by slender pillars, and the strip of water set to reflect them and the ten ancient palm trees, fronds spraying from gigantic bases so like the scaled shells of pineapples. And then, beyond again, in the third fashion of this land of mingled peoples past and present, the four-sided tower, the Westerner's stone defense, dominating the edge of the cliff. And behind this, the sea.

But the cliff was dangerous—Valia had learned that. And the tower crumbled. And tiles fell like rain from the walls of the house, and the water was stagnant—

"Did you enjoy the wine?"

Roilant started, his heart flexing. A tall slim figure had appeared from the alleyway ahead, and now leaned on a house front across the street.

"Wine—?"

"The wine in the black flask I bought for you. Do you tell me that the brat ran off with the fee after all? It seems the

King's soldiers no longer have any knack for frightening small children."

Roilant had recovered, and was registering the blond soldier of earlier acquaintence, Foy, who had pretended so superlatively to drunkenness.

"You sent the wine? Yes, I received it. My thanks," said Roilant cautiously.

Foy smiled.

"We nabbed the odorous rabble-rouser in the act, and I took him in, with a couple of others to help me, for he wriggled like an eel. I felt I owed you something. Whiskers was useless in the fray, naturally, and is now sleeping off his drink. Officially, he questions witnesses."

"And are you," said Roilant, "a soldier?"

"I? What else?"

"Then that," said Roilant, "is my last hope gone. I thought the wine came from Cyrion, possibly." Roilant nodded acceptance to the unkind spirit which, he felt, dogged him. "Your friend, by the way, is asleep in the Honey Garden."

"Is he now?" Foy was tickled. "Went back for more, did he, warlike fellow? When I left Whiskers he was prostrate under the sweet-seller's awning on Sweet Street. And he confided a dread secret before he swooned." Foy grinned. "The despicable barber had shorn half his moustache. Whiskers, poor mouse, has no choice but to let go the other half to match. Then he terrorizes the barber into sticking both halves back on with hoofglue. I saw the proof with my own marveling eyes, since Whiskers tore the thing off and waved it about to affright the sweet-seller and all his tribe."

Roilant demonstrated politic astonishment. He did not, he was afraid, care one way or another for the fate of Whisker's facial hair, whether lopped, glued back, ripped off or glued on again. Roilant thanked Foy once more for the wine, and walked away up the street.

Turning into the winding alley between two walls that marked the street's end, Roilant went briskly. Law in Heruzala, by day, was supportive in the better quarters, yet thieves were always liable. Roilant, who faced death in the near future, found his involuntary prudence ridiculous. Had he not, by now, started to go about unescorted and dressed as if for the court? For if someone inserted a knife between his ribs, what odds? Actually there would be a certain nasty satisfaction in dying so, and thus avoiding—

The footstep behind him was very definite, as if meant to be heard. It might be innocuous, or it might not. There was the choice of running, or of turning to confront whoever followed. The alley was a long one. Armed with a stylish dagger, in the use of which he had no talent. Roilant could still draw it, and threaten.

Resigned, he turned. And, despite all resignation, all ironies and futilities, gave a grunt of relief.

Moving quietly toward him through the narrow space the high walls had created was the dwarfish Whiskers himself. Minus his moustache.

Visually engrossed by this omission, Roilant could not take his eyes from the clean-shaven upper lip and the long and chiseled mouth that had hidden beneath the foliage. Only when the soldier had come within two yards of him did Roilant notice something else had changed. The extremely short Whiskers was now some inches taller than Roilant himself.

Roilant made a sound of inquiry, unluckily translatable as a cough.

The soldier, however, had halted, smiled seraphically at him, and then with a lean and articulate left hand, on the long fingers of which at least seven rings glittered, drew the light steel cap from his head.

The hair was unmistakable. More than merely blond, it was almost white, white satin threaded with gilt. Now the cap was removed, it reached his shoulders, and outshone a mail shirt of a quality far superior to the mail of the hapless Whiskers. Halo-ed by the supernal hair was a supernal face, daunting, recognized at once, for who else could look like this? One of the hellish angels of Lucefael the mason had suggested in his narrative. Conceivably the only apposite description.

The eyes, large, clear, beautiful, and reminiscent in their colour of Daskiriom steel, had fixed Roilant, and now did not deviate from him.

Roilant opened his mouth, and said flatly:

"This time, it *is* Cyrion."

"This time," said the musical voice, familiar as if remembered, "it is."

"And I hope you enjoyed your trick. Very clever."

"Thank you. I should perhaps tell you, there was more than one."

"Surprise me," said Roilant.

He was awarded by a gentle laugh.

"I was not," said Cyrion, "playing these games solely to distress you. When I hear a man has been asking frantically all over Heruzala for me, I become curious."

"And guarded?"

"Perhaps."

"And then I rush into the Honey Garden and offer gold. I admit, I would mistrust it all myself, if I were in your place. Can I deduce the mason is either your accomplice or your spy, and left after telling his parable in order to inform you?"

"You can, of course, deduce that. But it may alternatively have been the innkeeper. Or one of his slaves. Or the lady who left the inn immediately after you entered it—the lady who sometimes wears male attire. Or could it be the gentleman who sometimes dresses as a lady, and to such sumptuous effect?"

"I am past debating on that. I *do* understand that you returned dressed as this Whiskers, and clad in his—whiskers. I assume you robbed him of them."

"Not at all. I suggested their removal, and offered the going rate for shorn moustaches. Our friend accepted. The rest of the gear is mine."

"And I, looking for you everywhere, thought I saw only what I had seen previously."

"A common error. But you also missed me before."

"The scholar."

"Rather humbler than the scholar."

"The caravaneer."

"Dear me. This is, after all, becoming a game, I served you your dinner. My chief obscurity was a tunic over the mail and a headcloth. You did not take note, even when I thanked you for your kind words on my dealings at Teboras."

Roilant thought back, and grimaced.

"I conclude the inn slaves are in your pay."

"Not at all. The slaves missed me, too. They were busy squabbling over which of their multitude of pet dogs were to get some bones."

Roilant said, rather belligerently, "and each of the stories is factual? Even the Remusan ghosts?"

"Oh, I think you believe a substantial part of those tales, and any others you may have heard. Otherwise, why seek me so earnestly? By now, I also accept your own sincerity, you may be pleased to hear."

"I am prostrate with gladness," said Roilant grimly.

"Prostration can be irksome. Come to the inn where I am staying. You will be revived by a cool courtyard where they will serve iced wine."

"The Eagle?" Roilant hazarded, with little hope.

2ND PROLOGUE—*The Olive Tree*

The Olive Tree lay on the side of a hill, half a mile outside the old walls of the city. They reached the spot as the passengers of a cart en route to the olive groves which on every side surrounded the inn.

Roilant, aware Cyrion could easily have walked the distance, delighted he himself did not have to, kept his own council. He also, predictably, studied the new-found subject of his search with stunned and rather disapproving interest. Cyrion, half reclining on some sacks, his hands behind his gilded head, his swordlike eyes on the uncomparative blue of the sky, seemed relaxed as a cat. Roilant knew by now that, as with a cat, the pose could alter in the blink of an eye.

He had observed, too, a metal band clasped on Cyrion's tanned left forearm, which had not been mentioned in the stories. Or maybe it had. It was, for a third of its length, and half its depth, of a strange antique and greenish gold—the rest of the metal was silver. The more Roilant looked at it, the more it called to mind a woman's bracelet set into a larger armlet made to fit a man. The slighter piece being, therefore, the adornment from the slim wrist of Sabara?

The inn, whitewashed and deceptively modest, boasted a restful inner court, arbored with vines. The wine came, with crystals of mountain snow heaped in the bottom of the jug.

Roilant drank, gathering his wits. He had spent so much time in exclaiming over his urgent need to find this adventurer, it had now become difficult to speak coherently. Here the legend sat across from him, fabulously bright, as legends in the flesh rarely were. Nevertheless real and—presumably—human.

Cyrion himself, while not at all discouraging him, gave no help.

Eventually, a fawn cat stole from a shadow and began to roll, purring, at Cyrion's booted foot. Cyrion became engaged with it, apparently absorbed, and Roilant thought of the history of Berdice. It had touched rather near home.

"I had," Roilant said, "better admit why I have been trying to locate you."

Disarmingly amid the cat's paws: "I am all attention."

"Let me say first, I am prepared to pay—whatever you wish. In coins, in gems, in other goods—in charitable works. Whatever. Let me say also, that my family has connections with the royal house. Secrecy will be appreciated."

Cyrion, caressing the cat, regarded him.

"You are afraid of becoming a character yourself in yet another 'fiction'?"

"Perhaps. I really mean, I think, that while your aid to me might gain the approval of King Malban, I can expect none from his majesty."

"You should have approached the Queen-Mother."

"Who rules the youthful King as the King only appears to rule the city and kingdom of Heruzala. That is, if the infamous fanatic Knights of the Angel do not rule in stead of everyone. Yes. I know the version. I shall ignore your inference. In any case, this goes beyond statecraft. You see, in a nutshell, I have the misfortune to be contracted in a diabolical marriage—" Roilant stopped. Cyrion waited. "I will begin in good order. At the beginning."

The beginning was with Eliset. Beautiful Cousin Eliset. The beginning and, quite likely, the end.

Once upon a time, (as the priest had said), there were three brothers, of an illustrious family, the house of Beucelair. Roilant's father, and Roilant's two uncles. And the two uncles had short-sightedly become involved in a certain court intrigue here in Heruzala, in which the last king, Malban's father, had apprehended them. Matters had been smoothed. Offenders spared, oaths re-sworn. (A handful of years after, in any event, the old king had died in battle, the ultimate conflict between Heruzala and Kyros, before Malban and peace took control, under the auspices of the Queen.) However, pardoned and re-sworn, the two brothers still fell from favor—nor was the favor ever restored to them, even on the old king's death. Their wealth dwindled and their status declined.

Only the third brother, Roilant's father—he who had kept aloof from the plot—retained imperial partiality, and prospered.

When Eliset was born, Roilant was one year old. Eliset was the legitimate daughter of uncle Gerris, Master of Flor. One must stress that legitimacy, since there had been another daughter, two years before, the child of Gerris' amour with a servant woman. This woman he had subsequently installed in a small house in nearby Cassireia—which house, as the debts piled upon him, sank to the level of a hovel. The daughter had been named, aristocratically, Valia, legalized and taken into the mansion at Flor. There she had grown in close proximity to Eliset, who might perhaps have been rather jealous of this invading cuckoo that her father seemed to prefer. The two girls were also as unlike as was possible in their physical appearance. Valia's eastern blood was appreciable in her olive complexion, dark tresses and early plumpening of shape to the contours of womanhood. Eliset was daffodil-haired, snow-skinned, boyishly slender. Both however, were reputedly fair.

Then, comparison ceased to matter.

When Valia was eleven, Eliset nine, Valia vanished.

It was generally reckoned she had fallen from the cliff behind the house, though there were also those tales that often accompanied the disappearance of a child or young maiden—phantoms, demons or wandering magicians had carried her off as victim or slave. Nevertheless, servants had seen her playing on the cliff, and chided her not long before. The area was unsafe, she had always been told so, and the sea below the cliff very deep. Eliset, too, had always been warned from the place, and was nowhere near it just then, but sporting under the hornbeam tree with her nurse.

Valia was mourned, at least by her mother, who died soon after of grief, and by Gerris. Who himself did not live to see Eliset's fourteenth birthday. By then, the estate of Flor was all that remained to him, his business ventures having come to nothing, his wealth virtually gone, and royal consideration a mirage of the past.

The estate near Cassireia had then progressed, in all its encroaching ruin, to Gerris' brother, Roilant's second uncle, Mevary. However little it was, it was more than Mevary himself had retained. He became the guardian to Eliset, and her cousin, Mevary's son of the same name, became her brother. They were of an age, and dwelled harmoniously together. Intellectual pursuits they shunned, and rode wildly through the hills—while horses were left to Flor. It was a pity these two, so prettily complementary, he brown for her blondness, strong for her fragility, might not have wed. But there would be no sense in that. His lack of pecuniary advantage made him no catch. Her own poverty would negate the chance of her marrying among her peers, therefore at all. Unless—there was one other avenue.

Even Gerris, before he died, had put the proposition to Roilant's father. The only Beucelair left in funds should be generous to his reduced relatives, and surely felt some avuncular duty toward the innocent virgin daughter, if not to Gerris and Mevary the erring brothers.

Roilant had stayed at Flor twice, as a child. The time spent had been brief, and Valia already dead. Eliset, a year his junior, had struck him as a dull little girl, with whom, for some reason he could never fathom, he had always been uneasy.

The mansion and the wildering grounds he had, on the other hand, enjoyed. They had a certain magic for a pudgy little boy who failed in all the manly arts of combat, and preferred to sit reading about other people. Even as a child, Roilant had been aware that he had disappointed everyone, including himself. He would never be a warrior or statesman, he did not even have a particularly cunning head for business. While, unlike the two other cousins, he was stodgy and plain, and had laughable ginger hair—or, at least, it was always laughed at.

When Gerris was dead, the elder Mevary had raised the marriage proposition with Roilant's father once again. Roilant's father had packed off his tiresome son with a: "Go look the wench over. If you like her you may have her. We do not need a dowry."

So Roilant made his tertiary visit to Flor, and on this one, smelled the stagnancy of the cisterns, saw death preying on the palms, and how the orchards ran amok. No longer wishing to imagine himself a Remusan tribune, he stood on the ruined wall and admitted the fortress tower above the cliff was going the same way.

At dinner that night, he met uncle Mevary and Mevary's son, Mevary, and hated the pair of them at once. Mevary I was unwholesomely bitter, and sly. Mevary II was handsome, heroic and insufferable. At fifteen, he took care to make the fifteen-year-old Roilant feel eight years of age, and incompetent to boot. Then, came Eliset. Eliset was like a sunrise. She broke through the miasma and transformed everything. While Mevary I lamented on the lack of good things at Flor, adding the while, "no doubt you miss the luxuries of home," and Mevary suggested a board game, knight-and-castle, and beat Roilant five times, Eliset was kind, and winsome. She even, in the two days which followed, drew Roilant away from the others, finding pretext upon pretext to be alone with him, even her maid sent off on some errand. It might have been unseemly and Roilant, conscious of the proprieties, was sometimes nervous. Yet Eliset remained a model of decorum. She implied she trusted his gallantry. She made him feel gallant, a sensation so novel he did not quite know what it was. She made him feel clever, too, and once, when he killed a wasp that was maliciously pursuing them, valiant. He had thought her dull? She dazzled him. She laughed like bells at his occasional vague flashes of humor. She admitted she was unhappy, grieving still for her father. She was brave. She was like a figurine of jewels. She was perfect. And when he left, while saying nothing to him of the suggested marriage, still, she wept.

Roilant returned home and announced that, yes, he would be thrilled to have her. And spent the next three months writing private terrible poems to her sunshine hair and twilight eyes.

They were betrothed by letter. It seemed she was so delicately reared it would be best to wait a year or so. Roilant, dashed and also rather relieved—to wed one's love was a scaring prospect—accepted the plan. A year passed. Another. A few pressed flowers reached him, with two or three words, signed "Eliset." And once, a cheap pair of gloves, that did not fit. He knew how she was placed, and treasured them. Sent westward to complete his sketchy education, Roilant delved amid the culture of that cold clime, and was for a long while away from the eastern kingdoms his forefathers had won over the sea. When he went back to his father's estate at Heruzala, he felt worldly, and had begun to consider his marriage with impatience. The few women who had enabled him to feel this way had only reinforced the memory of Eliset's charms.

There was some news. The elder Mevary had died. The younger Mevary was busily spending what little (very little) Flor had left.

About to embark on a rescue mission, Roilant's scheme was interrupted. His own father, then with the young King's court, had ridden out with them on an otherwise quite unexceptional hunting party. During the course of which his horse threw him, and left him at the gate of death. As he was a notable horseman, the accident was perplexing.

Hurrying to the city, where his father lay dying, Roilant journeyed in a cloud of superimposed, respectful gloom. There was no love between father and son, and no rapport. Yet it would be the done thing to pretend to both at such an hour, and both of them duly pretended to it.

In a darkened chamber of the palace they spoke awhile. Then came a startling revelation.

"Listen, boy," said Roilant's father, shifting with pain in the soft bed and restraining a curse, "you are my heir and I have some frank advice for you."

"Yes, father?"

"You recollect the betrothal to your cousin Eliset?"

"Why, yes, sir. I was about to—"

"Do not."

Roilant, astonished, stared.

"Do not?" he stammered.

"Have I bred a parrot? I tell you, do not. Nothing was ever properly formalized. With a bribe here and there, you will be free of it."

"But she is a Beucelair, and destitute. And you promised her father and her uncle—"

"And I sent to the girl herself last month, telling her I would direct you against the match."

"Why?"

"Why?" Roilant's father glowered. "You are worth more than that. I have been hearing things, and found out others for myself. You are a young man of sturdy character. At heart we have always understood each other. Trust me. Get yourself a nice homely girl, who will appreciate you. One who has a decent dowry."

Roilant began to protest, but his father interrupted again.

"Damn this pain," he said, and died.

Roilant shed two or three tears, mostly because it was seemly, partly because to lose someone you have never known is often more frustrating than to lose a friend.

Duty was another matter. Out of duty to his father, Roilant, then, made no further move that summer toward his cousin Eliset. When an inexpensive talisman set with inferior jet arrived from Flor to "comfort his loss," he replied politely, and prevaricatingly.

It was not until the winter when he was nineteen that he learned for himself an array of rumors both about the young lady who was to have been his bride, and the life now lived at Flor.

The man who gave him access to these rumors was a person of rank and high esteem at the King's court, and they were contained in a letter, brought by a messenger in this person's employ. The letter itself was unsigned. It would seem Eliset was neither charming nor chaste, since she was the doxy of her brown-haired cousin, and of others besides. But this was nothing to her other practices. Roilant's informant was unclear on these, and self-excusive, now and then dismissing items as the "superstitions of the ignorant"—without even naming them. Fumbling between the lines, Roilant came to understand Flor was haunted, and Eliset herself belonged to a clandestine sisterhood of witches of whom her old nurse had also been an enthusiastic member. It was said (O oft' repeated and irritating phrase) that the death of Valia had been induced by witchcraft when Eliset was only nine. And that the deaths of Valia's mother and Eliset's own father and uncle had next been engineered at suitable junctures. Even the death of Roilant's father came in question. He, a peerless rider, had been thrown—immediately after he had denied the girl the wealth of Roilant's branch of Beucelair. The letter logically ended with the remark that any rich man who wed Eliset might expect to die himself, rather swiftly and without issue, leaving his fortune to his wife.

At this time, Roilant had not really believed in sorcery. And yet, a nagging, inexplicable doubt grew in him, a doubt he then accepted had been planted at his father's death. He did not ponder the matter unduly, but he resolved upon three things. Firstly, that he would not yet tell Eliset he no longer meant to honor the betrothal, secondly, that he would *not* honor it, and thirdly that he would make her, thereafter, a legal allowance to assuage his guilt.

So much was done, or not done, as the case was. Eliset for her part wrote thanking him for the allowance with total gracefulness. Only one tiny sentence jarred, that in which she looked forward to their future meeting.

But years, again, passed. Roilant settled to the knowledge that he preferred women who were not overly beautiful, and certainly not overly demanding, while finding a genuine happiness in female company. Eventually, he became aware of an ideal match, well-born, of ordinary appearance and meager dowry, but with a gleaming sound common sense, a calm vivacity, and a lovely disposition to mirth that uplifted Roilant, for it was never directed at himself. Not moved to write her a single poem, Roilant yet discovered himself saying to this lady one day, in her father's prettily dilapidated garden—when they had been speaking of some hypothetical traveler lost in the desert—"if I were lost there I should somehow have to get back. I should miss *you*—" By which, and the lady's quite unlooked-for but gratifying blush, he knew the time had come for certain arrangements. He therefore made the acquaintance of a lawyer or two, and was in the process of undoing the tenuous betrothal of nine and a half years before when—

There was a lengthy pause.

The fawn cat sat bolt upright on Cyrion's shoulder and stared at Roilant. Cyrion did not stare, but neither did he look elsewhere.

"—When," Roilant finally said, "a number of things took place that I should be hesitant to relate, if it were not that you, I gather, are familiar with the occult."

Firstly the letter which the lawyers had drawn up and sent to the estate at Flor was returned, during the night, by a messenger no one could describe, to Roilant's house on the Beucelair estate near Heruzala. Opening the letter, Roilant found the legal parchment, somewhat altered. It had been torn in many small pieces, and as these fluttered to the floor, they spontaneously caught fire. In a moment, cinders were all that remained.

"I thought I must have imagined it," said Roilant. "As one would."

"Would one?"

Roilant said, "Then, I would. And did."

The next thing to occur was that the shoddy talisman of the jets somehow unearthed itself from one of Roilant's chests, and came whirling in at him through an unshuttered window, badly contusing his forehead. When he picked the thing up from the floor, it burned his hand. Thoroughly alarmed, he had hurried from the room, only to return an hour later with the theory someone had stolen it and thrown it at him, having first heated it in a fire. He found the talisman in fragments, had them swept up, and tried to put the business from his mind. Which was quite easy as, that very night, something much worse had happened. Roused about midnight, he had initially thought himself awakened by a violent rain storm clamoring outside. But then he had become aware of a vile sensation, as if a host of insects were lightly crawling over his face, brushing him with their wings. Flinging up and clawing at his skin, he had escaped them—only to perceive, by the flame of a hastily kindled candle, that they were nothing more—or less—than the pressed flowers that Eliset had sent him after their adolescent meeting, brown and mothlike with age. Even as Roilant stood gasping and gazing at them, they flew in the air and scattered into dust. As the dust floated down, a figure came visible through it.

It was hard to see. The flicker of the candle, the riot of the storm outside, his own shock, made the amorphous visitation all the more difficult of observation. Yet it had been there, transparently printed on the air, like mist on a mirror. Slender and pale, the face a blur, but held within an aureole of daffodil hair. Then it spoke to him. Not audibly, but in words written slowly and brilliantly across the dark beyond the candleflame. They said:

The bond is made and may not be broken. You are mine and must come to me before the month is over.

"In the morning," said Roilant, "I thought it a nightmare."

"Of course," said Cyrion, kindly.

And for the first time in his life, Roilant felt a fool for not believing in the supernatural.

Sheepishly he said, "This same thing then happened every night, for seven nights. Then I *did* believe it. I was—I was terrified, I admit. And the freakish weather, the endless rain, depressed me in a way I have never known before. I called in a man noted in the nearby village for his grasp of magical lore. He examined my bedchamber, and said he smelled sorcery everywhere in it. I could smell only the rain. But I asked what I should do, and he offered to study the matter. He went off and I did not see him again, even when I went to the village. It seemed to me he was as frightened as I was. What came next? After seven days, the apparitions had ceased, and nothing else replaced them. Though I was constantly alert by then, for something. However, if I journeyed to Flor, this same sorcery that had called me, would presumably be used to kill me. It seemed safer to stay put. Then, there was news from the city."

The lady in Heruzala who had taken Roilant's fancy had been sitting quietly on her father's terrace, when part of the roof above her had come away and fallen with a crash. She was unhurt, but only the breadth of a finger had differentiated between herself and death. It was very odd. The masonry had always been considered sound. Her father, who had sent this information ostensibly to reassure Roilant, should he hear the event otherwise mentioned, in truth to stir the suitor's ardor, was rather mortified to receive Roilant's reply. Roilant expressed great joy in the young woman's safety, and chagrin that he would not be calling on them for some while; on the next occasion he hoped to bring his new wife.

"For me, there was never much choice. Eliset might sorcerously murder me, if I wed her, or if I did not. But when my dear—when the lady I alluded to was also threatened, I dared not delay any further. I sent a letter to Eliset that very evening, and bribed the messenger to ride in record time to Flor."

"And the message said?"

"Why, that I would be at her side on the last day of the month."

"Which leaves you scarcely any margin at all to get there."

"I have spent all this while looking for you."

"And here I am," said Cyrion.

Roilant frowned. "I am not a martyr. I do not want to die. Or to be cheated. But I would not risk—a lady's life. And since I promised to go to my cousin, everything has been placid."

"Am I to take it," Cyrion said, rubbing cheeks with the fawn cat, "that you also alluded to your lady in the betrothal-breaking letter sent your cousin?"

"Yes. An imbecilic act. I thought she would tolerate rejection better on such grounds. I added, of course, that not seeing Eliset for more than nine years had dimmed my recollection of her beauty."

"Most tactful," said Cyrion. Roilant looked at him narrowly, guessing this might mean the reverse, as he himself had latterly suspected. "At least," Cyrion elaborated, "Eliset did not learn of your new interest by sorcery. If she had done that, she could also have learned in the same way that you sought for me."

"God defend us."

"Quite so. I think, however, these powers are of another sort. The mind is used to protect the energy of the will. The spell works only through what is already, mundanely, known."

The plump gentleman spread his arms in relief, and knocked over his wine cup. He looked at the result in distaste. The fawn cat, however, sprang approvingly to the table, and began to imbibe. "You see how I am," said Roilant candidly. "No well-coordinated man of action, no sharp and racing wit. But, till they thieve it, I *am* rich. Will you assist me?"

"In what way," said Cyrion, "do you suppose that I can?"

Remembering such queries from the tales, Roilant refused to be thrown.

"*You* are the legend. Therefore, you decide," said Roilant firmly.

The cat finished the wine. Unsteadily it puttered back to Cyrion across the table, and fell into his arms.

"Three libations should be lucky," said Cyrion. "But I still predict you will have to start for Flor tomorrow. And travel quickly."

CYRION IN STONE

ONE

Where the road turned toward Cassireia, it casually threw off a subsidiary track which, curling uphill, overtook rocks and woods, and passed incidentally across two rambling villages. In the second village, overwhelmed by adventure, the track stopped.

A mile farther on a break between a pair of hills showed the orchards of Flor, and, rising from them, the grassy ascension which ended in the house and the tower, against the demarcation of the sea.

The villages had strayed closer in by-gone eras. When the Remusan fort had dominated the countryside, there had been a village at its foot. But now, the small settlements seemed sensibly to have crept away, taking their goats and their red oxen downhill, and riding to market in the city, where once the palace of a Cassian emperor had been built above the ripe blue waters of the bay.

To one not an emperor, the journey to Cassireia might well be irksome. To turn off at the track, to go by the villages and be stared at, to reach the cleft hills and look down, then up, to Flor—perhaps more irksome yet, and a cause also, maybe of apprehension, should that traveler be Roilant of Beucelair, riding hither to claim his bride. Theoretically, with the bride came Flor itself, her only dower. The beautiful wreckage of the place might repay renovation with interest. If such a thought had even been in the mind of the arrival it could well have departed on sight of the cluster of dead fig trees that introduced the orchards. A blight, a blasting irreparable. Next came a depressing cypress tree, long since slain by lightning. And then a torrent of healthy trees, burgeoning too soon and out of rhythm with each other, boughs bent to the ground, boughs flung around each other for support, the rogue fruit inviting swarms of insects so the whole area throbbed and thrummed madly in the thick green light. To fight a way through this jungle sound-box was neither easy nor entertaining on mule-back. To emerge at last among the ultimate trees and gain the slope, brought one to the Remusan wall, insultingly almost as intact as it had been nine years before. While the mansion, drawing closer over the brown grass, was little less than alarming.

The gates, missing many of their studded metals, were open and looked as though they might nevermore be shut. Within, the entrance court with its cistern, pillars and palm trees—a faded rose, whose petals rapidly fell. Smashed tiling, descended from above, lay in the barren trough that once had been a cloudy mirror of water. Lions of stone, blue with lichen, stood desolately at its corners. The lions, the walls, the pillars, the trees were universally scabrous.

Under a dead palm couched a ragged servant boy—asleep, and vagrant wasps and flies from the orchard buzzed fastidiously to and fro. No other live thing was apparent,

The arrival sat his horse in the gate, looking about him, the westering sun fiery on his fiery hair. His awkwardness in the saddle had been momentarily minimized by a stance of bewildered affront. To know was one thing, to *see*, another.

Behind him, the two Heruzin servants and the baggage hovered on their mules. Finally, one of the men inquired:

"This is Flor, my lord?"

"I grieve that it is."

The other snorted, just audibly.

"Should I wake the urchin?"

"It seems to be necessary."

The first man, bulkier than Roilant, yet with an undercurrent of pure muscle, swung from his mule and walked over to the sleeping boy. Taking him by one shoulder, the man shook. The boy came to his wits and began instantly to pummel his attacker, presently sinking his teeth in the man's sleeve and refusing to let go. The second Heruzin dismounted and ran to help. Something of a skirmish ensued as two further unkempt adolescents sprang from the raddled trees and landed with whooping cries amid the fray.

The plump young man continued to sit his mule, seeming dumbfounded and might have done so indefinitely as the fight indefinitely went on. However, one of the leaves of the central door beyond the pillars presently gave signs of having moved, very grudgingly, ajar, and next a figure appeared, stepping from shade to light.

Two white hands flashed as they were brought smartly together.

"Stop this! Harmul—Dassin—At once, Zimir."

Two of the boys hurtled aside and fell to their faces on the broken stone beyond the cistern. The third boy seemed undecided, before bolting away and into a narrow archway at the end of the court. The Heruzin servants were left in wild attitudes, scowling.

It was apparent the mistress of the house was here in the person of the girl with white hands. And it seemed she possessed authority, for one unruly youth had fled, the other two lay motionless, as if in abject fear, before her. When she spoke again, her young voice was like a thin knife.

"For shame. You should be beaten. If my father lived, you would be lashed. Get up. Go to the gentleman and his attendants. Beg their pardon."

The youth who had begun the brawl raised his head, and plucked at her gown. It was of a high-sheeny topaz silk, the exact color of her hair.

"One struck me," the boy avowed.

The girl with the topaz hair said nothing, she merely regarded him. Slowly, the boy rose, his companion with him. They slunk around the empty cistern and now cast themselves down before the redheaded man on the mule.

"Pardon, lord!"

"Pardon us!"

The redhead was clearly flustered.

"Granted," he muttered. "Now get up and go away."

"They cannot, alas," the girl called to him. "Zimir has run off, but these must see to your mules. They are the only grooms we have."

The plump young man maneuvered himself, stiff and ungainly, from his mount, and surrendered it with blatant misgiving. "But leave the baggage here—my own servants will see to it."

As the muscular Heruzin servant followed the boys and three mules in the direction of the narrow archway, the other Heruzin proceeded to unload the baggage from the fourth beast. Their master turned then, and let his eyes rest on the lady, a slim daffodil against the back-drop of sun-burned decay. He seemed unable to speak, and it was she who came forward, her movements fluid and connected as a dancer's.

"Roilant," she said softly. "Is it really you?"

"Oh, yes," he assured her foolishly.

She smiled up into his round face.

"How fine you have grown. I saw you last a boy, and now you are a man. And I, have I changed so very much?"

He was flushed and flustered again, and his wavering eyes seemed to note for the first time the worn places in her gown that had dazzled from a distance. Her allowance from Heruzala then, had been spent on other needs.

"You are," he said with an effort, "as pretty as ever."

Her eyes widened, possibly at his ineptitude, but she smiled still. "Then, if I am," she said, "it is from my joy at seeing you. I thought you had forgotten me. I am so glad that you did not."

His own eyes were tired and puffy and perplexed. It was not, perhaps, good policy to say: But you know you sent for me, a summons I could not refuse. Coercion by black magic. He only said, "It has been hell, the journey."

"Forgive me. I will send someone to prepare the bath-house—in the Remusan style—do you recall? And do you remember, too, the story? That a Remusan legion buried a treasure of gold there. . . . You and I searched for it. We did not find the gold, did we?" She put out one of her white hands, as if to rest it on his arm, then drew her fingers back timidly. She had no jewels, except her eyes, her hair, the pearl teeth, the white jade skin. "Your hostess fears she chatters. But she is so glad—oh, Roilant, it is so wonderful that you have come back. Please. Enter the house. And—" she lowered her lashes in long strips of bullion—"Overlook what cannot be helped. It is not as it was in Lord Gerris' day. Or even as in my uncle's."

He blurted bluntly, "If you wed me, it need not trouble you much longer."

"No," she said, very low. She was the picture of delicious humiliation, asking mutely to be spared the embarrassment of receiving his pity and aid too openly. Even Roilant, possibly, would have, at such an instant, the urge to slap her. But one did not risk one's neck with a sorceress, if one was astute. The hands stayed firmly clasped behind the pudgy back. He walked behind her, into the house, the servant with the baggage struggling after.

The entry—a sort of tunnel, once painted and ornate, now sprung with weeds and blown with dust and various debris—led straight into the second, inner, court, about which the body of the mansion clustered.

When Roilant had come here at fifteen, the fountains had still played, if unreliably. Now the basins were drying swamps of spilling moss. Dead leaves crackled about the court, and one insane spindly orange tree grew beside the stone stair that led to the upper floor, and thence to the roof. Posts of delicately carven ivory had supported the roofing of the veranda that ran along the second floor. Now, like carious teeth, several were cracked, or missing.

"Do not look at it," she said. "I have tried not to. I have tried to remember it as it was."

A fat and elderly man, imaginably a slave, came waddling from the opening that led through to the kitchens and servants' quarters. You might wonder what there was for him to have stayed fat on.

"Jobel," Eliset called, "prepare the bath for lord Roilant. Then fetch wine, if you will."

The fat slave emitted an uneasy grunt, and went off reluctantly in the direction prescribed, many times glancing over his shoulder as if hoping to be commanded back.

"I suppose it will take some while?" said the proposed bather.

"I fear it will. These you have seen are the only servants we have, the boys, the slave. And I have one maid—a luxury Mevary procured for me; I seldom use her. I gather her life has been hard."

"Mevary *procured* her—" the unfinished sentence—it ended: procured with *what?*—was out before he seemed able to stop it. He looked mortified, or perhaps nervous.

Eliset had parted her lips to reply, when a firm male voice smote down on them like another falling tile.

"How exact you are still, Cousin Pudding. Not procured with cash, then. I won her in a dice game from a muleteer, who kept her as his skivvy, and whipped her like the mules when he wished to ride."

The ginger head had gone up at once and the pouched eyes fixed. Leaning rather unwisely on some of the remaining veranda rail above, a young man looked down on him, in every sense of the word.

Mevary of Beucelair and Flor was of sinuous, athletic build, gleaming with healthful tan and walnut-colored hair, and two eyes of the yellowest and most wolflike hazel. His garments gleamed healthfully, too. Now you saw where some of the allowance had gone.

Eliset laughed.

"Mevary, come down and be courteous. Your sight is affected by distance. Our cousin is no longer a little boy, but a tall, strong man."

"He looks the same as ever, to me," said Mevary.

He walked noncommittally to a place where the rail had ceased to exist and leapt suddenly over, like a great brown rock-cat, landing on springs, flawless and unwinded before them. Eliset clasped her hands, and laughed brilliantly now.

"Oh, is he not clever?" she asked the third party, who plainly had never practiced such acrobatics in his life, and would have broken his neck if he had.

"Very."

"And you," said Mevary insultingly, "are *you* clever, Cousin Pudding?"

"I think," said the other, slowly, "I am not a complete fool."

"Merely a complete pudding. Such a lot of nice juicy meat, if ever he falls into the paws of wild beasts."

"Mevary!" she said sharply. But he met her eyes and smiled. They were lovers, he had no need to fear her supernatural wrath, as the three boys had seemed to do, not while he could please her. And patently he did please her. The lines of their bodies, apparently unconsciously, flowed toward each other like plants beneath water.

Then the yellowish eyes looked farther, and he said, "I take it that oaf is your servant."

Again the ginger head snapped about. Roilant's servant

was indeed standing over by one of the dead fountains, the baggage at his feet.

"Two men came with me."

"Then they may go away again. They cannot be housed here, they must put up in the village, and you can pay to feed them there. Do you reckon we can afford to cosset you *and* your wretched fan-bearers?"

"Very well." He had held his breath until his plump face reddened into the hair, staring at Mevary. "And am I allowed an apartment, or do I sleep in the cistern?"

"The cistern is already gifted to a large number of lizards. You will get the chamber that was my father's. I hope you enjoy it," Mevary said sweetly. "He is supposed to be haunting us."

The Remusan-style bath, though long delayed, was tepid, both hot pool and cold. There was only one truly awkward incident in the bath house. Abruptly anxious for his cousin's happiness and comfort, Mevary swung in, light-footedly. But it seemed the ginger imbecile had acute hearing at least; he was already swathed all over in a voluminous robe, which he clutched to him in a determined (successful) endeavor to conceal. Mevary's obvious attempt to catch him flabbily and disadvantageously in the nude had failed. It would seem it was one thing to be murdered, another to be humiliated.

"Jobel should have come and scraped you down. Or I suppose there was not enough steam anyway," said Mevary. "What a shameful house this is. We are dining at sunset, on the roof terrace. I noticed you drank none of your wine. Are you afraid we shall poison you?"

The muffled bather glared at him.

"Yes."

"Oh, well then, you shall have a taster. Dassin shall do it. If you are careless, he will eat your entire meal. But really, my Pudding, dear, there might have been poison in the water of the bath. Or in that robe. Or sprinkled over the dolphins on the floor, only waiting for your little shapeless pink feet to patter upon."

The feet in question, actually neither little nor shapeless nor pink, stayed on the dolphins of tattered green mosaic.

"My betrothed," said the owner of the feet. "Why has she

not used her allowance to repair the house, or to clothe herself decently?"

"Do you think the pathetic yearly purse you sent her would stretch to that?"

"It has stretched to kitting-out you."

"Well. But she is fond of me." Mevary prowled, a weird wolf-cat, about the pool, about the tense bundle of robe that currently represented his cousin. "It is a sad thing that you still desire to wed with Eliset. Or I might have—" Mevary paused significantly—"had her. You know, of course, you will have to live here with her when you are joined? Here with Eliset, and with me, darling Cousin Roilant."

Darling Cousin Roilant said he did not know anything of the sort.

"You will kill her if you take her away. Break her heart. Gerris is buried here, not to mention my own lamented sire. Kindred quick, kindred in the ground—how could she bring herself to part from us all?"

Before any new answer or denial could be launched, Mevary strode from the bath house.

Halfway back along the stone corridor, however, he paused a moment, as if in thought. The corridor, a partly covered way which once had been itself a narrow courtyard, led directly to the inner court of the waterless fountains. At the corridor-court's center, against one wall, stood an ancient well older than the house, a monstrous magnificence of twisted stone pillars and a mosaic back-frame, dimly visible while daylight negotiated openings in the roofing above. Mevary seemed to be pondering the flowers and fish of the mosaic. The well-shaft itself was long dry, a dead thing, like so much at Flor.

What exactly caused Mevary to grin was not obvious.

With the end of the day, a murmurous fire flowed inland from the sea, where the sun floated just above the horizon. Crimson clouds massed like a fleet on the edge of the water. The ocean itself was dyed from curving rim to swerving shore line with the tint of cherries, and the surfaces of all things which faced that way were similarly dyed: The walls of the house, the unstraight tower, the cascading downfall of the cliff. Even the figure of Eliset was carmined, a figure no longer particularly boyish, but decidedly eye-catching. She had changed her gown.

Mevary watched her as he moved in and out of the doors of the roof-pavilion. The pavilion, an octagon, possessed eight doorways, and had possessed eight doors. Now only five remained, of thin, stained latticework ivory, and these stood open so the pavilion might partake of the sunset and the expected cool of night.

"After ten years, what did you think of him?" Mevary inquired at last.

"He has improved. He is taller than I had thought he would be."

"Tall?"

"I had thought he would not grow as tall as he has. His hands are well-shaped. And his chin has firmed."

"Unlike his guts."

"Well," she said, turning about with a serpentine motion of gown and unbound hair, "all men cannot be as beautiful as you."

Mevary smiled. He walked from the pavilion and across the roof-terrace. He advanced until his body touched hers, and laid his hands, one on her waist, one on her breast.

"He will," she said, "be coming up here, and may see you."

"He would expire at once of the shock."

Eliset laughed a low consuming laugh, and raising her hands, ringed his neck with them. "He must surely marry me first, must he not? But oh—" she murmured, "how shall I lie with another after you? *How?*"

"Remember what is to be gained. You will do it."

"For you, then, I will manage it. You are my only god, Mevary."

Slowly, slowly, he bent his head, and more slowly yet savored the kiss he took from her. When he lifted his mouth from hers, the sun was suddenly gone, and a transparent blue wind rising from the sea, winging upward, brushing over the roof on its way to seek the wooded hills inland.

Out of the dusk there came a stumbling footfall. Mevary and Eliset slid apart.

An unseated stone tread dipped and crunched below, and then their guest appeared on the top of the stair, tottering and puffing.

"These steps are dangerous."

"Alas, yes—" Eliset.

"Oh alas yes indeed—" Mevary. "But they have this advantage; one knows when someone is coming by the noise."

Then, judging by the scrambling sounds, someone else was coming also.

No sooner was the first climber off onto the roof than Harmul bounced into view. He proceeded to race about inside the pavilion, disordering the low tables and cushions, discovering and kindling lamps with a great deal of smoke.

In the raw light, as the dinner began to trail up to the roof in the hands of the two servant boys and the pantingly obese Jobel, Eliset's dress was revealed. The cream silk was sculpted by hands of intricate patterning described with chips of nacre and heliotrope. The girdle, which crossed at her waist three times and once at her hips, before descending to her feet, was of purple and pearls.

Eliset said softly, "this dress if of your bounty, Roilant. I wear it to honor and to thank you."

Zimir whipped the lid from a huge dish of shallow viands, and a large moth hurtled from the darkness and crashed into a lamp.

The dinner was interesting, not in itself, but in attendant particulars. Dassin, called in by Mevary as unofficial taster for Roilant, gorged himself on what there was. Eliset seemed troubled, both by the joking act and its underlying inference. But the more her ginger visitor denied there was any need for a taster, the more Mevary waved Dassin forward. Dassin obliged joyfully. Until, evidently resigned, his involuntary employer ceased protesting and handed Dassin the wine cup himself.

"And so you see," Mevary said, "we shall have to dispense with the idea of poison as a means of getting rid of him. Or else lose one of our precious servants into the bargain."

Eliset vacillated between a smile and a look of despair.

"Do you really think of us so?" She asked. "We, who are your blood kindred, Roilant, to try to harm you?"

"It is a possibility I was warned of."

"Who warned you?" She cried. She seemed stung and was very alert for once.

"But," said the unattractive dinner guest, rinsing his surprisingly admired hands in the tarnished finger bowl, "I dismissed such low gossip. Why else should I come here? I mean to make you my wife. You will be interested to know I dreamed of you often. Strange dreams, which reminded me of my duty—and, er, naturally—my pleasure in honoring the betrothal our fathers arranged for us."

"Dreams," said Eliset. Her face, turned from Mevary to him, seemed of the same creamy silk as her gown, her eyes cold and flat as the heliotropes. "I do not see you, Roilant, as one to be influenced by dreams."

"This, however, was very definite. The same dream on several nights. Something to do with the pressed flowers you sent me long ago—and the little talisman on my father's untimely death. And there you stood, motionless and pale. *The bond may not be broken*, you said. *Come to me before the end of the month.*"

Eliset forced a laugh. It was noticeable to her observer that she forced it, though its sound was glittering and natural as a falling stream.

"But was I so forward?"

The plump narrator seemed to realize the impropriety of his words, and huffed into his napkin. The lean tawny cousin said, smooth as honey: "Perhaps some hidden desire in your sleep, Eliset, sent you to visit him, chastely recalling him to his vow."

"I do not believe in such things," she said. She was agitated and striving for control.

To confront the witch and her witchery was, after all, turning out to be interesting.

"And yet you do believe in the hauntings of this house," said Mevary. Changing the subject? "We have more ghosts here, Roilant, than people. We are outnumbered by the restless dead. Shall I enumerate? My father, supposedly. Eliset's old nurse, Tabbit. Then, a whole legion of Remusans comes and goes, glowing trumpets and chanting military parade songs. The bath house is decidedly a hotbed of phantoms. The servants will go nowhere near it after dark, and dislike doing so by day. Am I not correct, Dassin?"

Dassin swallowed most of a large fig and said, rolling his eyes, "We have heard sounds. And seen lights, in the corridor that was the old courtyard—and smelled the smell of perfumes rising." Dassin's horror seemed real. He had paled, but that might be only indigestion, or perhaps the first symptoms of poisoning. "A month ago," said Dassin feverishly, "old Jobel fell asleep, hiding nearby from his work. He woke in the dark and a light shone up from the wall. He went and looked down into it and beheld sudden water there, and on it—a tiny ship, no bigger than my hand, blazing with little torches and with a little red sail—"

Mevary caterwauled mirth. He rolled across the cushions until his head rested in Eliset's scintillant lap.

"You should not scorn these phenomena," said Eliset quietly. "The world is full of strangeness. I, too, have sometimes heard the voices of these ghosts and the blowing of horns—and known them for uncanny things."

"Weeny little ships skulling in the well—" spluttered Mevary.

"Yes, yes, master," said Dassin excitedly.

"Be quiet," said Mevary. "Go away. Lord Roilant has finished with your services. Go and be sick, or expire of venom."

Dassin snatched two handfuls of bread and fruit from the tables, and flew from the pavilion and the roof.

There was a silence, during which the sound of the sea reached them, somehow not only from beyond the walls, but from within the confines of the house, a low, mystical singing. Inland, a nightingale also sang, the miniature music carried by the open bowl of the night, clear as the crystal of Flor was not.

"The beauty of this place," said Eliset, suddenly, remotely. Her eyes were two blue flames. "I would do anything to keep it. Even when all the roofs have fallen, when one stone does not remain upon another, I shall live here in the ruin. And when I die . . . yes, my spirit also will wander here. I shall not want to rest."

"Roilant has decided you will live at Heruzala," said Mevary.

Her gaze faded. She looked at her avowed future husband not with distaste, but with an objective tenderness. He had seen such a look on the faces of executioners, just before they raised the sword.

"Then, of course, I should obey him. It was my heart speaking, not my brain. Pay no heed to me, Roilant. I will leave without protestation. Providing one may be found to tend my father's grave—he lies here, beside the tower. Tomorrow, if you will permit me, I shall show you the spot."

At this cheerful prospect, he seemed hardly uplifted.

"Have I not," he ventured, "seen it before, during my last visit?"

"The stone figure had not been added." Plainly, this made a difference.

Soon after, the guest pleaded the rigors of his journey and excused himself.

"If *my* dead father wakes you," Mevary called after him, "render him my filial surprise. Sleep peacefully, Roilant."

At midnight, Roilant, very far from peacefully asleep, sat under the hornbeam tree that stood between the orchards and the mansion of Flor. The moon had long since passed over the house and now was moored out to sea, its light here obscured by the intervening masonry. Under the tree was, therefore, blackness, a blackness to which Roilant did not take kindly. Having come to superstition late, he was unprepared for such nastinesses as fear of the dark. The sight of Flor had also evoked curious feelings.

Waiting for Cyrion, who had arranged to meet him here, Roilant's mind was full of adolescent memories of Eliset, and potent misgivings. Perhaps, after all, the vision had not been a threat, merely interpreted as one; the fall of the roof a coincidence—the rain had been very heavy that day. Perhaps Eliset's hope of being rescued from poverty, of being given status and respectability, had somehow, of itself, sent him the message. Not sorcery at all, but the energy of a strong will, imbued by fierce longing.

And perhaps—

Confused already, Roilant now became startled.

A shadowy figure had emerged soundlessly from the trees behind him, and was sitting down beside him on the grass.

"A beautiful night," said Cyrion.

"You did not come from the direction I anticipated."

"My deepest apologies. My route was circuitous."

"In case any watched?"

"I rather think none did. Dassin, who was supposed to guard your door, succumbed to the powder that fell in your wine tonight. It made him rather talkative, but later he slept with entrancing serenity. As for the circuitousness, I was simply exploring the ground."

"How did you manage the powder?"

"In a ring," said Cyrion. "An old trick. Remember Sabara? I had another plan if Mevary should detail one of the other three."

Roilant shifted a little. He stared intently at Cyrion, letting his dull night-sight investigate what was to be seen. Eventually he said, "And is that how I look to you?"

"No. It is how I assume they think you would look."

"An exaggeration, then. I am not a vain man, but—"

"But this is rather clownish, and purposely so. You and I are not alike, and they have seen you once or twice, however briefly and however long ago. That I am taller than they expected is credible, young men do grow, though Mevary does not take kindly to the fact that you are now one whole inch taller than he. I suspect tomorrow I shall meet him in well-heeled boots. For the rest, the body padding is overdone, and nearly proved my nemesis in the bath house, except that I reckoned on being caught unawares. The cheek padding in my mouth is hardly much safer, and a trial. My admitted fear of their poisoning me has been enhanced by my slow unenjoyment of eating with them. The pouches under my eyes itch. I am sure you are glad to learn of it."

"And I suppose you dyed your hair to resemble an orange?"

"The caricature of an orange, I do assure you."

Roilant smiled, then laughed unwillingly.

"I probably deserve the blow to my limited self-esteem. You are risking your life for me."

"Am I?" Cyrion, facial padding removed, began to eat one of the untimely peaches of Flor. "Meanwhile, how does your own side of the business progress?"

"My servant found the religious you told me of. It is being arranged as you specified."

"Your other two servants have been sent packing to the village, as I forecast they would be. Mevary wants no unnecessary witness to whatever goes on. They have been instructed to become sullen and presently ride to Cassireia, having first attended to local gossip."

"I played my part of the hooded traveler in the villages both. But the only gossip *I* heard was frankly poetical. There are apparently female demons, part siren, who rise singing from the sea about the cliffs. They steal ships, when able to snare them, and small children likewise, while sacrificing men to their goddess."

"A dull if messy way of life. And what of Flor's buried treasure?"

"Which treasure?"

"Your cousin Eliset mentioned one. The hoard of a ghostly Remusan legion, located suitably in the bath house."

"I think," said Roilant vaguely, "that was a game I played as a child, no more." A pause, less vague. "You will consider this odd—or maybe not. I just recalled, I once thought I saw a ghost myself, when I was in the bath house, a boy with a cloth wound about his head—it vanished into the corridor in an instant. I was only a boy myself and on a visit. I never mentioned it." Another pause, until Roilant, wondering if he was listened to, demanded: "What now?"

"Nothing now. The moves of this phase of the game are mostly theirs. Simply be ready. You recollect your own part exactly, I trust?"

"Oh indeed. It has a certain bitter humor. You are going?"

"I leave you to the beautiful night."

"Wait—"

Cyrion paused, standing there with the utmost elegance, despite the new and unbecoming silhouette the padding lent him.

"Is she," said Roilant, "is Eliset—all I judge her?"

"I heard a snatch of conversation on the roof terrace, between your cousins. She told him he was her only god, and their subsequent embrace was unfraternal. She also mentioned that you were not supposed to die until you had wed her."

"Ah." Roilant bowed his head. "It is not I want her. But, it distresses me to think of her in this way."

"Then, my friend," said Cyrion, "do not think of her in this way."

With the faintest brush of the grasses, he was gone.

The simplest route by which to leave the house had been via the little compound that flanked the bath house, and the comparatively low compound wall, whose declining and misplaced stones now offered generous footholds. Returning,

Cyrion reversed the method, hesitating only a moment to peruse the lookout tower some eighty feet away, almost at the brink of the cliff. The last gaze of the moon threw the edifice into relief, its pronounced leaning, its jagged parapet, the two or three black slits of its eyes. *It* looked more haunted than anything, while close on the near slope before it, a scatter of stone boxes revealed the graveyard of Flor. The perfect addendum.

The cumbersome figure went up the wall like running water, swung over into the bath house court, and so out of the fading grey moonlight through a side entry into the gloomy interior of the bath house itself.

Within, all light quickly died, save for the least substantial glimmer of liquid, left undrained from the kalidarium, and caught by one high unshuttered window.

Moving around the pool, and its emptied fellow, Cyrion avoided an ornamental basin with a graven sea serpent, and turned into the stone passage which led back to the inner courtyard of the house.

Halfway along it, just as Mevary had done earlier, Cyrion stopped beside the impressive, defunct well.

He had noted a lamp previously, hanging on a brass hook above the well, but it would offer too much show through the apertures in the roofing above. Instead, a flint, tinder and piece of candle were utilized. Presently a diluted color woke from the enamel and mosaic fish and flowers of the well's back-frame.

Cyrion's examination of the upper part of the well was thorough, if inconclusive. (Mevary's reaction to the well, though noted, as he had not reckoned it to be, had lent no clues.)

The twisted pillars upheld a roof, no longer needed once the court itself had been roofed over on that side. The chains that would have lowered great buckets were gone, though the brazen fitment which had held the chains was still in place: The angry heads of two lions with huge rings through their jaws. Through the rings passed a thick loop of corded rope, which then hung down into the well-shaft, taut as if weighted, but which ended without purpose flush with the shadowy rim of the barren stone floor some thirty feet below. It shone clean and smooth at its center, that floor, and void. No water mysteriously rippled, no tiny spectral ship appeared. Idly,

Cyrion took up one of the dead leaves which had blown in from above to litter the corridor. He let it fall into the well and watched it slowly spiraling, unimpeded by anything, to the bottom.

A few moments more and he had extinguished the candle. Surprisingly, the light did not go out with the flame.

A phantasmal glow was fluttering across the corridor-court toward him. In its midst, a dark shape suddenly bloomed.

The candle slipped into his tunic—padding made useful storage—Cyrion began to travel toward this second light. He was almost to the archway that led into the inner courtyard, when the whole of the light, and the dark within it, collided with him.

There was a swirling backward. The darkness flung up a wing, and something gleamed. A chilling voice whispered: "*Demon or spirit, dispel and sink, I command you by the power of this.*"

Cyrion, ginger, owlish, all padding in position, was captive in the glare of a small antique oil lamp, whose floating wick gave off a dense yellow brilliance. The slim hand which held the lamp was steady. The other slim hand steadily held up a large scarab of polished green stone engraved with magic eyes and similar symbols: A talisman, by whose efficacy the wielder seemed to set much store. She was also female, and very beautiful.

Cyrion looked into her face, and, being Roilant, gaped. She looked into his and gasped. The steady lamp became unsteady, and oil dripped on the dead leaves underfoot.

"My lord—it is my Lord Roilant, is it not? Pardon me, my lord,"

"Oh—" said Cyrion, at a loss, still gaping.

"My lord, I saw a light moving. They will have told you, this part of the house is subject to—supernatural things. I was afraid. Rather than let the thing pursue me, I ran toward it, trusting this amulet, which has protected me in the past."

"I," said Cyrion, "could not sleep. Remembering I had left an item of clothing in the bath house I—went to fetch it. It was my light you saw. Seeing yours, I was taken aback."

She watched him intently. If she believed him was not certain, but she now made to him a graceful obeisance, the eastern bow which, as the light of her own lamp slid and lingered over her, displayed her to great advantage. She was not only very beautiful, but of an unnusual, arresting coloring, her smooth olive skin set with two eyes of the coolest, most silvery grey. Meanwhile, hair of a thick and lustrous somberness hung unbound to her knees, and now, shawling forward and streaming back, the lamp found on it an elusive coppery sheen.

"My lord," she murmured, "I am Jhanna, the slave of the Lady Eliset. My lord—" she looked into his face once more, closed her eyes as if praying, opened them wide and said rapidly: "I entreat you, do not tell her I was wandering here. I—am afraid of her, my lord. She will beat me, or worse. Far worse. I beg you—" abruptly she was on her knees in the leaves and dust, none of her dignity lost, glorious, her night-robe slipping from one satin shoulder, her eyelids quivering, and her wrists, so the lamp faltered. "I have heard of your kindness. Take pity."

Cyrion fumbled for words, frowning. At length, words were found.

"Get up. I hardly require you to kneel. I will say nothing."

She rose at once, like an empress. Her fervor had ceased.

"I believe you, lord. You are a true friend to one helpless and alone in a nest of vipers."

Cyrion frowned harder.

"Who are vipers?"

Her teeth were furiously white, and the smile that revealed them, as furious.

"You *know*, my lord. Your cousins. He a vicious despoiler. She a harlot. And—a *sorceress*." The sentence was hissed, as she had hissed her occult dismissal behind the shield of the scarab. Her eyes, like those of a young warrior, met Cyrion's greyer, currently less-attractive ones. "Come," she said, "I am at your mercy. You may be honest with me, who am less than nothing. You would not have ventured to this cess-pit of evil if her wicked spell-making had not forced you here. I have heard of you. Your decency, your wise aloofness. That you were to wed another, a pure virgin in Heruzala. And would you turn from that to this? She has ensorcelled you with her will, and now does so with her physical allurements. Are you lost, lord? Or can you yet escape her? Is there any way?"

"I hardly think," began Cyrion pompously. Then his manner gave way under her dauntless stare. "This is scarcely the arena in which to debate it," he finished lamely.

Jhanna lowered her eyes, then raised them. She looked like a princess. She said proudly, even arrogantly: "You are welcome to follow me to my chamber, lord. I trust you to do me no harm. And if you do, what odds? Long ago my chastity was nullified by the gentle Lord Mevary, who raped me, and keeps me still his unwilling paramour. I tried to kill him once. This was the result—she turned her head suddenly and thrusting back her hair, she disclosed her right ear, its charm greatly marred by the absence of the lobe.

Cyrion swore softly.

"With the knife," she said, "I would have used upon *him*. He is just, sir, you will note."

"Your room," he said. "Rest assured, I would not—you need fear nothing from me."

"Come then. I will tell you now, I lied. I came to seek you tonight, and God blessed me in finding you. I will pledge myself to your aid in any way I can, to protect you, and to destroy those that I hate."

Her face, during these last words, was naked. No man of any wit or awareness would have doubted what she said. Even Cyrion had no doubt. The force that came from her was like a blow.

Then she touched the talisman to her brow, and doused her lamp.

"Follow close. *They* will not know. They are together in her bed."

Cyrion did not thank her for this jot of information. He was already well advised of it.

They went very stealthily and quietly across the inner court, skirting the nearer basin, and keeping to the wall. It was not until they had passed through the short passage which led to the sunken kitchen court that Cyrion clumsily stumbled over a worn stone. Even then, he made a minimum of noise.

In the sunken court was a well, the last well of Flor, and about the yard the kitchen stood, the wash house, and the shadowed apartments of the servants and slaves. Once, this had been a busy place, even at night, and through another arch, horses might have been heard, but no more. Now, only a desiccated vine rustled on the wall. No lights shone forth.

The girl led him through a low doorway and into the utter black of the space beyond. Here she knew her way by familiarity, and closed the door, first with a screen, and next by the drawing over of a curtain. The lamp was rekindled.

It was a windowless chamber. The cell of a slave. A few scraps of furniture had been gathered, a chest, an ewer and a cup, a stool. The bed was the only portionally sumptuous item, a mattress flung with pillows, rugs and a heap of three or four scarves, the topmost of which was a sheeny pale yellow. To this couch she pointed, and said, coldly, "when he is here, he likes to lie soft." She indicated the stool, next. "I can offer you no other seat."

"I will stand. Nor will I stay here long. These things you have said—you need not be anxious I would betray you. Indeed, in some respects, my predicament is all you say. I felt coercion, was summoned, and must arrive. But," he said, "it was still my duty. I had shirked it, the betrothal. I hope that when I have honored my side of it, and married her—"

"Why then," said Jhanna, pityingly, "she will kill you. It is all the wealth of Beucelair she wants, so he and she can squander it, and ruin all else as they have ruined this estate. Just as their noble fathers ruined it before them."

Cyrion looked at her with worried attention.

"Well," he stuttered," it seems—seems I cannot evade my fate."

She breathed quickly. She said, "You might kill her."

"I do not—"

"Scruples, against her foul witchcraft? Do not have scruples, my lord. She is a witch."

"Well . . . what weapon against her witchcraft, then? And how to avoid detection?"

"Why," she said, "you are quicker than I thought."

"A desperate man." He shrugged woodenly.

"I did not mean to be insolent, forgive me. But you are more swift of understanding than I looked for." She was like a fire, burning low, yet burning, her eyes no longer seeing him, "Well, then, there may be a way to subdue and punish her. Will you hear me through?"

The podgy figure moved toward the door. And sat down on the stool there.

"I will hear you."

TWO

It was true. Eliset was like the morning. The clear gold morning of her hair, today with a flimsy eastern veil adrift on it like a pale shining vapor, the white peerless skin and the white dress. Her first appearance in the tarnished gown had given an impression Mevary must have warned her from, after the comment in the bath house on the discrepancy in the cousins' apparel. Perhaps she had hoped to touch his heart the first time. (Strange notion—to touch the heart of your fearful victim—presumably part of their mutual game, her deceit, his self-deception.) There had been a sort of empty-headed coquetry and simpering on that occasion, too, which had since disappeared.

Eliset had grown more sure of him, her biddable Cousin Roilant. Or less.

Now she stood under the scattering shadow of a little tree with saffron blooms, her hand stretched out, its ringless fingers resting on the oblong of grey stone.

"This is where he lies, my father, Gerris."

"Ah, yes."

"There was a place for my mother at his side. But she died in Western lands, far away, and is buried there."

Heavily solemn, he stood over the tomb with her, as if checking for evidence of occupancy. The only evidence there was being personified in the solitary stone figure laid out on top.

"The graveyard here has always been open," she said. "My father wished to build a chapel, there, beneath the tower. But his fortune was lost. There was no chapel. And when I was thirteen—"

"Yes. Of course."

"His death," she said. "It was inexplicable and cruel. A physician was called, from Cassirieia. We paid him in gold. All we could afford. And more. But the man could do nothing. Nothing. No doubt foolishly, there was talk of sorcery, Roilant."

If this was intended as a threat, it was most implicit. Her pleasing voice delivered it harmoniously, with little trace of emotion. And yes, after a delicate pause, her face was lifted, her eyes fixed on him, and she said, "I must broach this openly. It *is* your intention to wed me?"

He flushed. (Like many women, Cyrion had long ago mastered this trick; a gloss on his fine performance.)

"Forgive me," she said, "it is improper that I speak to you so, and I know it. But, placed as I am—"

"Eliset, my—dear—Yes, I do indeed intend to honor the vow. Despite the legal letter which I sent to you and which you returned, so singularly—and about which I had such a curious dream—"

"A letter?" She was guilelessly puzzled. "I received no letter from you, save that which promised you would come to me here."

"There was a letter. It does not matter now."

"But yes. A legality, you say? And that I returned it?"

"I may have dreamed that, too. I told you, my dreams have been bizarre, warped by guilt over this lapse between us."

"But Roilant—" Suddenly she smiled. The move, it seemed, had been played to its end. She was content. "But, let it be as you wish it. We will forget this letter."

"Yes." He cleared his throat, and examined the stone body on the tomb, its pointed feet, and hands clasped on a sword, and bearded, sleeping face. Farther down, moist stains crept from the base of the tomb, and a whitish lichen, eager to weave a coverlet for the statue. "There is this problem. Our marriage, which I very much desire, must be circumspect. I regret there are . . . rumors about your life at Flor. The very fact that you have lived here at all after the death of your guardian, with Mevary . . ."

Her eyes no longer guilelessly swam. They stabbed.

"And where else was I to live? I have no other kin alive but you."

"Perhaps, with some sisterhood."

"Some sisterhood? Flor had passed to my Uncle Mevary, but Flor was to be mine on my marriage. And I should leave it to the care of Mevary's *son*? Never."

"When you are my wife, you will live at Heruzala."

"Yes," she said, recalled. "Yes, I shall lose Flor forever then shall I not? My legal dower, which my cousin will inhabit. And devour." She drew her hand from the tomb, and put it lightly to her eyes. "But I have no care." As an actress, you had to admit, she was expressive.

"I must have this clear, Eliset, while hating to grieve you," he persisted doggedly. "You must agree to a modest wedding, a secretive wedding, even. Living as you have, it is not possible it should be otherwise."

"Is it not?" She let down her hand. She smiled at nothing. Supposedly, an enchantress might enforce any sort of wedding she wished on him. But no, maybe it was politic of the enchantress to let her victim win in little things, letting him fool himself, fool that he obviously was, tutoring himself that the spell which had ruled him was no more than dreams and an attack of conscience. One might imagine her thinking all this as she stood there, and then moved her gaze wondrously back to him.

"I will do," she said, "whatever you want. With gratitude. And I will be a good wife to you. An honorable wife. You will have no complaint."

Probably, dead husbands rarely did.

They walked between the grouped and weathered tombs. There were not many; the family had held Flor a mere century. The tower was close, sunshine changing its stones to apricots, showing where the flowers rooted at its base. The reason for the marked leaning was discernible, two walls had risen, and two sunk. They did not enter, but walked by and came to the brink of the cliff. It was reputed to be unsafe, here among the parched grasses. You could picture the child-girl, eleven-year-old Valia, Gerris' legitimized bastard daughter, wandering at the margin of the tower, lured by the blue and bronzy flowerlets, lulled by the indigo band of the sea beyond the fatal edge . . .

Perhaps the witch remembered, and did picture. What had the sorcery been *that* time? The vision of a sea demon, maybe, rushing toward the girl with her flowers, boiling out of the air—and with a shriek she had fallen, down and down, into the depthless sink below, her black hair like a dying smoke.

The acting cousins looked out to ocean. There was no beach below to break the sweep of water, the blueness ran sheer to the rocky bases of the cliffs. An oared ship was coming from the north, her white sail furled, and her passage rimmed in glinting spray, making most likely for the bay and port of Cassireia. She stood not an eighth of a mile out from land, illustrating the deepness of the water below, and she was small as a toy, illustrating also the height of the high cliff.

"Dreams and departures," said Eliset. "Once I dreamed such a ship took me from Flor. I held out my arms to the land, but the land sailed far away."

As she spoke, conceivably seeking to burnish her performance with a gesture, as Cyrion had done with a flush, she took a step forward. Where he sole now came down, the grassy ground tilted. A clump of violet flowers burst upward, their roots rising with them, and shivered away over the brink, a bouquet thrown to the sea. A stream of rock and thin soil showered after them, and Eliset, unbalanced proceeded to follow.

The bulbous figure of Roilant moved in a blur of speed that should not have been possible to it. In the second she fell she was snatched, spun into the air and returned to earth some feet inward of the edge. She had not cried out, she looked quite collected, and thanked him politely. Then began to tremble in his grasp, a response that seemed, and probably was, genuine.

The ginger young man, still holding her, made no comment. Her voice shaking, too, she said, "This cliff is dangerous, the ground unsettled—even the graves shift. One day the tower will fall into the sea—How did you manage to catch me back in time—"

He said then, with great and infuriating and irrelevant portentousness: "You are to be my wife."

Now her voice shook with laughter. Trembling with shock, contemptuous and entertained at once, she looked up at him, and he in turn down at her. Something she found in his face, then, silenced her, and gradually stilled the palpitation of her fear. She made a sudden attempt to move away and he, rather than let go of her, drew her closer. The red head was lowered to the blonde one.

Her body stiffened to resist one moment, next, recollecting its duty, grew pliant, acquiesced. And then, amazing itself, flowed, dissolved, was borne away, as if on the waters of the sea itself.

His disguise was less than skin-deep. Somewhere within a succession of instants, and not comprehending it, the senses of Eliset had discovered as much. And, deliriously drowned in a single kiss she, even if she had summoned spirits, might well reckon he, or she herself, was possessed.

When he drew away again, she opened her eyes on the same pudgy cheeks, puffy eyes, carrot hair. She stared, and to her alarm, discovered she was once more trembling, though now at a different kind of fear.

Only as he became rapidly embarrassed was she able to command herself. With a wildly tumbling heart and a cool carelessness of person, she turned and retraced their way down the slope toward the mansion.

Presently he came up with her.

"I have," he mumbled, "made certain arrangements. If you are prepared to fall in with them, I will ask you to accompany me to Cassireia, tomorrow morning. At noon, we should be in a particular building, and there a priest and witnesses will be supplied. We shall then, husband and wife, travel directly to Heruzala."

The love scene might never have happened. It took her a moment to realize what he was saying, and as she did, she cried out almost involuntarily: *"No!"*

Her denial was vehement, tinged by panic.

"No?" He stopped.

She waited, her back to him, then turned to face him nearly more pale than in the aftermath of her rescue from death.

"Roilant, I cannot leave Flor so swiftly. Knowing I may never return here—I cannot. You must give me some consideration."

"Then what are we to do?" he asked frigidly.

"All else I accept. To be wed in such a way, and to be hustled out onto the street afterward without any delicacy. Yes, this means little to me. I see it must be so. But I must return to Flor, at least one short night. There will be things to discuss with Mevary. He will be my steward here. I had hoped—"

"Hoped?"

"You would confirm his stewardship by some form of gratuity. In that way, Flor may not suffer so greatly in my absence. But aside from all that—Roilant, I shall be newly your bride. The first night we are together . . . I would far rather it were here, at Flor. Where I was a child, where I became a woman. Will you, out of your undoubted generosity, grant me this?"

It was interesting to ponder if she thought even him idiot enough to suppose she would come to his bed a virgin. Perhaps she did think him idiot enough, and this was an appeal of fearful naïveté rather than nostalgia.

Cyrion gave a rough unwilling nod.

"Very well. One night."

Her face relaxed and the color came back into her lips at least.

"My dear, you are very kind to me. I promise you again, though you think me such an imperfect match, I shall not disgrace you."

He grumbled something cloddishly gallant. They walked the rest of the way down the slope. As they threaded among the dwarf tamarisks that clustered about the outer wall of the bath house compound, a weird noise became abruptly audible to both of them.

There was a blur of shouting, which rose and died, then rose once more. There was a startling crash like breaking pottery, and a thin shriek. Then came the original noise again, a horrid continuous yelping and squealing.

"Oh, God, what is it?" Eliset whispered.

She gathered her long skirts in her hand and began to run light as a white flame around the wall. Her plump companion went after her with surprising quickness and only the occasional organized blunder.

An unbarred door gave on the old stables. Thrusting it aside, she sprang in here, and so through the derelict yard, under another hollow arch and thus into the sunken court. It seemed she knew unerringly the source of the sounds, and here indeed it was.

Seen by daylight, the kitchen courtyard was the dusty, leaf-blown square one reckoned it to be by night, into which, from the kitchen itself, various utensils, such as baskets and pots, had spilled, piling against the well and the butchering block.

The scene which occupied this theatre was, as they entered it, in momentary tableau, as if to aid the new arrival in assessing it. In the open entrance to the kitchen stood the boy Harmul, clutching a long and lethal meat knife. Nearby, another of the boys, Zimir, lay sprawled on his face amid a smashed oil jar, oil and clay spread from him in all directions. The last boy, Dassin, was missing. Only two other persons were present. By the door of her slave's cell, Jhanna was coiled almost flat against the wall, as if nothing could pry her away. Her eyes were huge with terror and her long, long hair, like true copper in the sun, having been bound upon her head seemed to have been torn down. Her homely dress showed a great rent across the bodice, which she held closed with her hands.

On the coping of the well was Jobel.

As Cyrion entered the court, the fat and elderly slave was fixed in a crouching position, but a second later he jumped upright, nearly falling into the well, but somehow sending himself on into a ferocious leap that took him back into the courtyard. His belly slopped, his arms waved. He began to make again the terrible yelping noise they had heard from over the outer wall. As he did so, pink froth erupted from his mouth. His eyes were bright and blind.

Seeing Eliset, Harmul rushed to her, the knife still firmly gripped.

"Lady—he is filled by a demon!"

Eliset stood like ice.

"No," she said. "I have seen this thing before. It is a madness that may infect others. I saw a dog die in this way, and later a child the dog had bitten."

"He attacked *her*." Harmul pointed at Jhanna. "He ripped her dress and pulled her hair. But then he ran this way and lifted the jar of oil and flung it at Zimir—"

Jobel, the old fat slave, shrieking, cast himself against the yard wall, beating and slashing at it.

"Harmul," Eliset said. She seemed to try to catch her breath. She said, "Poor creature, he will die anyway, and is a threat to all of us until he does. He is already mindless and in an agony that can only grow worse. You must kill him, Harmul. Throw the knife."

Harmul stared at her, eyes starting. Then he nodded.

His skinny arm went up and the meat knife flew from it.

It caught Jobel in the back, and the blade was long enough, sunk to its handle, to penetrate all that fat and enter the heart.

With a gurgling screech, Jobel thumped down. He spasmed, rolled. The foam was now red as it poured from his lips. Incredibly, like some nightmarish acrobat, he struck the back of his skull with his own heels. And died.

Harmul gave a low cry. In her doorway, Jhanna hid her face in her hands. Zimir began to crawl from the ruin of the oil jar.

"Be careful," Eliset said. "Do not touch the spit which has come from his mouth. It is poison. Where it has fallen, sprinkle oil and let the oil burn. If his teeth have anywhere grazed you, the wound must be cauterized. And he, poor wretch. You must not undress or wash him for fear of infection. Wrap him in rugs or sacks as he is. Let their air do its work, do not put him in the ground until tomorrow." Her face was white and calm. She laid her hand on Harmul's shoulder. "You did well," she said, and he turned as white as she.

Eliset walked straight out of the yard and through the passage into the house court. Cyrion moved after her.

As they reached the empty basin of a fountain, she put out her hand and leaned there.

Cyrion looked up, and saw Mevary running down the stair from the roof terrace, producing slight clopping sounds. The reason was the high-heeled tasselled boots he was today wearing, a fashion of the Auxian region, that lent him two inches in height.

Despite his footgear, he came level with Eliset and caught her, before she dropped to the ground in one of the most excellently feigned faints Cyrion had ever had the joy of beholding.

"She sent me to you with this."

Cyrion looked dubiously at the amber rose in Jhanna's slim brown hand. Tied about the stem of the rose when, rather reluctantly, he accepted it, was a slip of paper. Which read: *My dear, forgive me, I shall not dine with you. That I should be well and strong for our journey to Cassireia, I find I must rest tonight. Thus, until tomorrow. Eliset.*

Having read the note he let it fall, and examined the rose. Its sweet scent came from it like soft music, and mated with another, more somber perfume, emanating from the slave-girl's hair. Smooth now, and pinned upon her head, it matched her present composure. Even when, very quietly, she said:

"The old slave, Jobel. A vile death. I, too, have seen men die of that sickness. But oh, the coldness with which she ordered the boy to kill him. And took care to swoon directly after, to mislead you, if she could. She is evil."

"Yes," he said, and put the rose aside.

"But that she sent me here to your chamber is good. She suspects nothing in sympathy between us, nor does that jackal, Mevary. And see, I have brought what I promised you."

Cyrion held out his hand and took from hers a small black vial.

"Do you think—"

"My lord, do not falter. I have told you what this drug will do. A pity she does not share her meal with you tonight. But tomorrow, when you and she are wedded, that is the time of danger, and then you can act. And I, Lord Roilant, will do anything in my small power, will risk my very life to cheat them of your death and your wealth, and give them to judgment. You see what I have risked already, stealing this potion from her witch's chests."

"Will she not miss it?"

Queenlike, she dismissed his feeble fears.

"Among so many foul medicines as she has? Never."

Jhanna stood before him in a shaft of westering sun, her hair haloed with flame.

"You stress your risk," he said. "Why risk anything?"

"For your sake."

"By which, I guess, you mean you wish for your freedom, and certain funds in recompense?"

She smiled, almost laughed at him.

"They are little things to me now. To live as I have lived. To endure what I have—I wish only for revenge upon iniquity. I wish for the justice of their fall."

Cousins Mevary and Roilant dined alone upon the roof, waited on by Harmul, who seemed distracted and soon disappeared.

It turned out Dassin had done the same, but rather more permanently.

"Jobel's death will have frightened him. They do not understand the cause of such things. They think demons kill the victim and then animate the body, an idea ridiculous."

"Oh, indeed," said Cousin Roilant, seriously.

"Either that, or Dassin has expired in some hidden place of the slow-acting poison I plied you with last night, and which he—greedy taster that he was—absorbed more of than you did. I do hope, by the way, you did not require your food tasted tonight? You seem to eat very little, dear cousin. How can you have got to be such a nicely rounded pudding on such piddling little mouse portions?"

"I would ask you not to insult me. For the sake of Eliset, if nothing else."

"Because she is to be your loving wife by tomorrow afternoon?"

"Yes. And there is something which should be discussed between us, Mevary."

"Ah." An expectant acid gleam was in Mevary's eyes, that faded when Cyrion went on.

"The matter of your stewardship of Flor."

"And I thought for one delicious moment," said Mevary, "you were about to question me on my own relationship with Eliset. I have, of course, been as a brother to her."

"You have, of course, shared her bed, and this I know quite well, as does half of Cassireia, and the King's court at Heruzala, for the matter of that." Mevary's mouth opened, and closed. Cousin Roilant said, "It makes no difference to me. If it had, you might suppose I would not be here now."

"But I thought uncanny dreamings and desires drew you here like a magnet," said Mevary gloatingly.

"I have no time for superstition. I am here because I intend to honor a bargain. Providing my wife behaves blamelessly after we are wedded, I shall raise no quarrel and harp on no past adventure. And for this, amongst other reasons, I shall expect you to remain far off from her. You will tend Flor, her property and mine. Money will be sent to improve the estate, and you yourself will receive a generous stipend."

Mevary yawned. He was frankly no longer thrilled by stipends, the hope of gain being rather different.

Cousin Roilant looked offended.

"You may conclude you will live better than you have done."

Mevary laughed. He drank, and laughed again.

"I do trust I shall. Well, I never anticipated such kindness, dear Pud. I toast you. To stipends." Mevary could barely restrain his mirth.

"My thanks. I shall now return to my room."

"Oh, for shame. I was desirous you would stay and play Knight-and-Castle with me—I still have the board and pieces we used as boys. Do you recall them? All those exciting defeats—"

"Excuse me."

"Or a practice bout with sticks, or blunted swords, how does that appeal? I still indulge myself in knightly pursuits. No?"

"No."

"I concede. You have an early start tomorrow. God bless your night. Angels flap over your bed, and so on."

Mevary stood to see his kindred down the stair, towering over him now by half an inch in his Auxine boots.

Improvising a mis-step on the landing, and so arriving audibly at the veranda of the second floor, Roilant-Cyrion blundered unsilently back to his allotted chamber.

As he entered, he became aware of a pleasing scent. Shutting the door and walking around the carved screen, he saw nothing in the spacious room was changed. Save that the window-shutters had been closed against night-flying insects, and a squadron of candles lit.

Breathing shallowly, Cyrion went to each of the windows and unshuttered them. Turning, he doused the candles swiftly. Moving lastly to the bed, he picked up the amber rose he had let drop there, the token Eliset had sent him. It had opened its petals and their exquisite perfume had intensified to a remarkable degree, permeating the entire room. Going back to the nearest window, he threw the rose out of it, and stayed to watch it fall. And thereafter still stayed in a long perusal it seemed of the roofs and walls of Flor round about, and the downswept land beyond them, the cloud of darkened orchards, the cleft hills in the east where a blond moon was just now rising.

The drug in the rose, a soporific, had perhaps been activated by the heat of the candles burning close. He had been meant, obviously, to come in and, rejoicing in the charming aroma, sink heavily asleep. That his life was endangered tonight made no sense at all. Therefore, the lady who worked her sorcery with a flower had done it for some other reason.

To sleep was to miss something. Cyrion, spying the circle of the moon, had some conception of what.

Half an hour later, when the room was scentless, Cyrion closed the shutters. He then spilled a vial of sweet-smelling unguent around the bed, positioned himself amid the pillows, and awaited a visitor.

The visitor was not long in coming.

First, a gentle tap. Next, the door opening a crack. Then an almost noiseless footfall about the screen. A lamp or candle was lit, and the light strayed over him.

"Cousin," Mevary said anxiously, then shook him.

Cyrion grunted blearily and awarded the young man one eloquent, awesome snore.

Mevary laughed, briefly now.

"He sleeps like a hog, just as you said he would," Mevary murmured. "No wonder. I can smell the drug even now."

"Yes," she said from the doorway, the clever sorceress. It was more like the hissing of a cat.

The light dipped and went out. In another half minute, they were gone, the witch and her lover, leaving the silly pudding cousin leadenly still and stertorously breathing. And very much awake.

The death of Jobel had plainly been a murder. Though the foaming madness had in many ways resembled that invariably fatal ailment passed from beasts to men, in some salient particulars it did not. There had been, for example, none of the prior symptoms generally attached to the sickness. Nor had any animals themselves so afflicted been noted in the vicinity. It was more certain (it was certain) some poison, reproducing the disease in its effects, had been put to work.

To finish a man so doomed with a clean knife blow would appear to be a kindness. Or an extra insurance. Jobel had been very unwise to tell Dassin what he had seen that night in the haunted well. Dassin equally unwise to report it under the influence of Cyrion's self-drugged wine. That the boy now recognized his own unsafety was demonstrated by his flight.

Which left one, as the round moon climbed the sky, listening to catch the very vaguest sound, beyond the thrum of the sea.

The sound, when it came, was not vague in the least. It was low, but quite definite. And no doubt any innocent sleeping in the house, waking and hearing it, would pull the covers over their ears and shiver. Ghosts, particularly the Remusan ghosts who bivouacked in the bath house, were noisy neighbors.

A horn blew, somewhere as it seemed in the core of the mansion. Then a chanting rose, militaristic in its rhythm, words inaudible, a buried tidal hymn. Remusans, or perhaps the sirens, those local child-snatching mer-ladies of the coast. To whom, doubtless, Valia had literally fallen prey.

As Cyrion moved noiselessly down the stone stair into the inner courtyard, there was a profane shrilling that seemed to rush up from the basins of the two dry fountains.

No one was about. Of course not. Those with cause to be afraid were sensibly hiding. Those without cause were elsewhere.

Even before he entered the roofed over corridor-court, he beheld the shimmering glow that pulsed from it.

The sound of a horn came again, louder, blasting up from beneath his feet and striking against the upper air. There was a dull vibration in the stone flags.

He entered the glow, went through it to the well, and standing there, looked beyond it to the corridor's end. In the bath house, too, a faint sheen seeped from somewhere in the unemptied pool of the Kalidarium. Most of the wan, wild light was about him now, however, wafting like smoke from the huge old well, so the fish and flowers shone brightly in all their colors.

The lamp above had remained unlit and unneeded. Through the ringed mouths of the two lion masks, the loop of corded rope still hung down into the well, its lower ends pulled taut as if weighted below the surface of the water into which they ran.

The *water*.

There in the luminescent well it lay, in a black and glittering jewel, where previously there had been only the moistureless stone floor.

That there had been no dead leaves, no debris at all on the floor of the well had already given away some of its secret to Cyrion. The floor was removable, it could be made to retreat into the shaft, to allow the passage of things which climbed down or rose up from beneath. Directly under the false floor, now revealed, the shaft of the well widened, and became one with what lay below it.

The chanting dashed up into his face like spray. There came a viscous, fishy scent, and then, unmistakably, the tinge of incense, unfolding through the stone funnel in invisible scarves. Abruptly the light in the well intensified and gave birth.

Leaning over, the watcher saw long treads of gold sprung in the black water, and after these, a wedge of fire. The ship came from nowhere, out of the rim of the well-shaft. The miniature demoniacal ship the slave had seen, and so earned death.

The sail was diluted scarlet, the color—and the *size*—of an autumn leaf. Torches blazed at the prow and along the sides, mere sequins of flame searing in the water. There was a swirl of motion on the deck, and a cumulous of scented vapor meandered in the well, at length reaching the corridor, dusting it as if with mist. When the mist cleared from the well, the tiny ship had passed from view. Like magic.

It was not, of course, magical. Its smallness was due solely to perspective. The distance from the high crest of the cliff to the base of the cliff. All of which must separate the well-head from the cavern floor beneath. The sudden widening of the shaft under the round rim, where the stone ledge had formerly closed it, gave the impression water lay directly below. In fact it was the sea, carpeting the cavern perhaps some two hundred and eighty feet down. Then again, the curtailment of the hanging loop of rope had abetted the illusion that water filled the shaft at thirty feet—for this was where the rope-line mysteriously tautened and ended.

A large part of the mansion of Flor must rest above the cavern, the hollow gut of the cliff. The sounds that started in the echo chamber of this hollow struck up through every delving pipe the mansion possessed—the fountains, the cistern, the live well in the kitchen court. Even the bath house stood upon it, and so the hot-water pool, which must have developed revealing transparencies in its floor, was never fully emptied. Only when the cave was filled by torchlight did the kalidarium display its secret, as openly as the open well.

Something scuttered close by. A lizard, perhaps.

Cyrion did not appear to have thought so.

He was gone into the shadowy recess between one of the well's twisted pillars and the wall behind.

There was also another shadow, one which had not been evident a few moments before. It lifted against the whitish sheen in the bath house, swelled, and came out through the doorway. And strangely, took no light itself from the glowing ambience of the well. Nevertheless, it grew visible, as if from some other, inner, agency.

It was the figure of a man in middle years, well-dressed, and disfavored by a predatory wolfish face framed by tawny greying wolfish hair. He moved past Cyrion's hiding place, past the lit-up well without a glance. The eyes were wide and hungry, and oddly myopic. The body moved slowly. But the earlier noise must indeed have resulted from a lizard, or some other nocturnally active fauna of the house, for this man, who caught no reflection and cast no shadow, also made no sound at all.

The chanting in the cavern under the well had sunk to a murmur indistinguishable from the sea.

As the man reached the end of the corridor-court, he turned to look back, and for the first he seemed to note the well. A kind of mindless snarl arrested his face. Then, turning again, he passed on into the inner court of the house. Cyrion, who had actually planned a journey in the opposite direction, instead followed him, and as silently.

At the edge of the inner court, Cyrion halted. His dubious quarry stood at the court's near end, close to the mossy basin where once a fountain had streamed over against the stars. The man writhed his head, looking up toward the broken posts of the veranda and the rooms beyond. Then craned the other way, in the direction of the kitchen court. Toward the passage which led to it he now advanced a step—and stopped. And vanished.

The vanishment was decided. It was not a trick of any sort. There was also little doubt of his identity. From his appearance, the visitor had been none other than Mevary's dead father.

Some twenty minutes later, there arose a new noise, a persistent scratching and clinking from somewhere in the graveyard of Flor.

THREE

It was a delightful morning for the excursion to Cassireia. Birds in wayside trees sang or shrieked merrily. The path ran downhill, mostly with open vistas on all sides and a still, promising sky above, and then for variety here and there, a plunge to bathe among the dry green woods. Where the last windings of the track launched on the broad and ancient road, the white walls of the city came visible, and the violent dark blue of the sea beyond.

Roilant's two servants, they had earlier learned, had already made the trip, having absconded from the village at Flor. Obviously embarrassed, Cousin Roilant had himself procured mules, and hired men to bear the moth-eaten litter unearthed at the mansion. (Only Mevary had seemed unastonished that the two servants were gone. One might almost think he had asked after them in the village before.)

Eliset, guarded from the sun by worn gauze, occupied the litter. The ungainly figure of Roilant endured the foremost mule, and was endured. The bony Harmul brought up the rear. This, aside from the hired men, comprised their complete party. Even Jhanna had been left behind. "I shall scarcely need her about me," Eliset had protested—in fact, Jhanna seemed seldom about her at any time—"and since we are to be so circumspect, the fewer travelers the better, surely?"

No one commented, even obliquely, on the supernatural uproar of the previous night.

Eliset's vigil had left her pale but poised. There was no mark on her person of anything she had practiced or willed or worked upon during those hours when the well burned from within and unquiet spirits walked. A genuinely yawning, ill-tempered Mevary, with brown rings under his eyes, had been a nicer calendar of the occult festivities he had supposedly known of and conceivably attended. On the other hand, an approving bystander of his lover's black art, he might yet be debarred from its operation. His debauch could, after all, have been occasioned otherwise, in the wine cellar, and later in the bed of one unwilling but beautiful subject, who hatingly welcomed him because she had no choice.

There had been no sign of Jhanna that morning when they

set out. While, unsuitable omen for a wedding day, Zimir had been behind the stables, digging a grave.

They entered Cassireia through a high gateway, whose stones were white as blanched almonds in the sunlight.

The great market-place beyond, with its odors of raw and cooked meats, fresh fish, scented oils, burnt honey and ripe fruit, its clouds of powders, grain dusts and flies, and its strident noise of music and argument, engulfed them, Making their way, with some altercation between Harmul and a drover of oxen, they wound around a mobile pottery, negotiated a billowing sea of sheep, and turned into a side lane known as Silk Street, where gilt-threaded raiment poured from shop fronts like golden rain.

Present and past held the city in equal measure. Looking up on every hand, one saw the elevation of partly ruined palaces. There the crumbling cake erected by the slaves of the first King Hraud, and there another put up to honor that Hraud who had been the stepfather of Zilumi, the terpsichorean sorceress. While, along the sea's blue hem, ran the colonnades of the Cassian Emperor, which at sunset still blazed with Imperial Purple.

At the end of the Street of Silks was the Street of Birds, and beyond this, the Street of Smokes, from which the small procession emerged, half-drugged, into the cave of a tunnel. The mouth of the tunnel opened on a small square with a water basin. A stable and a couple of inns crowded in with a pie-seller's and a fortune-teller's bazaar. Across the square, grave, graven and gracious, a small temple, with a pale mosaic dome and pillared entry. A temple reconsecrated and sanctified, for across the lintel was written, in two languages and letters of gold, the words common both to east and west: *There is no god save only God.*

The litter was set down in the shady portico, and Eliset drawn forth. The hired men were dispatched to one of the inns with the mules for company, and Harmul, a disreputable figure in his rags, stationed with the greatest reluctance on all sides, at a convenient pillar.

Cousin Roilant led his bride into the temple-church, pausing only while they removed their shoes, in the eastern manner, on the threshold.

The place was luminously cool, and the altar glistened with its gold and silver vessels. Doves, branches of olives and a rainbow were worked on the curtain, in token of the first punishment and the first forgiveness. Eliset and Cyrion turned, at his much-muddled directions, into a side chamber.

Here, a group awaited them by the secondary altar. A man bowed, and introduced the hired witnesses, with a mention of their suitability. As Cyrion nodded, Eliset waited aloofly, still as one of the clear shafts of light shot in through the windows. Though plainly dressed and without jewels, she had veiled herself in a thin embroidered gauze, and this veil now hung over her face, mostly concealing it. Only her hands gave her away, knotted together at her waist.

Finally, through a side entrance, the priest came in with a boy bearing parchment scrolls.

A somewhat pastoral prayer was offered, and the marriage ceremony began, just as the bell from the citadel rang for noon.

The rite, as was soon apparent to anyone who might know, had been pared to its bones, and the bones were being hurried. The priest, a white-robed, heavily bearded man, with fierce dark locks springing from beneath his shawled head, gabbled in places, and in others hesitated. He seemed also vastly unenamored of the red-haired groom, while mournfully fascinated by the veiled bride. When he symbolically bound their hands with the strip of fringed silk, he fumbled. The attendant boy caught the silk before it reached the floor. At the exchange of rings, it was the groom who fumbled, and metal rang on the paving. To the mismanagement of both priest and cousin Eliset remained impervious. Presumably, she herself did know enough to know enough had been said to espouse them, and that when the clumsy ritual mumbled to an end, though having been denied its dignity, she yet understood that she was sheltered by its legal power.

Documents were signed. The leader of the witnesses was presented with their fee, and they spilled in a gently bleating herd out through the temple into the square.

Cousin Roilant, seeming nervous of his new relationship, informed Eliset, as they walked more slowly through the holy building, that he had taken a room at the inn opposite, where she might dine and rest, before they returned to Flor. Eliset thanked him politely, and nodded politely to all the other little mutterings to do with her comfort, and the muted assurance, implied rather than spoken, that he would have an hour or so's business in the city, and would not be sharing the room with her. Some ten yards from the church door, Eliset burst into a peal of wild laughter that rang upward into the dome.

Her husband looked at her in alarm, clearly pondering if the day's excitements had proved too much.

Recovering herself, she only said, "Did you sleep well last night, Roilant?"

"I? Oh, yes—very deeply, in fact."

Through the veil, she seemed on the point of some revelation, some sinister promise, perhaps, but restrained herself.

"I am hungry," she said.

So they went to the inn, and there he left her, going off to attend to his city business.

Part, if not all, of his city business was sitting at the other inn across the way, a cup of wine before it, a bundle at its side in which were packed a priestly vestment and a dark intermingling bush of false hair and beard.

As Cyrion sat down, Roilant-Veritas, with yet another wig pulled fast on his head and sweat starting under it, looked up.

"I did not," announced Roilant, "enjoy that."

"You wished to be discreet. The fewer players the better, so you must play one part yourself. Besides, I thought you rather expected to. Enjoy it. Something about 'bitter humor.' "

"I mistook myself. It was also hellishly difficult. The old priest had agreed to my hour of private prayer in the chapel, then, when I arrived, began to make objections."

"So you doubled his bribe."

"Tripled it."

"Ah."

"No, I do not find it amusing. That is the first time I saw her, since I was fifteen. Even through her veil—Cyrion!"

"Well?"

"I cannot believe her capable of this villainy."

Cyrion rested his rounded face on his lean hand.

"You can always go back in my stead and make full confession, my dear. She would no doubt love it. She herself has quite a tart sense of humor. On the other hand, if your other suspicions are correct, tonight should confirm them."

"They will attempt to kill you."

"No, they will attempt to kill *you*, as gleefully represented by myself. For murderers, their way of going about it is intriguingly gross. I cannot think they would be any more subtle in their timing."

Roilant woollily scowled into his wine.

"I botched the service."

"Of course. You were meant to, surely? The whole essence being that it should, in all ways reasonable, be invalid. However, it was close enough for the layman to think it sound. I was, incidentally, captivated by your prayer. To compare our union to the mating of bees. You know, naturally, that after mating, the male bee is shed like a glove, and drops dead upon the ground?"

Roilant had paled. "I did not—Do you suppose you should continue with this? The danger is considerable."

"As each of us has known for some while. The plan proceeds toward a goal of discovery. And it would be a shame to spoil their fun."

"But Eliset," Roilant broke off. "Tonight she thinks herself your wife. Cyrion, you will not—"

The long hennaed brows rose like the wings of angels. His look, even in disguise, was so quintessentially Cyrionesque that Roilant was defeated by it, and grinned.

"I suppose," conceded Roilant, "she is scarcely innocent."

"You may also suppose that I will scarcely be allowed to get so far."

Alone in her private room, Eliset had taken off her veil, but did not rest. She paced about, now to the table with its half-eaten repast, now to the narrow window with its uninformative view of the inner courtyard. Her step was light and volatile, and her eyes had a look of banked fire. Only once did she glance at the couch that had been prepared for her should she wish to lie down on it. Without inflection then, but aloud, she said: "Whoever I may bed with tonight, Cousin Roilant, it will not be with you."

In the later afternoon, some four hours of daylight left in which to undertake the two-hour homeward journey, the wedding party deserted the inn. The order of advance remained the same: Cyrion, floppily piled on the mule, next the four hired men with Eliset's litter, and Harmul bringing up the rear. Having not profited by other example, Harmul was drunk. The four hired men were not entirely sober. Somewhat unevenly, therefore, the small cortege passed from the square, swayed through the arched tunnel, and wandered dreamily along the Street of Smokes, among the incense vapors and the poppy fumes. Thence through the Street of Birds, where Harmul saw fit to imitate each whistle and tweet, and thus down Silk Street, where Harmul inefficiently stole a floating, banded scarf with silver stars worked on it, yells and curses broke out, and Cousin Roilant, with a heavy-eyed frown, reimbursed the shopkeeper and wondered loudly what Harmul could require with such an item. Harmul haughtily did not vouchsafe either answer or thanks. They resumed.

Amid the striped awnings of the market-place, a new commotion ensued.

It happened very suddenly. A basket of dates fell in their path, another of figs, and another of oranges. A fruit-seller in a panic followed, and an un-cage-full of incontinent doves. Picking over the sticky litter on one hand, and with feathered and other debris whirling about their heads, the mule and Cousin Roilant were discommoded, the hired men pumped their free arms and the litter joggled, while Harmul screamed at the world and God. In the midst of invective, squabbling, laughter, fruit and fluff, a meaty muscular man hurled himself from the crowd and, with a single grab, pulled Cousin Roilant from his mule.

They landed on the dates, squelched, and rolled, grunting. The amusing scene, which most of the bystanders had stepped back to admire and encourage, changed its character as a long grey knife sliced upward in the air. Screams came then, but no aid. The strong and weighty man pinned the floundering redhead beneath him, pummelling the podgy face into submission, flinging up the arm at the end of which the knife had readied itself, like some horrible iron tooth, to bite.

The fang tore down.

There was a complementary wail from the crowd, followed by a gasp.

The ginger young man, who had seemed beyond redemption, had somehow incredibly twisted himself away. The bite of the knife had met with full impact the hard surface of the ground—and the blade snapped from the hilt.

With a cry, the big man leapt up. Without a backward grimace, he dashed into the crowd, tossing obstructions inanimate or human from his path. He was soon lost to view, and if any pursued, they did not catch him up.

Cyrion, in the person of Roilant, got to his knees. Holding a date-stained cloth to his mouth, he climbed to his feet. Thereby rather muffled, he thanked the litter-bearers and Harmul, with surprising dryness of wit, for their help.

Eliset had at last persuaded the bearers, formerly too interested in the fight, to put the litter down. She thrust through the curtains and went to her cousin, ignoring the gapings of the throng.

"Are you hurt?"

"Not to death. My regrets."

"What?" she said.

"A broken tooth or two. He did not kill me. As you hoped he would."

Her face through the veil was flamingly cold.

"Neither a seemly time, nor place, to jest," she said.

"You mean this was not your plan? It did seem somewhat crude. Also a little premature. I had thought you would wait for the modesty of darkness. . . . .cool refreshing steel slipped between the sheets."

"Roilant," she said, "the man was a thief."

"Who stole nothing, nor attempted to steal."

The crowd was enthralled. It stood about and smiled upon them, the angry aristocratic young woman with a torch of hair and cheeks which burned as if to set her veil on fire, and the tall yet dumpy young man whose hair had already caught."

"Are you telling me," she said, "you judge I wed you only to have you assassinated?"

"Why not? That is what all the rumors promised."

"We have had this out before. You discounted rumor as base, I thought."

"Did you?"

"If not, why are you so stupid as to be here, and to have married me?"

"A death wish?" murmured Cyrion. "For sure, wifey dear, now we are as one, my life is not," he gazed at the detritus about his boots, paused unworthily before the obvious, and added, "a fig."

And then, stunning her worse than if he had slapped her, he removed the cloth from his lips and bestowed upon her the most beautiful and malicious smile she had ever beheld. So beautiful, his whole face changed and ceased to be Roilant's, so malign, she took half a step backward before she knew what she did. And, to her absolute and inappropriate horror, trod on a fallen orange which promptly burst, causing the crowd practically to expire of joy.

Controlling herself with an effort, yet succeeding, Eliset—having been white, next scarlet—was now grey.

"If that is what you think, then," she said, "or if it is your joke, either way, you are contemptible. The damage is done, but may be undone. I am your wife in name only, and will remain so, in name only. Come to the door of my chamber and you will find it barred." A few in the crowd cheered lovingly. She ignored them. "Go back," she concluded, "to your fine estate at Heruzala, without me. Go court some mindless woman who will accept your suit, if any is fool enough. Yes. You shall have a divorce. Gladly. And nothing else." At which she turned on the goggling, wine-muzzy Harmul and cried: "Get down."

Harmul, with a dizzy nod, sprawlingly dismounted. Eliset, with a glorious acrobatic agility that managed three instantaneous things—to mount in a sea-wave of skirts, to achieve and maintain a side-saddle posture with only one fixed stirrup, and to uphold the while total decorum—won the ultimate heart of her large audience. Raging, she smacked the mule into a gallop, carving an exit through the market and out of the gate, amidst a hail of adoring flowers.

Flor had been decked for celebration in an abstracted way. Brown palm branches and rangey flowers stood in urns, and a perfumed candle burned within the roof pavilion, surrounded by dead moths.

"It was before half the city he said it."

The girl's voice trembled with alarm or shame, or both.

"To the delight of Cassireia." Mevary.

"But do you take my meaning?"

A pause.

"No one," said Mevary, "will remember the gist, only the show."

"If he is suddenly dead," she replied, steady now as the iron shine on the assassin's blade had been, "if that happens, Mevary, they might."

"Then," said Mevary, "we must wish our darling Cousin Roilant a long and healthy life. By God, what a nuisance he is becoming. How one wishes the wretched dagger had not broken."

There was after that a wide silence and a kind of crackle on the air of the roof, that made itself known, along with the smell of scent and flutter of dim lights across the dusk, to anyone who might be standing on the stair below the terrace.

The new wife had come home to Flor alone, and exhausted, almost a full hour before her husband trundled up, with his lower face wrapped in a cloth, Harmul walking sulkily a quarter of a mile behind, and neither bearers nor litter with them, or due.

Eliset, by then, was in her apartment. Mevary had leaned over various carious balustrades and sticks of crumbling furniture, and interrogated. All signs of debauch had left him. It was Cousin Roilant who seemed in need of medicine.

"I was attacked, probably by some fanatic or cutpurse. Being shocked, I said something irrational."

"So I gather."

"I hope she will forgive me. I meant it as an irony, and was taken in earnest. I suspect also a tooth has been broken. I can hardly move my lips for the pain."

"You had better save your talk for Eliset, then. I think she means to freeze you to death tonight."

What was visible of Roilant's face around the cloth, moped.

Now, washed, combed, ringed and dressed untidily in unsuitable splendor, the survivor of the Cassireian murder attempt stood on the stone stair, heard out the brief drama above, then went into his habitual announcing stumble.

"That stair," said Cousin Roilant, tumbling up on to the terrace.

"Its dangerous?" asked Mevary, helpfully. With the lit and latticed pavilion behind him, he was a figure of elegant menace, clad in the fourth set of impeccable new clothes he had so far sported. His eyes looked yellow as the lamp flames, and heightened as they did, as the dark blue of the sky became black.

Cousin Roilant went forward.

"Is she—?"

"Here? Yes. I persuaded her. I told her you were sorry."

"*I* told her I was sorry."

"Well," Mevary was bashful, "she has known me longer."

"And I am her husband."

"*Yes!* So you are. And how is the poor assaulted face?"

Cousin Roilant touched it, nervously.

"The gum has swollen. I shall undoubtedly lose the tooth."

Mevary tutted.

Under the—now clean—continuously patting napkin, the round face indeed seemed rounder still, the lips pushed up by the inner swelling and unable quite to close. Cyrion-Roilant's speech was also thick, and accomplished with difficulty.

"And on your wedding night, too."

Cyrion went by him, and entered the pavilion.

Eliset sat in her robe of cream silk and heliotrope, outstaring a lamp. He mumbled. She acknowledged the mumble with a frigid nod.

"A toast," said Mevary, stepping in, refilling his cup, beaming. "To love."

The cold dishes were already on the tables, kept at a suitable temperature maybe by Eliset's glances. The rest of the dinner arrived shortly with Zimir. His head was haphazardly bandaged from the cut the breaking oil jar had given him. Between himself and swollen Cousin Roilant (as Mevary pointed out), the place began to resemble a hospital.

"He fears," said Mevary to Eliset, "he will lose a tooth."

Eliset said nothing.

"He fears he will also lose a wife," said Mevary. "Come, my duck. Having drawn him here by means of magical force, you really have to put up with him."

Her head went up. She stared at Mevary.

He turned away. "Look how distraught you have made the poor man. He will eat and drink nothing."

Eliset rose and walked out of the pavilion on to the terrace. There she stood, lamp-brushed on the darkness, ignoring them.

Mevary grinned. "Try this raisin loaf. It really is almost edible."

"I am finding it very difficult—"

"To eat. Drink, then. Dull pain and heartbreak with the blood of the vine."

Without a sound, like a gazelle, a second female figure appeared on the roof, dark for the other's gold. Jhanna, who bore in her hands a great curved dish of basted meats. She came into the pavilion with it, and set it down in the midst of the tables.

Mevary seemed displeased, his smooth surface ran off him.

"Go wait on Eliset, not here."

Jhanna bowed low, eastern fashion. The obeisance was so complex as to be a caricature.

"It is for my lady to dismiss me."

Still and straight as Eliset outside, Jhanna poised herself before him.

"Then she shall."

Mevary strode out on to the roof.

Jhanna, a sable lily, swept down toward the table, brushing Cyrion with her perfumed hair.

"*Lord.* Do you have the vial I gave you?"

"Uh—oh, yes, I have it somewhere."

"About you? If so, then use the potion in the enchantress' cup. Now, before they return."

"I have already," said Cyrion, carefully through his swollen face, "used it."

She drew in a deep breath. Her hands glided over the table and she offered him, for the sake of pretense, a dish of bread.

"You are wise, lord. Wise."

Cyrion glanced toward one of the doorways. Mevary's voice was spilling on the starry air.

"I, care for that slut?"

"Slut," Jhanna whispered. "Yes, a slut when he is by. Watch them well, lord. And watch your cup."

She glided out, and was gone down the stair like a ghost.

Cyrion leaned forward himself, now, making a brief tally, so it seemed, of the plates and cups set at the three places. Flor being Flor, though each cup was matched with the others, each, due to wear and tear, had some distinguishing mark. That set before Mevary's place had a sizable piece missing from the brim, and that set before Eliset's, unsipped, boasted a white pock on the bowl. The cup Zimir had laid out for Roilant, and which Mevary had filled—both before his arrival—had a roughness high on the stem, invisible but immediately discernible by touch.

Since he would eat nothing, and the jugs were communal, a murderer would have to see to it the physic was dropped in his goblet. There was now, since the fiasco at Cassireia and his public declaration, every good reason for an intelligent murderer to see to it Cousin Roilant's death appeared natural. With the widow's fortune, the law might be bribed, but it would need some seemliness to back it. Which meant a death without a wound, a death by poison. And doubtless a story to add ballast: The ill-starred Roilant had been exposed to the infectious madness of which the slave Jobel had perished. It was not uncommon in such cases for more than one to succumb.

Still on his own, Cyrion took the opportunity to sniff at his cup. Nothing unusual seemed to be present in it, as yet, but then, the overpowering odor of the scented candle would blot anything out. He considered which of them might have lit it.

Outside, in the humming, glittering dark, Mevary and Eliset had drawn very close. There was a faint crystal rasp—the pearly girdle coming unknotted and falling down.

Cyrion exchanged his rough-stemmed cup for Mevary's chipped one. And sat back to wait.

Mevary soon after returned; Eliset, minus the girdle, a minute later. The meal was resumed, in as much as it had ever begun. Mevary continued to eat. Eliset and Cyrion continued not to.

In a moment or so, Mevary reached for his cup. He raised it, looked at it, and raised his eyebrows instead. Putting the cup down again, he turned to Cyrion with an arch smile. "Oh, indeed?" said Mevary.

Cyrion was blank.

Eliset was an icon.

"It would seem," said Mevary, "I do not have my own cup any more. Do you have your own cup, Eliset?"

The icon glanced down, and glazed her wine with a layer of frost.

"I have no idea."

"And you, my ginger pudding. Whose cup do you have?"

"Absurd," muttered Cyrion from the side of his swollen mouth.

"Hmm." Mevary did not drink.

Without warning, awful squeaky music came skidding from below and from some form of implement—conceivably, from the quality of the noise, a plucked mousetrap.

Rising with an oath, Mevary left the pavilion and shouted down into the court. The uncouth melodics ceased.

"Roilant," said Eliset icily, "I see you are still intent on this pose—our victim." She leaned forward across the tables. With a deft movement, she exchanged Mevary's cup, which had been Roilant's, with her own. "So, we will poison you?" She lifted Roilant's cup, her eyes resting on 'Roilant' balefully. As she drank his wine he came to his feet. Then checked. Slamming down the half-empty cup, she said, "Then, if it was doctored, I shall die, shall I not?"

"Yes," he said.

"I am a fool then. As I was a fool to marry you. But married we are, I believe. No. I shall not lock my door against you. Mevary has—persuaded me I must be dutiful. So, you may come to me when you wish. If you are not altogether too afraid of me."

Taking her snowstorm with her, she went out, passing Mevary as he reentered. This time, she moved on down the stair.

Mevary looked at the cups.

"Now," he said. "Let me get this fixed. You have my cup, I have Eliset's, and Eliset has yours. Since she and I are the poisoners and Eliset has obviously sampled your cup, we can deduce your cup to be safe. Mine, which you now have, should also be safe, since I have been using it since sunset. Eliset's drink, however, now passed to me—this seems a little cloudy. Can it be, dear Pud, you yourself have taken up the poisoning trade?" And Mevary poured the wine from Eliset's goblet indiscriminately on to the floor and cushions.

"Thus," said Mevary, with unreassuring briskness. Going back to the door of the pavilion, he yelled, "Zimir, Harmul, more cups. Lots and lots of them. You really are," he added encouragingly to Cyrion, "much sharper than I gave you credit for."

Cyrion looked affronted.

He looked more affronted still when the ragged servants came scampering up the stair with ten or so cups between them, all a match, and all randomly pocked and chipped and roughened, and dumped them on the central table. Mevary, pushing the dishes of food out of the way, filled the goblets broadcast from an upturned jug. He then, spilling and clinking, moved them many times about each other, his own and Cyrion's own, and even Eliset's, now refilled, included in the clanking medley.

"Now," said Mevary, "we each pick a cup, dear cousin, and drink it down."

Cyrion rose, with a spluttered avowal of departure.

Mevary snapped his fingers.

The surprisingly strong hands of Zimir descended on Cyrion's shoulders, and set about thrusting him back in his seat. Cyrion sat. As he did so, a thin dirty knife blade manifested two inches from his left eye.

"It could now be any cup, could it not? Any cup could contain that lethal ingredient I added by sleight of hand in front of you. "Since," said Mevary, you reckon me a felon, I will no longer make a mock of you by dissembling. She has wedded you, she will get your goods when you die. All your entrancing little fortune. So, *drink*."

"No—" Cousin Roilant struggled, and the filthy knife came an inch closer.

"It seems it must be 'yes,' " said Mevary, woven all of silk.

Cyrion stopped struggling. "All right." He went limp. "Which?"

"Oh, any, any. This is play, remember. You shall have every cup on the table, until you reach the deadly one. Then you shall have that."

Harmul giggled with nervous excitement. Zimir could be felt to be smiling.

Cyrion picked a cup at random. It was not Mevary's—there was a chip missing from it, but at another place. He bore it upward and flung it over his shoulder into the face of Zimir.

There was an explosion of activity behind Cyrion, and the threatening knife went away. Rushing up from his chair, Cyrion went after it. As he took the blade from the boy's flailing grip, Mevary, with a howl of scorn, drew his sword.

"Knife to my sword? You should have come to table armed in the old barbaric way, Roilant, dear."

He stepped between Cyrion and the table, and the sword drove Cyrion back.

"Meaning to spill *all* the wine? Oh no. Too easy, sweet Pud."

The dainty first motion of the sword, the second driving arc, informed one at once Mevary was a swordsman of some excellence. Cyrion moved backward, defending himself, as in a recent story, with the hopeless knife. The sword spat toward him and he glanced aside. Harmul dived from the area with a yelp. Latticework went by.

Cyrion was out of the pavilion. Mevary, kicking Zimir and a table from his way, hastened after him.

On the roof, under the large black sky with its spangled audience of stars, the soft air pleasant after the fug of the candle, both men paused, as if to appreciate their new arena.

"Of course, my sword might be envenomed too."

Mevary flirted his blade across the night, pointed a star with it, and sent it stooping like a falcon's wing.

Cousin Roilant, with unexpected agility, avoided its edge. Then he threw the knife.

It should have hit Mevary, and would have done if the wolf cousin had not been so very agile himself. He was gone like thought, and the knife went over the parapet of the terrace, into the night. Mevary, too contemptuous to be amused, leapt forward, the sword singing as it led the way.

Cousin Roilant, in a beautiful backward spring, eluded him, and met with something else. Something dimly shining, spooled out at ankle-height from the parapet, and across the terrace, like a long and slender serpent. Feet snagged, Cousin Roilant went down and Mevary, stalled, amused after all, strolled to him. While Zimir and Harmul bounded from the pavilion, dutiful thralls, and fell on the prone man, ignoring the flailing of his booted feet that had been snarled by Eliset's girdle of purple and pearls.

Cousin Roilant stopped fighting. He lay and was jeered at, while Mevary went back to the pavilion. But when Mevary returned, bearing a cup of wine, Cousin Roilant began to show fresh tendencies to leave.

Mevary kneeled and offered the cup.

"I found the right one. My cup. Which you exchanged for your own. As obviously I intended. Either I poisoned it then, when I had finished drinking, or just now. I wonder which. Whatever it is, drink up. *Enjoy, celebrate*. It is your wedding night."

Cousin Roilant battled a while longer, the two boys rolling on his arms like dogs, barking and cursing him, until Mevary's unsheathed sword came back and kissed the fighter's windpipe.

"Either you drink," said Mevary with great seriousness, "or I open your neck and force it down your throat *that* way."

Cousin Roilant appeared to give in.

Released by Mevary's servants, he sat up and held out his hand, with livid, bulbous dignity, for the cup.

"Quaff it all, now," said Mevary. "Like a good little boy."

Tilting back his ginger head, Cyrion poured the entire contents of the cup between his lips, closed his mouth, and swallowed with a dry strained gulp.

Mevary stepped back.

And stepped back even farther as the plump figure, eyes starting, gained its feet and hurtled by him and, for once sure-footed, went tearing down the stair to the inner court.

The two servants, hooting, pelted after him. In a moment, there was a scuffle below.

"We have him!"

"Trying to put his fingers down his throat—"

Mervary looked down from aloft.

"One sip," declared Mevary, "would be sufficient. Too late to try to bring it back. Better go to Eliset, and die in comfort."

Harmul and Zimir, letting the unfortunate go, careered between the empty fountains, honking with mirth.

On the roof, with the swordsman's elegant economy, Mevary sheathed his sword.

A quarter of an hour afterwards, the bridegroom smote on the chamber door of his bride, and on being admitted, crooned the romantic words: "I am poisoned."

"No," she replied with asperity, "*I* am the one who is poisoned."

Cyrion shut the door and leaned on it. The swelling seemed to have gone down, and left his face to its recently normal pudgy state. He said, "Gentle Cousin Mevary openly threatened me and—shall I say?—invoked me to drink the cup of wine that had originally been his. He had predicted all my moves, it seems. The exchange was intended."

"Unless we had also poisoned your own cup for good measure."

"You would not have drunk from it if you had."

"Would I not?" She regarded him with disdain. "Is my life so lovely I should cling to it? Perhaps I no longer cared what became of me."

"If you reckoned on dying, why are you dressed for the nuptial couch?" inquired Cyrion.

Eliset stared a moment, then lowered her eyes and turned away. The diaphanous robe turned with her, and the bright veil of hair.

"And if you yourself expected to die, *Roilant*, why are *you* here?"

"One has," said Cyrion sensibly, "to spend one's last minutes somewhere. Why should I spare you the theatre of my final agony? I may even, in my death throes, manage to damage some of your sparse furnishings."

"No matter. I shall have all your estate at Heruzala soon to comfort me."

"Shall you?"

She turned back to look at him.

"Or can it all have been a lie? Perhaps you have no estates. Perhaps your widow will be penniless."

She seemed schooled now, and gorgeous, the center of the amber candleshine that filled a room which, even with its signs of decline and decay, drew from her a curious depth of beauty—the power of sorcerous illusion?

"Why not," said Cyrion, seating himself in a high-backed chair, "lighten my ultimate moments with a few fascinating truths. Why not tell me about Mevary."

"Mevary—is Mevary."

"Excuse me. I meant the first Mevary, his father. Your uncle."

In a strange gesture, for she had made no sound attempt at modesty before, she pulled the folds of the loose robe together, so they became opaque.

"He was my guardian until I was seventeen."

"At which time he died. How was that?"

"He drowned," she said softly.

"At sea."

"In the bath house. In the kalidarium. He—" she looked away a second time and moved toward the window. "He was a drunkard, and disgustingly drunk he went to his bath and drowned there. Disgustingly, I am sure."

"You loved him dearly."

"As you perceive."

"Did you kill him?"

"No. I had dreamed of it, now and then. I did not do it."

"His ghost walks about the house, did you know?"

"I have heard it does. His ghost. Old Tabbit's, who was my nurse. Remusans galore, and sea demons who claw their way up the cliff by night—" she swung about and came hurrying back to him, dropped to her knees, bowed her head and said, through the fall of glistening hair, "You deserve the truth. Your damnable stupidity deserves it. Should Roilant be told? Yes, he should be told. I never meant to deceive him." She looked up and met his gaze sardonically. "I will tell you. Mevary will have intimated I am no innocent. But not, I think, that his father made me his mistress on the day I was fourteen. It was less than a month after my own father's death. It happened here, in this chamber. Over by that chest. My uncle came into the room, and inside five minutes he had forced me. When it was done, he asked if I had liked it, and if I loved him. When I said 'no,' he struck me. Then he asked me again, and I said, 'yes.' I learn quickly, do you see. For three years I gave him the lip-service his vanity required, and what his flesh required I gave too. I welcomed him always eagerly. I even learned the customs of his appetites. You will find me knowledgeable, if soiled."

"And the second Mevary," said Cyrion stoically. "How did he find you?"

"As you say, he is my lover."

"That you love as your god."

She studied him with a keen blue intelligence for some while.

"So you heard that, too? And believed it as he did? No. He is not my god. I do not love him or enjoy him, or even like his company. In the tradition of his kind father, he raped me. I was used to it by then. Like his father, also, his lovemaking is little better than a rape. And like his father he is petty, jealous, a beater of women and horses, and one who responds well to worship. So, I worship him."

"Why?"

"Did I not just now tell you why? How else was I to live here? How else was I to live?"

"Ah, yes. You could not bear to let the inheritance go, any ruinous inch of it. So you endured. And waited for me to honor my vow."

"You." She glared now. "I had hoped that marriage would bring me the gift of peace."

"After you had dispatched me."

She shook her head as if confused, searching. "I almost feared Mevary might consider such a thing. But I do not think he has the metal for murder. Anything else, but not quite that. It asks a kind of vile strength I do not judge he has." She sat back on her heels, frowning at Cyrion, then growing very still. Finally she said: "What is it?"

"What do you think it is?"

"You are ill."

"I told you at the door what I was."

"Poison? I do not credit that."

"He told me I should not get rid of it. It seems he was correct. Aesthetically, you have little to worry over. It will not resemble Jobel's demise. What splendid luck for us both."

She stared in earnest now. The low lamp, the candles, picked out the threads of sweat which were slowly running from his hair, across his cheeks and throat. His hands gripped the arms of the chair. His lips, so speedily cured of their swelling, were nearly the color of slate.

"What," she said, "should I do?"

"A suitable prayer?" he got out. It was now becoming noticeably difficult. "I would not advise you to kiss me farewell."

The pain, for demonstrably there was pain, must have increased. His body stretched, contorted, his face buckled around the rictus of his mouth, and his eyes froze in their sockets. A trickle of blood came from one corner of his lips, which closed in a smiling grimace.

The last Cyrion saw of Eliset, as the considerable agony dissolved his vision, was her upright figure backing away along the room, gold into gold. Then the terminal link snapped within him like the breaking of a stem. The world went in a blaze of black lightning, during which he undoubtedly screamed.

Eliset, having reached the window again, halted, the scream raw in her ears. She seemed to be waiting.

When she went back to him to be sure, he had relaxed, falling sideways across the arm of the chair, eyes shut, faintly smiling, his breathing ended and his heart stopped.

FOUR

The sight of a solitary rider trotting up through the orchards of Flor in the glass-edged sunlight of midmorning, did not serve as a tonic for the tumbled household. The night before, there had been an unusually energetic coming and going, opening and closing of doors. Not everyone was in the picture. Those who were, were not necessarily sanguine. The lone rider with his charge, delivered without mercy at the gate into the unchoice paws of Zimir, turned out indeed to be a harbinger of fate.

As Zimir eddied toward the stable-arch, he was apprehended suddenly, and in rather sinister mode, by a tawny figure. The packet, being demanded, changed hands. It proclaimed itself the property of Roilant of Beucelair and was promptly opened by Mevary. For the very good reason that Cousin Roilant would no longer show much interest in it. It contained two papers. The first, a parchment signed and sealed by three lawyers, bore witness to the validity of the second paper, which was but the copy of another, secreted in the vaults of some suitable edifice at Heruzala. The second packet bore Roilant's own seal, and was duly opened in turn.

With hindsight, it required perhaps no genius to guess the contents. Roilant's paper, with many a flowery legal phrase, gave notice that, at his sudden death—should it occur—all his estates, moneys and chattels would devolve upon no lesser person than King Malban, his esteemed liege lord, for the benefit of his armies, his charitable works, and the maintenance of his kingdom of Heruzala.

It was the one and only and utter way in which a rich man might cheat his heirs and his dependants of any right to his wealth. To leave all either to God or to the King. The King, being nominally there in person, was the safer bet.

Maybe an hour later, voices rustled in the jungle of the orchard, under a mulberry tree sticky with wasps. It was hard to be sure of the two persons, male and female, who sizzled there in the hot shadows, like a couple of wasps themselves. But the voices were remarkably like those of Mevary and Eliset.

"I gave him nothing. The coward died of fright," said the

man who sounded like Mevary, and with all Mevary's irritability.

"Did you not, beloved?" the woman said caressingly, with just the same hint of venom as had been evident about her that other night, when they had commented on a supposedly drugged sleeper.

"No, I did not. He only thought I did. And choked of fear. Unless you—"

"*I*?" A wealth of innocent astonishment.

Testingly, he: "Why *not* you? Oh sweet lady cousin, you have an odd way of going on."

Passionately, she: "You know I adore you. You know I worship you. Could I go against your wishes? Do I not deny all things and all people and all faith, that you shall realize your desires?"

"Oh, very well. But to get this damned legal nonsense—the king to have the fortune of Beaucelair."

"And we not to have it after all?"

"Look a little further. If the Pudding made such a will, wresting all from his widow and relations for the king, it means bloody Malban himself must see Roilant suspected us. No sooner is Roilant known to be dead, than we are branded his murderers."

Arrogantly, she: "The widow will be branded before you are."

Jaundiced, he: "Too fine a point. With our plans where they are, to bring in any uncertain element—"

"Then bring in none."

"What?"

Between the boughs thick with leaves and fruit and stinging insects, the flash of two pairs of pale eyes glaring at each other, sensual, antagonistic, eager.

"If Roilant's death will bring present trouble," she said, "let him, for the present, not die."

"You are late for that."

"Not at all. He is in residence, or he rode away—depending on who sends after him, or if any do. Meanwhile, put the body to bed and forget it."

"And reveal all with another new grave?"

"No. There is room in my father Gerris' stone tomb, is there not, an extra place, unfilled? Put the corpse in there tonight, and close the lid again. Harmul and Zimir will not anyway dare to speak. By your account, they are well-incriminated. While that woman you keep as your slave, that simpering bitch, you can order her and hold her silent. Can you not?"

A laugh. "Yes. You are very clever, dulcet love."

Then other sounds, and her voice like a needle: "Here? My bucolic lover. Do you recall how you raped me, first?"

"And you," he said, "do you recall how well you liked it?"

Her own laugh was very like the brush of cat's fur, and all the green shadows ran together.

The shining sea, running into the under-cutting of the cliffs, blue as the dyes of Tynt and garlanded with foam, sought caves and funnels and mysterious avenues, filled them, and then was drawn away again. The day leapt from the brink of the land and raced across the water. The horizon drank the sun, a sea-goddess taking bloody sacrifice.

That night at Flor was marked by tidal swells and ebbings, a nightingale or two, and some metallic clinks, some levering shifting noises, three or four unpleasant grating sounds, a thud, a further period of grating and levering, and a stony *crunch.*

In Cassireia over the hills, such an interlude might have been less audible, where all the city night doors and shutters slammed, mounted men rode pell-mell on the governor's business, drunks rejoiced or regurgitated, dogs complained and insane cockerels, constantly misled by the endless rekindling of lights and occasional minor arson, crew urgently. To this orchestration Roilant had been listening, as on other insomniac nights at the temple inn. As the dawn began to come and the cocks began once more to scream, either in embarrassed discovery, or affront, he rose, sat, and started to pen a letter to his lost lady at Heruzala. But the words would not come. Between himself and the calming, unexceptional image, another inserted itself like a slender knife. Eliset.

The dawn, according to the writings of the prophet Hokannen, was a time of purity and blamelessness amongst the creatures of the earth. The lion stole to the desert pool, and lapped there harmlessly beside the deer. The bird flew to greet the sun, the returning promise of God's love and forgiveness. Sunrise, like a great water, brought a washing away of all sins. It was possible to begin anew.

In the desert, where the prophet, in the fashion of most prophets, had dwelled so long, accompanied perhaps by the bronze-haired Zilumi, such a vision was conceivable. The coming of the day demanded only meditation, prayer and inner debate, now and then augmented by expeditions for the purpose of robbing bee's nests, or the devouring of defenseless locusts.

In Cassireia, dawn brought only further cacophany, and presently Roilant's unwritten letter was put aside.

Heavy feet on the stairs demonstrated the move had been wise. Loud knocking on the door added to the conviction. Roilant opened it, and a large man, composed of pressed fat and muscle and the rigors of a longish ride, entered the room.

He was recognizable as the larger Heruzin servant who had accompanied Cyrion-as-Roilant to Flor, gone off with the mules, and then gone off to the village, and later gone off altogether to the city. He was also recognizable, being now reasonably static, as the mad attacker with the knife who had dragged Cyrion from his mount in the market, and failed to stab with a pre-arranged, breakable knife blade. He had been, at Cyrion's suggestion, Roilant's hired servant for five days.

"What," said Roilant, "has happened?"

"The worst that could," said the hired man. That was his courtesy, he was merely doing a job of work. It was all one to him, so long as he was paid.

"What do you mean, 'The worst'?"

"Something odd went on, during the wedding night, and not odd in the proper way, either. There were all sorts of runnings about after that. Next day, Mevary was busy. Then I lost him. Found him again coming back alone from the orchards—he had some other business there, I should think, him and her. Funny how some of them like the open air. . . . Then evening came on and finally the moon set. Shortly after, a party of four went out of the back door, by the bath house, into the graveyard, and opened up one of the tombs with iron levers. In went a new body."

"My God. Whose?"

"Whose do you think?"

"You mean he—"

"There was precious little light, but I had myself up in that leaning wreck of a tower, and saw it from above. There was a small tree in the way, but that delicate fancy kind; easy to look through the branches. I could tell your Cousin Mevary, and the two boys. And she was there, even without the moon, her fair hair showed like a banner. The body was wrapped up in a sheet, but it was full of holes and his face was uncovered. I could see enough to know *him,* and then there was a dull shine from the rings on the left hand, even in starlight. He was heavy. There was some bother between him and the lid. She had to help. Then Mevary and the two boys pushed the lid back on, and they went away."

"Merciful God. *Are you sure?*"

"Sure as sure. I was only about fifteen feet above him, and not far off. It was Cyrion, and he was dead as a dead man can be."

Roilant sat down again. His hands were shaking.

"It—was always a chance. He admitted that."

"He left you a contingent plan, then."

"Yes. Oh God. I hoped to keep out of it. And Cyrion—I reckoned him indestructible."

"A tricky devil," agreed the hired man. "But even foxes get caught."

"I blame myself."

The hired man was bored. He had been a soldier, and was used to sudden death as a commonplace rather than an occasion.

After a dose more dialogue, Roilant dismissed him to the agreed lodging, and himself began to pace the room. He had the awful feeling of a man who has inadvertently caused a major calamity. Cyrion. That Cyrion was dead was unbelievable. Roilant did *not* believe it. He recaptured, frantically, the caravaneer's tale of the Knights of the Dove. How Cyrion had feigned profound unconsciousness. Assuming such magic were feasible, might he not be equally able to feign death?

If Roilant had witnessed the sequence on the terrace roof, he might have laid even these hopes aside. The wine had been very definitely poisoned, whoever would not admit to poisoning it. And Cyrion had poured the entire contents of the cup into his mouth, following the move with a huge and painful gulp. With a small amount of fluid in the mouth, it might be possible to swallow and take none down. But Cyrion had absorbed in bulk. Nor was it wise to disregard Mevary's playful words—"one sip would be sufficient." If the bane were truly that inimical, (and many were), even sucked in and immediately spat forth, the residue that had touched the inner mouth and tongue, mingling with the saliva, would be fatal.

A later drama, acted out behind the closed door of Eliset's apartment, might additionally have unreassured Roilant. During the drama, Cyrion's body had been subjected to many sorts of test then current for the ascertainment of life signs. But, pummelled, tickled, burnt and pierced with pins, it had stayed flaccid, and the mirror held against the face never once misted with breath.

There was also a further objection to Cyrion's problematic survival. One living, having been interred inside the airless tomb, would very quickly suffocate. It had required three pairs of hands to move the tomb's cover, and tools besides. The stonework was solid, and had also a prone stone figure on it to help weight it down. One who wished to leave might find himself detained. Dead or alive, Cyrion's future did not seem very rosy.

Jhanna had been weeping, quite violently, yet virtually in silence, a method she had learned perforce long ago. The ecstasy of tears had also been controlled for some while; this being the first leisure and opportunity she had had, since the death of Roilant of Beucelair, to give way to her emotions sure she would be undisturbed.

Her hysteria began and ended, however, with comparable suddenness. She was accustomed to deceptions, it had been essential to her, placed as she had been most of her life. She also possessed, when prepared to exercise it, enormous self-discipline. Once the summit of her passion had been reached, she diminished it. A minute more, and, dry-eyed and impervious, she turned to face the curtained doorway of her cell. As she did so, the mildest rasp sounded at her threshold. It might have been no more than a drift of dismembered foliage shuffling past in the afternoon breeze. Jhanna, wise in many things, knew it was not.

Soundless herself, she crossed the chamber and flung back the curtain. No one was there, yet lying on the threshold beyond the screen was a small folded packet. With caution she took it up, her light eyes wide, and her fingers sensitive. First the packet was turned, then sniffed. Then, gradually, opened.

A skein of glitter fell to the ground. Jhanna looked at it, then bent and picked it up again. A long silken scarf, sewn with stars, danced between her hands. The sort a lady might use to drape her gown or her hair. Ignoring her poor dress, sewn and patched across the breast after Jobel's maddened attack, Jhanna lifted the silk into the air and let it float down upon her head. The silver stars blinking, her silver eyes unblinking, she stepped over the sunken court and entered the open kitchen.

Harmul was busy at the ovens, clearing out the burnt charcoal. Or pretending to. After a moment or so, during which the girl said nothing and made no noise, Harmul, with apparent unwillingness, turned.

"Do you like," said Jhanna, "my veil?"

Harmul winced, and studied his unclean toes.

"Is it like the veil of a great lady?" inquired Jhanna sweetly. "I found it by my door, just now. A demon's gift. No one was there. Should I accept such a thing?"

Harmul writhed.

"I heard you say," said Harmul, "that you would like—would wish you had—might care for—" He faltered.

"A veil sewn with silver," said Jhanna, very very low. "But where did you come by such a veil?"

"In Cassireia. On the Street of Silk. I stole it."

"Ah!" True to her slavish childhood, she appreciated this. "And is it for me?"

"Yes."

"Then I thank you. But what do you desire in return?"

Harmul, in an attitude of frenzied worship, fell on his face.

Jhanna laughed again; this laugh was colder.

"Insurance for my love?" Because he was not looking up, he did not see her do it, he only heard her strong hands tear the veil in two fraying bits, which presently she dropped before him on the dirty floor. "I am not bought so easily," she said. "I know who it is you truly serve. Beware of me."

Harmul gave a frightened mumble. Before he could repeat or elaborate upon it, or Jhanna spit upon him, which she seemed likely momently to do, someone began to shout from the front of the house. Both recognized the voice of Zimir.

Harmul dashed up and sprinted away into the stable-yard,

and so through the other inner arch into the painted courtyard that faced the mansion. Jhanna followed more slowly.

Zimir, bored with casting stones at one of the blue lions of the cistern, had climbed up into a dying palm tree. From this position, he scanned over the mansion wall and out toward the orchards. He was not looking for anything in particular and so was rather surprised when something in particular emerged.

Glancing behind her, Jhanna perceived Mevary had come recklessly to one of the partly ruined long windows above the pillared entrance. He wore yet another ensemble of clothes, these the yellow of burned reeds, to match his eyes, possibly, and stood there, arrogant even in uncertainty. He had no eyes for her, and she, gazing at him, savored in that moment a vision of his death, bloody and conclusive.

Then she too looked out of the cloven gates, to see who or what approached.

They left the orchard trees in that intent, and riding rather quickly, entered the discerning range of her sight. Nine horsemen sprayed out three by three. At their head, two men, also well-horsed, one married to his steed with indifferent beauty but evident horsemanship. The other had an awkward seat and a sloppy appearance as he jounced there, heavily plump in his satins, his rings flashing. And the sun striking orange radiance from his hair.

It was enough to make the heart of Jhanna sear as if scalded. Enough to make her long for the talisman of green stone with which she protected herself from ghosts.

The hired soldier spoke first. With the addition of two days' growth of spectacular and genuine beard, he went unknown to any who had glimpsed him before in the person of servant or impromptu assassin. Flor to the hired soldier, however, which he had now ridden to thrice, and spied on in between, was becoming irksome.

He addressed in distaste the guttersnipe adolescents he had formerly skirmished with, since once more they were the only occupants of the painted court—Mevary and Jhanna had both disappeared.

"Go to your master and your mistress, and tell them Lord Roilant is here."

This time, the guttersnipes were not showing signs of fight.

They stared at the plump young gentleman of the ginger locks, and presently bolted.

It had been difficult, at a casual glance, to be sure who looked the more nervous, Harmul and Zimir, or Roilant.

From within the passages, courts and chambers of the mansion there now issued a disorientated deluge of eerie wails and door-slamming. Eventually, Zimir returned. He beckoned from between the leaves of the entrance, then fled once more.

Roilant dismounted. He was not quite as messy in this operation as Cyrion had been when portraying him. But almost. Three of the nine guardsmen also dismounted. The remaining six waited in attitudes of stern preparedness. They really were fighting-men. Though common mail was strictly illegal unless one's men were riding to the defense of the kingdom, under the aegis of the king, these wore sleeveless coats of quilted linen capable of resisting even arrows, iron caps, and generally bristled with blades. Over all was inscribed the crest of Heruzin Beucelair. Not merely guards, but Roilant's personal quota, armed to the teeth and obviously able to commit murder.

Roilant, with the hired soldier and the three guard, squeezed through the jammed-ajar doors, through the passage, and into the inner court.

Mevary was standing by the farther of the dead fountains. His tan, too, looked rather yellow, but he swept an insultingly pretentious bow, straightened, and held his ground. Wordlessly. His eyes went over Roilant, over and over again. Despite Cyrion's tactful denials under the hornbeam tree, he had made himself sufficiently superficially like the plump third cousin as to cause slight terror, in these circumstances.

"You, sir," said the hired soldier. "Are you Mevary of Flor?"

"Probably," said Mevary. "But I would like to know who this is, and why he cannot utter for himself."

Stung, Roilant regained some of the angry backbone that had got him here.

"I can utter. I am Roilant, your cousin."

Mevary's eyes twitched. Then he smiled.

"We were expecting you some days ago."

"And I arrived some days ago, did I not?"

Mevary became transfixed, mastered himself, and waved one hand in the air.

"Did you?"

"You supposed that I did. A man, calling himself by my name, and looking somewhat like me."

Mevary took a breath, and a risk.

"You mean," he said carefully, "that was an *imposter?*"

"No. He was my representative. He came here to impersonate me to you, and to our cousin—" Roilant wavered, but got the name out intact: "Eliset. He acted as I had instructed him. Now, I should like to know where he is."

"Oh." Mevary paused. He squinted at the bright ether, then looked Roilant in the eyes. "He rode off yesterday. We thought it curious. He had," very careful now, "made an offer of marriage to Eliset."

"I do not believe you."

"It is completely true. Thinking it to be you—what a perverse notion this was of yours, Roilant, dear—she accepted him."

"I mean," said Roilant leadenly, "I do not believe that the man rode off. I believe he is here still."

Mevary spread his arms.

"Search."

"I shall."

Mevary's jaw dropped.

"The man I sent here," said Roilant, "acted as my agent because I had certain misgivings. I reckoned them unworthy, yet the warnings had been so far specific that I took heed. I had been told that you and—and Eliset would attempt to kill me, once I had wed her, in order to get my wealth for yourselves. I now understand that, since you credited my agent to be me, she went through with the marriage to him, and he was then slain."

Mevary seemed displeased, and said nothing.

"Should I require proof of your villainy," Roilant went on, gaining a sort of dismal power with every sentence, "this unfortunate young man's death, when acting in my place, will furnish it. You will agree, I have only to find his body. These gentlemen will then escort you and your—and Eliset to Cassireia, where I have already alerted the justices of the governor."

Mevary was now decidedly pallid but, wolf-fanged, managed to sneer the final challenge.

"As you say. You have only to find the body."

A girl's voice came from the air like a crystal dart.

"Mevary, are you such an optimist? If he knows so much, he knows that, too."

Mevary flung back his head to regard Eliset standing on the veranda above.

"Be quiet, you bitch."

"No," said Roilant, with unusual force, "you be quiet, you mannerless dog. I *do* know." He looked at Eliset, pale and still beside the collapsing ivory, then looked away. "You slung the body in beside her father, without even benefit of proper wrapping."

Mevary backed off, having forgotten his back was already to the fountain. With a curse he moved aside instead.

"You are a lunatic, Roilant. Crazed."

"And she, of course," said Roilant, more quietly, "condoned it."

"Yes," said Eliset. She walked along the veranda and began to come down the stone stair. She moved steadily. Her face was itself like death, and strangely compassionate. "I did condone that ghastly, vulgar burial. I am as guilty as he." Reaching the court, she hesitated, then took a step toward Roilant. "As your hostess," she said, "I will lead the way."

Roilant blanched. Mevary did much the same.

Eliset, whiter than either of them, went into the sunken court, and was duly followed, via the stable, to the hillside.

Roilant was five or six paces behind her, the hired soldier a pace behind him. Mevary, originally of half a mind to flee (it would seem from one galvanic stride toward the orchard), had been interrupted by the three guard. Aware there were nine more close by, Mevary had fallen in with the plan and now came on just ahead of his three almost-captors. He was smiling, teeth bared, in extreme derisive horror. To be undone by idiots was obviously not to his taste.

They went up the sun-blasted slope, where the little saffron tree shone out like a beacon.

Entering its lacework shade, Eliset positioned herself at the head of the stone figure, and gazed down on it without another word.

Roilant, Mevary, the soldier and the guards positioned

themselves around the slab and stood waiting, as if about a conference table.

"My lord?" the soldier asked at length.

Roilant swallowed.

"Open it."

As the levers were produced, and began their grinding, grating work, another figure appeared, far down the slope among the tamarisks by the bath house wall. Jhanna, watching like a shadow with eyes.

There were still only three engaged in the labor, but, on this occasion, all full-grown men, and strong. It was the business of a minute and little more before the tomb's stone lid, already loosened somewhat by its prior move, scraped raucously upward.

Roilant's pulses clattered. He had had some inchoate, ridiculous hope that, getting here as fast as he might, he would be in time to save Cyrion from asphyxia, providing he had—fantastically—escaped death.

The lid was pushed and heaved away. The contents of Gerris' tomb were revealed not to the moonless darkness, but to the full and pitiless glare of day.

The soldier and the guards peered in from curiosity. The other three nerved themselves and did likewise, from grim need.

Eliset made the first sound. It was a small, expressionless sigh. Mevary made the second. Turning to Roilant, Mevary shouted: "There, pudding-brain. And where is your proof?"

Roilant looked down at the muffled body, which lay to one side and was instantly dateable by its state and smell as that of Gerris of Flor, and also down at the broad, darkly stained and webbily-cracked stone of the adjacent side that marked a place for one more corpse. Other than these things, the tomb was empty.

FIVE

To predict the conclusions of an oblique mind, and the deeds which proceed from them, is sometimes less difficult than to judge the course of the simply rational.

With Cyrion, conceivably, a grasp of the oblique ran concurrent with a sensitivity to the occult.

He had predicted that, on the night of the spurious

wedding with Eliset, the being of Roilant, that he personified, would be poisoned. It had accordingly been fair to assume that from the moment he arrived on the roof terrace he was open to assault by any dish, flagon or goblet that came his way. Mainly for this reason, Cyrion had seen to it that he was set on in the market at Cassireia. Though the attack had also served a number of adjoining purposes. First, it had given the about-to-be-attempted true murder a public dress-rehearsal, informing Eliset, and thus any other interested party at Flor, that a large crowd had heard what Roilant feared might happen to him. Secondly, and rather incidentally, it had thrown a spoonful of extra confusion into a cauldron whose recipe, until that moment, had seemed mostly that of the conniving cousins'. Cyrion had additionally been able to note Eliset's reaction to the unforeseen alarm, an entertaining, not uninformative sideline. The third reason why the affray had been staged was bizarre but vitally important. Having been smashed, apparently, repeatedly across the face, poor Cousin Roilant had every excuse thereafter, on that inauspicious evening, for finding it impossible to eat and very difficult to drink through the obvious and inartistic swelling of mouth and lips. All of which had been rather necessary. While to have achieved the injury, by the slight device of announcing one had walked into a door or fallen down a flight of stairs would not, under the suspicious circumstances, have done at all. To be beaten to the condition in view of several score people served much better.

The actual cause of Cyrion's swollen face was not, of course, either the beating or the broken tooth it was claimed to have instigated. The hired soldier, like most excellent fighting men, was a master at make-believe combat; Cyrion another. The date-stained napkin had been used to conceal a lack of bruises rather than their nativity.

In the privacy of his chamber at Flor, Cyrion had removed the cheek-padding his role had asked of him, and replaced it with another set having something more cumbersome still attached. It was a kind of small stetched bag, formed of thin, treated leather, rising at the sides into leather pouches and at the open end into a rough semblance of the inner portions of the human lips. Inserted into the mouth, it held its place by a measure of suction coupled to sheer lack of room to do anything else. Once the device was in position, the lower physiognomy came to resemble that of a pensive baboon. To eat was unthinkable, and to talk was a trial, for though the tongue could maneuver it must do so under the leather of the bag, and though the lips could move, they were hindered. The teeth were out of the picture altogether. The charm of the whole horrible thing was, however, that having allowed oneself to be felled and forced to drink, any poison, even of a corrosive nature, providing it was poured in clear of the outer lips, had no contact of any kind with any part of the mouth, let alone reaching the intestines. To remove the bag was more simple even than to insert it. One reached in and gently pulled. The contraption coming free, the potion unspilled and having harmed no one, it might then be taken off and examined. All this had been done. Cyrion had been most intrigued when he identified thereafter the poison that had been in the cup.

The next move was rather less easy and considerably less delightful. He had been expected to sup bane, he had obliged. Since it would now be expected of him that he should die, Cyrion had every intention of being equally obliging. Assuming that he would consequently be carefully tested for death in the furor, he knew that the mere appearance of demise, however convincing, was not enough.

It was true, Cyrion knew the techniques sometimes attributed to the nomads, sometimes to the prophets and magi, or else laid randomly elsewhere, disciplines reckoned to be magic, that concerned the control and subjugation of the flesh. There were, among these techniques and these magics, more than two or three forms of apparent physical death, and only one means of inducing real physical death—a real physical death that, providing mind and body were healthy and abnormally well-tuned, could be supposed temporary, and reversed at the adept's will. This means related to a system of natural bodily galvanics, located in the spinal cord and brain, and known to the nomads, at least, as The Serpent. This 'creature', which was pure energy, might be roused and elicited from the nerves of the spine. Passing up the vertebrae like a rearing snake, the charged electricity would eventually reach the brain and explode there—the striking of the serpent's fangs. It was also quite like being struck by lightning. The heart was stopped, and all complementary functions ceased. The body lay in stasis, and was, in any physician's parlance, dead. While to any of the most betraying tests ever divined to establish mortality, it remained impervious.

The consciousness, nonetheless, persisted. Initially, of course, it was stunned and would go out like a candle. (And, in one unadept, stay put out until it found itself severed and unable to return.) Cyrion, an adept whose skill spoke for itself, was once more aware in less than an hour, and so kept a lookout, from the darkened watchtower of his skull, on what went on. The instant the testing was done, and the dead body proven beyond even the wildest doubt to be dead, he reactivated the organs and currents of his frame into the most gentle and imperceptible quickening. Now, had any tried for it, they might have found a heartbeat, faint and widely spaced though its soundings were. They might, too, have noticed an indefinable breathing. But only if they had come back to study him once more in pedantic detail. And by that time, any who had been likely to check the cadaver had done so. And in the words of the nomads themselves: What man sets fire to fire?

So, for part of a night and a day and a second night, Cyrion lay on the edge of life, perfectly in command of himself, and was spoken of as a corpse. This subtly just-breathing corpse was presently cast into the ill-smelling box of Uncle Gerris, and the lid firmly replaced upon it.

To predict beforehand where they would throw him was not such a long-shot. Eliset herself had specified the vacant space in this tomb. That, unlike the hapless Jobel, he would not merely be bunged into the earth, would spring from the arrival of legal papers addressed to Roilant himself. As Mevary had intelligently fathomed, to convert one's property from one's rightful heirs to the king, implied one's suspicions of said rightful heirs. To broadcast Roilant's death was not, therefore, advisable. Not to leave handy evidence in the form of new turned ground for any who might shortly come to see.

Cyrion had subsequently visited the tomb under the saffron tree, on the night of the ghosts. He had worked there some while with a mallet and chisel, until a quantity of small holes had been made at various points near the base of the tomb. The stone, tilted and eaten away by damp, had not proved enormously resilient. The resulting holes, though modest in size, were decidedly sufficient to admit life-giving air to any live thing immured within.

No one had prepared Cyrion-Roilant's body for its resting place. As Cyrion had also deduced they would not. For one you may be accused of slaying, such honors are a mockery, and are also inclined to set the teeth on edge. While, the weather being warm, eventual haste was advisable. For these reasons, the padding of Cyrion's bodily disguise was never come on, nor those useful articles which that padding had, during the ultimate events, contained.

Cyrion in stone was to be a fleeting concept, not a permanent condition.

Once the tomb-lid grated home, blotting out the starlit night, Cyrion's remote yet steely consciousness set about restoring his body to its total capacity. That he had practiced such exiling and such restoration before is definite and logical. That a certain disorientation and mystic inebriation should also attend the rite is credible. But if so, such items were dismissed by the adept on his return. Having unfolded himself from the tomb's floor, Cyrion proceeded to regain his freedom. This, too, was logical. The only unusual aspect being that, rather than strive upward to force the lid, he had elected to continue down.

There was a water-course under Gerris' grave, so much was amply obvious—from the condition of the tomb's base, the lichen, and from the flourishing little tree which had sprouted there when all the cliff top would otherwise support were the burned grasses and the handful of dry flowers. There might have been a water-course, too, under the haunted well in the corridor-court, and this in turn had led into the great cavern which seemed to undermine all that section of the cliff. There was also the interesting visual information to be gleaned on the depth of solid material which separated the open cavern below from the topsoil above. Thirty feet of rock seemed the separative depth directly under the well, for that was roughly the level of the well's original, now movable, floor. On the other hand, the depth under the bath house must be less, otherwise the wearing of the upper strata would not allow the lights in the central cavern, when lit, to shine up through the hot pool. Then again, the mansion, though in dire decay, seemed reasonably well-lodged on its foundations. Once beyond the compound wall of the bath house, however, and everything set on the ground was shifting.

The tombs stirred, dragging their sides from the earth. The tower was positively precarious, leaning at a humorous angle. It was not irrational to guess that the area of rock beneath the tomb of Gerris, faulted besides by its freshet of water, was neither dense nor particularly sound.

Having ignited the first of the slender candles removed from his stomach padding, Cyrion conducted the dead corpse, with whom he shared his temporary abode, quietly into a corner. It turned out that the tomb floor under the body was more eroded than that on the other side, perhaps due to the interplay between absorbent rotting flesh and the mildewy stone. While nine and a half years had sterilized most of the uncongenial aspect of the former, they had only allowed the latter to get worse.

Cyrion went to work, pacing himself with care, for though there was air now, it was limited, and the tomb remained foul and close. Where commodious, he labored also in the dark, saving the candles, of which there were three. The implements, mallet, chisel, and a scatter of levers and wedges, plus a few other things of worth, were produced from chest, back and arm padding. Along with a generous coil of rope.

The task was heavy, but never hopeless. In the first five minutes a large piece of stone, coming up in a plate, brought the smell of wet earth. Two hours later, a shiver of air came trickling up. It no longer had the scent of fresh water, but the fishy odor of an inner sea.

When the last candle was almost through, part of the quite respectable hole beneath gave way in a rush. The sounds of falling matter lasted some while.

Cyrion tidied the floor of the tomb. Having hammered an iron hook into the rock directly under the ragged opening, he fastened the rope to it, and himself to the rope. Letting himself through, his feet braced on the stone, he reached back and brought the candle down to him, placing it on a jutting fist of rock for convenience. He then reached back again and pulled the useful corpse into its former station on the tomb's southern side. It and its draperies covered the new exit wholly and beautifully.

Cyrion swung down then, into the increasing blackness.

A moment later, he encountered the shallow roister of the little freshet, which he had been hearing for some time. It provided a cold but hygienic means of involuntary washing off the dust of the grave. The stream accompanied him a brief distance in his descent, before finding a sideways channel too slight for him to follow. Soon after, the receding light of the last candle fluttered out, and only the intense blackness remained.

The length of the descent was moot. It might be blocked by some further natural floor, or, much more likely, pass straight through, by cramped twists and turns, into the body of the cavern, thence to the water at the cavern's bottom. Even as he walked sideways down the narrow funnel, held only by the hanging rope, he was aware that the treacherous rock, so easily penetrated by metal tools, could just as easily evict the iron hook and so dislodge him into the debatable voids below.

The complexity and danger of the enterprise were, nevertheless, considered essential to the plan as a whole: To discover what he wished to, by his own and undetectable means, while leaving as much chaos and doubt in his wake as he might.

That Roilant himself had been left out of this stage of the affair was purposeful. Roilant's theatrical ability was slight. To convey his belief in Cyrion's probable murder he would need to believe it for sure. That Roilant had, on his own initiative, sent the hired man to spy, Cyrion had half suspected, but while the soldier set up his watch, Cyrion had been so far immersed in his own poisoning and its effects that he had no leisure to spare on such hypotheses as spies from his own camp. In fact Roilant, failing to receive pre-arranged communications from Cyrion, had been intended to arrive with his bombast accusations, and to instigate a wracking upheaval of the premises in search of Cyrion's remains. Because Roilant had known exactly where the corpse had been flung, the synopsis was somewhat spoilt.

Cyrion, however, had hauled the bones of Gerris over the exit hole as a bit of fastidious insurance, similar to locking a door upon departure. Luckily, and not entirely astoundingly, the several persons had been so enthralled to find Cyrion absent from the tomb, they had omitted a rigorous investigation of the smelly and ill-omened box. Instead they had fallen to frenzied examination of the landscape round about. To conclude the prisoner, if able to escape, would seek upward, that was psychologically inevitable. There was no immediate evidence to suggest the contrary. Mad speculation, not untinged by supernatural fear, wondered how the demon in disguise had raised the weighty tomb lid alone, and vanished without trace.

All this Cyrion, if he had paused in conjecture on the outcome of Roilant's spy, would have predicted. The subsidiary illusion, however slight, would do.

An artist, Cyrion went on artistically descending via the rope, through the eyeless black of the inner cliff.

He was now some five yards below the tomb, but the falling material earlier dislodged had seemed to drop considerably further. The end on the descent remained theoretical, while the iron hook, that might well be working loose, took all his weight.

Before the hook—or, for that matter, the length of rope itself—could fail him, something else happened. His feet, seeking for fresh sliding purchase, encountered open space. Lowering himself, with more emphatic caution, into this openness, he found himself arrived in a short curving corridor, some geological passage through the rock. As his feet touched a solid, though sloping, floor, the smell of ocean came thickly in to him from a point not far ahead, and with it a dull shimmering of light. It was the light which enabled him to see as well as to feel the security and angle of the ground. On this the rock debris had crashed, and down this it had continued to slip, thereby giving the impression audibly that it had cascaded through the air far longer than it had.

Cyrion thrust what slack remained of the hanging rope out of sight in an interstice of the rock, as he had similarly stored the padding and the tools of egress en route from the tomb in crevices directly under it. This too was the security of minor door-locking. That anyone should come on them was unlikely.

Cyrion walked toward the light.

It had a shape, an oval, pearly now, and flickering with the motion of water. And with the light, there came the low, restless vibration of the sea. Wet plants dripped on the rock.

A minute more, and, coming through the oval of light, which was the mouth of a cave, Cyrion stood on a winding ledge, some ten to twelve feet in width, a gallery that ran a third of the way around the womb of the cliff, and gave a vantage of almost everything.

It was dramatically reminiscent of the Belly of the Whale. Above, the ribbed stone, luminous and colorless. All about, the swooping walls of that enormous hollow shell, pocked with a hundred caves, and curiously, patchily shining, with a tarnished metallic glow. And maybe two hundred and fifty feet below, the cavern's bottom, a plaque of water, not black, but blackly, opalescently green.

At its western end, the cavern eased itself into a narrowing vent, which no doubt gave at length on the open sea beyond the cliff, in the guise of some slim and inconspicuous cave. But this did not represent the source of the light which caused the walls to shine so oddly. The sun would not yet have risen.

The source of the light was in fact a series of small fires, which burnt far down in the vertical pits of lower caves. These fires gave little brightness, yet between them and what must be their reflections on some substance in the rocks, the whole cavern had a milky luminosity, vague, undeniable.

Unpaddedly elegant, though clad in the gaudy garments of his wedding supper, Cyrion began to tread the slimy, down-sloping ledge. He had seen something to his left and farther on along the path. It appealed to him almost as much as the incandescencies in the cave mouths beneath.

A long unbroken loop of thick rope came down and touched the ledge. Following it upward, one saw a peculiar brazen cage poised up against the cavern's roof. Beyond the cage, and to one side, a hole showed in the roof, from the shaft of which another, lesser, pair of rope-lines extended. Where they left the hole, they were pulled tautly over until they reached the jut of adjacent rock, into which they had been pinioned by iron bolts. Looking down from the *top* of the shaft, the ropes would appear to terminate in midair—or, optically, in the water far below. The cage-contraption itself, being to the side and under the widening roof, would not be visible. The head of the shaft was, of course, the haunted well in the mansion's corridor-court.

Cyrion studied the cage, and all the ropes. It would seem certain acrobatics would be called for from one descending. First negotiation of the double rope down the shaft, next an unsafe swinging across and away from these ropes into the mostly openwork cage. Once the cage had been achieved, it was clear from the uncomplex pulley attendant, that the cage rope could be operated by the cage's occupant to haul the strange vehicle down to the ledge. Ascent would be in a complementary vein.

Far up, in the gut of the well-shaft, came the softest little sound.

Having already deciphered the method of travel the rope-lines and cage offered, it seemed Cyrion was also to be given a practical demonstration. Displaying graceful interest to a thoughtful fate, he stepped back into one of the shallow pleated fissures of the rock wall, and prepared to observe.

Presently a pair of long legs evolved from the shaft, and after these a torso. Two slender hands gripped the taut ropes, picking down them with enormous physical control, the whole lithe weight of the body slung from them as the feet kicked free. Reaching the ropes' ends, the feet kicked out again; they went in at the top of the cage, and brought it swinging back under the well-shaft. As the cage came directly beneath the opening, the figure dropped fluidly down into it, taking fresh hand-holds on the bars as the vehicle shuddered and dipped. Unsafe indeed, yet managed with the agility of a marmoset. Or, the agility of a human well-used to clinging, balancing, the intrinsic laws of a reckless yet mathematical fearlessness.

The cage steadied, and the being in the cage waited for this process to be complete before applying downward pressure to the loop of rope. One might have taken the cage's occupant for a boy, Zimir or Harmul, for it was dressed in like garb. However, you soon saw upon the head a coiled arrangement of sheeny pale yellow, eccentrically pinned to keep it from coming loose. Both this and the clothing were plainly sensible precautions for the journey.

The cage grounded obediently on the ledge. The girl stepped out of it, and the rogue light of the cavern caught her a moment in silhouette. If there had been any lingering doubt as to her sex, this moment would have dispelled it.

Leaving the cage, the yellow-headed figure proceeded down the slitherous slope of the ledge. After a while, apparently coming on an anticipated path, from Cyrion's vantage invisible, the girl swiftly vanished downward.

At this point, Cyrion assumed pursuit.

The invisible path shortly revealed itself. It wound down across the inner face of the cavern, jumbled with old falls of cliff material. To Cyrion, as to the girl, this way was completely usable. He slowed only when the pale topaz bob of head came back into view.

The idea that she would seek the fire-lit caves was not really the result of Cyrion's exceptional deductive skills. Anyone might have fathomed it. Unless she wished to throw herself for an icy swim in the murky waters, there was patently nowhere else to go.

The first six caves she passed. They were dark.

The seventh, revealed by a turn of the path, glimmered with its witch-light, a carious unholy tangerine. The crackle of flames echoed in the drumming stillness, losing all pretentions to normalcy.

(The water was closer, perhaps a hundred and sixty feet away. Overlays and the bulging spill of the rock hid the extent of its incurving edges. Somewhere out of sight, beached on the basin's lip, must be the weird ship.)

The girl had stopped before the lit cave. Its malevolent, etiolated glare described her rather well at last, the beauty, the jewel eyes, the aristocratic turn of head, of body. Then she stepped through and again disappeared from Cyrion's gaze. But almost at once, he heard her speak, in the musical voice one would recognize, not seeing her at all, as the voice of Eliset of Flor.

"Greetings, Oe-Tabbit."

And the elderly voice, like dry broken bread crusts, responding: "Greetings. Why are you here?"

"To report and express my joy to you; so to our sisterhood."

"One is dead, then."

"Yes, Oe-Tabbit. One is dead."

"But you recall the pledge to the Green Mother, the Lady of Great Ocean?"

"Of course, Oe-Tabbit. He shall be mine only because he is Hers. My offering to Her."

A long pause. Then the voice of the sea-witch, she who had been the nurse of Eliset, and of the lost Valia, a woman old even then, steeped even then in the sorcerous membership, probably old in its own way, old as the cliff, or nearly, which had given Flor its legend of sirens and enchantresses reaching from the waves to steal and slay.

"Remember, too, daughter, that this scheme of yours is allowed you simply at Her whim. You are Hers. You have no life but the life She grants."

Somewhere within the fire-lit cave, a girl's sharp laughter.

"I have known that thirteen years. And have I not given Her sacrifice before?"

"So you did. She recollects. Only be wary. There is a smoke over this thing, a mist. One other element which may not be contained and which will not reveal itself. This may be the meddling of another human. Are the servants under your sway?"

"That, or dead."

"It is another, then. Some stranger."

"Or a ghost. Sometimes still my Uncle Mevary manifests. I have guarded myself against him as you recommended. I think he wishes very much to harm me."

"This is no ghost. The shells in the fire show a man with white hair."

"As white as yours, Oe-Tabbit? I do not fear him. Let him come to Flor, and perish with my other enemies."

"Gently," said the eerie, smashed voice of the ancient witch in her nest of stone and fire and sea. "You are young to play with death."

"Young," agreed the young voice. "But did I say I only *played*?"

Tabbit made a crooning noise. She said, "It will be dawn, soon." Then, a whisper: "Go see if any followed you."

When Gerris' daughter, proud and violent and doubting, stepped out on the path to look, the way, and all the upper cliff, were empty.

A short space later, the cage was hauled up again, and a female figure in male attire acrobatically navigated the well-shaft.

The sun also rose.

Thereafter, Jhanna wept in her cell; Zimir spotted an advance of visitors; Roilant burst in person upon the impressed household; Mevary blanched; Eliset led the way to her father's tomb. The tomb was opened to reveal a miraculous omission.

While, some hundred odd feet under their soles, Cyrion sat in a cave, eating the small portion of food and wine he had provided himself, and watching the occasional witch-crone straying to and fro on the rocks below.

Following the discovery of the vacant tomb, there had occurred a mildly diverting scene.

Amid the dilapidation of a downstairs salon, furnished solely with two wooden candle-stands and an empty birdcage, Roilant had confronted Mevary. Outside in the central court, two Beucelair guardsmen leaned by a fountain.

"I say again," Mevary said again, "where is your proof?"

"The absence of my agent is proof enough."

"Is it so? How if I remind you the oaf rode away? Took your cash and duped you."

Roilant was flushed and his hands shook. He was in an indeterminate state between rage, alarm and guilt. Nor did the presence of Eliset beside the door aid him at all. He felt peculiarly embarrassed to be accusing her of murder and infamy, while from Mevary he burned to get justice, by fair means or foul.

For his part, Mevary was strung up, elated and uneasy at once. The uncanny vanishment, having let him off the hook in one direction, posed weird problems from another. If the wretched duplicate-Roilant was alive and had escaped, then how, and where was he now, and doing what? A certain abstraction on Mevary's side, a certain lack of proper attention to Roilant's demands and inculpations, due to the fact that Mevary's brain was in full cry after the quarry, trying to run Cyrion to earth, trying to learn how one who seemed carrion had really been quick. There was another possibility. That Cyrion *had* been as dead as he seemed, and that some other, some third party, had stolen the body for personal ends. But he would need darkness and the deficit of the confounded red cousin before he could investigate.

For what of something better, Roilant announced:

"You are a damnable liar, and your lies will see you at a rope's end."

To which, for want of something better, Mevary had made a suggestion as to what Roilant might do with a rope's end.

At this juncture, Eliset spoke for the first time in an hour.

"Roilant, I comprehend quite well that I am equally implicated with Mevary. But I wonder if you would, of your clemency, permit me to seek my room? You have my word I shall not abscond. Indeed, where might I go? Your guards are set at all exit points. And in any case, I have little money with which to purchase shelter should I evade them. Though you may also, if you wish, place a guard at my door. I am, believe me, very weary of all this."

Roilant regarded her. Her face was haggard, almost destitute of its beauty in a manner that must invite sympathy. It could scarcely be an act. She looked as if, along with enduring the stresses of the day, she had not slept at all on the previous night.

"Yes, by all means," he said. "No guard at your door will be necessary. I regret that this—I regret—"

"Regret is superfluous," she said. And then, with an unemphasized dignity that wrung his heart, "you are very kind."

She went from the salon, and Roilant followed, instructing the guards by the fountain not to detain her. The sunlight caught her hair as she turned towards the veranda steps, and hesitated a split second there, noting the orange tree had died in its pot. Then she went up, with such grace, and he saw a worn patch in her shoe. Seldom had a potential murderess been so reverenced and pitied by her victim.

In her chamber, Eliset barred the door. She was genuinely exhausted, and going to her bed, she lay down on it. She had taken in the death of the orange tree with deadly recognition.

She did not expect to sleep, being too wrought up by events, and at first drearily listened to the usual and unusual noises in the court, and beyond the house on its farther side—the sea, birds, the distant domestic clink of a jar filled at the kitchen well—and the bored laughter of the guards distributed about, the sounds of their horses (bringing a memory of former days), and once or twice the disharmonious wrangling of Roilant and Mevary flaring up from below.

And then, sleep after all began to cloud her senses, and everything drew far away. There seemed nothing else she might do, and so she let go of all of it, and the afternoon light faded from her.

When she woke, it was to the world of night. The sky was full of stars, and the moon rising—it must be, she reasoned, at least an hour after sunset. The escapism of sleep had proved too seductive.

With a nervous intuition that she had missed some crucial happening, she left the bed, lit a brace of candles, then moved to the chamber door. But her hand already on the bar, she checked. The medley of sounds was done. The house seemed disturbingly quiet, as if it lay in wait for her.

With no preface then, there came the lightest of tappings on the door, and she barely restrained a cry. It was some moments before she could ask: "Who is there?"

"Roilant" came back a harsh whisper.

Perplexed, she poised, her hand still on the bar, still not lifting it.

If Roilant were here, their conqueror, why need he whisper? She had the preposterous sudden notion that he had come secretly to help her escape from himself. With an uncertain amusement, she accepted she was beyond caring for anything, and raised the bar, and opened the door.

The soft candlelight washed out and illuminated the figure of the caller.

Eliset took three involuntary steps backward, eyes wide.

"Who are you?" supplied the arrival gravely, coming into the room and closing the door on the night.

"Who are you?" Eliset obediently repeated.

"As Roilant may have explained, perhaps adequately, the person who was here previously and answered to his name was an impostor. This man's true name is Cyrion. I am Cyrion. Good evening."

"But," she said.

"But. Bear in mind that, aside from the lamentable tresses, I am no longer in disguise."

Having shut the door, he was leaning on it, casually, the candles gilding him, and the somewhat impaired garments she remembered from their wedding night. Otherwise, he was hardly as she recalled. A young man, tall and slender, with much of the lynx and the panther about him, a face like that of the Fiend at his most irresistibly prepossessing, long-lidded eyes like half-sheathed blades—and over all, the orange flag of hair. This, then, had mocked her, angered her, made a simpleton of her, made her afraid. He it was who had saved her from the cliff's edge—died in front of her in this room.

"If you are about to swoon," said Cyrion, "I recommend you consider I may not be as swift to catch you as Mevary."

She said coldly, "I never fainted in my life."

"I rather thought not."

"You are thinking of the day when Jobel died? I was tired

and sickened, and it has sometimes been expedient to pretend. . . . to jettison consciousness is an excellent way of avoiding wearisome questions. Not that my performance in any way rivals your own. You do not only faint, you die."

"Which also avoids answering questions."

"Perhaps you are a sorcerer."

"Or perhaps I am not a sorcerer."

"Did Roilant send you to me?"

"No."

"Then how did you reach this chamber without challenge? There are guards everywhere."

"Someone else saw to it they slept soundly."

She balked, then said, with a wealth of dislike: "And how did you get out of the stone tomb we had so misguidedly shut you in?"

"The lid of which, I noticed, goes unreplaced." Cyrion walked suddenly by her. Going over to the lights, he drew something from his shirt, and anointed it with a candle. "The reply to that, as to a host of other clamoring questions, I must restrain myself from giving you. Time, as they persist in saying, is short. However, perhaps you would be so good as to deliver this letter to your Cousin Roilant."

She glared at him, at the leaf of folded paper, carefully if idiosyncratically sealed with hot candle wax, which he was now extending to her.

"What is this madness?"

"The surety of your good name," he said. "When Roilant wakes, give it to him. He will be in a crochety mood, having been drugged. Speak low to him. That is for tomorrow. For tonight, keep here."

"Another jest."

"Not exactly. There is a slight possibility I may be delayed, or mislaid. It would be a shame for your innocence to remain in doubt, would it not?"

"Innocence? You believe me a villainness. Everything you said to me—"

"Alas. There is no more time."

Walking away from the candles, he passed before her, and leaning his iridescent head toward hers, kissed her lightly on the mouth before moving to the door, opening it, and going out again into the darkness.

Only as the door closed did she realize the letter had been

placed in her hand and that she had taken it, together with the obscure sentences and the phantom kiss, which even now left its electricity behind it through her flesh, her very hair.

Impulses sent her directly back to the door, where impulse directly delayed her. She looked down at the sealed paper in her hand. The seal would be very easy to break and then repair—the same wax was here to hand. And could she believe he had not known she would grasp as much? Restlessly puzzled, she let down the bar again across her door, and went slowly to her bed. And ran her thumbnail through the impromptu seal.

Having stayed as long within the confine of the hollow cliff, and witnessed as much there as was currently informative, Cyrion had returned to the surface. The cage, operable solely by its occupant, was now in its topmost position—against the well-shaft, where its former passenger had left it. Perforce, Cyrion utilized the hundred odd feet of slack that constituted the free stretch of the rope loop, the cage itself on the other stretch, and held against the pulley, acting as the counterweight.

This, and the last acrobatic transfer to the shaft cords, and so up the well and out of it, he managed at least with the dexterity of anyone else who had occasion to use them. Actually, with more dexterity.

The remaining scheme should have been simple. It entailed locating and imparting news to Roilant, who would by then be in the house.

Roilant was indeed in evidence, though in no condition to be awarded information. Certain other things were also to be seen. Firstly, two Beucelair guardsmen draped around and about a fountain; secondly a small wine flagon on the ground beside them. The smell of the dregs of this told its own story. They were drugged within an inch of their lives, just as were three others he found, just as Roilant was when, trying the door of a veranda apartment under which light stole and out of which came a dull masculine snoring, Cyrion discovered him.

Papers scattered on a rickety table helped put the irritating riddle together, Roilant, it seemed, had been in the process of writing a report to the governor at Cassireia, when his own cup of wine had sent him to sleep. He had already, as the papers showed, sent back two of the guardsmen to procure a detatchment of city justice. (Mild arithmetic demonstrated that of the ten men referred to on the paper, two more were still missing. Cyrion found them in the outer court. One was drugged. The other, the hired ex-soldier, had apparently scented rats and been rewarded with a whack aft of the cranium for his pains. Breathing, but senseless, he could as yet offer no assistance and no worthwhile facts. An effort to rouse him had only elicited the words: "Not now, Aishab, for God's love.")

It seemed, nevertheless, from Roilant's unfinished literary exercise, that having argued all afternoon, fruitlessly, with Mevary, Roilant had decided on glueing himself to the sticking place until judicial reinforcements should appear. He had therefore permitted Mevary to seek his apartments, as Eliset had been permitted to seek hers. And when Mevary had asked imperiously for supper, Roilant had allowed him to be served with it. Supper had also come for Roilant and his men, by the hands of a frightened servant boy or slave, incorrectly noted down as one, Zunir. Zunir's terror of Mevary had been obvious—according to Roilant; another incriminating factor. Conceivably this was true, since Zunir (or Zimir) had conveyed an unhealthful soporific to all and sundry, doubtless at Mevary's bidding.

Roilant's stack of paper, ink and quills had, however, provided Cyrion with the means to make another version of the story. To leave this in the unaware hands of Roilant was chancy. It was besides more entertaining to render it where he had. That Eliset would read what he had written was all to the good. Perhaps the most fascinating part of it would be the message that her half-sister, Valia, the dead child of Flor's legend, was now and then to be seen in the sea-cave under the house.

As with any worthwhile drugging, there was a sound motive for it. Mevary intended to be about on commerce. It hardly required the notes of his raised voice, ugly with annoyance and threat, to be detected from the kitchen court in order to gain such knowledge. Yet, Cyrion was treated to the noise. Halting en route elsewhere, he listened.

"Very well. I absolve them of appropriating the agent's corpse. Why not? But I still have dealings with them. I tell you, I will go, you wretched slut," politely avowed Mevary.

To which a girl's voice, stifled and anguished, cried out:

"*No!* It is not the time—"

Startlingly, it had sounded like Eliset's. But, "Curse the bloody time. What do I care for their superstitions? Have I not been kept dallying all these months for a pack of lunatic rites and mumblings? Long enough. Now I must have speed. And *will* have it."

A quarter minute later, Mevary came striding from the kitchen court. Cyrion was no longer to be seen. Not was he visible when, having perceived the way into the cavern was open, (an oversight Cyrion had earlier been charmed by—ignorant of the mechanism, he could not otherwise have used it on the road up), Mevary swung over into the well. With a wolverine twist of his body and a string of oaths, he disappeared.

The haunted bath house provided adequate concealment, and continued to do so. Cyrion stayed there a while longer, courteously allowing the lady of the party, after an uneasy stare or two about her, to hurry through the corridor and wind herself away down the well-shaft in Mevary's wake.

Cyrion granted them the space to get clear, before he followed.

SIX

The somber cavern still glowed. In their cave mouths, the scattered fires burned on, lurid record of the cavern's subterranean tenants.

So much Cyrion had seen previously, and rather more. Some twenty feet above the surface of the water, and in a direct line downward from the gallery on which he had first emerged, the rock shelved under. Its tiers, with their stony orifices, were held out in one bulging balcony by some freak of natural architecture. Beneath this granite overhang a half-moon of shale sloped to the cavern's sea-pool.

The way to this shale beach, as presumably to all the narrow strip of level or semi-level shore surrounding the water, went through inner passages, either sea-hewn or man-made many hundreds of years in the past. To these tunnels through the cliff walls, the witches' caves themselves gave entrance.

On his initial exploratory trip, Cyrion had located such a pass. This cave was unlit, and the way mostly lightlessly occult along its curve, though soon enough paling again at its opposite end. A heap of bones in a hooded garment of damp-stained cloth near to the egress point showed where the former owner had dropped down. It turned out, the eldritch sisterhood did not bury its dead.

On the shale beach to which the tunnels this side of the pool gave entry, lay the uncanny ship, as Cyrion had guessed.

Her scarlet sail, in portions thin as spider web, hung from the yard even ashore. It could scarcely have been taken in—one touch and it would, from the look of it, have shredded. The oars, rather than belayed, were leant against the sides. she was a very old vessel, antique, encrusted, scarred, nearly derelict, brought in from the open sea at some distant date, centuries before.

That she let water was but too predictable. That she had been used for ritual, more so. The torches stood up on their spikes, kept fresh and trimmed as nothing else had been. Sail and woodwork were dark with smokes. An oil jar stood on the deck, a common article out of place here. There were other utensils, set about a block of what seemed fossilized wood, in the prow. These were more oblique, more suitable, hinting at magic exercises to do with blood-letting—weird knives of stone, stone basins, each crudely painted with a fish that was also an eye. The sigil of the Lady of Great Ocean?

Formerly the area beside the ship had been deserted. No longer.

A fire burned on the shale, started from driftwood with the aid of oil and tinder. In its spitting glare, which now and then flashed blue-ish or clear green, hovered a collection of aged women.

They numbered between seventeen and twenty. It was impossible quite to count them, for though of different heights and unsimilar stances, they seemed of a regulation boniness, and were dressed each the same in the worn and dirty grey raiment that had come to denote their calling. Under the hood struggled worms of hair, filthy white or filthy grey, or none at all, indicating baldness. The faces poked out of the hair and hoods like tortoise heads from shells, or else shrank inward and were hidden.

At the forefront of the group stood one who could only be their leader, a female who went arrogantly unhooded, to display the full ruin of her flesh and features. Her whole countenance had fallen in, the eyes, the cheeks, the mouth. It was the visage of a skull, draped by a transparent shroud of skin, quite without color, except the colors which the fire painted on it, now amber, now turquoise, and now greenest jade. She might have been one hundred and fifty years of age. *She.* She might also have been genderless. Time had taken from her all soul of sex and everything of character. She had none. She had become a function. Yet, as with the block of wood upon the deck, she had been turned to carbon, and there were fixed in her the marks of all she had been, the habitude of her life, when she had lived, and upon which still she acted. And chief among these was shown to be a sort of patient wickedness. Her eyes held it yet, flares of an intelligence that remained active, but which no longer understood itself, not asked to.

Instead of the hood, across the strands of her white hair, and dripping down the broad forehead of tidal lines rising and falling, was a net of golden chains set with pearls.

There was also one further notable thing. On the woman's right hand, the little finger was missing.

Facing the apparition across two yards of shale was a young man colored in with wolflike shades, and with wolflike eyes, which seemed to find no trouble in meeting the evil, mindless eyes of the witch. In his hand a naked sword dazzles red, then blue, then green. Then red once more. Mevary, at his most uningratiating.

"Yes, you have said it all, Tabbit. The moon is not at full. This is not the hour for the ritual. *Then dispense with the bloody ritual.* What do I care if your bitch-mistress in the sea mislikes it? Let her. Let her give up her gold, this gold you've shown me in bits, this treasure from the cavern. Then if she wants, I'll call her pretty names. Perhaps."

Tabbit, titled by her acolytes: "Oe" (some mystic prefix of their order, incomprehensible) drew the seams of her sunken lips apart. The voice came out, the same voice which Cyrion had heard within the cave, speaking to Gerris' daughter.

"It is not only the full of the moon that must be waited for. It is the season, which is not yet, but will be, soon."

"Damn the season. Have I not told you, old woman? I can no longer while away my time here, waiting on your goddess' convenience. I must leave Flor—tonight. If you will not assist me, only tell me where to delve. I can row this water-logged kindling alone I would hazard, if you can move it with your decrepit crew back there. Come on, you senile hags. Do as I say." He raised the sword. "Or do you think you can run faster, all of you, than this?"

The women rustled, closed together like a colony of grey bats. They did not seem afraid. Tabbit, called Oe-Tabbit, did not seem to be.

"And you, daughter. What do you say to this?"

Mevary sprang round. And saw the shadowy figure which had stood behind him some while, having already dogged him out through the tunnel passage that led from Tabbit's cave.

"You," he said. "Well, what *do* you say, doxy dear? Do I get this gold you and your sweet old nursie promised me? Or do I go back and confess to Cousin Roilant, and go be hanged in Cassireia?"

"It is true what he says," the shadow murmured. "I was mistaken in Roilant's death. It seems he has an accomplice, who played him. For sure, Mevary will be in the governor's custody if he returns above."

Soft as brick-dust, Tabbit inquired of her.

"And do they search for you, up there?"

"No. I gave the boy Zimir a drug to temper their wine. And another brave, Mevary brained with a candle sconce. All sleep save the girl. And she has learnt to obey Mevary's whims."

Tabbit lowered the corrugated lids of her eyes. She seemed in meditation, but only for a second. The awful gaze came straight back to Mevary.

"Then, though it is not the season, it shall be."

Again, there was a rustling behind her, skeletal hands waving like spiders through the air.

"Be still," said Oe-Tabbit. "She will receive in mercy. She knows the times are not always to be observed by those that have been persecuted, by those who, shut in this stone, may only worship as they can, not as they wish. Consider, sisters, how long she has waited, and how long hungered to have the ritual completed. She will forgive, She will be content if it is done, although it be done in the wrong season."

Sighing, hovering, they relapsed, grew silent.

Mevary stood blazing in the firelight, his eyes bright with malice, greed, mistrust.

"She is eager, you say, to give me her gold?"

"We have told you often, the Lady has no use for gold. Come then, my daughter," Tabbit said, looking beyond him to the shadow. "The shells in the fire told me you would return tonight. We are here, we are waiting, as you see. Step among us, put on your robe. Become one with us, Valia, my daughter."

The shadow moved. It slid past Mevary and into the light of the fire. As it did so, it pulled the scarf of pale yellow silk from its hair, and the pins which had secured the silk rained unheeded to the shale.

Valia stood a moment then, between her cousin and her sisterhood. Something in her stance revealed she felt no great love toward either. And yet, toward the old women she expressed, through every angle of her body, a compulsive returning. In the boy's disguise, which she found most handy for climbing the ropes of the well, much of her slim voluptuousness was lost, though not all. Burnished by the fire, the fierce copper glaze that sometimes revealed itself on her dark hair, flamed up, making her in fact a redhead, displaying surely her links with the House of Beucelair, with blonde Eliset, tawny Mevary, ginger Roilant. Her grey eyes, too, owed their origin to Gerris, but her olive complexion was her mother's legacy, the woman he had installed in Cassireia, and who had died of grief soon after Valia was lost.

Valia, the demon-snatched child of Flor. She had passed her infancy in that little house Gerris had given her mother, and now and then seen her father arrive on a visit. At which time he would look askance at her, force a smile, toss her some cheap toy—and then she would be bidden to play. To play and not to disturb the mother and the father, who had other matters to attend to. This, in her most formative years, was all that Valia saw of her father, and all that he represented to her; that she was sent off, being superfluous and unwanted. And later, when the cash diminished at Flor, and the house of Gerris' mistress became a hovel where rats chirruped instead of caged birds, Gerris came to represent this also. It was not surprising she hated him.

One day, there was a change. Gerris' wife had died, far away in a land whose name Valia did not even know. Gerris succumbed to a strange guilt. He resolved to give up his mistress, now when it barely mattered, since he had not sought her for over a year. The morning he came with the news, Valia was playing in the yard, swinging upside-down from the dead fig tree. She was incredibly limber, and also incredibly dirty and ragged, and covered all over by the bites of ferocious insects which now infested the walls of the house. She recalled vaguely, even to this day, the upside-down red-blond man staring at her as he sat his upside-down horse.

It seemed his guilt had taken an extra turn about itself. This sore-plastered urchin was his. He must expiate his sin. He must save the child.

He saved her. He adopted her. He took her from the hovel where she had been at home, if not happy, and put her into Flor, where there were still servants to swear at her and abhor her, and a priest to lecture her on the love of God and beat her for her fault of not remembering it. And where there was another sister, younger than she, like a golden lily, reed thin, placid as a reed, legitimate and not legitimized, a perfect thing suitable to the house, as Valia frankly was not. And there was Gerris, showering upon Valia now a false theatrical affection, a mountain of presents (still cheap, money was short), shrinking when he came near her and driving himself to embrace, to extol—she did not comprehend, but she nevertheless gauged his weakness and his unlove, and his fear. And only hated him the more. Hated all of them, and everything. Except—

The old woman, the golden sister's nurse, *her* nurse also now. . . . Generally, the old woman paid her very little heed, though once, climbing the hornbeam tree, loose and skillful, Valia had noticed the old eyes watching her. Thereafter, finding her occasionally alone, Tabbit would tell stories. They were beautiful stories, of a wonderful palace of crystal and emerald beneath the sea, where dwelled a goddess forgotten by men, but reverenced by a few, the chosen, the elite, and these only women. And she would bestow power, it seemed, this goddess, on those who served her. Power to make others, men and women, one's slaves. Power to punish and command.

Tabbit was old even then. Very old, and one of her little fingers was missing. Tabbit explained the committment she had made to the goddess in the sea, the Mother of Great Ocean. The severing of Tabbit's finger had sealed the commitment. There were other tokens which might be offered Her. A toe, the lobe of an ear, a nipple, even—Valia, whose breasts had already begun to grow, thrilled with horror. Ah, but what (said Tabbit) was a little morsel of tissue in exchange for such power? The sorrow was, so few were suited to the retinue of the goddess that her devotees had shrunk to a mere handful. That the order might survive, one had gone forth, both to supply the sisterhood with such provender as she could obtain, for they too grew old, and could no longer very well seek it from the ocean. Also, to search the earth for one shining child, fair and wise and strong enough to enter the temple of the Lady and receive her blessing of supernatural genius.

The process had been subtle, far more subtle in the doing than in recollection or recital. It had eventually come to the two inevitable climaxes. Tabbit's revelation of herself as the searching priestess. Valia's passionate wish that she be worthy to be found.

She had never been anything special. She had been an unwanted birth, a superfluity to lovers, a bribe to God. She had no standing, or felt she had none, and she was unloved. She loathed Gerris, and she loathed the golden lily, Eliset, who was all Valia was not, and who, mistakenly, had sometimes tried to be kind to her, so inciting her animosity to new heights. Valia longed for the blessings of the goddess. She got them.

Tabbit finally told her how to reach the temple, which was nothing but the dismal cavern itself. The way through the well, the cage, was also unveiled. This route had been extant, Tabbit said, time out of mind. An eastern lady of an earlier house, upon whose foundations Flor now stood, had been a member of the sacred sect. She it was who had sheltered the sisterhood when they had gone to ground in fear of persecution, and later joined them in their rites below. Through this means of the well, Tabbit had afterwards also passed to and fro, stealthily and intransigently supplying her sisters with stuffs stolen from the house. Agile as a monkey, though aged, was Tabbit, yet her agility grew less. Youth was needed now. Youth constrained by that same maniacal loyalty and obsession which fired every one of those other women rotting away underground, man-haters, world-haters, *life*-haters, all of them. Yes, Tabbit had recognized the qualities in Valia that the witches' goddess desired. Not wisdom, or shining strength, but the sly tenacity of deception, the ignition of paranoia.

In the end it was settled. Valia let herself be witnessed by servants, near the tower and the brink of the cliff. When alone, she ran to the bath house wall and climbed it. She hurried from the bath house to the corridor-court, which in those days was unroofed. She opened the well as Tabbit had instructed, and climbed down into the luminous shade below. Tabbit came a little later and closed the way. Accustomed herself to climbing ropes, she entered the corridor-court by means of one, having got from a window to the wall-top. She returned in the same manner, quite unseen, and was soon under the hornbeam tree with Eliset, playing her usual role of age and immobility, convincing the girl she had been there longer than she had.

So Valia passed into her new domain.

She had looked for pulchritude and grandeur, something to rival the dreaming sea palace of the goddess. Again, she discovered herself betrayed. There was no grandeur, there was slavery. Slavery for several years, in fact, during which, only by climbing along treacherous ridges of the cavern to its outermost limit, or by swimming through the icy pool, did she find the thin break in the cliff wall and so glimpse sun, open sea, the air and any horizon not a rock.

She had, of course, rebelled, but rebellion was useless. She had done vile things, but these, too, brought neither relief nor recognition. When she attained the outer air, there was no escape. She was not strong enough to row the antique ship to liberty. And above, the well was kept closed. There was no chance either, that way.

Tabbit came after the first month, and Valia railed against her. Tabbit stood impassively, framed by the shimmering darkness of the shale beach. And when Valia's fury failed her from overuse, Tabbit turned her and made her look out toward the sea-pool. And then Tabbit spoke words, and a miracle happened. A green shell rose from the black water, glinting with stars of brightness. In the shell, beautiful women drifted like aquatic butterflies, and there was the scent of a thousand flowers, and a melody like a harp fashioned from water. . . .

The vision died quickly. It was merely an illusion, and cost

Tabbit much. Her beginnings were not so driftingly ethereal as she had given out. She had been born to service in the house of Flor, and when the household grew lax, found her way among the witches, a tradition of the female side of her earthly kin. With age, her magic faculties were deserting her. Only the power of command would soon be left her, and now she commanded Valia, who turned back to her, bemused, trembling. "You shall summon greater wonders than I," said Tabbit, "and perform greater sorcery. But only if you remain with us, learn from us, render your soul to Her."

And Valia, who had been nothing but other's fears and duty, obscurely noted that here she had become something in her own right.

So she resumed her slavery with a reluctant willingness.

Thirteen years she suffered it. She learned magic, and that she was no adept was cunningly kept from her until she came, with the egotist's true and always-to-be-relied-on blindness, to believe herself an adept. Meantime, she fished from the waters, tended the herbal and fungoid druggist's gardens, and made bread from the flour which she herself began, in her fourteenth year, to steal from Flor above. And when she journeyed above, and saw now the free earth, she spurned it, rejected it, for it had given her nothing but contempt and dismissal, and false emotions. The witches had seduced and thieved her. They had really *wanted* her. She stayed with them and grew wise and shining in the dark, or thought she did. And when Tabbit at last told her masters she would go home to die, and instead travelled below, then Valia became her daughter, her witch-daughter, bound to her by a spillage of blood—just as, in her fifteenth year, Valia was bound to the goddess by the amputation of her ear lobe.

And yet. All the while she shone there in the darkness, she knew that life went on above her in the house and on the land about Flor. It became the world the other side of an immense door, unlike the world she climbed or swam to, that lay beyond the cavern entrance.

She saw *them* too, when she was above. The first Mevary—her *uncle*—strutting, leching, drinking. The younger Mevary, ugly in his beauty, which some part of her heeded and so scorned. Eliset. Valia's neglectful mother had died long before, herself of neglect, and despair. Gerris had died. Valia credited herself with his death, for she had willed torments upon him—though not for her mother's sake. Sometimes by night, on those rare occasions when she was above and not spying on the living, she went to his tomb and spat on it, and wept in a strange agonized joy that she had harmed him. She saw Roilant once. A plump boy, uneasily bathing in the bath house when she had come up from the well incautiously. She took care he did not see her in her filched boy's clothing, her scarfed hair. She perceived his *red* hair as the description of a cousin. And hated him, too.

Somehow it blossomed in her, from the death of Gerris onward, that she would like to be the death of all of them. All those who had had as a right (and had yet) what had been given to her as a penance.

There was a love of shed blood among the sisterhood. In the time, centuries before, of the religion's glory—if so it could be termed—males had been sacrificed, one a year, to the Mother. Valia came abruptly to the notion that the practice might be honored still. Not on the water of the sea, it was true, and yet, maybe *through* water—

Tabbit indulged her as all the sisters did, now she was theirs. She was their star, their moonrise. And even Tabbit had no love for the house. She had used them, and she was mad. The old leader was dead, and Tabbit had become the leader. She swathed herself in her fanaticism, hardening, calcifying. She consented.

Valia waited for some while in the bath house, until Uncle Mevary, intoxicated and late, came to bathe. He was a lusty man, but drunk—and he was very drunk—strengthless, crippled, unable to aid himself. When the girl appeared he grinned and grunted, beckoning her. And she came to him and pressed suddenly against his nostrils a little scrap of cloth with a pleasant smell. The drug was vital, as he was not. In another minute he was unconscious and Valia stood upon him in the kalidarium, holding him firmly under the hot water until he should be entirely drowned.

She was just nineteen.

It was a number of years afterward that the ultimate plan came to harvest in her mind. She was by then a mighty sorceress; the witches had told her so, and she believed them. Their senility, of which she was contemptuous, if outwardly respectful, meant little to her otherwise. She overlooked the inexorable fact that they cared no longer for the things of life, its morals—however warped—its duties—however extraordinary—did not involve them. They clung to existence merely, and so, merely existed. They flattered and cajoled the shining star of Valia from force of habit, and from some dim, resentful fascination with her youth. They had ceased truly to be concerned with her, or with anything. Taking her had been their last tribute to their religion. Keeping her—why, they forgot she had not always been there. And Valia, in her own form sightless as they, did not notice.

It had come to her she was now ready to abandon the sisterhood, however, and live above on the open land. She foresaw herself a priestess of occult mysteries, spreading her own fame through the idea of the goddess. What heights could she not, with her powers, achieve? That the goddess was quite real for her was no hindrance in the matter. The goddess would smile upon Her chosen. And if Valia judged she should be free to practice her worship, and should become an empress thereby, then the goddess would smile upon the enterprise. For the goddess was only a figment of Valia's inner pantheon, which she herself ruled, an adjunct to Valia. As magic was. Which might explain why her talent was so poor.

Not knowing this, she dreamed of the history before her. Quite suddenly, escape and vengeance came together. She took her theme, edited on the matter of escape, to Tabbit. Thus:

Though Valia was witch-priestess before all things, and lived piously only to serve the Lady, yet Valia was driven by a wish to bring justice to those who had spurned her as a child. Did not the goddess Herself advocate justice and the exacting of dues in blood? Valia had conceived a strategy; it had come from her almost as if the goddess herself had been speaking in Valia's ear. She would, for a term, go above, insinuate herself openly into the dilapidated household and, while still acting as supplier to the witches below, watch an opportunity to destroy her kindred. Eliset's death might be easy to encompass. Mevary's death should be of dual purpose.

The goddess had gone too long without a sacrifice of masculine blood. Now, the breach might be filled.

The only problem, Valia commented, would be in discovering some tactic whereby to lure Mevary below into the cavern, not once, but many times, that all the proper stages of the pre-sacrificial ritual be observed.

"There is," said Tabbit, "the Remusan gold."

One dusk, walking back from the village where he had been drinking, Mevary met a woman. She was sinuously beautiful enough that he took heed of her, and she smiled at him with a familiarity and knowledge that were somehow intriguing. At first she did not tell him who she was, nor did he ask. But he allowed her to accompany him among the orchards of Flor, where soon enough, he pushed her down. Valia was not unprepared for this, either mentally or physically. Though carnally a virgin, in the flesh she was not—she herself had been her own most ardent lover. Now, Mevary's lust had titilated her. It was a strange dark triumph to lie with one she meant to slay, a device which also existed in certain of the old goddess rites. She found therefore a perverse delight in the rape, aroused by what he did to her not to sexual pleasure but to a sense of glorying omnipotence. He had done all she predicted. He thought her his victim and minion. He was in error.

When Mevary was done with her, feigning rapture, she confessed to him who she was—none other than dead Valia come back from the grave. It seemed she had been stolen away as a child, and though enslaved, saved thriftily, at length purchasing her manumission. Now she returned to claim her birthright. At this, Mevary was highly amused. Then she told him what the birthright really was: a fabulous golden hoard secreted in a cavern below Flor. Her old nurse had advised her of it. Her old nurse, with other madwomen, now guarded it. They must be humored, but she could surely do this, and so could he. Would he help her to the prize, and share it with her?

She convinced him. To convince him of her love for him was no problem; he was, in this regard, exactly like her, an egomaniac. Nor was the tale of treasure too hard to substantiate. She had brought him some scraps of antique gold, enough to garnish her words—Remusan coins, a fragment of a breastplate. The bulk of the hoard, she told him, lay in a sub-sea cave of the cavern and must be fished out. The women knew where it was, and a method of raising it. If their foolish rituals to appease a sea goddess were followed, then they would be obliging.

Mevary had been poverty-ridden some while, a thing which did not suit him. He had reckoned to wed Eliset and get what he could that way, making certain the little Flor had to offer stayed with him. Lazy and self-assured, he had not speeded this aim. Now it seemed he was in line for something much better.

He took Valia into the house. Since she did not wish to reveal her identity elsewhere, he said she was a slave he had won at dice, a lie which tickled him. It tickled him, too, to award her to his other bedmate, Eliset. Presently the girl, who for expediency had called herself Jhanna, the name of her own dead mother which few but Gerris had ever known, led Mevary down the dangerous shaft into the cavern. And on the first visit, as if to test his unlove of his blonde cousin, not to mention his unawareness of the dark cousin's cunning, "Jhanna" had taken with her a present for Oe-Tabbit. It was a gold and pearl hair adornment thieved from Eliset—her final valuable. Certainly, Mevary did not seem to mind; certainly he did not wonder that the gold-lusting Valia should give such an item away. He might have read the clue from it—that Valia did not really care for cash, or treasures, or property. Her goals were more aesthetic.

However, the pact was made. Accordingly, on nights of the full moon, Mevary climbed to cage and cavern, was put in an unseaworthy boat, torchlit, chanted over, rowed about, daubed with soots and inks and fish-blood. He bore with it all, waiting for the hoard to be drawn up and pressed upon him. The goddess despised the gold, it seemed; it polluted her. And now and then oddments of gold were produced, to keep him sweet.

He was exasperated, but he was hopeful. Being lazy, full of self; these elements also helped render him docile. Then something happened which Mevary did not see, nor for that matter, Eliset. A letter was brought to the mansion intended for Eliset, and was conveyed instantly, true to recent custom, into the hands of Jhanna. It was Harmul who brought it, Harmul who went in terror of her. She had taken pains to evince her witch-powers to him and threaten worse. Valia had seen he admired Eliset, as did the other boy, Dassin. They followed her with doglike eyes, paled at her touch, were fatuously in love with her—but Jhanna had counteracted that spell with implied spells of her own. Swiftly cowed by her malignity, Harmul, Dassin and even Zimir, Mevary's creature, tended to bring her placatory tokens.

The letter, being opened, proved to be Roilant's legal casting off of Eliset. He wished to marry another lady, it transpired.

Jhanna paced about her slave's cell—the slave's cell equipped with luxurious pillows and vials of scent no slave in her position would have been possessed of. In the midst of her villainy a fresh villainy had occurred to her. She had heard mentioned, as a joke of Mevary's, the long-ago betrothal, never reckoned now to be likely of fulfillment. The communication, rather than shore up this lack of faith, presented a means of reversal.

Jhanna tore the letter across and across, and doctored the several pieces with a particular chemical known to the sisterhood. Replaced at once in their external wrapping, and the wrapping resealed, they would lie dormant until brought back to the air—at which instant they would spontaneously burn. She sent Harmul off with this novel package, instructing it must go to Roilant at Heruzala. Eliset herself would pay for the messenger; she was to be told Mevary had required one to take his excuses somewhere over some gambling debt. Eliset was accustomed to financing Mevary in all he did, and would question nothing, wishing to avoid the blow in the face he had given her on her last inquiry.

Valia was appreciative of her own wit. Such a return to Roilant could be interpreted in only one way: *I reject your rejection*. He would think the reply came from Eliset, of course. He would have, thereafter, no choice but to come to Flor in person, either to argue, or to change his mind and honor the adolescent bargain. And to that end, Valia bent her powers on him, a geas that would draw him thither. He would indeed be moved to marry Eliset. Instead, he would die with her.

This neat extra caused Valia an ecstasy. The three of them to perish. The entire tribe of Beucelair, saving herself, wiped from the world's face. The most appealing format was this: she, Jhanna-Valia, should kill Roilant. For this Eliset, due to benefit as his widow, would be arraigned. She would be thrown, aristocratic lily, into a vile dungeon, and from thence be conducted, stripped to her shift, to some ignominious and public execution.

Roilant duly arrived at Flor, primed with supernatural intimations.

Mevary was naturally uneasy. The last thing he wanted at this time was the presence of an interfering ginger cousin whose wealth, compared to what seemed set to be dredged from the sea, was unimpressive. Eliset minced and mewed. And Valia herself had met the overweight numbskull one night. Seeing Roilant's light emerging from the bath house, she had thought herself under attack from the elder deceased Mevary. Since her semi-permanent sojourn at Flor, the thing had begun to haunt. She protected her sleeping place, the kitchen court, by talismans Tabbit prepared for her. Beyond these it could not go—but caught in the open, she had sought to ward it off—which had instigated a hilarious muddle. She had subsequently charmed Roilant, nevertheless, the booby, clouded his judgment, fed his fears (it had enchanted her to paint Eliset with her own sorceries), at length given him a phial of perfumed unguent, making out to him it was a potent drug. It would enable him to rule Eliset, the wicked witch of Flor, since it would render her malleable and vacuous, should he but let it slip in her drink. This he claimed to have done, but must have balked. A dreadful bout of vomiting would have been the result if any had swallowed the dose, a visitation it would have been gratifying to lay upon the exquisite Eliset. Then again, that night of the wedding supper, begun in triumph, ended the succeeding morning in horror and confusion.

When Valia had borne the dish of meats into the pavilion, Mevary himself had seemed wary of her, and made a great show of dislike for Eliset to see, a game he sometimes played between the two women. When he had gone, Valia managed to tip the poison she had brought with her into Mevary's own goblet, unseen by the ginger-nob. She had then warned the ginger-nob to watch his cup. The way things lay then, she was positive the suspicious Roilant would attempt to switch cups with Mevary, whom he mistrusted even more than Eliset. Meanwhile, she had previously suggested something of this sort might happen, to Mevary, who would then look out for it. Being Mevary, he would push the gambit to its logical conclusion, forcing Roilant to drink from everything on the table.

If, on the other hand, Mevary imbibed the poison, Valia's

dream was not unduly shaken. She meant them all to die, at one time or another. If the chosen sacrifice expired at dinner, the witch in her might be cheated, but the murderess would remain content. She would finish Roilant herself thereafter, and still leave Eliset the obvious perpetrix of the carnage, Mevary as obviously undone by his attempts to help. For the sisterhood and the goddess, there might still be the treat of Harmul, lured or threatened into the cavern. The ritual would have to be done over, and perhaps Valia might not linger to see its completion. But it would be her parting gift to Tabbit. And the goddess, Valia knew, would be lenient. So Valia's schism worked, the witch in her bowing to the woman, the woman to the witch, as it was needful.

In the end, the alternatives were unnecessary. The goblets were exchanged as she had gambled, exchanged and exchanged. . . . At last, a scuffle, and Mevary doing the right thing by all of them, forcing Roilant to drink the one predestined cup.

It was not the poison she had used on Jobel to silence forever his wagging tongue. After Mevary's report of Jobel's story-telling, it had been essential the old man's death seem due to natural if nasty causes. With Roilant, death should appear anything *but* natural. The tincture was an acid, searing to the insides. She had looked forward, had Valia, to hearing his prolonged screams. Somehow, there had only been one, that muffled. She was sorry about that, but happy in his death. She had gone down into the dark to tell Tabbit of it. Then, returning to her privacy in her slave's cell, Valia had wept with wracking joy, as once she had joyfully wept above the tomb of hated Gerris. Oh, she would leave the cicatrice of her power behind her in the world, like the claw-marks of the tigress.

And then. Then she found she had not dealt with Roilant, after all. Had not duped him, frightened him, charmed him, killed him. Possibly had not killed anyone.

A terror of the wheels of fate sliding from their allotted and predetermined grooves overwhelmed her. What must she do next?

Mevary solved this problem.

He proposed that she prepare a drug for the wine of Roilant and his guards. He knew her skill with potions. She had drugged Roilant—who was not Roilant at all—before.

With a yellow rose, on the night of the full moon, when Eliset's written message had handily furnished an excuse for such an offering as a flower.

Roilant's men out of the way, Mevary suggested he should himself fly the premises. He was all but incriminated, *wrongfully*, in the death of the agent, he of the missing corpse—Valia's advice that Mevary should hide the body had turned out full of ill repercussions. She had had to assure him the sisters had not stolen it for unholy practices. Meanwhile Eliset was doing her best to facilitate Mevary's conviction. Mevary had pronounced her tame, as had Valia. She had shown no spark of anything formerly. They were both a little astonished at this brand new suicidal streak that seemed intent to see herself, and Mevary with her, tried before the governor.

But Mevary must not disappear. Valia reminded him of the Remusan hoard. At which Mevary decided to force it from the old women in the cavern, and take it with him on his flight. The witch in Valia had protested—again, the schizophrenia of her two selves. The sacrifice was not yet to term, the rituals incomplete. Then it came to her, as to Tabbit, that a sacrifice out of season was more fortuitous than none. And then, her other self cried in Valia's heart, silencing the priestess. What after all did she care, as long as this the hated handsome beast of her perverse adolescent fantasies, bloodily died? What matter *when*?"

Valia stepped forward, and the witches parted to receive her. Curtained by their hooded forms, she sloughed her boy's garments and put on her robe, here and there spotted and rotted as were their own. She despised its smell, as she recoiled from the smell of the old womens' decades-unwashed bodies. And yet, there was a comfort of homecoming to that odor. It was her security. She would miss it in the fragrant conditions of her future life.

Even as she laced the robe, her mind had skipped sensibly beyond the moments of the wondrous blood-letting, to her last exit up the rope and through the well. Some minimal reason—anything—would do for Valia's departure following the sacrifice. Only when she omitted to reappear would they realize she was free at last of all of them, even of her sisters. Or else they might think she had died. But of course, she would not die. Valia had been painstaking, even in the person of Jhanna, that no incrimination could get purchase upon her. It would be apparent to all, the family had slain itself, along with a couple of innocent bystanders. She would see to Roilant when she emerged later tonight. She had not done it already for fear Mevary would note the fact and become cautious. To kill a man once was one thing; Mevary had blamed circumstance, or even Eliset then. But twice—ah, no. Only with Mevary himself dispatched could Valia conclude her trade with Roilant. Leaving Eliset to suffer for it. As for Mevary, his remnants would never be found. Harmul and Zimir Valia should probably silence also, Eliset's work, naturally. A pity Dassin had run away, but he was nothing. . . .

She was ready now, and the light of purpose burned up suddenly within her, dizzying her. To be at liberty at last, how wonderful, how fearsome. But firstly, to exact the retribution she had thirsted for, more than thirteen years. Her spirit came back to the present and dwelled there in its glory.

On the contrary, Mevary stood scowling. Sweat glittered on his forehead. It was not from his proximity to the clammy fire. Some part of him was warning him, but deeds and greed had become mechanical. He could not evade her now.

"Come," she said. "The ship."

Gerris' dark-haired daughter stepped from among the witches and led the way toward their cranky vessel.

The old woman filed after, numbers progressively less sure as a trickle of others slunk from their holes to join in. The torches spat and fumed. With an almost obscene strength, the increased collection of crones thrust their burden toward the water, floundered into it, took up the oars.

The effect was laughable, a hideous farce.

Mevary was the last aboard.

Creaking and lightning, a thing of ruinous timber, fire, peculiar ancient energies, the ship moved out on to the water, its antiquated crew furiously skulling. Mevary was rooted in the stern, the lean sword still in his hand. Tabbit had advanced slowly to the prow, where she brooded over the fossilized altar, and the instruments of sharpened stone. The man's sword glinted unseen, ignored, behind her. Her wicked, soulless eyes, that seemed to have looked upon the world for aeons, gleamed now, not with the birth of anything, but with a resurrection. Close by, Valia began the soft and pitiless invocation. These arcane words, like the accolade "Oe," had ceased to have any individual meanings. Only the gist remained, which, if you knew it, was appalling enough. Valia, saying and knowing, had assumed a calm and theological elation.

Her mood would have changed considerably had she also known what, this very instant, somewhere far over her head, her blonde cousin was reading and incredulously rereading, in the light of two candles.

The ship, groaning and taking on water, achieved the center of the cavern. Here it began to drive aimlessly up and down, the old sinews of oars and hags dragging it. Two of the sisters, leaving their posts, had wisely commenced to bail. Round about, the cavern walls shone dully and patchily and endlessly with their luminescence.

Tabbit lifted her gold-sprinkled head.

"Well," said Mevary sharply. "Let us get to it, grandma."

"Hush," Tabbit responded, almost caressingly. "Soon you will receive what the goddess keeps for you. Soon, now. Do not interrupt the invocation. The words must be said. The horns sounded. The chants rise."

Mevary came forward, balancing with scornful adroitness on the tilting deck. The rowing witches looked at him, as he passed above them. Valia's voice murmured on and on.

"How is it to be done?" Mevary said to Tabbit, standing directly behind her now, mocking, sweating. "You told me of a cave below the water-line. Do you employ a magnet? A fishing rod? Or will you draw the treasure by a stunning spell?"

"Hush. You will see."

"I will not *hush*." He lifted the sword and rubbed its flat along her skinny arm. "I am the master here. Remember it."

"No. She is master. The goddess—Master-Mistress—who will be honored, and obeyed."

"Damn the—"

Mevary stopped abruptly. One of the bailing witches, leaving her task, had come up in turn behind him and now suddenly gripped his arm. The grip was surprisingly strong and steely for one so brittle and so elderly.

"This is all such delightful fun," said a young voice, not

only musical but undeniably masculine. "However, every treat must come to an end."

Mevary's sword arm fell. He spun about and was allowed to. Tabbit turned also. Valia too, the invocational words trailing from her mouth, and no additional sentences replacing them.

The second bailing witch was obligingly dropping her grey habit on the deck. To reveal a glamorous courtier, blazoned by orange hair. It was not the first time Cyrion had borrowed the clothing of the dead to effect a disguise; he had not always, though, stripped it off bones in cave tunnels.

Mevary, who was in many ways a fool, had still the quick immediate wit of those incapable of prolonged deduction.

"Roilant's agent," he exclaimed.

"Roilant's agent," Cyrion agreed. "And you, of course, are Mevary. And you," bowing to Tabbit, "the nurse-sorceress, Tabbit." The cool eyes came to the slave-girl Jhanna, and rested there gently. "And you must be the Lady Valia. I am so glad to see you well."

Valia sucked in her breath. She did not look away from him as she said, "he must die also, Oe-Tabbit."

Tabbit's mouth moved. No sound came out. Her face seemed bound together. Her goal had been before her, clear, uncluttered—now this. The pure order of her will was outraged by the mess.

"Did you understand they brought you here to die, Mevary?" Cyrion wondered. "No? I am afraid so. A snack for the goddess, who drinks the blood of young men with her watery lips. But you thought they were about to draw up for you the treasure hoard of the Remusans. That would be the only thing that could have induced you to take part in any of this." Cyrion smiled at Valia, at Tabbit, at Valia. "Do I have the space to explain to him? Does the goddess grant me the time?" No one spoke. At the oars, the sisterhood rowed, even as they craned to see, held like their leader in the wilderness of the unforeseen.

Cyrion said to Mevary, his eyes moving slowly from Valia to Tabbit, from Tabbit to Valia, "I think it must have been this way. Centuries ago, a group of soldiers deserted from their legion, having relieved it of a quantity of gold. Next they stole a small ship, and rigged it, since it had no sail, with a brace of their own cloaks. There is little left of it, but that is the red of Remusa's legions, faded by salt and wear and stained with smoke. They either knew, these men, or found out, this cavern, and rowed in here to stow their loot until times were safer. But, in the act, one of the earlier orders of the dedicated sisterhood came on them, and killed them for the goddess. That must have been a happy evening, Tabbit, must it not? You may have noticed," Cyrion said, incidentally, to Mevary, "the walls of the cavern gleam here and there. This is partly from the fungus-gardens these dear ladies cultivate for unwholesome drugs and poisons. But there is another source. In a number of places, the bones of men have been fastened to the rock, quite an impressive quantity of them, and these give off their own phospherous. The gold of the dead legionaires," Cyrion added, "was, it goes without saying, thrown into the sea-pool as a further offering. It would be virtually impossible to retrieve it. Only a fragment or two is sometimes washed up on the shale by a freak of the tide, alongside the odd chip of armour. The ship, however, is very useful for the ritual. It takes the servants of the goddess jollily out upon her bosom. So, patently, they have kept the ship."

Mevary leered.

"So," he said, "it makes good sense at last. All a trick, eh?" He too looked from Tabbit to Valia, and he grinned like a wolf. "And you adored me, did you, darling cousin? I thought I should watch my step with you. I never guessed it would be such a tussle as this. But then, you are crazy, are you not, my sweetheart." Not glancing at Cyrion, Mevary said, "and you, agent to the Pudding. If you solved this did you solve the rest? Though I buried you, I was innocent of the murder attempt. Innocent as an angel."

"I know you innocent of murder, certainly," Cyrion said.

"Then you can help me back into Puddy's nicer books, and we can maybe share his bestowals—"

Mevary broke off. Valia, whom both had been watching, had altered her stance. She had taken from the altar a stone bowl and a knife of razor-like flint. With one of these in either hand she began to tread, a slow, gliding step at a time, toward her cousin.

Mevary laughed. It was a genuine laugh, of derision. At the same moment he shortened his grasp on the sword. He was quite ready for her.

"Well now," he said, "and do you actually believe you can come at me? I mean to give you a beating, dearest. With steel, if you like. One more step, and your head goes from your body. Credit me, my duck. I can do it. I *will* do it."

Valia halted. She stared at him. Against the dark of her hood and her olive skin, her light eyes showed almost white. They were full of lust. He, the youth she had seen from her hiding places, the fantasy of her pubescent years, the first and final stirring of carnal bewitchment which she must cauterize. Valia did not like to be ruled. Tabbit did not rule her. The goddess did not. Mevary, who was the sexuality she had herself diverted, never had and never would.

If she had moved the hand with the knife, he would have slashed out at her instantaneously with the sword. But it was the other hand she moved, the hand which held the stone bowl. It went toward his face, and from it flew a blackness, straight into his eyes. It was the ink they would have used to daub him for the ritual, and it blinded him.

Instinct is not always an ally. In this case, it was a man's instinct, blinded, to raise his hands to clasp and defend his eyes.

Mevary's sword swung wide. And Valia, darting under the swinging sword, plunged the flint knife a third of its length into his breast. Then, letting go the bowl, using both hands, she hammered the blade, in one further stroke, home to its hilt.

The sacrifice might have been different. Its gloating quality suggested another scenario. But to hit the heart was simple. Very few did not know its precise situation.

Mevary, proud aristocrat, brutal lover, parasite, swordsman, bully, gamester, man of fashion, fell back. There was just room for him to sprawl between the prow and the lines of the rowers, while their intent grey faces bent and jutted forth to see.

Valia, too, looked intently, first at the man she had slain, next swiftly toward the other, the man who had stood just behind him.

Cyrion had not shifted. Those who knew Cyrion, or knew of him, might have been interested by that. His mercurial speed, his reactive abilities, these were all part of his personal mythos. And yet, he had not been quick enough to prevent the death of Mevary of Beucelair, from a death blow he might have been anticipating.

Valia looked at Cyrion, her face one meaningful blank.

And Cyrion, with the politest of noncommittal smiles, looked back. Then, herself a thing of quicksilver, Valia sprang for the ship's side and went over, dropping into the gold-reflecting water, and so through into the black water far beneath.

The witches cried out at their oars, a thin wailing sound. There began to be disarray.

Cyrion did not spare a glance for them, and only the most momentary for the sea-pool into which the girl had flung herself. That she had learned to swim here, he had no doubts; it would have been a challenge she set herself. After the momentary glance, he glanced back, and sidestepped the second knife Tabbit had, predictably, thrown at him. It fell behind him in the boat with a clatter, and she dredged her lips from their sink and snarled at him.

"The ritual has been profaned," she said. "But still, there is you. You that I saw in the fire, white-haired then, whiter than I."

"My hair," said Cyrion in a confiding tone, "was once the gold of buttercups. The ghastly distresses of my life turned it white when I was a boy of seventeen. A thing not generally known. I hope you will keep the secret."

Tabbit threw her arms into the air. They were cruel arms, and the hands were cruel, the whole posture maleficent.

"Leave the oars, my sisters," Tabbit called. "And take hold of him."

There was at once a threshing and plunging, as the host of women at Cyrion's back scrambled from their benches, already reaching out, their arms, their clawlike hands as cruel, as mindless, as Tabbit's own.

"He," she said, "shall appease our Lady with his prolonged and bloody death."

"I regret not," said Cyrion.

One second he was between them, the priestess and her crew, the next he was at the side. As he went, he pulled one of the blazing torches from its spike, and dropped it methodically in the oil jar.

With a perfection of skill none of them appreciated, he clove the water, and two breaths later the oil jar exploded.

Valia's dark head would long since have broken the water. Cyrion, emerging from the same subaqueus gloom, did not bother to search for it. Though the illumination was now improved.

Neither did he investigate what went on behind him, roughly at the sea-pool's center. So he missed the screams, the smoke, the conflagration, the total capsizing of that mildewed, grimly omened craft, under its leaf of flaming sail. Nor did he behold the sisterhood crashing like a parcel of yowling sticks into the water. Some most likely had a knack for swimming. And some had not. All were aged, all scorched. Though they might, in their insane piety, lug the oars of a ship, they were poorly equipped to deal with this sudden plunge in icy turgid water, the suck of its undercurrents. Worse equipped to thrust their frail bodies, undernourished for so long on the sight of the rich blood of men, toward any of the rocky, slippery, unwelcoming shores. Some perished at once. Others, their non-swimming sisters plastered screechingly to them, flailed for sanctuary, and went down. It was not beyond the bounds of logic that a couple gained the beach. Cyrion did not pause to wait for them when he himself gained it.

The glare of the dying ship was already nearly out as he made his way through one of the tunnels of the cliff. When he came out on the rock above, only a slight trace of burning oil still flecked the pool. The splashing flotsam seemed all gone.

There had been, however, enough noise about him that he had not picked up another. It was not until he reached the gallery above the caves that he found the toppled cage, its sides crushed inward by its fall, amid a heap of severed rope. With the rope cut and the counterweight of the cage removed for good measure, it would be impossible for anyone to climb up into the well. Valia had done her very best to cancel pursuit.

Cyrion spent less than a heartbeat by the wreck. He stepped over it and went on along the gallery.

In the blackness of the corridor-court, Valia did hesitate, leaning against the well to catch her breath, laughing a little, venomously. She had achieved her aim, despite the interference of the stranger. What had happened in the ship she was uncertain, though she herself had looked back at the explosion of light on the water all about. There had been a struggle, obviously. And Tabbit—what had become of Tabbit? At the thought that Tabbit might have burned, Valia felt a dreadful release, as if a bar of lead had dropped from her soul. And with the release, a fearful loss. And with the loss, a malign delight. And with the delight—

Valia shook herself, chiding herself excitedly. Though she had seen to it the clever dolt of a stranger was trapped forever below, still she must get on. There was Roilant's death to be accomplished before the night concluded. And then her own leave-taking, clad only in her rags and her powers. What she had done to Mevary, she would wait to enjoy, as was her way, in private. And she would weep there those tears of hysterical pleasure that she was wont to shed at such times. She was only sorry his death had had to be so abrupt. But then. No doubt she could linger here a short while, and study Roilant's demise. And, at Cassireia, or wherever Eliset would be condemned, might Valia not be a watcher in the crowd?

With all the unawareness of her shuttered intellect, she failed to perceive a dozen flaws within her plan. Those she sensed she knew would not ultimately matter, and how right she was.

The faint sheen, when it began, alarmed her. She took it for the dawn.

Then the sheen coalesced. It wrapped itself about a shadow, became the shadow, and the shadow started to move toward her.

Without visible light, yet he was quite discernible, as if lit up from within. A man in middle years, with tawny hair that greyed, and the face of Mevary, some twenty years older and forty years more debauched.

Valia grew cold. It was not from the chill of the night, the icy swim in the cavern. It was the cold of utter terror. Nevertheless, her numbed hands fumbled in her tunic, clutched and brought forth a carved green stone, the amulet Tabbit had given her against this apparition—which in life had been Valia's uncle, Mevary's father, Mevary. That dear relative she had drowned in the kalidarium.

Never had she been this unprepared to meet the thing, this far from her magic safeguards, which had kept the phantom away from her, even when she came here, almost to the very area of the murder. Yet the green stone was powerful. She had seen it repel the devils Tabbit once or twice summoned. Why was her fear so uncontrollable?

"Demon or spirit," she hissed, holding the stone before her, "dispel or sink. I command you by the power of this."

There was one small difficulty. The power of all the safeguards, and of the stone—if there had been any—had come from Tabbit. It must be assumed that Tabbit was now dead.

Though moving sluggishly, the ghost reached Valia. There was no pleasure in its face, or rage. It merely took her and drew her to itself. And while it had no substance, yet she could not fight her way from its embrace. The awful cold of terror was now augmented by the drawing cold and torpor the undead spread about itself and her. The scream she attempted to voice died in her throat. Her body seemed to sag, to founder, to lose consciousness. Her brain, alas, could not.

With a slight *crack*, the talisman hit the paving of the covered court, and broke in two sections.

It was in the bath house that Cyrion came on Valia somewhat later, in the half-light before sunrise.

His own route aloft had been uncomplex enough. Returning to the cave from which he had previously entered the cavern, he negotiated the slope, uncoiled the slack of rope from its storage, and climbed back through the rock and the freshet into Gerris' busy tomb. The iron hook was indeed working loose, but could be said to have done its work more than adequately before he pulled it free. Forced to shuffle the corpse of Eliset's father aside yet once more, Cyrion replaced it with decency before vacating the grave, the lid of which, in yesterday's mayhem, had not been replaced—as he had mentioned to Eliset earlier that night. Things remained otherwise pretty much as he had left them on that former call. The drugged guards and Roilant slept. And no horse had been made off with.

The kitchen court yielded only dead leaves. Harmul and Zimir were absent, having perhaps run away in the most sensible tradition of Flor.

The search led, at length and not unreasonably, to the bath house. And there she lay, Gerris' other daughter, her dark hair looking black now under the never quite emptied water of the kalidarium, and drifting goallessly as ink.

She was herself quite goalless at last, lying there on her face on the pool's floor, all her hopes and dreams, and all her mighty magics gone for good. For the second and final time, Valia had drowned.

EPILOGUE

In the rose-bloom of the early morning, emissaries from the governor of Cassireia arrived. After a rather befuddling and not entirely amiable discussion with Roilant of Beucelair, they rode off again. An hour later, after an even less amiable discussion, the ex-soldier became Roilant's ex-hired man, and rode after them.

Sometime approximate to noon Harmul, who had crept back from temporary accommodation in an apple tree, served a light repast in the roof pavilion. The day was very hot; arrows of sunshine pierced the lattices and stuck into everything, scratched wood, worn silk, tired flesh. Roilant, nursing a nauseous headache, regarded the food and drink with aversion.

"Is it safe this time, do you think?"

"Quite safe," said Cyrion, and began to consume bread and cheese.

"Even the wine?"

"Even the wine."

"I should have been more careful."

"Indeed you should. I was rather astonished you were not."

"But I looked for harm direct from Mevary and—and from Eliset."

"And now you know yourself mistaken."

"I can never—What must she think of me?"

"You had better ask her."

"This report you sent to me," Roilant murmured. "You say Eliset will have read it?"

"Oh, I should think so. She has protected herself by acting a fool and by keeping herself ignorant of most of what went on here. But she is neither ignorant nor foolish."

"And Valia—these details you give of her life and motives. How in God's name did you suspect Jhanna *was* Valia—and that she was the guiding principle behind all this?"

Cyrion drank sherbet. He said, "Her voice gave her away inside two minutes."

"Her *voice*?"

"Beautiful, of course, and almost identical to Eliset's. A thing not too uncommon in sisters. Even where one parent is different.

"There were other clues. Her unusual coloring, between easterner and westerner, and the red in her hair that reminded me at once of your clan. While for the abused slave she represented herself, her demeanor was somewhat arrogant. That she was a murderess suggested itself when the poison was handed out at the wedding feast. Earlier, she gave me another drug, meant for use on Eliset—to protect me. I tested this and found it was simply a perfumed unguent that would cause intestinal violence, but no more. Jhanna was intent on mischief. Her gift proved useful none the less. She tried to put me to sleep with a medicinal rose. Having rid myself of it, I used the unguent so thoughtfully provided to replace its scent about my room, and so avoided any dream of subterfuge. Then we came to the poison banquet. Even the most unsubtle murderer would not have served me a bane so obvious in its post mortem effects—which are singularly unpretty. I reasoned then whoever desired to kill you had no aversion to the murder being, not merely suspect, but proven. And if so, why so? You see," said Cyrion, "the whole initial pattern was, as you rendered it, too pat. Rumors fasten like barnacles around any event, tending to take familiar shapes. An adopted sister vanishes under strange circumstances. The legitimate sister was envious and dispensed with her. An impecunious woman marries a wealthy man. She must mean to despoil him of his wealth. I came here eager to alleviate the tedium of rumor with some other text. I found it."

"But to guess Valia lived."

"It occurred to me at once she might. While the legends of sea-dwelling sirens who stole children seemed to lead somewhere. Then I learned the well was in use as a doorway. Alas, a touch too near the haunted bath house, for Valia's continued good health. Uncle Mevary's ghost was plainly hunting someone. I wondered who it was."

Roilant shuddered. "I will have to credit your ghost," he said. "I saw her in the kalidarium."

"Justice," said Cyrion blandly. "She had rather put him out, you should not forget. It would seem, too, it was her wish to slay the son that incited the father. Her success in the wish appears to have given uncle his ability to slaughter her in turn. One feels father and son did not adore each other. Probably it was the spilled blood that spurred the old fellow on."

Roilant took a gulp of wine, considered whether he could retain it, did so, and sighed, one iota improved.

"And you recognized Eliset's verity from the first. Would that I had been so sensible."

"Not from the first. But having come to believe she was not an imbecile, I was surprised to hear her make jokes about your being allowed to die only after you had wed her—when she might suppose you almost in the vicinity, on your way to supper, and agog at any mention of yourself. If such a scheme were in the offing, she would have been more canny. Mevary also, one would think—the other tack is a fraction too delicate for him. Whatever hold she had on you, would either gamble you would not overhear and bolt prudently for Heruzala? The way I played you, you had only got there through telling yourself they meant you no harm. An overt threat would have sent you flying. No. Her concern on that occasion was to remind Mevary of the grant he might look forward to on the wedding. And his concern was to encourage her to that wedding. Which proves he never told her any alternative road to riches was likely. There was, nevertheless, a similar scene later, when I think she did warn Mevary from any act against your life. She had begun to fear some more than average plot was hatching, and wanted to save you, if she could."

"She did?" Roilant stared. And palely flushed.

"You see," said Cyrion nicely, "how uncomplex it is for you to trust her. Despite your adolescent misgivings."

"They may have been only my—my uneasy dawning affection for one I—But then there was my father. *Why* did he defame her, on his very deathbed?"

"He had heard the rumors, too. As had your later informant. She had taken lovers. She practiced sorceries."

"And his fatal toss from the horse?"

"An accident. Unless he had enemies at court who were with him that day."

"He was reckoned a notable rider."

"In his own words? He was still capable of misjudgments. Why not with a horse?"

"Yes. My father was somewhat of that sort. Not that I am denouncing him. It was his nature. Then only my Uncle Mevary was the victim of a murder. Or was there another? There was?"

"I see you are learning to read me like a scroll. I cannot swear to it, but I think Gerris, also, was packed off before his time."

"By Valia?"

"No. By merry Uncle Mevary himself. He wanted Flor, his own estates being, by then, nonexistent. He could have killed to get it. If so, Valia became the ironic avenger of her hated father."

"I recall how he—my Uncle Mevary—having got the betrothal and its benefits, put off my marriage to her, hanging on to the guardianship of Flor as long as he might. And using her into the bargain. A monster. As his son was. I cannot mourn for either Mevary, uncle or cousin. Although, my Cousin Mevary's death was undeserved."

"It removes him, however, from doing further harm to those around him."

Roilant frowned. "There was no chance of saving him, in any event."

Cyrion, his meal finished, had leaned one elbow on the low table. He met Roilant's gaze with two eyes more clear than the clearest winter sea, and rather colder. "None," said Cyrion, gently. The combination of supernal blamelessness and demoniacal sweetness had never been more blatant. For a second Roilant was agitated. Almost repelled. This man he had given stewardship of his lifes and fortunes, what in the name of God was he?

"Tell me," Roilant said, "tell me truly, what you have got from this affair?"

Cyrion smiled his angelic smile.

"The delight of aiding you, my dear. Plus whatever delirious fee you mean to press into my outstretched hand."

"A fee you have never attempted to discuss with me."

"Have I not? A sad lapse."

"Which implies you do not care what you are paid, or *if* you are paid. Which in turn implies—"

"The thrill of the chase is its own reward?" Cyrion was fastidious. "How disastrously inane."

Roilant came to his feet.

"I am due to see the governor. Valia's body has been—is ready for traveling, I understand. I shall probably press on directly to Heruzala afterwards. There seems little point in dawdling here. I shall be sending letters to Eliset, of course, and money. The full allowance she has long been entitled to."

"Should you not," said Cyrion, "tell her this yourself?"

"I think I have done enough. I told her Mevary was dead in the cavern, and that Valia—Eliset has shut herself away. She will have nothing but scorn for me. Hatred perhaps. I could have had her as my wife. Everything she said was the truth. Yes, I am aware she has had lovers. Damn them. What do I care. But then. I am—or I was—contracted to a lady in Heruzala, who will tally with me far better, having—"

"Having convinced yourself your worth is so negligible only a plain and undemanding woman will tolerate you," supplied Cyrion mercilessly.

Roilant gave way to an unusual violence.

"Be silent!" he shouted. "Confound you, what are you? A daisy crossed with a razor—some kind of hybrid of Heaven and the Pit? You have done my work. This is no longer your concern."

"Actually—"

"*Silent*!" roared Roilant again. And picking up the wine jar, he flung it at Cyrion. Who leisurely ducked. Meeting one of the five intact pavilion doors, the jar smashed through it, and took it tidily off its hinges. With a bang, the door fell out on to the roof and ivory splattered.

Roilant, without another word, stalked through the new doorway he had made, thus giving it all a purpose. At the edge of the roof he said, "your remuneration will be sent to you."

"Oh?" said Cyrion, "and where will you send it?"

"To the Olive Tree Inn. So you had better get back there."

Ten minutes later Roilant, trailed by his guard, was riding toward Cassireia in one of the most explicable and least common foul tempers of his life.

Untouched by all these things, the decadent landscape of Flor burgeoned through the morning, stilled and drowsed into the depth of afternoon. Inside the thick green walls of the orchard, the orchestrated insects buzzed, glutted and fell dizzily down; the fruit smoldered on the boughs and in the grass, sending up its winey smokes.

Eliset, no longer shut in her chamber, but shut instead within this viridian sun-cellar of propagation and rottenness, stood like a white statue green-jeweled by light through leaves, breathing, being, gazing, as if she had opened her eyes on it from a hundred years of sleep.

Green-gold her hair, too, gilt where the sun directly hit it, and the wakened eyes dark with their awareness. Her dress was the shabby dress in which Cyrion had first seen her, stained now across the hem with the liquors of the broken fruits. If she was joyful, or if she was serene, or if she grieved, these things were not written anywhere about her. She merely was; a matched facet of the place and the hour.

And when Cyrion, without a sound, stepped through a break in the crowded trees ahead of her, she made no move toward him or away, or anywhere.

"You create," he said quietly, "a most captivating picture. It needs now only a pagan god to come out and startle you to make the tableau complete."

"A pagan god," she mused. "Surely, one has."

He said, "Roilant has gone to Cassireia."

"I know. It seems I must presently effect mourning, after all. Mevary and Valia. A show, nothing else. I do not mourn. The business will, in any case, be hushed up."

"Without a doubt. I gather even Harmul has been bribed and sent away. Zimir and Dassin one predicts would fare likewise, if unearthed."

"And so I shall be unencumbered at last, to pursue my life, alone—in this ruin. You see, I have had to face the truth. I love Flor, but Flor is dead. I have been clinging to a corpse, thinking I should lose it. Now, it seems I am condemned not to. How ungrateful. Yes, there is beauty here. My past is here. Perhaps I can be content. But there have been too many battles on this ground. Every sweet thing I see reminds me of some other thing, which is bitter."

Cyrion said nothing.

"I imagine," she said, "creature of action that you are, you must find me despicable. My great fault all along has been that I have deliberately averted my glance from everything that went on here, made myself, as best I could, unknowing. It seemed the only manner of survival. To agree to everything. To simper, to praise, to do all I was bid—even to assisting at an illegal burial. Ah, my blind reliance. I had faith that if I did not note it, the nightmare might pass me by. It has. And I am left with—very little. Well, I shall haunt here, then. With the ghosts."

"In which you believe?"

"I believe there are ghosts here. Oh, not those others I paid lip-service, those riots I assumed to be orgyings of Mevary's and Jhanna's—Valia's. I feared some obscene practice of witchcraft, also, and hid from it, of course. When you related the dreams which had brought you—brought Roilant—to Flor . . . I wondered if she had somehow set them on you, at Mevary's direction. You see, I do not credit magic, but the force of a dedicated, evil mind—that I do credit, and she, Jhanna, Valia—I feared her from the moment she entered the house. His strumpet, as I was, as he had made me, waiting on me, trying to prize from me any confidence, any weakness. I gave her nothing. She was like a cold whispering at my back." Eliset waited a moment. Then she read, "there is another cold whispering now—my father. I read your letter, as you knew I would. It made no mention of Gerris. Was he poisoned?"

"It may be."

"By my uncle."

"I see you do not ask it as a question. He is the most likely candidate."

She turned very gradually away from him, averting her glance literally as she had metaphorically described the gesture less than a minute before. Presently she said: "I recall, when I snatched your wine at our hideous wedding banquet, you seemed disturbed. Did you reckon me poisoned, also?"

"It was possible. Someone had sugared one of the cups. I was at that point unsure which."

"So, you had accepted my innocence by then, after our dramatic dialogue in Cassireia market-place?"

"Not exactly. There has, Eliset, always remained one fragment of this charming puzzle that stayed stubbornly unhoused.

This item has tended to implicate you. A riddle. Regardless of your radiant unblame, I could not swear you were not a sorceress."

"And can you swear it now? Should I tremble?"

"I said, a riddle. I trust I have the answer to it."

"And I am absolved."

"You are absolved. Except, it may have some bearing on your future life."

She waited. A bird began to flute among the leaves. Rather than tell her the solution to the mystery, Cyrion began to tell her about the bird, the method of its song, its colors, its migrations.

Eliset listened in astonishment. After a short interval, she found herself walking beside him through the fermenting heart of the orchard. He informed her of the properties of a variety of flowers they went by, and catching a glimpse through the tangled trunks of the old Remusan wall, he spoke to her of the Remusans.

His voice, so melodious and so flawlessly articulated, almost hypnotized her. The lessons were easy. In some extraordinary way, she felt she would never now forget how that little bird flew to Kyros and Askandris in the winter, or that the white flower reckoned a cure for insomnia, or that a Remusan officer, enervated by midsummer heat, had cut into the stone of an antique cook-shop at Teboras the words: *Legionaries roasted here.*

But then she said, "This is a curious conversation we are having."

"Oh," he said, "I think there has been enough blood and pillage for a day or so. Sameness is a fearsome thing."

At which juncture, they broke from the orchards entirely, and came out on the dry lawn before the slope. Ahead, the land rose, browning, to the faded hornbeam tree, the ramshackle mansion, the leaning tower, the vista of the sea beyond, which abashed the rest by its unruined splendor.

Eliset took in the view.

"The dowry of Flor. Only consider. If you had honestly married me, instead of by a sham, all this might have been yours."

"And only consider what a worthless husband you would have received in exchange."

"I supposed you were Roilant."

"Did you?"

She looked at him, into his eyes. "You know I did."

He acquiesced, "I thought you did. In retrospect, I wonder. But I have neither proof nor logic to back me, this time."

Her eyes were lowered. "Very well then. Since you make no demand you shall have it gratis. Naturally, I continued to perform my part, to ignore my discovery as I ignored all else which might be dangerous. It could have been some game of Mevary's. Or Roilant's. For I knew you were not he. It was more than intuition."

"What gave me away?" he said. And then, so softly she scarcely heard it, "Eliset?"

She raised her eyes again. The sun filled them with every blue nuance current on earth.

"On the cliff," she said. "Your kiss betrayed you."

"Because he would not have kissed you."

"Because it was not the kiss of Roilant."

"And still you wed me, an impostor."

"I guessed by then the ceremony would be invalid. Though I was afraid enough that I begged you to remain that night at Flor."

"Dreading I would claim a husband's rights."

She said, "Not afraid of that. A succession of men have forced themselves upon me."

"And I merely one more."

"And you, at last, one I would have chosen, gladly."

Her pride, her equilibrium seemed untouched by what she had said, only her heartbeat flashed whiteness from her throat like the shaking of a petal to and fro.

Cyrion's hands, no longer those of a swordsman, now those of a musician, came lightly to her brow, her hair, her mouth. She closed her eyes as his lips followed them. As his arms came about her, she drifted, and just for an instant remembered that pleasure is only the passing of a season, before she forgot everything save the man who held her. Forgot even the warmth of the distant sun, the singing of the small bird that in winter would fly away into the desert.

On a certain street of Heruzala named Fortress, owing to its proximity to an old Remusan prison, stood a selection of ornate houses now in decline. Once a fashionable area, the high walls and heavily barred gateways, spoke of riches past. One house on Fortress Street was of unique concern, to Roilant of Beucelair, if to no one else. It was the domicile that contained his elected lady, she whom he had renounced only that he might protect her from the spells of Eliset—or, in recent parlance, of Valia.

Very early on a summer morning, Roilant's lady was thrown into a flurry by the announcement that a red-haired gentleman had called on her.

She was thrown into a greater flurry when, on entering the room, she discovered another than the one she had looked for.

Cyrion bowed exactly.

"Excuse me, Madam," he said. "I am ashamed to admit I may have gained an audience under false pretenses."

Roilant's lady recovered her composure rapidly. Her unbeautiful, pleasant face realigned itself. She said,

"Indeed, I should have guessed it was not Roilant. His letter stipulated he would be here at noon. He might have been a little late, but certainly never indecorously early. My maid, also, is not given to evasive jokes. Rolling her eyes and squeaking of a red-headed visitor seemed somewhat unnatural, not to mention unaesthetic."

Cyrion smiled.

"You are being very gracious, in the teeth of your disappointment. For I realize how severe your disappointment must be that I am *not* Roilant." Cyrion gravely paused. "You gather, of course, he means to ask you to be his wife, at last."

"I—" the lady flushed. "His letter appeared to indicate this would be so. His betrothal to the Lady Eliset—"

"—Seems to have proven invalid. I trust you will not judge me forward should I offer my felicitations?"

"Not—at all." The lady's mouth grew firmer. "And certainly not, if you will explain who you are and why you are here."

"We may come to that," said Cyrion. "But indulge me a moment."

"Why should I, pray?"

"Because what I recount may be of value to you."

Roilant's lady folded her hands and sat down. Nothing gave her away, except that her fingers were a jot too tightly interlaced, as if anxious something might get out between them. Or in.

"Well?"

"Well," said Cyrion. "Roilant will not have troubled you with this matter, but before he abandoned his—dare I say?—his sincere determination to protest affinity to yourself, in favor of his betrothal vow to Eliset, a number of abnormal events occurred. Firstly, it would seem the Lady Eliset began to haunt him, reminding him of his adolescent promises. Along with the haunting went a variety of oddments—talismans whirling through the air, dried petals falling on his pillow."

"Perhaps," said Roilant's lady, grimly, "the phenomena were caused by a guilty conscience at his desertion of her. And may therefore still plague him, may they not?"

"The phenomena were caused by witchcraft," said Cyrion. "A very adept witch, able to bend illusion to her will, and with the energetic power to put inanimate objects into motion. I will admit, I am impressed by her skill."

"Yes," said Roilant's lady, "if you believe in such things, you would be impressed. On the other hand, allowing for magics, such items as those keepsakes Eliset once sent to Roilant might well be imbued by their own vitality, and able themselves to reproach him."

"Then you knew the talisman, the flowers, were keepsakes she had sent?"

Roilant's lady checked. Again, she reddened.

"He told me, in confidence, some of what passed between them. And that these things had gone to him."

"The talisman, then, and the flowers. But a pair of cheap gloves seems not to have been mentioned. Otherwise, I am sure, you would not have omitted them."

"Gloves? No, he did not say she had given him gloves. But what concern is this of mine? Of yours?"

"Tell me," inquired Cyrion, "are you really prepared to condemn yourself, and him, to a miserable match, simply because your father somewhat likes the notion, and your sorceries have failed?"

Roilant's lady came to her feet. If she had been in a flurry at the onset, she was now in a tumult. Her cheeks were scarlet and her clasped hands bloodless.

"What are you saying?"

"You know quite well what I am saying." Cyrion moved to admire the view from a window that looked from its grill on a disheveled garden of rose briers.

"I do not. I—"

"To be plain. Though you have been most adroit, there are one or two avenues you missed. To begin with, even pragmatic Roilant, seeing visions, unsuccessfully ducking amulets, suspected not his conscience or God's foible, and had them investigated. The fellow who did so assured him witchcraft lay thick upon the chamber. This settled, Roilant must suppose Eliset the witch. I take it you never heard sorcerous rumors concerning the lady, and that Roilant honorably did not mention them, or you might have thought of this yourself. Now, Roilant has discovered that Eliset is guiltless of spell-making, and blames another lady. But I myself have seen that particular lady's magic in practice. It was not much. Without resort to chemicals and portions, her talent was sadly limited. Though she might have boasted to herself she had the force of will to accomplish what was accomplished against Roilant, she did not. And there is another thing. Since definite objects were employed in the psychic visitations—talismans, flowers—one must deduce whoever worked the spell knew of them. Eliset naturally knew. She had sent the gifts herself. But Eliset was not the sorceress. While the second lady I spoke of is highly unlikely to have known. Roilant could not have told her. Eliset would have kept them secret both from the woman and from her other cousin, Mevary, neither of whom had she any reason to take as confidant. I was also struck by the form of the vision, which made Eliset slender and golden-haired, yet left a blur in the region of her face. Neither did she, in the vision, say a word. Her declaration was written, most spectacularly, on the air. A problem then. Who might be privy to such details as Eliset's coloring and Eliset's private gifts—and yet understandably without such details as the physiognomy and voice of one never met?"

There was a slight delay, during which Cyrion courteously examined the roses, while a series of expostulations took place. Then, resuming, "These, I am afraid, are the facts. But what can be the motive? It seems you do not desire to wed unlucky Roilant after all. When you saw the way the wind of his affections blew, you flushed with alarm, just as you are doing now. Which unfortunately, he took as a blush of consent. Thereafter you utilized your most impressive powers to send him from your course back to the old one. Recall his duty, marry Eliset, and he would not bother you."

The mouth of Roilant's lady had come open. Rather than stay in this position, she spoke.

"*Who* are you?"

"Ah, yes. My name is Cyrion. Does that help at all?"

"You—you rogue, you monster! Do you accuse me of unlawful acts?"

"Your witchcraft does not interest me, save in this one respect. You may glamorize snakes from the ears of King Malban and you will hear nothing from me, except perhaps, some muted applause. In this case, however, I am bound to inform your intended lover. Or, there is one other solution."

Roilant's lady compressed her lips. She was pale now.

"Money. You wish to be paid."

"I wish to prevent a desolate marriage. The other solution is that you should reject Roilant yourself, as all this while you have been wanting to do."

She began to upbraid him, and then suddenly left off. Her good sense was showing her that argument was done.

"Yes," she said at length. "Yes, yes. It is all as you say. Roilant is a good man, but I have no hankering to wed him. Or anyone. What I have hankered for all my years is to travel, to study—*alone,* unhindered. Roilant wants from me what he thinks he beholds in me: My father's daughter. Decorous, mannered, cheerful, obliging. And this I have been for my father, and will be while he lives. But eventually I hoped for liberty. To do as *I,* not a man—husband, father—desired it. Oh, my father is eager for this wedding. We are not opulent as once we were, though we do well enough. But he tells himself he pines for luxury—the multitude of servants he used to forget we had and ask nothing of, the costly clothes he never wore. In his memory he was only happy then. And how to get back to it? Why, a rich husband for his child. I am dowdy, and thought I should escape, but it turns out I was wrong in that. Roilant stumbled on something in me to plesae him, though he never loved me. It was Eliset he loved, and loves, so much was flagrant. He could never, poor soul, leave talking of her." Roilant's lady, who was not his lady after all, shook her head. "Hapless Roilant. I liked him excellently. But is that a wonderful reason to wed? I like my cat excellently. And my old tutor. Am I to wed them? Why is it," cried the young woman in obvious chagrin, "everyone believes a plain girl will leap at the first man who wants her? And I was so pressured. My father—Oh, I was driven mad to take the match. And so. I worked my magic on Roilant. Naturally it was infamous. I have censored myself over and over. But having studied such arts, and having a little ability—a *very* little ability. My control was not beyond reproof—I fear the talisman grew hot and struck him—while the petals seemed to terrify—I was truly sorry, seeing him in my crystal in such agitation. . . . .But then, knowing he did not want me, wanted her alone, I felt justified in forcing him guiltily to go to her and be happy. That was all. And it is sure, he never told me anything of her that might make me guess he would think her a sorceress ensorcelling him. He said only his father forbade the match on his deathbed, because she was poor. As I am, indeed. But it seems I have been an idiot. Dear me. What is to be done?"

"What I advised. Tell him you will not marry him. The magic can stay your affair. As I mentioned, another got the blame for it, but it does not disconcert her."

"He has suffered so many rejections, it seems. And my father will sob and complain. Heaven! Must *I* renounce Roilant?"

"You must. You do not want him."

"But, so much trouble. Weeks of it."

"Against a life of it."

Cyrion had turned back from the window and the garden, although a modest heap of rubble on the brier-rotting terrace had previously claimed his eyes.

"I imagine," she said slowly, "since you have found me out, I have no choice."

"None."

"And on the rest you will be circumspect, if I keep my half of the bargain."

Cyrion stunned her with a luminously honest smile.

She touched her hair, her gown, as if righting herself after a physical struggle. Cyrion was already leaving her. At the door he halted.

"There is one final question I would like to ask you," he said.

Nervously, she peered at him.

"What would it be?"

"When the rain brought down that portion of the terrace roof, were you anywhere near?"

"The roof—" she stared. "Not at all."

"Your father, I am afraid to tell you, phrased the event differently. He wrote Roilant a letter to the effect that the tiles had missed you by a finger's breadth."

The young woman, who was no one's lady now save her own, pealed with a vibrant and wholesome mirth.

"*Did* he so? Well, my gentleman named Cyrion, when the roof fell, I was in the library of my aunt's house, three streets away. I never even heard the crash."

In the rose-fall of the sunset, the rose-red ashes of the sun had powdered the roofs, and doused the courtyard of the Olive Tree. There, a rose-red cat chased a little rose-red ball in which a miniature bell chimed and clinked. Under the dark red vine leaves, the roughed shadows of a man and woman had talked a while, she with hair of sun-flushed fires, he with sun-flushed hair that defied description.

"No," she said, "I cannot nourish myself any more on dreams. You, like all the rest, would vanish when I woke. You are not what I want, Cyrion. My whole existence has been insecurity, the collapse of bricks and hopes together. I do not want to love and so be wounded. I want—I need—to be safe at last. And he is a kind man, with intelligence and sensitivity there in him, if only they were allowed the chance to thrive."

"And you would award them such a chance."

"I would try. Whatever else, I should not betray or befoul what he could give me. In return for my harbor, my anchorage, in return for *peace*—I could render him a sort of love. In a way, I have for many years."

"And will you be content with that, Eliset, my douce?"

Yes. As I should never be content should I let myself love you. What is easy is often stupid. It would be stupid to love you."

Cyrion regarded her through the ending of the rose-red

light. He did not reply. So she said, "For you would leave me, Cyrion. Gods and angels both are noted for their transience, their infidelity. You would leave me."

"Yes," he said, with a strange and unalterable tenderness, "I would leave you."

"Then, our paths are before us. And they are not the same."

The light perished soon after, going out, designating the blue of evening to recolor everything; indigo sky, blue leaves, blue playing cat.

When Roilant entered the courtyard (with, if less pretty than, the first star), he stared about and found no tranquility in the evening. His mood was already dejected. Having sent word beforehand he would meet Cyrion here with his wage, Roilant had kept the pledge in spite of his great desire only to ride swiftly to his Heruzin estates and grow very drunk there. For Roilant's bridal choice had turned him down. She had been dulcet, tactful, adamant. Of all men, had marriage been her goal, she would have taken him, she said. But marriage was not her goal. She was a scholar, and would be happier solitary. Her depressed father, skulking in the corridor, had only added to Roilant's anguish by bemoaning his daughter's "decision." Patently, he had no plan to coerce her. Nor did Roilant wish her to be coerced. He had thought she was *willing*—

Now, with this load of disillusion on his back, this brand of utter failure on his ego, Roilant came into the yard of the inn and searched for Cyrion and did not detect him. Roilant accordingly gave vent to a vociferously vulgar and fairly uncharacteristic ill-wish.

Which, somewhat shockingly, received a response.

"I think he is already on the road for Jebba, and will hardly stop to do *that*."

Roilant swallowed his next breath and choked on it. When he had done coughing, he walked cautiously toward the darkened arbor from which the voice had come.

"Eliset?" he asked the blue vine leaves, without any conviction.

Then a light flowered suddenly in the house behind him and a warm goldenness flowed by and opened the shadows. In the heart of which, framed now by lampshine and daffodil hair, the mirage of his boyhood and his adult years sat smiling.

And the one he had always wanted, and from whom he had been stringently kept by liars and cheats, and games and fools, and rumors, and self-deception, now murmured, "Yes, my dear. I followed you." And held out her hand to him.